USA TODAY BESTSELLING AUTHOR

DALE MAYER

A Psychic Visions Novel

SNAP,
CRACKLE...

SNAP, CRACKLE...
Beverly Dale Mayer
Valley Publishing Ltd.

ISBN-13: 978-1-773364-83-4
Print Edition

Books in This Series:

Tuesday's Child
Hide 'n Go Seek
Maddy's Floor
Garden of Sorrow
Knock Knock...
Rare Find
Eyes to the Soul
Now You See Her
Shattered
Into the Abyss
Seeds of Malice
Eye of the Falcon
Itsy-Bitsy Spider
Unmasked
Deep Beneath
From the Ashes
Stroke of Death
Ice Maiden
Snap, Crackle...
What If...
Talking Bones
String of Tears
Inked Forever
Insanity
Soul Legacy
Coveted

Boxed Sets and Bundles
https://geni.us/Bundlepage

About This Book

Remember …

The haunting refrain torments Bethany, almost as much as the horrors of what she's forgotten. Chased, terrified, and injured, she races away from a gunman into the woods, determined to once again escape those after her.

Hunter's first meeting with Bethany reveals an injured, exhausted, and possibly dangerous psychic. Plus she was uncooperative, barely civil, keeping everyone at arm's length. Only she needs help, … and he is the one available. Time for the hunted to turn hunter, and that is his domain. Especially if he gets to champion the underdog, which, in this case, is a prickly and way-too-beautiful woman, whom he doesn't want to let out of his sight.

Not only is she being tracked but they want her back as a captive. A captive to do their bidding. And they've enlisted another of their group, her ex-best friend Lizzy, to hunt down Bethany.

They want, no *need*, her to remember who she really is …

With Hunter at her side, Bethany fights for survival, racing toward an explosive reveal that leaves them all gasping, as their world turns upside down.

Sign up to be notified of all Dale's releases here!

https://geni.us/DaleNews

CHAPTER 1

BETH METLOMAR WAS dying, and the window to reverse that was quickly closing.

"They were close, too close." She shook her head, the rain and wind pelting her from every angle. "No, *she* was too close," Beth murmured, meaning Lizzy, her ex-best friend, now her nemesis. Fear and panic snuck through Beth's body, exasperating her already fragmented energy problem. She tried hard to pull herself together, but slices of her were dissecting, disappearing into the ethers. It was all she could do to keep herself together.

"No," she cried out to the vanishing energy bite, "get back here."

The pieces refused to obey, were harder to control these last few days, directly related to her waning energy. Finding out she was being hunted did that to her. Being on the run wiped out the rest.

She shifted her weight off her sore, wet feet, as she huddled underneath a tree. Hell, there was no reason for them to follow her at all, but they had.

How had they known where she was?

Her survival instincts had pushed her here. One step in front of the other—her only possible direction. Following the one thread that she'd kept close all these years. He was the only one who could help. But would he?

She had traced his energy to this location. He was home. But he wasn't alone. That was a consideration. Would he remember her? He'd helped her a long time ago, and she'd never forgotten his compassion or his truth. Few were like him. Had he changed? She had. So why not him?

Everything was at stake. But she had no choice. Not if she wanted to survive. She'd been running for weeks—or months maybe—after hiding in plain sight for years, while appearing to be normal.

Cold from her wet clothes, her wet hair dripping down her back, Beth shuddered, her slight frame trembling harder than before, as she fought to pull herself together again. She needed a source of warmth and soon. The blood seeped down her side, a steady drip from a bullet wound two days ago, right out of the blue. A shot fired from behind, while she had been enjoying the morning sun. She'd managed to escape capture, but it had been a hard-won effort. Even now she looked down gratefully at the cat at her feet. The huge jet-black Maine coon mix wouldn't leave her side, even though she'd tried to get him safely away. He refused.

He was stubborn like that. Nocturne would survive, if Beth didn't make it. She wasn't sure she would do the same though, should their roles be reversed.

The rain and wind continued to whisper around her, even under cover of the huge tree, and she searched the darkness enveloping her world. Other energies were out there, hunting for her, reaching through the darkness, searching the ethers to find her scent. Even a faint remnant of Beth left behind was enough for them to grab on to.

She focused on her goal, on the house she sought. Besides the man who had helped her long ago, there was *him*. Someone she saw—or rather felt. Someone she thought should have seen her. Should have felt her, yet he didn't.

Was he an innocent? Someone who had no idea of this insane shadow world? Or maybe she was sending signals that weren't strong enough to be picked up. She was certainly fading quickly. She slumped against the tree trunk, wishing she didn't need yet another rest. The night wouldn't last forever, and she needed to make headway while she could.

Just the thought of getting back on her feet defeated her. Still, she was so damn close.

Just not close enough.

A few vehicles were on the road below, with traffic moving smoothly, zipping along in the darkness. Normal sounds of civilization. Except everything felt and sounded *off.*

Her senses strained for signs of the danger she knew surrounded her, but her ears couldn't be trusted right now. None of her senses could. Everything was too fragmented for that, impossible to pull them back. She could handle one sense—maybe—but she couldn't use up her dwindling energy reserves, or she wouldn't make it to the house.

She struggled to her feet, wincing as her spiritual energy plus her life force drained from her into the puddle of blood at her feet. She'd been forced to use so much energy to keep her spirit from completely fragmenting outward that her body would just have to wait, eventually no longer having any protection for it.

With another bitter laugh, she pulled her hand free from the oozing bloody wound on her side, desperate to keep her soul conscious but also she didn't want to lose this physical existence, if she didn't have to. Forcing herself to move, she trudged forward one more step and then another, leaving a heavy blood trail behind.

At her side, Nocturne moved quietly, his ears up, his tail

twitching, as he searched the surrounding area. Nobody would see him. Nocturne was the darkness of night, but then so was she.

She tossed her jet-black waist-length hair over her shoulder, wishing she had a moment to braid it. But lacking food, water, and even a bandage to hold in her blood's life force, a braid was the least of her worries.

"Nocturne," she murmured. "You go to him if I don't make it."

A tiny meow came from beside her. She felt it more than heard it. They'd always communicated like they were soul mates. So here they were, a broken-down fugitive and this precious soul that stayed at her side, no matter what.

SITTING COMFORTABLY IN Stefan's living room, a surge of electricity shot through the room, shocking Hunter Brill. "Whoa," he exclaimed, jumping to his feet.

Another electric influx had the power surging inside the home, then sparking. Hunter turned to Stefan and Celina. "Will that storm cause a power outage?" He'd only stopped by for a quick visit, not even sure of the impulse that brought him here, but he had been long used to listening to it. Yet the power surges going off and on over the last hour were something different. Something he'd never seen before.

Celina shook her head. "What is going on?"

Stefan walked to the massive wall of windows at the back of the living room and whispered, "It's not an electricity issue. Something, someone, is out there."

Another spark lit up the room.

"Did you see that?" Hunter walked closer to the wall of windows, certain he saw an image out there. He narrowed his gaze, studying the energy, but it acted like live electricity, still sparking in place. Bizarre. And that said a lot, coming from him, a man who lived bizarre.

"I did," Stefan murmured thoughtfully, "but I'm not sure what."

Another flash lit the room.

In the fading light, Hunter caught sight of a woman.

"Is she ... a ghost?" Celina asked, stepping closer to Stefan. "If she is, she's not like any I've seen before."

"No."

Stefan's words synced with Hunter's. "It's like a holographic image."

"She's young."

"Midtwenties, hungry, afraid, ... and injured." Hunter wished the image had stayed long enough to learn something else. Something helpful, outside of the massive dark pain in her gaze from her white face. He turned to look at Stefan. "I have no idea what's going on. I've never seen anything like this. Have you?"

"Yes, and no."

"A little more detail would help," Hunter said, with a note of humor, even as the light flashed again at a different location, showing the same woman, only slightly different. "Can we tell if this is in real time? Are these slices of her past? Is she close? Is she headed here? Lord, she's not teleporting, is she?"

Hunter seriously hoped not. It looked like something out of a horror show, and the end result couldn't be good. The next flash came faster, then another and another, completely surrounding them in the living room, as the three stood in wonder and, yeah, on Hunter's part at least, ... in horror.

The images and flashes were constant now.

"Is she in danger?" Celina murmured. "Or dangerous?"

Stefan wrapped an arm around her and held her close. "We are all dangerous in different circumstances," he said, but his voice was barely audible over the crackling electricity.

Then suddenly it all stopped.

And silence reigned.

Until a knock sounded on the door.

BETH LEANED AGAINST the wall adjacent to the doorway—well, more like sagged against it. But she was vertical. The trip had been horrific, yet she'd done it. But what waited for her? Other energies were here. She hadn't expected that. She hadn't allowed herself to consider it. She'd been solely focused on her friend of old.

Nocturne meowed at her feet.

"Sorry, buddy. I just need a moment."

What if she was wrong? What if this person wasn't who she thought he was? What if he didn't care? What if he didn't remember her? She leaned heavily against the wall, loath to reach for the door. She felt another piece of her soul splinter outward. Only this one moved into the house. She smiled upon seeing the beautiful open, airy space with the huge wall of windows. A beacon in the darkness—the ever-encroaching darkness—as her own vision narrowed down to a small pinpoint of light, then to almost nothing. And now the effort to stay upright was too much, and she did a slow slide to the ground outside the door.

Of course, outside. She was always outside.

In the far recesses of her consciousness, she heard a hard knock on the door. She wanted to run, to cry out a warning, but too late.

The darkness choked her before she could say a word.

Splintered as she was, multiple sensations poured through her soul, overwhelming her in sights, sounds, emotions.

A slurry of light shone down on her. Strong arms reached for her. She was lifted, carried inside. Light warred with the darkness. Softness warred with the extreme hardness of her world. Compassion and caring opened up old wounds that leaked with pain and sorrow.

She wanted to cry out a warning, but somehow they already knew.

She wanted to let them know why she was here, but somehow it didn't matter.

She wanted to tell them who she was, but somehow they didn't seem to care.

With the last of her strength, she opened her eyes, checking if she were safe or if she'd bet on the wrong door.

Fear struck her heart as she struggled to free herself from the stranger who carried her. "No," she cried out. "No, it can't be."

"*Shhh*, you're hurt," he said gently. "Let me help."

"No, it's you. You're a hunter." There. She'd said it. The reality of losing it all crashed into her, tears leaking from her eyes. *Over.* The war was won. She'd lost.

"I am Hunter, yes," he said, staring down at her in his arms. "That's my name. I'm not, however, hunting you."

"No," she whispered. "Not yet."

With the last of her energy, she whispered, "But you will."

CHAPTER 2

B ETH OPENED HER eyes, her sight blurry, her heart slamming against her chest, as fear immediately gripped her soul. A voice whispered close to her, "You're fine. Just relax."

But relaxing was something he could suggest but she could not do. She'd been on edge, too alert and wily for too long. She didn't say another word, letting her eyes drift closed, hoping that whoever was beside her would see her as sleeping.

"Good," he said calmly. "You need rest."

She shifted in the bed, loving the absolute softness against her skin. And then remembered Nocturne. Her eyes opened wide, she bolted upright. Immediately hands grabbed her shoulders and gently pressed her back down. She stared up with a wild gaze. "Where's Nocturne?" she demanded.

Stefan—and there was no way not to recognize him—stared down at her in surprise. "You arrived at my door alone," he said.

She shook her head frantically, only to wince, as the inside of her brains pounded against the bone. "No," she whispered, "I was not."

At his startled exclamation, he said, "I will check," and he disappeared.

She sagged back onto the bed and sent out a message.

Where are you? Where are you?

Nocturne's calming voice whispered right back, *I'm here.*

She sighed with relief. *Don't do that to me,* she said.

I'm here. Just rest.

And she drifted back under again. When she woke the next time, Stefan and the hunter stared at her. She frowned. "It's very odd to be stared at like that. You make me nervous."

"Good," said the man who had carried her in.

She knew him. Or knew his type. She couldn't be sure which. She felt his energy wafting her way, the anger and the worry. She studied him closely, but she didn't recognize him. "Why do you want me to be afraid?"

He shook his head. "You are already afraid. I just want to know why."

"You want to know many things," she murmured. "That doesn't mean you get the answers."

His eyebrows shot up. "You came here for help."

"You are not the one to help me." She shifted her gaze to a woman, leaning against the doorjamb. Beth studied her carefully, as she didn't know who this person was, whether friend or foe. She looked around for Stefan, but he wasn't here. "Where is Stefan?"

The woman answered, "In the kitchen, making you tea."

"Tea?" she asked hazily.

"Yes, tea."

"What if I don't want tea?" she asked in confusion.

"It's medicinal, for your head, and he is very good at what he does."

Beth already knew he was very good at what he did, but nobody ever understood just what that was. She didn't know either.

Just then Stefan's voice called out and said, "I'm here. I'm here."

She looked at him, feeling the same sense of relief as when she had first laid eyes on him. "It really is you, isn't it?"

"It is," he said, looking at her. "But I'm afraid I don't know who you are."

She slowly closed her eyes, sinking deeper into the bed, hot tears leaking from the corners of her eyes. Of course he didn't know who she was. Why would she have thought that he could even think such a thing? But the betrayal, that sense of indignity that he didn't know her just ate at her. Finally she opened her eyes to see everybody still standing here, waiting for her to speak. "You do know me," she said, "but it's been a long time."

He studied her closely. "I'm poor with names," he said, "but I'm good with energy."

She gave him a twisted smile. "How about altered energy?"

His gaze widened and then sharpened. "How altered?"

"One-hundred-steps-forward altered."

"What do you mean?"

She didn't say anything. Wasn't a whole lot she could say. She waited to see if Stefan would be who she thought he was or not. And, if not, she needed to get out of here and fast. She waited as Stefan studied her. Or rather searched ... but for what? "What are you doing?" she asked curiously.

He shook his head. "I'm searching for someone I recognize."

She nodded. "Maybe not someone but maybe something?"

He frowned.

"Meaning, you don't recognize me because everything

has changed," she said. "They did that to me. But maybe you'll recognize this." She lifted her hand and slowly rolled her palm outward.

He stepped forward to study her offered hand. "What am I looking at?"

Despair washed through her. Had it changed so much? She looked down at her palm, spreading her fingers wide, and the same spiderweb network of scars remained.

He looked at it, and recognition slammed into him with a powerful jolt. He sucked in his breath and reached a hand to the wall for support.

Immediately the woman rushed to his side. "Stefan, are you okay?"

He didn't answer but turned to face the bed.

Beth stared back at him. She knew her soul was in her eyes, desperate for recognition. Desperate for somebody to say that she was who she was. Maybe that was her fear the whole time, maybe that was her horror—that she wasn't who she thought she was. How could she even explain such a panic? And so little that she could even do with it. She stared at him.

"Beth?" he asked, his voice raw and hoarse.

Tears came to her eyes, and she whispered, "Thank you."

"Why thank me?" he cried out. "What are you thanking me for?"

"For recognizing me," she said, "even though it took a bit."

"My God," he whispered. "What happened to you?"

She just gave him that flat stare.

"I went back, you know?" he said, walking forward. "I went back to get you."

Her eyes widened. "Did you?"

"You weren't there."

"Wasn't I?" She sent her mind back in history to that horrible place, where they were part of those terrible experiments. "I don't know where I was," she said sadly. "I don't remember much at all."

"And yet you remember Stefan?" Hunter asked, a note of doubt in his voice.

Him again. *Hunter.* She stared at him. "Yes," she said, "some people are unforgettable." As Beth looked at Stefan, she saw the shock and the pain in his gaze. "It's okay."

He stared at her. "It's not okay," he whispered. "No way I would have left you, if I could have found you."

"But you couldn't," she said sadly.

He stared at her. "My God," he said, walking forward to sit down at the side of the bed. He gently picked up one of Beth's hands to cradle in his. "How did you find me?"

"They didn't break everything," she whispered, with a bitter laugh. "And some of the things they tried to break had different results."

He winced. "Okay, that's enough for now," he said. "I want you to rest."

"By keeping me here, you're in danger," she warned.

"I'm always in danger," he said, almost absentmindedly, as if it weren't an issue.

She studied him. "Have you become so powerful?" He gave her a lopsided look, so apparently he had. She studied the woman at her side. "And you?"

"I am Stefan's wife," she said, "but I am nothing like him."

"Don't let her lie to you," Stefan said affectionately. "She's the other half of my soul."

"The woman of the stone."

His eyebrows shot up. "You remember that?"

"How could I forget?" she said gently. "It's the only time you would talk about her. Plus, you were so devastated to not see her."

He nodded slowly. "I remember that," he said, "but I'm surprised that you do."

"Not much about you that I've forgotten," she said. "My life experiences were narrow. And painful. I kept hold of the good memories."

The other man, Hunter, stepped forward. "You were tortured?"

She looked at him and asked, "Why are you here?"

"Instinct," he said, in the same flat tone, crossing his arms over his chest, as if unwilling to give any information. But then, she was no different. She took a long slow deep breath, willing the pain to subside. Her hand inched around her body to the bullet hole. "Were you able to get the bullet out?"

"Hunter did," Stefan said. "I was busy stopping the bleeding."

"I lost a lot of blood," she noted. "Thank you for not turning me away."

Hunter said, "Yet all you asked about was somebody else who was with you."

"That's all right," she said. "I heard from him. He's fine."

At that, all three of them stiffened, but she didn't offer anything else. Her gaze went from one to the other, like they were on one side of this room, she on the other. Not the welcome she had expected.

Hunter stepped forward. "Why are you here?"

She gave a bitter laugh. "I was dying. I needed help."

"Do you need other help?" Stefan asked quietly.

"Yes. But I don't want to hurt you or to put you in danger." That's the last thing she wanted. If she could heal, revitalize her energy, then that was enough.

"And why would you think that would happen?" Hunter asked.

She rolled her eyes to the side. "I don't like you."

"Doesn't matter if you like me or not," he said, his tone hard. "I'm here for an unknown reason, and I suspect it's you," he murmured. "But what I don't know is why."

"None of us know the whys anymore," she said, as she studied him. He was a couple inches over six feet, maybe more, and filled out, yet he had a panther-like grace as he moved. "You're a hunter," she whispered, "but why are you *here?*"

"I wasn't hunting," he said, "but now that I'm here ..." And he let his voice hang.

She turned to look at Stefan. "I'll leave now," she said and slowly sat up, pushing the blankets to the side.

"Whoa," Stefan said, "you can't go anywhere."

"Yes," she said, "I have to."

"Why?"

"Because they're coming," she whispered. "Thank you for healing me." She didn't even look at her wound to confirm. She didn't have any doubt that Stefan had done what he said he'd do. She might not be 100 percent, but she'd take it. "I'm much better now."

"Yes, you're better," Stefan said quietly, "but you're not good enough."

She stopped, looked at him, and said, "It has to be."

"You weren't this stubborn before."

"Times have changed," she said quietly. "Things got a whole lot worse."

He winced at that, as he stared out over her head. "My God, it would have, yes," he said. "I swear you weren't there when I checked."

"I was there," she said, "being held somewhere else."

"I'm so sorry."

She nodded slowly. "I forgave you a long time ago."

He seemed relieved but then doubt took over. "What can I do to help?"

"You've done it," she said. "I'll survive now that you've closed the wound."

"Survival? Is that enough?" Hunter asked in a harsh tone.

She glanced at him and said, "Sometimes it's all we have." He seemed frustrated by her answer, frustrated by everything going on around him. She understood, but clearly he hadn't come to the point in time where he accepted that some things in life one couldn't change. She had come to that conclusion a long time ago.

"I want to help," Stefan said.

She shook her head ever-so-slowly. "Nothing you can do."

"That's not true," he said. "There has to be something. Otherwise why did you come? Besides to heal, tell us who shot you. Let us help."

"Why?" she asked, not comfortable talking with the others here. "You could do nothing all those years ago. Why would that have changed?" It's not the answer Stefan wanted, but the only answer she could give him. She slowly stood, happy that at least her body didn't scream in agony, though she worried at the weakness, the lassitude that filled her. She staggered, taking one step and then another.

Stefan immediately stepped in front of her and said, "Beth, you're not healthy enough to leave."

Her gaze dark, so deep, she whispered to him, "And yet I'm too healthy to stay." And, with that, she took another step forward. Stefan placed a hand on her shoulder. She immediately felt energy draining from her. She gazed at him, her eyes wide. "Why?" she whispered, her energy quickly withdrawn from her.

"You aren't strong enough," Stefan said.

"I have to."

She collapsed, only to be gently positioned right back in bed where she had been. As Stefan tucked her under the covers, she stared up at him, some of the paralysis easing that he had instilled.

"We'll talk tomorrow," Stefan said. "For tonight, just get some rest."

She closed her eyes. "You'll be sorry."

"Maybe not," he said. "We too have skills."

She nodded. "They've been looking for you since you left. I didn't want to lead them here," she said, "but I may already have."

And then the darkness claimed her once again.

HUNTER STORMED AROUND the living room. "Jesus Christ, Stefan! What the hell is going on here?"

Stefan sat calmly in his chair, a cup of tea in his hand, as he studied the massive windows. "Events from my child-hood," he said. "I managed to escape before she did. I tried to find her, but no sign of her was anywhere. I was torment-ed for a long time because I couldn't get her out, but I didn't dare go back either. It never occurred to me that she would have taken the punishment for my escape. Then they all would have, I suppose."

"Why would she have?" Hunter asked.

"Standard torture techniques there," Celina said to Hunter, then gently turned to Stefan. "And you did what you had to do."

"Of course I did," he said, "but it cost somebody else I cared about a great deal. Did you see the condition she's in?"

"She's lost." Hunter shoved his hands into his pockets, as he crossed the room once again. "She's a lost soul, but that doesn't mean that she's your responsibility."

"No," Stefan said sadly. "I wish she were. Then I would force her to stay where she is, until she could heal. As it is, she has a certain amount of ..." He stopped, shrugged, and said, "I don't want to say *bitterness*, but maybe bitterness is the correct word."

"Well," Hunter said, "just think about what may have happened to her."

"I don't want to," he said quietly, "because I have a pretty good idea. My escape would have just made it that much harder on her."

"Of course," Celina said. "If they thought she had anything to do with it or thought that you were coming back for her ..." And she let her thought hang there.

"Exactly," Stefan said.

She nodded slowly. "So, what do we do? Just wait until she wakes up the next time?"

"She'll wake up guarded," Hunter said. "She knows you put her under."

Stefan nodded his head. "I know. She is bound to wake up, kicking and fighting." He smiled at the thought. "That would make me feel better than this fragmented soul she has become."

"How much do you remember about her?" Hunter asked. "And do we even trust her?"

Stefan shook his head. "Absolutely not," he said. "I trust the person I used to know, but I don't know this one at all."

"Is she so different?" Celina asked.

"Yes," he said quietly. "She's very different."

"In what way?"

"Her energy for one. I've never seen anything like it. She is in pieces, and she's holding herself together with a very thin spiderweb of energy."

"Why though? What exactly is she doing?" Hunter asked, as he studied Stefan. The man had experience in this like nobody else. But even Stefan hadn't seen everything. Hunter had done all he could in the last decade to help gifted people—like himself, Stefan, and, yes, even Beth. Something was so odd with her. Something affected him so strongly about her; maybe that she understood what he was.

Maybe she understood who he was on the inside, but her assertion that he would be hunting her shook him. He did spend a lot of time hunting people, not to cause injury but to help. She didn't seem to get that part of it, and that bothered him too. He could only hope that, when she woke up, they could talk a little bit. Hopefully she would be less cryptic and more open. But somehow he doubted it.

"I think she's been alone a long time," Celina said. "I think she's been alone since Stefan left."

"Not possible," Stefan said, "but she probably felt alone. I know how rough it was for me back then, and to think of that as just a fragment of what she faced seems terrifying."

"She seems to think that she has brought trouble here,"

Celina said quietly. "Do we need to worry?"

"I'm scanning for anything out there," Stefan said, "and, so far, the answer is no."

"But we don't know what that means, do we?" she said, slowly wringing her hands together.

He walked over, placed a hand on top of hers, and said, "No, we don't." He asked Hunter, "Do you sense anything?"

"I'll go out and take a walk," Hunter said. "I'm definitely sensing something, but I'm not getting a negative threat from it."

Stefan nodded. "No, I'm not either," he said, "but I don't know what it is, and I'm also not sure what she meant about not being alone. And having already communicated with them. But her energy is a mess, making it almost impossible to read."

Hunter nodded. "I was thinking the same thing." He walked to the front door, shoved his feet into his boots there, grabbed his jacket, and said, "I'll be back in a bit."

Stepping out into the night, he didn't go far. He just went enough away from the house itself and the strong energy beacon that Stefan ran high and loud and large for those who needed it, plus the silencing shield that Stefan had put out for the other energies of those looking for him. Hunter had to get far enough so that he wasn't distracted by those energies. As he took several steps forward, he felt something. He looked everywhere and couldn't see anything. Unnerved, he took several more steps farther out, hoping for answers and looking for something *wrong*. He didn't have to go far to find it.

A black cloud was up in the hills behind Stefan's house. Hunter suspected it's where she had come from. He studied the energy, finding hers, and then slipped through the trees, taking the long way around to see where this came from and what they wanted. Because one thing he knew for sure, when he hunted, he didn't leave any of the prey behind, if he could help it. As he'd learned from Stefan, the prey and predators came in all different forms.

Never a day passed that Hunter didn't get a chance to find something new and completely different out there. It was shocking really, and the rest of the world had no idea what went on. And, in this case, Hunter wasn't sure he understood himself. Did Stefan? Hunter had no explanation for the crazy energy-field flickers they had witnessed. No explanation for so much of what they had just seen happen, and yet the woman who had answers didn't seem prepared to cooperate at all. She appeared ready to run, but from what?

She was right in the sense that Stefan had healed her enough to survive. And knowing him meant knowing that he would help her. So that explained why she came. But now, rather than stay and give any explanations, she was prepared to leave in the middle of the night, if need be. Hunter shifted, climbing up the hill. Behind the house he sensed Stefan's curiosity, that probe on his part, asking if Hunter had found anything. He answered calmly enough. *Energy, black energy on the hill behind the house.*

Recent?

Yes, recent. They were looking for her.

Well, they found her, Stefan murmured in Hunter's mind. Neither had any expectation about the world around them. Hunter didn't think Stefan would want to let Beth go, not in any way, shape, or form, no matter what she had to say. Hunter wasn't so sure she could be trusted, but then he had trust issues himself.

Just as he walked forward, a crackle sounded beside him.

He looked down, thinking he saw something, but it shifted in the wind. He called out a *Hello* on an energy level and got one in return. He froze, looked down, and whispered, "Who are you?"

No answer.

But he could sense the energy. Small, but a powerhouse. Like the woman crashed in Stefan's spare bedroom. He stepped back and slipped against the trees, until he blended in with the silence around him, waiting to see just what was going on. But found nothing related to the crackling energy. He did find another energy, a black energy, old but stale. Left by somebody who didn't care if his presence was found or not. A predator who didn't give a damn. A predator who was dangerous, indeed. Hunter searched the area and sent a message to Stefan. *Whoever was here is gone now.*

Hunter turned to look around and sidestepped a sudden shift in energy. He pivoted to stare at the darkness around him. "What do you want?" he cried out. No voice, no answer. Nothing was more perturbed than he expected it to be. He studied the silence around him in the darkness, looking for an answer.

"Who are you?" he called out. And again nothing. Frowning, he slipped off to the side and waited and watched, and, when there was nothing, he waited longer. Determined to win this waiting game, he waited more and then another ten minutes beyond that. Then he noted a gentleness of an energy separation, and something small and black moved toward him. An animal. A voice reached into his mind.

Is she okay?

He couldn't see what he was looking at or what was talking to him, but he answered readily enough. *Yes.*

Good. Keep her that way.

And it disappeared. Was that the stale black energy that he'd sensed? No, this was loving energy. The other was not.

What the hell had that been? Still Hunter had a sense of danger, of old energy dispersing, as if a hunter had moved on. Much out there was unexplainable. Change was happening. And he didn't understand at all what was going on here. It unnerved him, but it also pissed him off.

"You shouldn't hunt for an innocent woman like that," he yelled into the darkness. The response was almost like a mindless laughter or a sound of mockery, and then another voice, a different voice, crept to him through the darkness.

"Whatever you think of her," came that voice, "an innocent young woman, she is not."

Just like that, the dark cloud cleared up, and a bright star shone in the sky above, lighting Hunter's way. Absolutely nothing was around him, nothing to see or to feel. Whatever had been here was now gone. Only the remnants of the voice remained and a sense of warning that, whoever Beth was, she wasn't what she appeared to be.

HOURS LATER HUNTER and Stefan stepped back from the sickbed, as Hunter looked down at the sleeping woman. "Do you think it's safe to leave her alone?"

"No," Stefan said. "We'll need to set up a camouflage."

The room had big windows, only one interior door in and out, yet the en suite bathroom had another window.

"I'll work on the security," Hunter murmured. He shifted, so he could set up an energy field all around the outside.

At that, Stefan placed a hand on Hunter's arm. "Dr. Maddy needs access in and out."

He gasped and said, "Right. Shit. So how will we do

that?"

"We'll figure it out."

Hunter nodded and continued with the work, knowing Dr. Maddy and Stefan would tweak the field as needed, and then Hunter stepped outside, searching the darkness all around them. He'd already sent out feelers and alerts to see just what was following Beth. Something weird pulsed in the woods, but he couldn't figure it out. Energy, yes, but then everything was energy. If somebody could harness the actual soul of the trees, that energy field would be so vast that nobody could get through it. Thankfully, so far in life, that hadn't come to pass.

As Hunter stepped back inside, he looked at Celina's worried face. "I didn't see anything out there."

She relaxed slightly and nodded. "I want to go to sleep, but I'm worried about her," she said. "We need to clean the wound, and I know Stefan is working on it, but she's a mess," she said frankly.

"In what way?"

"Her stress level, her muscles." She tilted her head. "Even though she wore boots, her feet are injured. She's badly bruised and scratched all over. It's like she has been on the run forever."

"My understanding was just for a couple days, just since she got shot," he asked cautiously.

Celina shrugged. "I can only tell you what I see, and I think she's been on the run for years. Stopping to heal, then maybe getting 70 percent back and moving on."

He nodded, then eyed the bedroom doorway with a different viewpoint. Stefan was in there even now, and Hunter saw a blue glow coming from the room. "It's amazing what he can do."

"Maddy is helping. Besides, it's also amazing what you can do," Celina added.

He laughed. "I'm utilizing a lot of energy to source what's out there. I need to drop and recharge."

She nodded and said, "Go ahead to your room. We've got this."

He smiled, gave her a gentle kiss on the cheek, and said, "It'll be fine." He turned and headed off to bed. If he could catch a few hours of rest himself, he would be in a whole different state tomorrow. As he drifted off to sleep, he couldn't help but wonder about a woman who had been on the run for as long as she had. The big question loomed: What was she running from?

CHAPTER 3

B ETH WOKE UP with a start, her gaze darting around the room, struggling to understand where she was and what woke her. She was in a small room, a nice room, except for the weird energies floating around her. She shifted to see better, sending shards of pain down her body. She lay here, trembling for a long moment, hearing a female voice in her head say, *Be still.*

A sense of admonishment was in the tone, as well as care. Beth did as she was asked, but she didn't know who had spoken or where Beth was. She thought she was at Stefan's, but ... panic stepped in. She threw back her covers and stood. The motion itself forced her to lean against the wall, as the pain once again shafted through her. She had to leave. The inner sense was overwhelming. She must go.

Beth raced toward the window and looked out. The darkness was outside. Mindless black energy. No feel to it, nothing positive or negative, just there, staring at her, always hunting her. She shuddered and looked for her clothes, only now realizing she was nude. Nothing here to wear, except for the old bloodstained things she had had on before. She struggled to get into them, even as she heard somebody moving on the other side of the door. She froze, afraid they would come in. She waited in the darkness, studying the latch on the window to see if she could open it. She knew she could.

She used the bathroom, got herself a drink of water. When she stepped back into the bedroom, she looked around with a sense of sadness that she had to leave, but, if she didn't, it would get that much worse. She headed to the window and unlatched it. Even as she pushed it open, it slammed shut with a hard force that she hadn't expected. She cried out, and suddenly her bedroom door opened.

Hunter stood there, glaring at her.

She held her hand to her mouth, backing away. "Am I a prisoner?" she cried out. This was the worst possible outcome. She'd been a prisoner before—never again.

Immediately the look on his face changed, as he came forward, his hands out, palms up. "No, you're not."

"But I can't leave."

"You can leave," he said, "when you're better."

"But that's a *when*," she murmured, staring at him, her heart still slamming against her ribs. "Which means I am a prisoner."

"You're safe here," he said, motioning at the bed. "You need to lie down and to keep healing."

"I want to leave," she said. "You can't keep me against my will."

He hesitated and then gave a firm shake to his head. "No, not tonight."

"So, I am a prisoner," she cried out, her worst fears coming true.

"No," he said.

"How can it not be?" she asked, daring him to argue.

"This is best for you, for now," he said. "Please get back into bed and heal."

She shook her head slowly. "And if I refuse?"

He said, "Look at you. You're dripping blood every-where again."

Surprised, she looked down at her wounded side and winced to see that blood running down her leg and even now dripping onto the floor. "Damn," she said, wavering on her feet.

He raced toward her to hold her upright.

She looked up at him. "I don't want to be a prisoner ever again."

"You won't be," he said. "I promise." He picked her up, swung her off her feet, and carried her to the bathroom to sit on the counter.

Once back there, she felt rather than sensed him stand-ing beside her, as he checked her wound, applying pressure to slow the bleeding. He quickly changed out her dressing, before sitting back to stare at her.

"I'm staying," she said. "For a while."

"You are, indeed," he said.

She studied him in the darkness. "Why do you care?"

"You came here for help. Stefan is helping you. I won't have you run off on him."

She winced at that. "So, you're doing it for Stefan's sake."

"Maybe," he said, scooping her up and walking her to the bed where he gently laid her back down. "is there any other reason I should?"

Her back stiffened, and she shrugged. "No." She rolled over, shifting uneasily with her wound. Finally she got comfortable, and, even as she closed her eyes and lay here, she sensed him still in the room. "You can leave now."

"No, I can't," he said. "You've already shown you can't be trusted."

DALE MAYER

She hated that, hated that somebody could judge her for fighting for survival. Then he didn't know what she'd been through. "It's for the best."

"It's not for the best," he said in exasperation. "Now go to sleep."

She wanted to; she really did. But having him here was unnerving. "I can't sleep while you're sitting there, staring at me."

"Fine," he said. "I will leave, but, if you try that stunt again, you won't like the result." He turned and walked out, shutting the door hard behind him.

Still, she was alone, and, with that, she closed her eyes and slipped off into dreamland.

HUNTER WAITED OUTSIDE the bedroom door, not exactly sure what he saw, but definitely something was going on. He opened the door quietly and stepped back inside the room. A *woosh* of energy. No rhyme or reason to it. It flared and sparked. Hunter whispered, "What the hell?"

He didn't understand it, but this huge energy ball moved toward the window. Instinctively he knew that it was part of Beth. Was it her, assessing the window to see if she could get out, and would then go back and wake up the body? He knew it sounded like something from a freak show, but he didn't quite understand how and why her energy was everywhere. Like somebody had taken a high-voltage line and had plugged her in, exposing her to it, just shattering everything. But a part of Beth remained calm and contained in this outlying mess.

He couldn't imagine it would be very nice for her to live this way, but somehow she had managed. That's the thing that always got him, when he saw these gifted people with abilities. The things that they survived and managed to live with just blew him away. No real reason for her to have survived something so like a high voltage of energy.

But she had, and that brought them back to what Stefan had said about the childhood torture, the "training" that had occurred, and that she would have been a test subject. Stefan didn't explain too much about it, but enough grimness was in his tone that Hunter knew any further discussion would hurt Stefan to relive that time as much as anybody else. And Hunter didn't want to do that.

Stefan had done more for everyone in their psychic world than anyone Hunter knew. And Stefan was still fighting the good fight, but just so many bad guys were out there that sometimes Hunter wondered if it was worth fighting at all. And Hunter had to admit that, given what he'd seen of her, Beth probably felt the same way. And that had to be hard too. What were you supposed to do when everything broke down and became this constant torture? It's not what anybody would want for themselves.

Hunter watched as a huge ball of energy shimmered in place at the window. Neutralizing his own energy, Hunter stepped forward and made sure the window was locked. The energy flashed around him, and, whether pissed off or frustrated, he didn't know, but he quickly stepped out of the way. It reached forward and back, over and over, until Hunter had backed up against the door.

"Go back and lie down," he ordered. The energy shimmered in place and then headed toward the window. This time as Hunter went forward, he saw the window unlock. Swearing, he stepped forward but came up against the energy and immediately bounced back, as heat seared through his soul.

He shook his head. "That's not allowed," he snapped.

The energy shifted toward Hunter in a threatening move, but he stood his ground. "No, you're not leaving. You might get through that window, but you can't get through the energy shield."

It shimmered again in frustration. He was used to seeing energy; he was an energy hunter. He followed energy, hunted it down, based on its individual energy pathway. Just like a dog could scent a certain smell six feet under and miles away, Hunter saw it, and he could follow it, but he needed something specific to follow. He must have a signature, and this energy didn't seem to have that.

He studied it carefully. How would he possibly recognize it in the future? The best way would be to understand that it didn't have a signature at all. It just flared in a multitude of colors and energy patterns, and he shook his head. "That makes no sense," he cried out. "What the hell is going on?"

The energy stepped back, as if not liking his questioning. And he nodded. "You need to go back and lie down."

The energy shifted a little bit closer to the bed. He nodded. "Go ... now!"

At that, maybe the tone of Hunter's voice, maybe something completely different, but the energy turned and lunged toward him. Almost immediately, another energy stepped in place, blocking the space between them. It slammed up against him like a wall, flattening like a cloud of smoke hitting a pane of glass and spreading along the edges. Then another energy—and he didn't even understand what that energy was—touched the same energy, like a lightning bolt. It immediately shrunk down to almost nothing, then slowly drifted back to the form sleeping on the bed, where it laid down on top and slowly dissipated. Soon gone, the shield in front of him immediately dispersed too. Taking a long slow breath, he stared down at the woman, who even now twisted on the bed in obvious pain.

He whispered, "Dear God, what the hell was that?" He slipped from the bedroom and locked the door. Then he turned, finding Stefan standing in front of him, rubbing the sleep from his eyes.

"Are you okay?" Stefan asked urgently.

Hunter nodded. "I am. But what the hell is going on here?"

"I don't know," Stefan said, "but we need to find out."

"She's dangerous," Hunter said.

"We all are," Stefan said, giving him a lopsided look.

Hunter took a deep breath. "I get that. But I don't know what the hell just happened in there."

"And we'll find out," Stefan said, with a firm nod. "We will find out. It's okay." He nodded again. "You should get some rest."

Hunter looked at him strangely. "It's a little hard to rest."

"As long as she stays in there, we're okay."

Hunter shook his head and said, "How will you contain that?"

"I don't know," he murmured, "but I'm hoping she'll do it for us."

"Are you saying that wasn't her?" he asked in astonishment.

"Well, it was," Stefan said, "and it wasn't."

CHAPTER 4

W HEN BETH OPENED her eyes the next time, sunlight poured in through the window, adding a brightness to the world around her, a world she barely recognized. She was used to the darkness and used to hiding. Sunshine was a joy for her, something she hadn't had a chance to appreciate in a very long time.

And, when she had, look what had happened. She was so sure she'd been safe, so sure she'd made a new life for herself. One that nobody could track down. Yet not only had they found her but they had taken her out so fast. If she hadn't moved at the last moment and managed to keep moving, she would be dead by now. At that, she laughed bitterly.

No, she wouldn't be dead; she would be living a life much worse than death. She would be their captive again and forced to do their bidding because the only other option was death. And, even after her escape from the compound, they had found her, and now she couldn't do anything except live her life as they allowed her. Not a whole lot of good escaping did for her.

It was hard not to think on it now that *his* thoughts were in her head. And she hated her tormenter for it.

Showered, dressed in clean clothes, courtesy of Celina, Beth sat in the living room sipping tea, surrounded by the others. She didn't want to be here, and neither did she think they wanted her here, but it seemed like she had to deal with that right now. Finally she looked at Stefan and said, "You've done well."

He nodded slowly. "I have," he said, "but it didn't come without cost."

"Isn't there always a cost?" she asked. "It seems like the price is higher than most of us can pay."

"It's not higher than we can pay. It's higher than most of us want to pay," he murmured, studying her.

She shrugged, feeling oddly disconnected from the whole thing. A part of her didn't even think she should have come, though she wasn't sure what other options she'd had, if any. Obviously she needed his help, and he'd given it willingly, and, for that, she was grateful. "I need to leave, you know?" she said.

He nodded. "I know you believe you need to leave."

She gave a bit of a laugh. "What does that mean?"

He said, "I think there might be another way, but, if you're not ready to hear it, that's a problem."

"It's not that I'm not ready to hear it," she said. "You just don't understand how difficult this is."

"So help me understand," he said.

"No," she whispered. "You've already been through life on the compound. You need to stay out of it. You're getting me back on my feet. That's enough."

He gave her a deep blossoming smile. "What you don't understand is, I've been out for a long time, and my skills have gotten stronger, better, and faster." He gave a self-deprecating laugh. "No, I'm not Superman, but I am not the victim I was before."

"Good for you," she said, "but I don't have that same security, that same sense of assurance that I can do this," she whispered.

"And that's because you're still running in fear, and nobody would expect you to be running on anything but fear right now," he said. "Don't misunderstand. We don't expect you to handle all this on your own."

"Aren't you?" she said, shooting Hunter a veiled look.

"No, not at all," Stefan said, "and, of course, we don't necessarily understand all the ins and outs of what's currently happening, but you need help, and I'm someone who knows you, who knows what you went through because I've gone through it myself, and I'm willing to help."

"And why is that again?" she asked. "Why would you put yourself in a position where you could get hurt again? Or where those you love could get hurt?"

"I have safeguards here for my family," he said, "so I'm not worried about them."

"You should be," she said, quietly studying Celina. "It's obvious that she loves you."

"And that love will not die at the end of this lifespan either," he said, studying Beth. "You just haven't necessarily come to that same acceptance yet."

"It's a little hard to," she said, "when everything out there is so intent on hurting me."

"And that's something we have to fix. You need to have the same time to heal that I had."

"And how do I get that?" she asked, staring at him.

"Fearful?" Hunter asked. "Again?"

"Who wouldn't be?" she said, glaring at him.

"Hey," Hunter held up a hand, saying, "I'm not making this more difficult for you."

"Well," she said, "you couldn't prove it by me."

He groaned. "Look. We're not supposed to be at loggerheads here."

She gave him another flat stare. "Then let me go."

"I'm not holding you anywhere," he said, and she just stared at him. He frowned, then looked at Stefan.

Stefan said, "That's me, not Hunter."

She said to Stefan, "Then let me go."

"I can," he said, "but you'll just get hurt again."

"Maybe, and maybe it doesn't matter." She didn't know where all this defiance came from, but that feeling of being held captive would never go down well. She waited, edgy for him to answer.

Finally he nodded and said, "I won't hold you any longer. You've been held for too many years in your life. I just wanted you to know that you were safe here, could heal here."

"No, this is where *you* think I'm safe," she murmured, "but you don't know that."

"No, I don't," he admitted, "but I'd like to think that you are safe here."

"What you consider safe and what I consider safe are two different things."

"Does it matter?" Celina asked impulsively. "You're obviously still hurt, and people are out there after you."

"And how will you handle it when they come here and burn down the house?" she asked Stefan.

He tilted his head and said, "A shield is around the property."

She nodded. "There might be, but that won't help you in this case. They have somebody who can create all kinds of hell with fire."

"There will always be people out there who can do that," he said. "It depends on what kind of fire and whether it's that hard to put out."

"I don't know. I've never seen them test it," she said, "but I know he was working on all kinds of chaos with it."

"Of course," Hunter stepped in. "You keep saying *he*."

She hesitated and turned to Stefan. "I don't know who the boss was, much else the others. Do you?"

He shook his head. "No. I never did find out. And I assumed that you hadn't survived the last set of testing."

She stared at him for a long moment, the shudders working through her. "I almost didn't," she said. "One of those sets of testing, much later of course, turned me into the person I am now."

"And what does that mean?" Hunter asked, leaning forward. "We're tiptoeing around this concept, but what exactly are your abilities?"

"Maybe I don't have any," she said, giving him a flat stare.

"You evaded capture all this time," he said, "and whatever we saw with that electricity outside was pretty damn scary."

She frowned. "What was scary about it?"

"You should have seen it," Celina said. "The whole place lit up, like in the center of a large electrical storm."

"Well, that's not a bad thing," Beth said quietly.

"Maybe not, but we saw a holographic image of you flash time and time and time again, all in different places."

At that, Beth frowned. "In different places?"

"Yes, very much different places," Stefan said, looking at her curiously. "You didn't know?"

"I kept calling the energy back," she said, "but, when I'm tired, I don't have the energy to pull it all in as I need it."

"The fact that you can even separate it off like that is

amazing," he said quietly.

She gave a half smile. "Not really," she said, "it's basically a failure on my part."

"A failure, how?" he asked.

"My body cannot handle the lack of energy, the lack of focus. I was hurt and basically crying out, looking for answers, looking for help. And, when I did that, instead of a thought going out into the ethers, a piece of me went as well."

"But you can call it back?" Hunter asked in amazement.

She looked at him and said, "When I'm strong enough, yes." She was reluctant to tell him any more because she still held that inability to truly trust that he was who he said he was or that he was doing anything good for her. And how sad was it that her world had come down to that.

"So you were surprised to hear that we saw various slices of you?" Stefan asked. He was always the observer, always the one figuring this out.

She shrugged. "I don't know what I expected or what I thought exactly. I was dying and struggling to reach you. Nothing worked as intended." She released a heavy sigh, as she slowly rotated her neck. "It's hard to understand just how bad things can get," she said quietly.

"Not necessarily, we've all been there," Stefan said. "It's just that, in your mind, you're always alone."

"Because I always have been," she said, with a start.

"And I get that," he said. "I really do. But you have to remember that you're not alone anymore."

"Sure, I am," she said. "I'll leave here, and, although you'll remember me after I'm gone," she said, "it won't be long before you'll go on about your life as before. You may wonder, but you'll carry on as if it doesn't matter because, to you, it really doesn't."

Stefan stared at her in shock. "Yes, it does matter."

She gave him a mocking smile. "Of course it does," she said, with a long and drawn-out tone.

Hunter studied Stefan, then stared at his guest with a worried look. "Stefan cares a lot."

"That's because he feels guilty because he tried to help me. I'm the one he never could save."

"All the more reason that he wants the chance to help you now."

"Nothing he can do." She hopped to her feet, gave her body a quick shake.

"And what makes you think it's safe now?" Hunter asked.

"Well, it's probably not, but I think I'm okay to deal with it now." She walked to the front door, turned at the entranceway to stare at Stefan. "Thanks for not telling me to stay."

He gazed at her steadily. "I meant what I said," he said. "You were a captive for long enough. I won't cage you again."

She smiled. "And that is appreciated."

"However, I would still prefer that you stay."

"Well, I can't," she said. "Staying here won't help either of us. It won't get me someplace safe and free and clear of all this."

"What will?"

"Walking out that door and disappearing into the night again," she murmured. "This time I guess I'll have to go a little bit farther away."

"Is that feasible?"

"It has to be," she said, studying him carefully. "Only so

much anyone can do, Stefan. You've done what you can for me, and I appreciate it."

Celina patted Stefan, then nodded at Beth, sadness in her eyes. "I put together a small bag of clothing for you at the door. Be safe."

With that, Beth smiled, turned, grabbed the bag, opened the door, and stepped out.

HUNTER IMMEDIATELY SWORE and got up to go after her. He couldn't believe that she just smiled and left. "Stefan, we can't just let her go back out there again." No immediate shots were fired, but, as he hit the front door, he saw that she was gone, as in gone-gone. He raced around the vehicles outside, looking high and low for her. When he came back to the front door, he studied Stefan, standing there, with his hands on his hips and a frown on his face. "Did you expect her to leave?"

Stefan shook his head. "No," he said, "not at all. I had a field up. She shouldn't have escaped." Stefan stared at the field and said, "That's never happened before. Have you ever seen anybody cross the field?"

Hunter shook his head. "I didn't think that possible. How could she?"

"Probably because she's electricity," Celina said. "She's obviously dealing with a lot of electrical currents, so this either energized her or possibly was something that she didn't even notice."

"Energizing her wouldn't have been bad, but then why wouldn't she have gone out earlier?"

"She wasn't strong enough," Celina said, staring at him. "Did you see how she moved just now? Smooth, light?"

"I know. I know. I know," Hunter said, raising both hands. "I'm just frustrated."

"Can't *you* get through the shield?" Stefan asked, a tiny smile at the corner of his lips.

"I can," Hunter said, already reaching for his jacket. He turned, looked at Stefan, and said, "I don't know how long it'll take me."

Stefan looked at him, nodded. "It won't be as easy as you're thinking. Her defenses have kept her alive. She won't lower them anytime soon."

"So we do nothing?" he asked, shoving his fists into his pockets, as he waited for Stefan to answer him.

"No, not at all. You must understand that we were kept in cages at the compound. Anything that doesn't have wide open windows and an open door will feel like a cage to her. And I won't do that to her."

Hunter nodded. "I get that. But she's also a link to a group of people who are hurting gifted people like us," he said. "I can't live with that. We have to do something."

"And do you think there's no other way to do it but with her help?" Celina asked the two men nervously.

"Easier with her help, I would presume," Hunter said reluctantly.

"I think she's pulling the electricity from my field around her," Stefan said, with a sigh. "If I drop it, we're in danger of having somebody up in the hills fire back at us, and, if I keep it up, it's something that she can continue to pull on and to use to hide from us."

"Then keep it up," Hunter said immediately. "I'll let you know when I find something."

And, with that, he disappeared into the force field.

CELINA PLACED HER hand in Stefan's. "If that's the case, how can he go through it?"

"He's an energy hunter, so he can move through almost all mediums. Energy was one that took him the longest to figure out, but he can use it to track her."

"Is that wise?"

"Hunter appears to be on a mission," Stefan said, quietly sliding an arm around his wife's shoulders and pulling her up close.

"I like her," she murmured.

"I do too," Stefan said. "She was very young when I was there. I think only five, maybe six, but just a child, barely more than a toddler. She had no idea what was going on, but she never once cried for her mommy and daddy. I remember that. I tried to befriend her and did for a time, but there was only so much I could do as a prisoner myself. But I did try to comfort her, you know, help her sleep and ease her fear when she was locked up."

"Did she even have parents at the time?"

"I don't know," he murmured. "I don't remember."

"But she remembered you, and, even after all these years, she found you. That's what I find stunning."

"I think she experienced a shock wave, almost like a slice of her memory returned to her. Maybe because of all the fragmenting happening to her system. Regardless she somehow remembered me and managed to find me, which I don't understand either. I'm not sure she understands any better."

"Do you think she'll be okay?"

He squeezed Celina's shoulders gently. "Well, I can't tell you what tomorrow will bring, but, for the moment, she's okay."

"Why wouldn't she stay?" she asked, with a note of urgency, turning to look up at him. "We could have helped her."

"We are helping her," he said thoughtfully, still staring out the front door. "And I think Hunter will be the best thing for her."

"Why is that?"

"Because of the energy they share," he said, his lips twitching. "Hunter doesn't know it, but he'll get the shock of a lifetime when he figures this out."

"Figures what out?" she demanded.

He looked down at her, gently kissed Celina's forehead, and said, "They have a connection. A big one."

"What kind?"

"The best kind," he said.

She glared at him, and he shook his head. "I'm not being difficult. I'm asking, is a big surprise coming for Hunter?"

"Well, he has to find her first."

"Very true."

"And let's hope he finds her quickly."

"Why? What do you see?"

He stared off in the distance and shrugged. "Trouble. She's had a lot of it in her life, and it won't stop anytime soon."

"There's got to be something we can do to help her," she said urgently.

"We're working on it," he reminded her. He motioned her back into the house. "It's time to go inside."

"At least that bullet hole of hers healed."

"Dr. Maddy and I are both quite surprised by her ability to heal. It's phenomenal."

"I wondered when I saw it," she said. "It had only been

two days, and it looked like it had already healed for several weeks. Almost closed over."

"If she'd rest longer, even another day, it probably would have been."

"Do you know what they did to her?"

He hesitated and then slowly nodded. "I saw bits and pieces in visions," he said, "and I saw enough when I was there with her to have a good idea."

"Well, … will you tell me?"

He looked down at her and, with a serious tone, asked, "Do you want to have nightmares for the rest of your life?"

She winced. "That bad?"

"That bad," he said, with a nod. "Absolutely that bad."

"Why are people like that?" she asked softly. "That poor woman doesn't deserve this."

"No, she doesn't, not at all," he murmured. "And we've got to do what we can to help her, so they can't capture her again. I think they kept her as a tool—as a weapon—and now they want that weapon back."

"You don't think they did before?"

"Oh, I think they did, but I also think that they have a use for her again. Perhaps she took off at a time when they had no particular use for her, and now they do, and they're angry. I don't know. It's hard to say."

"Do you think that they let her come here specifically to lead them to you?"

He stopped, looked at her, and said, "I was hoping you wouldn't guess that option."

"I'm not a fool," she said, steadily looking at him. "When people come here, it's usually because you let them."

"Very much so," he said. "I always put that beacon out there, in case people need help, but that doesn't always mean

I know what's coming."

"And that's the concern," she said quietly. "Because you don't know if maybe this woman didn't lead some other element here."

"Well, it's not another element that she had any control over," he said quietly, as he locked the front door.

"And then you lock the front door," she said, almost laughing in dismay. "What good will that do?"

He said, "We have people who can walk through walls. We have people who can walk through doors, but still, if you put up an energy message that says, 'Keep out,' it's one more lock they have to figure out."

She nodded. "I know that. It just seems so pointless."

"It's not pointless," he said. "Let's go have tea."

"Tea doesn't solve everything either," she said in a wry tone.

"Nope, it doesn't, but it sure does make us feel better."

And, with that, she laughed and let herself be led to the kitchen.

CHAPTER 5

B ETH MELTED INTO the scenery around her, a particularly easy skill for someone like her. She hadn't told Stefan, and she hadn't wanted Hunter to even know, but wrapping in the energy of those around her let Beth hide almost indefinitely. But the thing about being hunted was that Beth had learned how to become safe as prey too. She knew what the hunter would do to find her, so she could counteract that somewhat.

As she leaned against the tree, letting her energy camouflage with the tree itself, she studied the surroundings, while doing a self-assessment. Her body's energy was at about 50 percent, the wound at 80 percent. She rubbed a hand over it gently, feeling the sore muscles and the puckered skin beneath her fingertips. A ball of healing energy added to the sensation.

"It's much better," she murmured out loud in surprise. She rotated her shoulders and her neck, even as she mentally called out to the bits and pieces of her energy to return. She just needed to get that 50 percent boosted much higher. She had a long way to go, even though she had no destination in mind. She had to get away from here, before her presence brought problems to Stefan.

Now to search for a new destination and to not do anything stupid. And definitely not get caught.

If she could utilize her system properly, she could pull more energy from Mother Earth around her. There was never any shortage of energy, but there was a shortage of energy she could use. Being so statically charged, she had to warm up the energy and then bring it into her system in a different way. As her body was still healing, that slowed down the process. Which is why, when she'd been injured, she couldn't do it at all. So, instead of her energy recharging, it had faded quickly.

She moved out of the trees, wondering where to get a set of wheels so she could travel faster. Money was another thing she didn't want to locate on her own. If she hit an ATM or a bank, they could track her. She had credit cards and cash on her, just not enough. It was never enough if you needed to disappear. She hadn't set up safe deposits anywhere, nor stashed cash at various locations. She hadn't had time, since she'd been on the run forever and, of course, obtaining cash was a whole different issue. As she took two more steps forward, a voice called out to her.

"You don't have to be alone, you know."

She froze and turned to look at Hunter, glaring at him. "Why can't you let me leave?"

"Because you're hurt and you're heading toward certain death."

Her eyebrows shot up at that. "Certain death is something we all have to face."

He nodded slowly. "And you've had a rougher time of it than most. But I don't want you to disappear right now. Not alone at least."

"I want to go alone," she said.

"I have wheels," he offered.

She froze, as she studied him carefully. "And?"

"If you have a destination in mind, I can help you get there."

She thought about it, wondering what the payoff would be and what he would want in return. "There's always a price," she said boldly. "What is yours?"

It was his turn to raise his eyebrows. "In this case, the joy of doing a good deed."

She snorted at that. "People in my world don't do things like that."

"Because you haven't had the right people in your world."

It was hard to argue with that. She'd had assholes and bastards around her for a very long time.

"Who's hunting you?"

"My captors." She shouldn't be telling him even that much.

"Someone in particular?"

"Lizzy," she said faintly as if giving voice to the name would give it more power.

"This Lizzy girl, will she be hunting you?"

"I didn't think she would bother me anymore," she said quickly, "but I no longer know."

"And would you blame her, if she is?"

"I don't blame her for anything she might do to stay alive and to stay sane," she said, "and nobody should."

"I get it," he said, holding up his hands in front of him. "I'm not accusing anybody. I do know what it's like to be alone and to have the world against you."

"You do, huh?" She studied him for a moment, seeing him nod.

"Different than your case, for sure," he said, "but we all have stories to tell. Most of us don't like telling them."

"Isn't that the truth. I do have a cabin I can go to," she said quietly.

"In that case, I'm happy to drive you."

She shook her head. "It's too far away, but, if you can get me where I can connect to a bus, that would be great."

"Where is it you want to go?"

"I was thinking up by the Canadian border."

He frowned at that. "Are you planning on crossing?"

"No plans at all yet," she said easily.

"A lot of land is between here and there," he said quietly, "not all of it easy."

"None of it's easy," she said simply. "I'm just looking for a way to get through this and to get somewhere I can hole up to heal more."

"So, the cabin would be temporary?"

"Very," she said, "every place will always be temporary."

"You can't spend your life on the run forever."

"Sure, I can," she said, with a half laugh. "It's all I know."

"You've never had a safe place to rest, have you?"

She shook her head. "No."

"Well, how about, instead of your cabin, you go to my cabin?"

She looked at him. "Where is your cabin?"

"Well, that's what makes it special," he said. "Whoever is hunting you doesn't know where it is. Whatever connection you have, they'll pry at, until they can get it out of you or whoever might know you."

"Nobody knows me," she said.

"But they tracked you here."

"Yes," she said, hesitating and looking back in the direction of Stefan's house. "I'll feel terrible if they get a hold of him. I needed his healing, or I'd be dead by now."

"Stefan can handle himself."

"You seem confident in that."

"Well, you knew him before, right?" Hunter asked easily, not taking a step forward but keeping his distance. "What was he like?"

"Tormented, like the rest of us, and driven to get out of there. Driven to succeed in a way that would ensure he'd never become a victim again."

"Well, in that case, he succeeded in a big way."

"Maybe, but everybody can still become a victim. You don't know how easy it is to get that mind-set all screwed up again, until you are one."

"Very true," he said quietly.

"And I don't intend on being one ever again either."

"Good. You should also know I have helped put away a lot of criminals."

"That's just making you cocky," she challenged. "How many of them have had abilities?"

"Some," he said. "Either way, I'm not prepared to back down from the challenge."

"You should," she said calmly. "You don't understand these people and what they're doing."

"There's got to be a reason why they're doing it though. What's their endgame?" he asked curiously.

"Control," she said instantly.

He nodded slowly, as if understanding what that meant. "Control of people, control of circumstances?"

"I don't know. He has high plans, and I think he's just looking bigger and bigger."

"As in government bigger or law enforcement bigger?"

"All of the above," she said quietly. "You don't know

how dangerous these people are."

"All the more reason," he said, "to put a stop to them."

"And again, not that easy to do."

"Maybe not …" His voice trailed off.

The smartest thing she could do was make use of his assistance and then leave him somewhere before he got caught. She didn't want him to get hurt, not after he'd helped her, not since Stefan obviously cared about him. "You understand it's a death wish to do anything with me, right?"

"I understand you believe that," he said.

She smiled. "Yeah, well, that's exactly what it is." She shook her head and said, "I get that you think you have the answers and that you can do something that's better than what anybody else has tried."

"Tell me," he said. "Have many people tried, or has he kept to the shadows up until now, while working on a game plan?"

"I think he has kept in the shadows," she said quietly, "but that won't last much longer."

"And can he do things, like rob banks or coerce people into doing things they don't want to do?"

"Well, they already have done the latter," she said, staring at him. "Did you not understand anything of what I said?"

"I think I understood it," he said, "but a lot of criminal activity is out there, and we don't know what people are up to."

"Maybe," she said, "but also a lot of people don't want to know exactly what others are up to either. For them ignorance is bliss."

"Very true," he said. "So, what'll it be? A ride in my vehicle or not?"

She nodded slowly. "I guess."

He smiled. "In that case, let's go."

"Where are we going?"

"I'll walk you down to the road. Then I'll go get my vehicle from Stefan's place."

"Will you tell them?"

"*Pfft*. Stefan already knows," he said. "That's one of the things about Stefan. It's pretty hard to pull anything over on him."

"I just want to keep him safe," she said.

"He knows and appreciates that, but, at the same time, it frustrates him because he's already in a certain amount of danger on a daily basis, so what you do won't change or affect that."

"It could make it a lot worse," she murmured.

"Maybe. But it could also be something that ends up being not a big deal."

She shrugged. "So go get the vehicle then."

He smiled, nodded, and asked, "You'll be here when I come back?"

Seeing the road ahead of her, she said, "I guess we'll know when you get there."

He hesitated and then, swearing, turned and bolted into the woods.

She smiled, and, as soon as he was on his way, she turned and disappeared again.

HUNTER SWORE, AS soon as he picked up the vehicle and headed down because he knew, in his heart of hearts, that she'd already left. "Damn it," he said out loud. "I shouldn't have trusted her."

She was so determined to get the hell out of here, and he'd wanted to give her a place to go where she could at least hole up and heal long enough to be in fighting form. But she didn't appear to believe in anybody. What a life had she gone through that this was her reality? It must have been pretty difficult in many ways. As he drove down the street, he kept hoping that maybe he'd see her.

Even though he knew she was gone, and her energy had somehow dissipated all around, he would find her. He wouldn't give up. He got out of the vehicle and leaned against it, as he studied the darkness. She was here somewhere. Using his peripheral senses, he studied the hills, looking for shifts in the energy. If she'd come this way, he would see the traces that she left behind. Energy spores, so to speak.

But he found absolutely nothing, which meant that she had gone up instead of down. He shook his head at that. She was obviously much more comfortable in the night, in the bowels of Mother Nature, than being around two-legged humans.

As he studied the area up ahead, he saw a road winding up around the back of a hill. On a hunch he got back into the car and headed that way. When he got to higher ground that gave him a beautiful view down below, he parked off to the side and hopped out. And he smiled because he could sense her. He called out, "The offer still stands."

She stepped out from behind a tree and glared at him.

He gave her a fat smile. "Did you think you could get away from me that easily?"

"Well, I tried," she said, then hesitated and looked at the vehicle.

"I know you're tired," he said, "and you don't have to

exhaust yourself just staying hidden. It burns up a ton of energy. It's not necessary." He motioned at the car. "Offer stands," he said. "Up to you."

She shot him a look, walked toward the vehicle, and got inside without saying another word.

He hopped in, holding back his smile. Round one had gone to him.

CHAPTER 6

THREE HOURS LATER Beth finally spoke. "Where exactly are we going?" She'd been pondering the route for the last few hours, wondering what their final destination was. She almost recognized part of the journey, but her memories weren't serving her enough to place it.

"Well, I have a spot on the Oregon coast."

She stared.

Hunter shrugged. "It belonged to my grandfather."

"Will they track that?"

"We don't have the same name, so I doubt it. He's also been gone for quite a while."

"Whose name is it under?"

He just looked at her and said, "You don't trust much, do you?"

"I don't trust at all," she shot back.

As they drove, he pulled into a small gas station to fill up, and he said, "We will need to pick up groceries for the cabin."

"Agreed." She nodded. "So a store large enough that we can get lost in."

As soon as the gas tank was filled up, he paid and hopped back into the vehicle.

Sitting in the passenger seat, she turned and asked, "Why are you doing this?"

"Because I believe in you."

The words were so shocking and yet seemingly so honest, she frowned, as she studied his profile, looking for any sign of deceit. She studied his energy, what little she saw. All of her abilities were completely decimated in direct proportion to her decimated energy. She couldn't see or read much from people for a while. Even then, that wasn't her strong point. She had to keep her energy focused on looking for the ones who were after her. She sagged into the corner. "You could be betting on the wrong horse."

"I've often done that," he said, "but I still learn in the process."

What could she say to that? He drove another ten to fifteen miles and then pulled into what looked like a community shopping mall. She tucked her hair inside her jacket and followed him into the grocery store. He grabbed a shopping cart and proceeded to put loads of fresh fruit, vegetables, and meat into it. She added a jug of milk, so she could have tea the way she loved it, and some cheese. When she stopped at the apples, she frowned.

He asked, "What kind do you like?"

"Galas are my favorite—or pink lady's."

He chuckled and said, "Let's grab both." And he quickly bagged up a few of each.

She looked at the growing pile of groceries in the cart and said, "How will you pay for this?"

"Money," he said easily.

"But I don't have any."

"No worries," he said. "I have plenty."

"Good for you," she said, "because I'm broke."

"Of course you are," he said, "but the fact that you even survived these last few years is amazing."

"I had a job," she said. "It was enough."

On the road again, he said, "We'll have another hour or so on the road, if you want to sleep."

"I don't sleep much," she said, studying the road as it disappeared.

He nodded. "We could talk."

"I don't want to talk."

He gave a bark of laughter. "Not a whole lot you do want to do then, is there?"

"I want to live my life without this added weight," she said. Surely he could understand that, at least she hoped he could. She sighed and said, "It's not your fault. I'm not angry at you."

"Aren't you?"

She shook her head. "I'm not, not really. I'm just, I don't want this for my life."

"What will you do about it?"

"Well, that's the trick, isn't it? If I don't do something, this will continue. I can hide my head in the sand as long as I want, but it won't change anything. I thought I was safe, thought they'd given up. But they hadn't."

He winced. "And I'm sorry for that. Living on the run is no fun. I'd like to see these guys caught and jailed."

"I would too. I would too," she said, staring out at the darkness and the trees all around them. A question burned on the back of her mind. "How long have you known Stefan?"

"A decade," he said simply. "Plus."

She nodded, yet frowned. "And you've worked with him that long?"

"Off and on. What you probably don't know is that Stefan has a whole team of gifted people like us."

"Like us?" she said, questioning.

"Energy workers."

She studied him. "So, what do you do that is special?"

"I don't do anything," he said, "and I especially don't do parlor tricks."

She nodded. "I figured that would get to you."

"Well, hardly the nicest question."

"Maybe not," she said, "but it does tell you what people are like."

"Maybe," he said in a noncommittal voice. "But to answer the question you didn't ask, I'm a good hunter."

"Meaning that you can follow energy."

"Sure, but lots of people can do that." He shrugged, showed his teeth.

She studied him and said, "A lot more to you than that."

"Maybe," he said. "A lot more to you than what you're showing us too."

"Sure," she said, "but I don't know what there is."

"What do you mean by that?"

"I spent so much time being tested and used to test others, that I don't know the full extent of what I can do."

"And you've never had to test the limits of your abilities?"

"Nope, not at all," she said. "Maybe it'd be better if I did."

"I don't know about that," he said. "Life is tough enough without coming up with answers for everything."

She burst out laughing. "Wouldn't it be nice if there were any answers for us?"

"True," he said, with a smile, "but obviously that's not happening."

"No." She leaned back, closed her eyes, and said, "I'll

just rest."

"Is that different than sleeping?"

Her eyes flew open, and she said, "I rarely sleep," she said, in a dark tone. "Best you remember that."

With that, she closed her eyes and zoned him out.

HUNTER HAD NEVER met anybody as prickly, as cantankerous, and as hard to get along with as Beth was. Did she really not sleep? He wondered about that because she had surely slept at Stefan's before. But maybe that was because she was injured and so badly overwhelmed by everything. That was certainly possible, though it didn't say a whole lot about her body's ability to function if she couldn't sleep because it also meant a lack of trust. But then she'd probably been sleeping with one eye open all this time, and that's more likely what she meant.

He kept driving, ignoring his passenger, as he tried to remember the pathway from this road. He'd taken a different entrance, avoiding all the main routes to keep them a little bit hidden. He also had managed to make a couple contacts and to send a few texts before he left. One to Stefan to let him know what they were doing and another to a friend, hoping that the cabin would have heat and power by the time he got there, as well as a stash of weapons he could utilize. Not everybody did this same type of work, but Hunter had enough friends in the private sector that he could get what he needed, when he needed it.

Finally he took the turnoff onto the road he wanted and drove down the rough gravel for a good ten to fifteen minutes. He wasn't at all surprised when he looked over to see her studying the area with interest. "The cabin's up there."

She didn't say anything, but she did sit up and pull her jacket a little closer around her.

"It will be colder just because we're at the lake, and the weather isn't supposed to be all that great for the next few days," he said.

She just nodded.

He frowned. "You don't have to go out of your way to be cranky, you know?"

"I'm like this all the time."

He shook his head and said, "Interesting way to get along with life."

"I don't plan on getting along with anybody," she said. Then she looked at him and added, "You don't have to stay at the cabin. You know that, right?"

He shrugged and said, "Let's get you healed up, get your energy back to normal, and then see how you're doing."

"And you won't hold me captive?"

"No," he said, "I won't hold you captive."

She studied him intently, then turned and completely ignored him again.

He pulled up in front of the cabin, happy to see that lights were on at several other cabins around.

"There are neighbors?" she asked in alarm.

"A few, but they don't know who you are. Remember?"

"But they could find out easily enough."

"Maybe, and maybe they don't care to. Not everybody knows or cares who you are."

"And yet enough do," she said, "and that, for me, is a problem."

"Maybe it's a problem, or maybe the problem is you being overly paranoid."

"Maybe not," she said, as she swung open the door and stepped out.

He watched her as she assessed the area. He saw the boundaries, the barriers going up, the energy probes going out, and recognized somebody who had been on the defensive for a long time. But something else was going on in there too, something he couldn't quite understand. Energy went off in directions he couldn't keep track of. He frowned at that but didn't say anything and just kept watching.

Finally she turned to him and said, "Will you let me in?"

He raised an eyebrow and said, "Absolutely. After you, ma'am."

Just enough sarcasm was in his voice that she glared at him. "I don't have to stay here."

"Nope, you sure don't. You are more than welcome to go wherever you want."

"What if I took your vehicle?"

"Well, I can't say I'd be thrilled, but it'd be easy enough to get it back."

"And how's that?"

"Do you think I wouldn't track it?"

She smiled and said, "Of course you would." She walked up to the front of the cabin and waited for him to join her. He unlocked the front door and pushed it open. As she stepped inside, he heard her suck back the breath in her throat at the view that opened up, as soon as she stepped through. "It's beautiful," she whispered.

"It is, indeed," he said. "This is where I plan to retire one day."

"One day? Why not now?"

"Because I spend a lot of my time hunting."

"Are you sure you want to do that?" she said. "It doesn't

sound like that great of a pastime."

"I'm helping people. Like Stefan helps others like us. What's not to like?"

"Maybe," she said.

He said, "Wow. You don't even trust Stefan, much less me."

She nodded.

"So you'll never share information with us, based on that lack of trust, right?"

She remained silent, gave a one-arm shrug.

"And you'll always be so cryptic?" She tried to hide her grin, and he burst out laughing at that. Suddenly he realized just how much of the problem was her inability to even recognize friend from foe and to relax in a circumstance that was well past what she was used to. He said, "I'm not here to hurt you."

"Well, you could have tried already, and we would have had this discussion with you pinned to the ground."

He looked at her with interest. "Well, I'm glad to see you think you have some skills."

"I do," she said absentmindedly. "And, if you keep pushing, you'll find out."

"Well, I hope I don't," he said, "because it would mean that I attempt to get you under control."

At the term *control*, she stiffened.

He cringed at his use of the term. "I didn't mean it in that abusive way."

She turned ever-so-slightly and looked at him, and he saw the huge black wells of pain on the inside. "Just in case you ever think you *will* use that term," she said, "I can tell you, right now, that you won't succeed."

He held up his hands. "Sorry. Like I said, didn't mean it

that way."

She studied him for a long moment and then nodded. "Good thing," she whispered, "I wouldn't want to have to kill you."

With that, she turned and walked toward the windows, leaving him standing there in shock, staring after her.

CHAPTER 7

B ETH DIDN'T KNOW why she was being so difficult, except that she was still edgy. The farther away from Stefan's place she got, the more nervous she became, and all she could do was not show it. Inside the grocery store she'd been one step away from bolting out to the parking lot, stealing the vehicle, and disappearing. She'd learned a few tricks in the last few years and had befriended a couple homeless guys. One had showed her how to boost cars, and another had taught her how to pick door locks. She was decent with both after many hours of practice, but it still wasn't the same as being safe. Having skills helped; it gave you power in a powerless world. It made you no longer a victim, after being a victim for too many years. But still, not enough.

She stood here, staring at the view, wondering how something so absolutely gorgeous could belong to one person. She shook her head, hearing him come up behind her.

"It's something, isn't it?" he said, his tone soft and calm, like oil on her troubled water.

She gave him a sideways glance. "I'm still struggling to understand how one person could own this."

"A lot of people own something like this," he commented, studying her directly.

She shrugged. "I've never seen anything like it."

"Many houses are up and down lakes, rivers, and ocean-fronts," he said, "and many are far more spectacular than this."

"But that's Mother Nature right there," she said, "so close you want to believe you can just reach out and touch it."

He walked to the left a few feet, and, as she watched, he opened up a huge sliding door that must be at least eight feet across, then motioned for her to step out with him. He stepped out first, and a huge deck ran the length of the house and around the corner. From there, steps went down to another level with another deck and a little bit of a walkway down to the lake below.

"It's so beautiful," she whispered. She sat near the top step, wondering if her knees would even hold her up after seeing such a place.

"Where have you been living?"

"Garages, basements, storage units," she said, with a wave of her hand. "They were all I was comfortable with."

"You were kept in a concrete windowless room?" he guessed.

She looked up at him and smiled gently. "Yes. So, anything other than that never quite felt safe. Odd, I know, since I was tortured in that compound, but somehow my room was not where I was *trained*, as they called it. Being held there for so long made me wary of anything else. Being out in Mother Nature, even like this, it took me a long time to venture out," she said. "To go for a walk or to feel the wind on my face, it was all so foreign. As much as I loved it, the lack of security made me want to run back inside again and shut the doors. I had spent all that time under their control, doing what I was told to do, without the ability to go anywhere, and then, when I got the freedom, I didn't know what to do with it. I couldn't reconcile safety with it in any way."

"But it's different now," he said.

She laughed. "It sure is. What's different is the fact that even more people are out there after me, more danger that I must find a way to get around," she murmured. "It's certainly not that it's any safer." She looked at the houses barely visible on the neighboring properties on either side. "When you see that people are right there," she said, "doesn't it bother you?"

He looked at her and shook his head. "No, not at all," he said quietly. "They aren't after us. They aren't after anything but peace and quiet for themselves. We don't bother each other. We're friendly when we need to be and always cordial, but, beyond that, I don't have any contact with them."

She nodded slowly. "And you trust that?"

"I do," he said with a smile. "And eventually you'll get there too."

"Not as long as I'm being hunted," she said quietly.

"Nope, but that state doesn't have to continue."

"Says you."

He shrugged. "Let's get the groceries inside."

She followed him back out to the car. She studied everything, as she moved through the motions of unloading, her gaze constantly searching and looking around.

"See?" he said, when they got back inside. "Nothing to worry about."

She just gave him an odd look and said, "I'm surprised you would say that."

"Why?"

She said, "Because danger's everywhere."

"Sure, but you can't just give in to it. You still have to live."

Her lips quirked. "I tried that, and then one morning I got up, went outside into the sunshine, and stretched, wondering how it could be such a beautiful morning, and I took a bullet in the side."

Stated so simply, it had more impact, and, although she didn't mean for it to come across that way, she heard him suck in his breath. Turning to face him, she said, "I didn't mean to bring that up again. It's just hard to forget that's how I got to be here."

"I get that," he said quietly, "and obviously you'll still deal with a lot of memories and issues on a daily basis."

"It happened just when I thought I was doing so well," she said. She turned to study the area around her. "I can stay here for a little bit," she said. "Maybe long enough to heal."

"On a scale of one to ten, where are you?"

"I'd say five. The stress affects me in an ugly way," she said, with a nod.

"So you need to make sure your time here is as stress-free as possible."

"So, how will we do that?" she asked, with a laugh, looking at him.

"Have you ever been fishing?"

She shook her head. "I'm not even sure what it involves," she murmured, as she looked out at the lake. It called to her in a way she'd never felt before. "Does it mean going out there?"

"It does, indeed. I have a boat down at the dock." He pointed off to the side at a small rowboat.

"Is that thing safe in the water?" she asked doubtfully.

At that, he burst out laughing. "Absolutely," he said, with a bright smile. "But we'll get to that later."

"Maybe," she said, "but how do you protect yourself when you're out there?"

He took a deep breath. "Well, you make sure that you're not being followed, before you get out there," he said, trying for a logical answer. "And then you just have to trust."

She winced at that. "Back to that trust thing again."

"I know it's hard for you."

"Very," she said, "but, if you think it's safe, I could consider it. You should have better instincts than I do."

"Oh, I doubt it," he said. "Your instincts should be phenomenal, after being hunted all this time. Nothing makes you more in tune to what's going on around you than that."

"Maybe," she said, "but it would be nice to get out for a bit."

"And we will," he said, "after we get some dinner and after you get a good night's rest."

She nodded slowly. "I won't let down my guard," she said, "so don't ask me to."

"I would never ask anybody to do that," he said. "That guard is what kept you alive all these years. Don't let it down on my say-so."

She smiled and said, "Okay, good."

And, with that, he asked, "How do you feel about pasta?"

"I like it if it's cooked," she said, "but the raw stuff is

hard to get down." He looked at her sideways, unsure what to say. She shrugged. "I didn't know how to cook when I first came out," she explained, with a smile. "It took a bit and watching lots of videos to understand that some stuff you had to cook, and other stuff was ready to eat out of the package."

He grinned at that. "That's a hard lesson to learn," he said, "but I'm sure you learned it fast."

"Yeah, I got it right the first time after that," she said, chuckling.

"What else have you learned to cook?"

"Lots," she said. "I have an affinity for it, I think."

"Good," he said. "I'll cook dinner tonight, since I'm rested up, and maybe you can cook dinner tomorrow."

"I can do that," she said, "as long as we have something that I know how to cook."

"That's always the caveat, isn't it?" he said. While she watched, he quickly put together a simple pasta with fresh tomatoes, canned olives, and parmesan.

"That looks good," she said. "I would never have thought to combine them like that."

"I like simple meals," he said, "especially if I don't have a ton of time. And, right now, getting a meal on the table quickly seemed like the best idea."

"I won't argue," she said. "Seems like a long time since whatever I ate at Stefan's."

"And that was nothing but a couple muffins and sandwiches," he said, "and nowhere near enough for your body to heal."

"My body heals all the time and from sources that you have no idea of."

"Should we have bought pet food then?"

At that, she froze and turned slowly to stare at him. "Why would you ask that?"

"Well, *you* didn't knock on Stefan's door," he said. "You told us that at Stefan's, and you haven't explained who did. You also weren't alone, but the companion energy is very different. I don't have a ton of experience with animal energy, but," he said, his gaze studying her, "you've also never mentioned anybody else being here. Not to me anyway."

"So," she said, "why would you mention it then?"

"Because I sense another energy with us. And I thought one spoke to me at Stefan's."

She frowned.

He groaned and said, "You can just tell me if you have a pet, you know."

"Do you think I would leave a pet behind?" Interesting he could sense but not see Nocturne. She waited until Hunter was focused on setting the table, then turned and winked at her cat. He swished his tail at her but stayed quiet. Was that in case Hunter heard Nocturne again?

Hunter shook his head. "No, I don't think you would have. The question is whether you managed to get him in the vehicle while I wasn't watching."

She just gave him an openmouthed look and shrugged. Then she picked up a spoonful of pasta and ate it. And just as he went to do the same, a huge black cat jumped up on the table in front of him and meowed. She laughed. "Nocturne, your timing is impeccable."

The big cat stared at her, then turned those massive golden orbs to Hunter.

Hunter stared at him in shock. "Where did he come from?" he demanded.

"And you're the one who had it all worked out," she said casually.

"He was in the vehicle?"

She nodded. "Of course. I brought him with me."

"What about at Stefan's?"

"He was outside, but I opened the window, and he came in and spent the night with me. But he always leaves before anybody else is around."

"So *he* knocked on Stefan's door, when you were unable to." She avoided his gaze. Hunter turned to Nocturne. "Thank you for watching out for her." He studied the cat, who stared right back, measuring him. "Yet he appears here now, before me and you," Hunter said, still staring at the massive feline. "Why is he visible now?"

"Because he chooses to be," she said, facing Hunter. "He's obviously checked over your energy and made a decision about you. Honestly I'm surprised. He's often been very difficult about making those kinds of decisions."

"Difficult?"

"Yeah, he doesn't like people," she said bluntly. "Especially men." Her gaze narrowed, as she studied the look on Hunter's face. "Particularly young men."

He looked at her, eyebrows up. "What difference does age make? Isn't it just about character?"

She shrugged. "Let's just say, he has his preferences."

"So, do I pass muster?"

"You're still alive," she said succinctly. "So, I would say, yes, you do."

CHAPTER 8

HOURS LATER, DOWN at the edge of the lake, Beth sat hidden in the brush beside the dock, a cup of tea in her hand, wondering how quickly her life had shifted and changed. But then it was the only reason she'd stayed alive. Hunter walked down the path onto the dock and out toward the end, as he studied the water and the horizon. He turned to look at her and said, "If you wanted to go fishing, right now is not a bad time."

She frowned. Damn, she didn't expect him to see her. "But I'm quite happy right here, with my tea."

"When we go inside, I have hair dye for you, so you can change your hair color too."

Her eyebrows shot up. "My hair doesn't change color."

He frowned at that.

"It's jet-black," she said, "very hard to change."

"I was thinking of a blue."

"You know what? That might work," she said hesitantly. "I've tried to dye it various browns and blonde, but it never works."

"I figured a blue-black might be okay," he said, studying her. "It is almost too jet-black to be natural."

She smiled. "And yet it is."

"Your skin is almost too white to be natural too," he said, standing in front of her, his arms across his chest, frowning, as if he didn't like the color of her skin.

She shrugged. "It's always been that way."

"Bloodred lips too," he said. "It looks like you've got on makeup, and yet I know there is none."

She just stared at him steadily. If he dug deeper, he would find out some of the secrets she didn't want anybody to know because, as soon as they got wind of it, it would mean more explanations, and she wasn't up for that.

She waited until he turned to look out on the horizon again and said, "Depending on how long we're here for, we can go fishing another day." He shoved his hands in his pockets, and she saw he was almost itching to go out. "Are you a fisherman?"

He tossed her a casual grin. "I caught the bug a few years back," he said. "And I promised myself I'd come here many times, but I just never managed to get here."

"Work?"

He nodded. "Work." But he didn't offer anything else.

She had to wonder what somebody who worked for Stefan would do. "Does he pay you?" He stiffened ever-so-slightly and didn't answer. She knew it wasn't that he hadn't heard but that he chose not to.

"We have more time to cook now. I'll go put some meat in marinades for the barbecue."

She nodded slowly. "Vegetables? I'm kind of a rabbit."

"You're not a vegetarian, are you?" he asked.

Such a note of shock was in his voice that she had to laugh. "You make it sound like that could be the absolute worst thing in the world."

"For me, it would be," he said candidly. "I am very much a carnivore."

"Good for you," she said, "but I've never been able to

afford much meat."

"Ah," he said, "now that's a different story." She raised an eyebrow. "I can afford meat," he said, "so I eat it."

"Good, and I certainly won't say no, if it's there." As a matter of fact, she felt her mouth watering at the thought of a good thick steak.

"Steak is food for the kings," he said, as if echoing her thoughts.

"I can't even remember the last time I had one."

"When you were a captive, what did you eat?"

"For a long time, it wasn't even food, at least not anything we would recognize as food. A gruel, with all kinds of supplements and nutrients in it. They kept us healthy, healthy, healthy, but with absolutely zero appreciation of what real food was, until our teeth weren't developing properly. Then they suddenly gave us food to chew, bread to bite on, bones to gnaw on," she said, shaking her head. "We had superhard baked crackers, just to give our digestion and our teeth and our jaws some practice. But most of the food was liquid."

"That sounds disgusting."

"Later," she said, "we had some changes in diet. We would get things like oatmeal and puddings, soft foods, but they could mix whatever they wanted into it, without us having the ability to taste much of it."

"Is that why they did it?"

"I think so. Some of us got more common food, but, if you resisted or caused them any trouble, you got mostly liquid food," she said, with a half smile. "So I spent a good half of my life on liquid foods."

He chuckled at that. "Not surprised at that, but I am surprised that you have any enzymes to digest food at all."

"It's one of the things I did when I left. I struggled with supplementation to eat naturally. But I survived," she said. "And beef hasn't been cost-effective enough for me to eat."

"Well, you get it now," he said. "Let's go take a look." He reached out a hand toward her.

She nodded, and, using his hand to pull herself up, she managed to straighten without too much pain digging into her.

"How is the wound?" he asked.

"Healing," she said, keeping her response short. She led the way up the hill, finding it a little bit of a climb. By the time she made it to the lower-level deck, he said, "We can go inside, if you want."

She shook her head and kept on going up the staircase to the left until she got to the upper deck. There she slowly sagged into one of the outdoor chairs. "You're blessed to have something like this," she said wistfully.

"How much understanding do you have of the real world? I don't mean to offend. It's a sincere question."

"Thank you for that. I understand quite a bit," she said. "We had to take lessons in economy and how the actual banking system works. How society worked. It's a good thing we did because, when I was finally free, it's one of the few ways that I could put my education to use."

"That makes sense," he said.

She wasn't sure when she closed her eyes, but sitting here in the sun in the late afternoon, as he sat beside her, waiting on the steaks, she felt her eyes drift closed. She would force them open, and then they would drift closed again, and finally she just dozed. Awake, asleep, awake, asleep. Somewhere in the distance, she heard a man talking.

"No, she's here. ... I know. I know it's a dangerous

time."

She frowned at that, opening her eyes and turning on her senses. She thought she recognized Hunter's voice, coming off from the side. She shifted her head to look around, and, sure enough, he walked a pathway on the opposite side from where the vehicle was parked, toward a neighbor's property. But Hunter was talking on his phone. His voice was picked up by the wind and moving for added clarity. She strained to hear, but, by then, he was too far away, until he started walking back. She tried hard to listen, but she still hadn't healed enough to do the job properly.

"Oh, I know. I don't want to tell her. ... Yes, I know. I will. ... No, I'll let you know if anything changes. ... Yeah, okay. I'll expect him." With that, he hung up.

She sagged back in her chair, and she wondered just what that all meant. Who had he just talked to? Was it Stefan or somebody completely different? She didn't want to be so nervous and so worried about everything but hard not to be when it sounded like he was talking about her to somebody she didn't know. He came up on the deck a few minutes later. She studied his energy.

He smiled at her. "You're awake again, huh?"

She nodded slowly. "So, are we alone here?" she asked bluntly.

He nodded. "I mean, people are in other houses," he said, motioning at the neighbors. "But we're alone here."

"Does anybody know where we are?"

His response was instantaneous. "Stefan."

She let out her breath, feeling something inside her untwist. "Is that all?" she asked cautiously. And then she saw the shadow that crossed in front of his face. And inside her, everything tensed, as she waited for his answer.

"No one else knows that I know of," he said. He gave her a bright smile. "I'll go check on the steaks."

She nodded, irate that he wouldn't tell her about the phone call and now must kiss the steaks goodbye. As soon as he was inside and out of sight, she got up and walked, as if going to the bathroom, then snuck around the corner of the cabin and headed for the vehicle.

As soon as she slipped inside, she released the brake and let it roll down the driveway ever-so-slightly, enough that she could direct where it would go. Then, as soon as she hit the bottom of the driveway, she turned on the engine, circled around, and tore out of there. She had no idea where she was going; she just knew she had to get away.

She raced back to the highway, not even sure where she was, but, without a phone or any navigation equipment, it would be a case of just getting as far away as she could, as fast as she could. She hit the gas as soon as she reached the highway, putting her speed well over one hundred, going back the way they had come. She didn't know how long it would be before Hunter noticed that she was gone or how long until he rousted a set of wheels, but it wouldn't be very long before he was on to her. She needed to exchange his vehicle for another one soon. She drove up to where they got the groceries, then pulled around to the parking area in back and checked the glove box for money or anything of use to her.

She found a twenty stashed inside and grabbed it, then tossed the keys under the floormat, where she'd found them, hopped out of his car, and raced into the store. As she walked in, she checked out the energy, looking to see if she were being followed. Nothing was here, not even any energy from Hunter. She moved through to the other side, grabbed a big sandwich, walked through the checkout aisle, and, as she stepped outside, her hoodie pulled down low, she shuffled off to the last row of vehicles.

As she moved down, she watched one guy walk off, without locking his vehicle. As he entered the store, she waited for the electronic *click* to say he'd locked it, but there wasn't one. As soon as he went inside, she moved forward, opened the door, and slid in, smiling. It took her way longer than it should have to hot-wire it, but she got it going, managed to put it in Reverse.

It was a standard transmission, which was a bit of a challenge, as she hadn't driven one in a while, but she pulled forward and headed back out onto the highway, feeling much better. It wouldn't be long before an APB was out for this one, and she'd be watching for cops on the lookout for a stolen vehicle, but that was a whole different story. She kept to the highway, going as far and as fast as she could, and eventually she felt herself falling asleep, so she pulled into a cheesy motel, wondering if it were safe, deciding the parking lot was probably a better deal.

She pulled in, parked the vehicle, but this shiny new edition would stick out like a sore thumb here. She checked the truck right next to her and, sure enough, found it unlocked. She crawled onto the bench seat of the old cab and crashed. She woke up when she heard noises outside, and cops were all around the parking lot. She winced because, of course, they were after the nearby vehicle she stole. Just as she opened the driver's side door to slide out of the dilapidated truck, she was grabbed from behind and pulled up tight, as a hand clapped over her mouth.

Hunter's voice whispered in her ear, "Don't scream. We have to get you away from here."

She sagged against him, then turned and shot him an angry look. He gave her a beaming smile. "Hey, a little bit of exercise is good for the soul."

She shook her head, but he picked her up and said, "Now, you better throw your arms around me and make this look good."

She glared at him and hissed, "Why?"

"Well, unless you want to go to jail as a car thief," he said, "you better do what I tell you."

She slid her arms up around his neck and burrowed her face against it. Inside, her heart was slamming. She knew he was a hunter, but this was pretty amazing. She asked, "How long did it take you?"

"About three minutes," he said. "Long enough for me to grab the motorcycle in my garage that I keep here for dirt biking around the hills."

She groaned, as he led her to the bike, yet was happy to see a spare helmet.

He put it on her head and said, "No funny stuff." He got onto the front and said, "Climb on." She slid onto the back, wrapped her arms around his waist, and he said, "Look. I know you don't like the scenario, and I know you don't want to be with me," he said, "but I'm still your best chance."

And, with that, he fired it up and pulled onto the highway.

HUNTER DESERVED A damn medal. He hadn't smacked her silly, and he hadn't roared at her. When he saw the cops surround the vehicle that she'd somehow hot-wired and got going, he thought he was too late. The fact that she'd boosted the vehicle had shocked him because he thought, *No way she'd get it running*, but she had. He'd been on his bike and after her, as soon as she hit the road. He should have grabbed her there at the grocery store, but she was too far ahead, and he was afraid of making a scene and getting them both in trouble.

She hadn't gotten too much farther ahead of him, but, after a good hour's drive, he was sweating it because he was on the wrong vehicle for a chase and didn't have tons of gas in his tank. Even now he needed to fuel up. With her securely on behind him and willingly with him, he soon pulled into the same gas station, where they'd fueled up before and close to where she'd lifted the car.

When they got back to the cabin, he got off the bike, without a word, and so did she. He motioned to the front door. She stepped forward, and he followed.

She unclipped her helmet and handed it to him, walked right through the house and back out to the deck where he'd seen her last and slumped down into the same damn chair. He walked out beside her, still so furious that he didn't trust his voice, when she said, "Does this mean you won't share your steak with me?"

Hunter stared at her, still fighting for control, but losing, and said, "What were you thinking?" And then that same fury roiled through him again. "You expended so much of your energy that could have helped you heal. Instead you fled, where you could have been captured. You could have been killed," he said. "Any number of terrible things could have happened to you," he roared. "Is it so bad to accept protection from somebody sometime?"

She gave a minuscule shake of her head.

Still not enough of a response for him. He wanted to

wring her neck or shake her shoulders, until he got the response he was looking for. But not only did she not hear what he was saying but it could easily have been that she didn't know how to comprehend it. All the heavy emotions drained from him, and he sagged into a chair across from her. "Seriously? Do you not understand the danger you're in?"

Her eyebrows shot up. "I think I understand the danger more than anybody," she said succinctly, her own ire spreading through her voice. "How could you even ask that of me?"

"You seem to have very little care for your life at the moment," he said. "Your actions make it very hard to believe your story."

At that, she glared at him. "And your actions," she snapped, "make it very hard to believe that you're the safe haven that you're proclaiming to be. I heard you on the phone."

His heart stopped, before slamming forward again. "My call to Stefan? Meaning, you don't feel like you can trust me?"

"Who says I can trust you? Stefan? His wife? I mean, who says I can trust any of you," she said. "I spent the last five years keeping everybody at arm's length to make sure that I knew who to trust and who not to trust, and I damn well needed to learn and to learn fast." She leaned forward and glared at him. "Just because you're sitting there in that physically fit body with whatever weird psychosis you've got going on in your mind that makes you think you're some hunter and savior doesn't mean I'm sucked into the same psychosis."

He settled back and looked at her, wondering just how

damaged her own mind-set was. "So, you don't believe that I'm here to help," he murmured, "or you don't believe anybody is?"

She stared at him for a moment and then shrugged. "It doesn't matter, does it?"

"Yes, it does," he said, quietly understanding. "You don't think you're lovable, and you're not even sure you know what love is."

"Oh, wow," she said, "that is not fair."

"I think Stefan leaving was very hard on you."

"So what?" she said. "That doesn't mean he's responsible for what happened to me."

"And, just so you know, as much as I appreciate the fact that you were happy to let him off the hook, I'm not sure he's so happy."

"He's moved on, hasn't he?" she snapped.

"You know that he did everything he could to break down that whole group, right?"

"Whatever," she said, with a wave of her hand, and then turned to stare glumly out at the world.

"Wow. You're incapable of accepting help or accepting love because you've deemed yourself unlovable, because you're so damaged no one could love you, right?" he guessed.

And *bam*, if that arrow didn't find a home. It slammed into her chest, like a physical blow. She sank back, taking the force, letting it flatten her against the chair, but she didn't say a word.

"You know that you're wrong, right?"

She turned to look at him, and once again that mocking look was in her eye.

He was starting to hate it. Yes, it was her defense against the world. He understood that, but it irritated him. He shook his head very slowly. "You know that just being obnoxious doesn't mean you get away with this crap."

She snorted at that. "Being obnoxious doesn't mean *you* get away with it either."

"What kind of a crazy world do you live in that you would even say something like that? I get that I didn't have the same terrible life that you did, growing up," he murmured, "and I get that there's probably a lot of anger and hatred inside you over all this." As she stared at him, he wanted to shake her out of her complacency or break through that protective shield. Even knowing that she was so damaged and had been through what she had, he wanted to believe that something normal was inside, something that looked outward with hope to find a world where she could live normally. He sagged back, stared around him, and said, "Nobody can understand what you went through," he said. "I get that. But not everybody is the same. And not everybody is to blame."

She started at that. "I never said that."

"You might as well have, and, by the way, with that runaway attempt of yours, were you planning on leaving without the cat?"

She looked at him. "Nocturne is special," she said. "I would never leave him."

But something was in her tone. He studied her for a long moment, then shook his head and said, "I don't know whether to believe you or not."

"That's your problem," she said. Just then her stomach growled loudly.

He stared at her. "Have you even eaten anything?"

"I bought a sandwich, before I took the other guy's vehicle, but I couldn't drive a stick that fast and eat too. Then I got too sleepy. You still planning on having steak?"

He hopped to his feet and said, "I will as long as you stay here."

"I'll stay," she said immediately.

As he walked past her, he checked out her energy. It had this smoothness to it, almost as if she had put a reflective surface on it, so he couldn't read it. If she could do that, he wondered just what the hell else she could do. Did she even know? He had to wonder at Stefan's comment about her being used for testing because that didn't sound very good.

He opted to grill the steak outside, where he could keep an eye on her, adding a fresh green salad and the green beans that they had picked up. He had dinner on the table in a few minutes. He motioned at the table for her to come join him. She got up and walked over, and he checked out her energy again. That same smooth surface, almost like a bubble of soap, with colors merging and shifting all over it, but with this glassy coating. He wondered about it as he sat down.

"Problems?" she asked.

"I hope not," he said quietly. "Only so many I can handle at once."

She gave a shout of laughter at that. "No, I think you're one of those guys who think you can handle everything."

"Everybody can think that," he said ever-so-quietly, "until they get something they can't handle." She studied him with a frown on her face, until he gave a quick nod and said, "Eat."

And, with that, she dug in. He watched in amazement as she plowed through the salad, the green beans, and then turned her attention to the steak. He knew several people who ate one food at a time, instead of mixing them up. But he wasn't sure what she would attack after the steak.

On that note, he got up and brought out a loaf of French bread and cut several slices. She took a bite of steak, then sliced up the rest of it, grabbed a slab of French bread, buttered it, and laid the steak on top, pouring a little juice from her plate all over it. He had to admit. It looked damn good.

"Now that," he said, "is a hell of a dessert."

She stared, then shrugged and said, "It's a little more filling this way."

"I've also got jam, peanut butter, honey," he said, "if you want more bread."

She nodded in acknowledgment and kept eating.

He enjoyed his meal but always kept an eye on her.

"You're worried I'll take off, aren't you?"

"Sure," he said. "Stefan trusts me to keep an eye on you. I'd hate to let him down."

At that, she glared at him. "That's blackmail."

"Whatever works," he said, with a wave of his fork. "I don't know why you think that you would be safer alone than you would be around somebody else."

"Because other people betray you," she snapped immediately.

At that, he slowly sagged back and stared at her. "That's a pretty momentous statement."

"Not really," she said, "just stating the truth."

"So, you found that safety in numbers meant that it only allowed others to betray you?"

"I was in a unique position in my group," she said in a mocking tone. "Others were sent in to befriend me, only to find out that they were stabbing me in the back, which meant that I kept everybody else out."

"Of course you did," he said, "but did you ever consider

they may not have had a choice?"

She stopped and stared at him, her eyes liquid pools of pain.

He nodded slowly. "If they were as much of a captive as you were," he said, "think about all the things that they might have agreed to for a chance at freedom."

"They would never get their freedom, not from the people holding them," she exclaimed. "They knew that."

"Hope is a hard thing to diminish and an easy thing to take advantage of," he said.

She nodded ever-so-slowly and continued eating but no longer with the same frenzied pace.

He finished his plateful, then shoved it back and relaxed a little bit. He wasn't sure how he would keep her in through the night, but he needed to. She needed several days to heal, while they formulated a plan. "We'll need more information about the location of this compound," he said, "so we can gather a group of warriors and go take it down."

She stared at him, shrugging. "Except I have no idea."

"What do you mean? You escaped from there."

"No, we were moving to a new location. That's when I got the opportunity to escape. The old place had more defensive measures than I could possibly break through."

"And the new place?"

"I would imagine it probably had even more," she said, "which is why I took advantage of the transit time, being on the road. Lots of Mother Nature with more energy to utilize," she said, "and I managed it."

"Did you have to kill anybody?"

Her face twisted. "I don't know," she said honestly. "I didn't stop and check. But I hope not."

"Good." He nodded in approval. "As much as it would

be nice to know that they couldn't come after you anymore, I understand that those vital seconds made the difference between getting away and not."

"I thought you'd called the cops on me earlier," she said, and once again he heard that thread of bitterness.

"Well, I haven't been known to betray anybody in my life," he murmured, "and I'm not about to start now. Besides, with the crimes that we see, the cops are usually more confused than anything. My call to Stefan was just updating him."

"You said, you would expect *him*. But I didn't know who *him* was."

"So you bolted, without giving me the chance to explain? I'm expecting a delivery guy with electronics. Sometimes we have to trust a little."

She snorted at that. "It's safer not to trust. And we had cops called in at the compound, and it's true that they have no clue what to do with our kind. One kid died during some of the testing. His body would have shown some pretty odd symptoms at the time of his death," she said. "I have no idea what the police thought about it."

"Who was that?"

"They called him Mitch," she said, "but I don't know what his real name was."

"Male?"

"Yeah, and young," she said. "I think he was about eight, maybe nine."

"What were they testing then?"

"Ability," she said. "Nobody would listen when I said he had none."

He stopped and stared in shock at what he heard and at the image of some poor innocent boy, with absolutely zero energetic abilities, being tested, then failing something he couldn't even begin to comprehend. "Did that happen often?"

"Depends," she murmured. "That's when they changed from commission-based bounty hunters to whatever they did afterward."

He got up, poured himself a whiskey, and offered her one. When she shook her head, he came and sat back down and said, "I think I need this." He tossed half of it back in one swoop. He looked at her. "Commission based?" he asked, his voice strangling at the words.

Her lips twisted. "They were struggling to find more people like me, like you, like Stefan."

"So they sent people out to look?"

"Every rumor, every bit of gossip, every newspaper article, every person called a psychic was investigated. Then whenever they had somebody they thought was viable and real, the hunters brought them back and were paid."

"And did they have quotas?"

"Not at first," she said, her eyes huge, "but, soon enough, when the boss wasn't getting in as many as he wanted, he put down quotas or else."

"And that's when somebody like Mitch would have been plucked up," he murmured.

She nodded. "Apparently one of the guys put a shroud around the kid to make his energy look possible, but, when they realized what had happened, I think they probably killed that bounty hunter too."

"Did you ever see him, the boss?"

"He had a lot of scars on one side of his face," she murmured, her gaze lost in on itself.

Hunter couldn't imagine the nightmares every time she

closed her eyes. If she ever slept, that would be a miracle. "Would you recognize him?"

"Of course," she said immediately, "but I haven't seen him in a very long time."

"But then you've been free for, like, five years, right?"

She nodded slowly. "Yes, that's true."

"So maybe in five years things have changed."

"Well, I'm pretty sure everybody is in their new compound, and the hunters are still out there hunting." And she used the term with a heavy emphasis.

"Listen. I might be a hunter," he said quietly, "but I'm not that kind of a hunter. Did they check out the mental institutes?"

"They did that for a while, but some of those people were too difficult to handle. One was shot right in front of me."

He swallowed hard, wondering at a world where people had so little value that they were either shot or killed in other ways because nobody cared or because they didn't possess that one quality that was sought. "Another child?"

"Nope, an older man. I think he probably did have a lot of abilities. But," she said, with half a smile, "he was pretty crazy. No way he could control anything, and he had a fascination with fire."

"So, a pyromaniac?"

"Whatever labels you might want to use don't apply to somebody who uses it to burn themselves. Particularly when using energetic fire."

Hunter stared. "I don't think I've ever seen that before."

"Well, you haven't been where I've been," she murmured.

"Well, that's a damn good thing," he said, and, with

that, he tossed off the rest of his whiskey, grabbed the dishes, and went into the kitchen.

Only so much of this conversation he could handle.

CHAPTER 9

BETH LAY IN bed, knowing Hunter was only a thin paneled wall away and no doubt listening for her movements. Tonight neither of them would get any sleep, which was too bad because he needed it. Well, she did too, but she was used to not getting it. She would feed some energy to her system to stay awake as long as she could, and then she'd catnap. Hopefully it would be enough. Nocturne had curled up alongside her, giving her both comfort and a sense of peace. As long as he was here with her, she knew that she was safe because he'd give an advance warning. Only because of him could she catnap at all.

She snuggled in close and murmured, "Thanks, buddy."

A tiny meow followed her sigh. She closed her eyes and let herself drift. She wouldn't drift far or deep, but just the process of drifting allowed her soul to expand and to relax. She doubted anybody even understood what that meant, although Hunter and Stefan might. She'd love to have the chance to talk to them about it, but what was she supposed to do? Bring more danger upon Stefan and his wife and his friend?

Even thinking that Stefan had found a partner in the midst of this craziness blew her away. She had always imagined him to be this strong commander, leading an army, and he was, in a way, but she'd also imagined him to be as broken as she was, incapable of forming permanent attachments and easily breaking, like her.

Yet she also knew that, as the child who had been there, she had always desperately formed attachments with anybody to keep herself alive, very much a survive-or-die system. She'd mentioned Mitch to Hunter, still a memory that hurt because she'd recognized immediately that the boy didn't have any abilities. Mostly because she recognized the energy around him as that of the hunter who'd delivered him. She wanted to think the hunter had some humanity left inside him, but the day he brought in Mitch, that was no longer possible.

She'd learned a lot about betrayal, the fight for survival, and what people would do to each other. She'd also learned a lot about greed. She was a long-timer, only one of a couple, like Lizzy, and they'd been there in the compound since forever. For all she knew, Lizzy hated Beth for having escaped, when Lizzy hadn't. Beth tried to talk to Lizzy about it every once in a while, and finally, when management realized the facility was becoming too visible, the bodies racking up so much that people were noticing, plans were made to shift the operation to a new location, and that was it. That would be Beth's one shot. She knew it, and she was willing to die to take it. Anything to get free.

Nocturne shifted uneasily in her arms, and she relaxed again, realizing that, as the tensions in her mind mounted, the tension in her arm had squeezed him too hard. "Sorry, buddy," she whispered, gently stroking his chest and furry body. She closed her eyes and this time slipped under.

Almost immediately she felt the enemy, the unseen enemy reaching for her. Those eyes all around, looking for her. The hunters would always be on watch, and she knew a bounty would be on her head. She also knew it would not be a case of bringing her back alive. Everybody related to the compound would want her dead because they all believed she knew too much, could do too much, and held way too many secrets. So she couldn't be allowed to live.

Yet her memories were gone, as were her abilities.

She awoke with a start, bolting upright, still fully dressed because undressing was giving trust to a situation that she couldn't allow herself to give.

Something was so very wrong about this place, yet something so wonderfully right. She heard the storm outside, the waves from the lake lapping against the beach, the creaking of the dock, and the trees whispering in the winds. But through it all she could also feel the fingers, probing, reaching for her.

And then she recognized one.

Surely not possible. The boss wasn't here himself, was he? But that voice? ... Please let that not be so. She sat on the side of the bed, pulling herself inward, yet that was the only way for her to look outward. She tapped the bits and pieces of her energy out in the world, looking for any sign of him. He was strong, so very strong, but more so because he utilized many people in his network; then he tapped into that network. Besides the boss, she also recognized Lizzy and her energy—that weird push-and-pull-back motion that she used.

The boss hated that tracking system and had tried since forever to make Lizzy change it because it was so recognizable, something so obvious that nearly anybody would know who was out there. And Lizzy had tried, but she was broken, just like Beth was broken, so Lizzy's abilities were all about power and what she could do with it, but controlling that power was a whole different story.

Even as Beth sat here on the edge of the bed, she felt Lizzy lock on to her, that energy flying toward the cabin. Gusts of wind slammed into the cabin, defying its ability to stand upright, and she was certain Lizzy was out there, shaking it hard. Beth knew she had to get out, and she didn't dare let Lizzy find her or know that she was here. So far, she'd managed to keep her energy low, mostly because of Nocturne, who would suck it up and use his energy as a cloak, but she needed more right now. Nocturne couldn't do this forever.

Knowing it was wrong, but not really having any choice, she reached out to Hunter. Seeing that he wasn't asleep, but in a very light doze, she gently sucked off a portion of his aura and slid it toward her, stretched it around her body, and tucked it around Nocturne as well, shielding herself between the two energies. It should hide her own easily enough, but, as long as she stayed, there was that taint, that smell that said she was here.

Suddenly she slipped out of bed, down the hallway, and into the garage, where she hopped onto the bike. The keys were still in the ignition, and, pushing it, she moved it through the side door and let it drift slowly down the driveway. As soon as she hit the highway, she turned on the engine and ripped off into the night.

WHAT WAS BETH planning on doing? Hunter wondered, as he sat in his car in the driveway—returned from the grocery store by his local friend—slightly rolling down behind her with his lights off. He'd followed her immediately, after letting her go, figuring out just what she thought she was doing. The storm was uncannily fierce outside, and something was odd about it. He couldn't detect too much, except that it was a strange conglomeration of weird lightning flashes and yet almost colorful.

He studied it, sensing the otherworldliness about it, something that had spooked her badly. Now he was already at the highway but, in the dead of night, maybe 2:00 a.m. If she found the main drag, she would need the headlight on his motorcycle, but he would drive his car in the dark without lights, following behind her in order to get as close as he could, without letting her know he was there. It was easy to follow her once he caught up.

He saw her headlight on now and knew she was booking it, though nothing in his research on her indicated that she could ride a motorcycle. It's not that hard, but pretty-damn easy to kill yourself once you got them going, especially if you didn't know how to control them. She whipped down the road, almost reveling in the speed, and it was all his old car could do to keep up.

When suddenly he kept going faster and faster and saw no sign of her headlight, he got worried and drove the car even faster but still saw no sign of her. He swore into the darkness, pulled over to the roadside, awkwardly made a three-point turn, heading back the way he'd come. Somehow the witch had lost him. How was that even possible?

He drove much slower going back, covering ten miles before realizing that the energy was different on this side. He crossed to where the energy shifted again, almost like driving through a slight field, feeling that she was here somewhere close by, her energy drifting. Maybe he didn't understand because, if she were hiding from the energy of whatever was in that storm, surely this would be a giveaway.

He pulled off to the shoulder, turned around again, drove up to where he thought the line divided, and stopped. He slipped into the trees, letting his senses open up. It felt so familiar, as if someone he knew were here, yet how was that possible? He sent out a message to Stefan. *Are you feeling this?*

Yes, watch your back.

Always.

And, with that, he slipped farther down, heading toward the long expansive river and the lake that followed all along the road. Here, as he made his way toward the water, he thought he heard something. He paused, stretched out his energy again, then shook his head at the same sense of knowingness, and then he saw her. She sat there, huddled up against a tree, something black in her arms.

It must be the cat, although he couldn't imagine how she could have possibly carried him on a bike ride like that. Unless she had a bag for him or some chest pouch. He hadn't even checked for something like that. Hell, he hadn't checked for anything because she hadn't had anything. He stepped forward, realizing she made no attempt to leave.

"Did you really think you'd get away?" he murmured.

"Well, I did," she said quietly. "At least from what I was trying to escape from."

"And what was that?" he asked, struggling hard to keep his anger and his disappointment shielded.

"Well, not you," she said. "Otherwise I wouldn't have used your energy to escape." She turned and looked at him, and he saw her eyes, brilliantly twinkling globes of lights. "Someone was searching for me in that storm."

"Are you sure they were searching for you?"

"Oh yes," she said quietly. "You never forget that sense of being hunted."

He winced at that because his life was hunting others. He nodded slowly. "Do you think you evaded them?"

"Well, that depends," she said, slowly climbing to her feet. He saw the exhaustion in her face. "It depends on whether you led them here or not."

And, with that, the storm caught up with them. As the thunder boomed, and the lightning flashed, she looked at him sadly and said, "You did, didn't you?"

CHAPTER 10

BETH DIDN'T KNOW what to do. She'd half expected him to come but had hoped that he wouldn't. She stood up slowly. "They'll find us here."

"Okay, then we'll go somewhere they can't find us," he said, his voice firm and not at all afraid.

"No such place exists," she said. "I've tried looking. I hid for a long time. I took energy from people, as I moved from shadow to shadow, and every time it seemed like I left a little piece of myself behind."

"There are tricks to pulling that back."

"Well, yes, there are," she said, "but some of me is—" She shrugged and said, "Not some, all of me is b-broken. I can't pull myself back in this condition."

"That doesn't mean there isn't any place we can hide." He hesitated for a moment, and she watched as the rain built above them in the dark skies. "We'll get soaked. Let's go grab the bike, get into the car, and we'll talk about it there."

Not knowing what else to do, she shrugged and said, "I don't think you can put the bike in the trunk of your car."

"You might be surprised."

He helped her up, and a strange feeling crept up her arm when his hand touched hers—a sense of connection. But, of course, that was his energy reacting to his own energy that she'd taken from him. She didn't pull back in any way but noted such an odd thing to hold somebody's hand. As they got up to the bike, he looked at it and nodded, then said, "I'll put it in the car."

She followed as he pushed the bike over, popped the trunk, and put it into the back, leaving the trunk open. He had a strap that he lowered the trunk lid with, securing the bike, preventing it all from bouncing. He motioned at the car and said, "It'll start pouring. Let's get in."

She slipped into the front seat, with Nocturne curled up in her lap. Hunter got in and stared at the cat, opened his mouth as if to ask, then thought better of it, and slowly closed his mouth again. As they sat here in the darkness, he asked, "Would you have any idea where you escaped from? The location, I mean?"

"Of course," she said, "a point like that is always indelibly marked in your consciousness."

"And how long after leaving the original compound was it?"

"Maybe ten minutes," she said. "Why?"

He said, "I'd like to find the original compound."

"Well, I would too, but I doubt we have the same reasons."

He looked at her and then shrugged. "Well, I was thinking it would be a safe place, where they wouldn't be likely to come looking for you."

She stared at him in shock. "You know what? ... That might be possible. The boss had all kinds of defenses set up, so nobody else could search for the place and find it. Nobody could come in without his permission, without him opening the doors."

"Do you know if it's still standing?"

She shrugged. "I have no idea. I was always inside."

"And when you were transported?"

"I was blindfolded," she said succinctly.

He nodded. "But surely you have a connection to that place."

"Of course."

"So, can you follow that connection back?"

"I don't know," she said. "I haven't tried, and honestly it never occurred to me. Mostly out of fear I suppose."

"Which makes sense. So, what was your reason for wanting to go back?" he asked her curiously. "You said that you wanted to find it too, but you doubted we shared the same reason."

"I want answers," she said quietly.

"Answers to what?"

"Who I am."

NOT WHAT HUNTER had expected. His heart slammed against his chest and then caved in on itself, as the shock finally receded. "Are you saying you don't remember your family?"

"I don't even know if I have a family," she said. "I don't know if I was kidnapped. I don't know if I was sold. He told me that I was sold, and maybe that's true, but I was only around four, so I don't have much in the way of memories. I also don't think Metlomar is my surname. I think it's one they gave me."

"Interesting." He put the key into the ignition, and started the engine. He opened the window a crack to stop the steam from their breaths from fogging up the interior. "Any idea how far away it is?"

She looked at him, gave him a brief smile, and said,

"Less than an hour from here."

"Good," he said. "Which direction?"

She stared at him for a long moment and then pointed down the road in the direction the car was already headed and said, "Down here, for about the first thirty-five minutes."

He nodded and started down the road.

"We shouldn't go back there alone," she murmured.

"Why not?"

"Because he might have left a sentry."

"I hope he did," Hunter said, trying hard to keep the virulence from his voice but not succeeding. "I'd like to talk with somebody."

"You don't understand. These are energy workers who have been bastardized into his creations."

"You make him sound like something out of ... *Frankenstein* or the like."

"His creations were," she said. "Look at me. I was a normal little girl, who became something very different."

"You haven't said what happened to you, but obviously you can manipulate energy at a level most of us couldn't begin to attempt."

"I don't know about that," she said. "The boss was always very good at finding people who could, although he had no energy skills that I'm aware of."

"He's still alive?"

"I think so. I do. I thought I felt him out there tonight." He gave a strangled noise. "Out in the storm." She nodded. "Along with Lizzy."

"Ah, Lizzy, the searcher."

"Yes, the very powerful one with a signature that's hard to even imagine."

"What kind of a signature?"

"It's very specific. A strong push and then she pulls back, and then she does a heavy push again, and each time that energy goes out with an almost military precision."

"Wow," he murmured. "I don't think I've ever seen that before." *Except ...* in Stefan's guest bedroom, the sickbed for Beth.

"You would remember it if you had. It's very distinctive." She looked around and said, "Do you ever wonder how all these people out there in the world can live their lives without even knowing that people like you and I exist?"

"I think they're happier that way," he said. "If they had any idea of the abilities that some people have and what they could do, they would be terrified."

"Maybe," she said, "There have always been psychics and spoon benders. There have always been people who saw into the future or read the past."

"Sure, but, as their people kept those numbers way down, they graced the newspapers for a day or two and disappeared."

"I never could bend a spoon," she said in a way that made her laughter burst free.

"I never could either," he replied, looking at her with a smile.

She grinned. "It's one of the tests."

"Seriously?" he asked.

She nodded, her green eyes flashing. "I don't know that he ever found anybody who could. He was always trying to disprove that guy so famous for it."

"And yet that guy was made famous because he could do it, basically at will."

"And that just means that it's possible, so, for the boss,

that meant he needed somebody who could do it."

"Was he looking for court jesters and party tricks?"

"He was looking for the unusual. He was looking for the special, for the powerful. And, when he didn't find it, he did his best to create them."

"Still, it's pretty ugly when you think about it."

"Everything about him is ugly. Even his face."

"What do you mean?"

"He was burned in a fire," she said. "Most people would have no idea who he was or what he could do."

"But you know who he is."

"Of course. I was part of his world, before he knew how important it was to be secret about it."

"And when did that happen?"

"I think after Stefan left," she murmured. "Everything changed then."

"That makes sense. The boss didn't realize he was vulnerable before that. Stefan made him vulnerable."

"Exactly," she said, "and it made him really angry."

"Do you think Stefan is in danger?"

"If he finds Stefan and his wife, yes," she said honestly.

"So why did you come to him?" he asked. "I'm not judging you. I'm just trying to understand."

"I did war with myself over that one. Almost too long, as it turned out," she murmured. "In the end, I didn't know who else would even understand me or what it is that I am. Not that anybody possibly could, but, if there are degrees of understanding or if someone could comprehend even a little bit, it was Stefan."

"Understood," Hunter said. "It's still sad to think that this boss guy had to put somebody else in danger in order to get answers."

"Isn't that always the way?" she murmured.

"Well, I hope not. We'd like to think that the world was a little more progressive than that."

"The only thing that's more progressive is technology and our understanding of our own personal limits," she said. "When it comes to greed, I don't think anything has ever changed."

"I hate to think that way," he said, "but you could be right."

"You know that I'm right," she said. "Everything about this world is twisted and messed up. That the boss could even survive as he has all these years is completely unacceptable."

"And have you ever tried to do anything about it?"

She shook her head. "No," she said, "and every time I even think about it, I choke up in a full-blown panic, realizing that I'll just be his next victim."

"Any idea how many victims we're talking about?"

She snorted. "I don't know for sure, but at least a dozen, if not dozens."

He sucked in his breath at that. "That makes him a serial killer."

"He wouldn't think so," she murmured. "He wouldn't see that at all. He wouldn't see himself as a murderer. He would say that they were all failures. People who weren't able to do what they needed to do in order to survive, which made them the weaker of the species."

At that wording, Hunter winced and said, "I hate to ask this, but was breeding ever part of his program?"

She looked at him and then slowly shook her head. "Not while I was with him, although that could have been part of the reasons for the move to the new location. I don't know."

Then she gave a shudder and said, "That's a horrible thought. Why did you have to put that into my head?"

"I'm surprised that anybody could put it in your head or that it wasn't already there," he murmured. "It's natural selection, and that's what brought it to mind."

"He used to talk about that all the time, saying that he needed strong warriors."

"That just brings us back to natural selection and how that comes about," he said, studying her.

"And that's just gross," she whispered. "How could he do something like that because it wouldn't be with anybody's permission."

"Are you so sure? People will do all kinds of things to survive."

She winced at that. "That just makes me think of Lizzy. She's so very unstable, but still she deserves a decent life."

"Sure she does, but that doesn't mean she'll get it, particularly at this stage."

"Well, couldn't you at least let me keep a little hope?" she snapped at him angrily.

"Would that help in some way?"

"I don't know," she said. "Everything is so black-and-white."

"Says you," he said. "But you're the one who firmly believes that he'll find us and that you'll be caught and captured and tortured again."

"Well, I will be," she said, her voice ever-so-faint. "But I'm doing my best to make it as difficult as possible for him."

"I'm surprised you even feel that there is safety for you, plus a way to get Lizzy out."

"I want to believe there is. I keep hoping. I survived outside for five years, so I know another five years is possible, but I was hiding in plain sight, using their energies to stay hidden. But now somehow they found me."

"Tell me what happened when they found you."

"I'd been renting a room from a widow, paying in cash. I had been working at one of the local fast-food chains. I'd asked to be transferred to another nearby town, figuring I was getting a little too comfortable with the locals in the first town. Becoming a little less aware made me scared, thinking that maybe my guard would drop, and they would get me."

"And so the fast-food company, they didn't have a problem doing the transfer?"

"Nope, not at all. Pretty common, it seemed. They always had people moving back and forth. Not even so much back and forth, but a lot of staff movement. I think it's typical in the industry. It's usually a pretty short-term deal."

"I'm sure," he murmured. "So what happened?"

"I got up one morning at the boarding house and went outside and stretched. A beautiful morning, so I raised my arms over my head, did a sun salutation to unlock some of the stress that's always burning deep inside, and I took the bullet in my side," she said quietly.

He sucked in his breath and said, "No honor among thieves, is there?"

"I never heard a thing," she said, "but, instead of falling, I bolted."

He turned, taking his gaze off the traffic light. "How did you manage that?"

"Practice," she said, "a lot of practice."

CHAPTER 11

B ETH KNEW SHE'D surprised Hunter yet again. But she
fell silent, hating the wash of memories going through
her. "I'll sleep now," she murmured. She curled up in the
corner of the car, closed her eyes, and refused to answer any
more questions. When he came to where she wanted him to
turn, she pointed it out and had him take the next left. He
didn't say anything but followed her directions in a smooth
manner, something that led her to realize just how good he
was at doing that. "You'd make a good leader," she murmured.

"How do you figure that?" he asked.

"You take directions when you need to, but you also
don't mind standing up and taking the front position when
necessary."

"There's a time to lead and a time to follow," he said.
"Every leader knows that."

"Maybe," she said, "the boss would never have allowed
something like that. He would think that a sign of weakness."

"Well, that's not how weakness works," he said. "Weakness is mental."

"Maybe"—she shrugged—"not that I know anything
about it."

"No, he said, "maybe not. You're the strongest person I

know."

She gave a startled laugh, looked at him, and said, "What?"

"You heard me," he said. "Don't pretend you didn't."

She shook her head. "I'm hardly strong," she protested. "All I've ever done is run."

"Run, sure, but that's what you had to do to survive. Surviving is all about doing what you need to do," he said. "That doesn't make you weak."

"Well, it sure feels like it," she murmured, not sure of his assessment of the scenario at all.

"Maybe, but, at the same time," he said, "you're strong. You're still alive, and you keep fighting. That is all about leading the way for others to follow."

Inordinately pleased but not prepared to show him in any way, she shrugged and said, "I think you're making it all up."

"Of course," he said, "because otherwise you would have to acknowledge that you've done something right. All you've been doing so far is castigating yourself for having done everything wrong."

"I survived," she said. "That was the right thing to do. The wrong part is to still be running."

"What do you want to do about it?"

She thought about it for a long moment and said, "I want to stop running."

"And how will you do that?"

"That's the part I don't know," she whispered. She turned, looked at him, and said, "Do you have any ideas?"

He nodded. "We have to go on the attack, instead of always being on the defensive. We have to go on the offense for a change."

She said, "We'll get killed if we do that."

"I don't think so," he said, with a gentle smile. "You have skills. I have skills. I'm sure between the two of us, plus Stefan and whatever team he can rustle up to help us, we can all get to the bottom of this and put a stop to these guys."

"Well, I would love to think that," she said, "but I think you're back in fantasyland."

He chuckled. "Fantasyland isn't such a bad a place to be."

"And again," she said, "that's because you haven't been there for the worst of the worst."

"Nope, and I don't intend to go there either," he said in the gentlest voice.

She nodded slowly. "Maybe not, but that doesn't mean you'll escape unscathed though."

"Maybe not," he said, with a smile, but then he stopped because she was pointing.

"Take a right." He took a right, and she said, "Okay, stop."

He pulled up to a crossroad; early in the morning, just enough light outside to see an intersection. Almost two wooded roads in the middle of nowhere. "Where are we?" he asked.

"Somewhere important," she said. "I escaped right here." She hopped out and wandered around, looking at the area around her. "It's hard to even believe."

"You mean, that you made it?"

She nodded. "Yeah, and that I still am free after all this time. *Always impossible*, something the boss had said over and over again."

"So that should be a good-enough reason for you to fight a little longer, a little harder than ever," he said, "because that was a lie, and you proved it."

She looked at him and then said, "You know what? You're right, and if he lied about that …"

At that, Hunter nodded with a smile and said, "You're getting it."

"We can't bring him down on our own," she said. "We're not enough. You don't understand how powerful he is."

"So, is it him that's powerful, or is he powerful because of Lizzy?"

She frowned and said, "Lizzy is incredible. She's a combination of a lot of other abilities but energized."

"And I presume she didn't come by that naturally."

She shook her head. "No, not at all. It was his doing, and he wanted all the abilities for himself, but, when he couldn't do that, he ended up coddling Lizzy, making sure that she was his secret weapon."

"And it sounds like it worked," he murmured.

"Oh, it worked," she said. "You have no idea."

"So, this is where you escaped. Where were you headed from here?" She stopped, looked around, and said, "The vehicle was pointed this way," she said, pointing back toward where their vehicle was, "which means it was still going this way."

"Do you know how you got out?"

She nodded. "The driver had to stop to go to the bathroom. I was supposed to be tied up, but I'd undone my bonds, and, as soon as he got out, I slipped out the other side and disappeared into the bush."

"And did he not look for you?"

"Well, he did in a panic, yes," she said. "And then, once he contacted the boss to tell him that I had escaped, it got scary."

"But you escaped anyway."

"Yes," she said quietly. "But he didn't. He was killed somewhere around here."

At that, Hunter sucked in his breath and said, "Where?"

She stared at him. "What do you mean, where?"

"Is he buried here?"

She slowly shook her head and said, "I have no idea."

"Was he killed right away?"

"I think so," she said. "I remember hearing a shot. But my memories can't be trusted."

"It would make sense. Failure is not an option, right?"

"No, failure is not an option, not in his world especially."

"So, the question is whether he's buried close by or if they did something with him elsewhere."

"I don't think the boss would have buried him," she murmured. "I don't think the guard would have been shown even that much respect."

"Ouch, so the boss is a nice guy, isn't he?"

She shook her head. "I'm pretty sure I told you repeatedly," she said cautiously, "that nothing's nice about him."

Hunter gave her a wicked grin. "That was sarcasm."

"Sorry," she said immediately. "I'm still struggling to adjust to some of that."

"You're doing just fine," he said casually, "but this might be something I can do. Let me see."

And he walked over to the side of the road to a large tree, where he closed his eyes and leaned up against it, crossing his arms over his chest.

CHAPTER 12

B ETH LOOKED AT Hunter in amazement, not sure what he was doing, but she felt energy stirring deep within. But not strange, like Lizzy's energy, just not energy that she recognized at all. The fact that she didn't recognize it made it scary too. Calming down, she took a long slow deep breath. They shouldn't be here; for all she knew, the boss had some safeguard set up, in case anybody came by.

She wanted to tell Hunter that, to warn him that they needed to leave, but he was so busy doing whatever he was doing, she didn't know how to tell him, without this interruption coming across as a complete shock. Finally she called out, "Hunter."

He held up a hand. "Just a minute."

She took another look around. "It's not safe to stay here."

"Nope, it isn't," he said, and then he moved forward.

"What are you doing?" she asked.

"Well," he said, "you were right about the driver. He didn't survive." And he walked purposely forward, to a large thicket of trees up ahead. She watched as he stepped into them and then disappeared from sight, but she heard him thrashing around, looking for something. She didn't want to think about what he was looking for, but it was pretty obvious. Finally he stepped out, his face grim, and he nodded. "He's here."

"What?"

"His body is here."

"Seriously?" She raced over to his side, and he held back the thicket, and, sure enough, a jawbone stared straight skyward—bones barely bleached from no sunlight but still had no flesh, since the bugs had done their work.

"Good God," she said, feeling herself getting a little faint.

He immediately walked her back to the car, leaned her up against it, and said, "Don't pass out on me."

She shook her head. "No, I won't." She looked up at him. "No way to know for sure if it's him."

"Nope, not a sure way, but you and I both know that it is."

She winced and nodded. "You're right," she said, "and how awful is that. He died because of me."

"Don't go there," he bit off, giving her a shake. "You don't know anything about what brought him to that point in his life. You don't know why he was there, working for the boss. You don't know anything, and don't you dare take that on."

"Says you," she said, "but a man died here because I escaped."

"You don't know the why of it," he snapped, "and you can't blame yourself. You were a prisoner, and you took the opportunity to run. The guard knew what the chances were, working for the boss, including the odds of failure. The guard also knew what would happen if he failed, and that's not your fault."

She took a long slow deep breath, realizing the truth of his words, yet still hating to even think that she felt guilt for his death on her soul. "Now what?" she whispered.

"*Now what* is easy," he said. "Now we carry on to the spot where you came from," he said, "and I'll bring in the authorities to look at this body." He marked it on his GPS and sent off several messages, as she watched.

"What good would that do?" she asked.

"Well, it'll give the body and the soul of this man some rest, once he gets a proper burial," he murmured. He asked her, "You don't have a problem with that, do you?"

She shook her head immediately. "No, of course not, but—" Then stopped, shook her head, and said, "I guess it needs to happen."

"And it would have happened eventually," he said. "So, if the boss cared about it being found, then he wouldn't have left the body here out in the open."

"It would hardly be found out here," she said. "Look at this place. It's completely deserted."

"Except we're here now," he said, with a fat smile. "And that'll change everything."

She sighed. "I hope so. I'm not sure you're right about it though."

"That's fine," he said. "Let's not get overwrought yet. Let's get back in the car and carry on."

As soon as he started up the engine, she said, "I'm not sure I can do this."

"Of course you're not," he said, "but you weren't sure that you could escape either, and you did that. I'm counting on you to stand strong and to do this thing."

"Nothing like a little coercion, huh?" she murmured.

He grinned at her. "Hardly coercion," he said. "Think about it being justice for the people who were hurt, like Mitch, like the other people who were lost forever into whatever nightmare the boss dropped them into," he murmured. "Think about the people who died and how nobody ever knew. Think about all those victims, yourself included. Think about justice and about stopping the boss once and for all. Now," he said, "which direction and how far are we going?"

She pointed the same way she had pointed earlier. "It's down there," she said quietly. "And I don't think it's very far at all."

"Any idea how far?"

"No," she whispered, feeling her throat freezing up, as the fear threatened to close it completely. "I'm not sure at all."

"Good enough," he said, pulling the car forward. "At least we have some idea that we're in the right location."

"And is that good enough?" she asked. "Is that enough to justify all this?"

"Not yet," he said, his voice turning hard, "not yet at all. But we stick to what we're doing and why we're doing this, and, if that's what you need to hang on to, then do that to get through it. This man is an animal, and we must stop him, before he hurts anybody else."

"And if I don't want to?"

He smiled at her and said, "Fear is understandable. Letting the fear stop you, not so much."

She glared at him. "That's a low blow," she murmured.

"Whatever it takes," he said, with a bright smile and an easy laugh.

"It's not that easy," she said. "I've been on the run for a long time."

"And you've been a victim for a long time," he said. "I thought we decided it was time to stop running and to take charge. Look at what we've already accomplished. A whole investigation will be opened up into this."

"So?" she said. "It's just one of many more dead bodies. I don't think this will change anything."

"If it won't on its own," he said, "then it's up to us to make sure it does."

She stared at him for a long time. "Does that attitude always work for you?"

"Of course not," he said cheerfully. "Does sticking your head in the sand always work for you?"

HUNTER HADN'T MEANT to push it quite so hard, so fast, but he couldn't have her back out and get cold feet on him. This was too important, and they were too damn close. Stefan's voice whispered in the back of Hunter's mind.

Take it easy on her. She's been through a lot.

I know, he muttered to Stefan. *I get it.* He also knew that Stefan was emotionally attached, and that, in itself, would be crippling.

It won't stop me, Stefan said, his voice a little snippier than Hunter had ever heard him.

Of course not, but you care, he said.

Stefan laughed. *You think you can do this and not care yourself?*

I always have before.

That's not true, he said. *Every time that you've cared, you've made friends.*

Nothing wrong with making friends.

Yes, but you weren't involved directly. You were always helping somebody else's partner, somebody else's friend, somebody else's special someone, he murmured. *This time nobody out there but the two of you.*

It's not that kind of a relationship, he said, *and, at the moment, I want to wring her neck.*

At that, Stefan laughed. *Of course you do,* he said, *and more power to you. But a note of warning, she's way stronger than you think. And, if you think you'll wring her neck, don't be surprised if you find your own neck being wrung when you least expect it.* And, with that, Stefan slipped out of his mind.

"What was that?" she asked, looking at him.

He frowned. "What are you talking about?"

"What did I just hear?"

He stared at her and said, "I was talking to Stefan."

She frowned. "What do you mean, you were talking to Stefan?"

"I was talking to Stefan," he said.

She looked around, as if for his phone.

He nodded. "That's the thing. I was talking to Stefan," he said, "but I was using my mind to do it."

Her mouth formed a rosebud. "Oh," she said and sank back.

"Not just you have developed while you were in that place. Also everybody else in the world," he said. "Stefan is stronger and more powerful than you could possibly imagine."

She looked at him and said, "I hope so. He'll need to be, and he'll need to help us because I guarantee we're up against something you've never seen before."

CHAPTER 13

B ETH STARED INTO the growing darkness around them. In a way the blackness helped, but it also gave her the heebie-jeebies. She'd spent years, almost two decades, in this horrible place. No good memories were here, and the thought that she was actively looking for that place of torture, the soul-sucking concrete building that had taken the life from her for all those years, was something she couldn't even believe she was doing. "Why?" she murmured.

"Why what?" Hunter asked beside her.

She glared at him and snapped back more because it was expected, not that she felt she needed to respond. "I wasn't talking to you."

"Well, that's too bad," he said, "because nobody else is around here to talk to."

"You were talking to Stefan. Maybe I am too."

He raised an eyebrow, looked at her, and she shrugged, then said, "No, I was asking myself why the hell I'm even here."

"Because you want to put an end to this."

She frowned and studied the windshield. "It can't be much farther," she murmured.

"And what are you basing that on?"

She thought about it and said, "Because it wasn't all that long after we left that I managed to get free. We were the last group leaving."

"Why?"

"Because my guard was one of the ones who locked up at the end of the day. So he was locking up as we left."

"That's fine," he said, "and it's interesting that you were the last one because it gave you a position to escape. If somebody had been behind you, it would have been much harder to successfully escape. Somebody would have seen you and gone into the woods after you."

She nodded. "I did wonder about that at the time."

"Wonder what?"

"If there was a reason I was last."

He took his eyes off the road. "What are you thinking?"

"I'm not," she said abruptly. Then she stopped and said, "Look. I won't be myself over all this, so maybe I should apologize in advance or something."

"I get that," he murmured. "But the more you can tell me, the more we can prepare for whatever we'll see."

She snorted. "I'm hoping it's a run-down old building that's dilapidated and collapsed," she murmured.

"That's possible," he said, "but these things tend to take on a life of their own."

At that, she turned to look at him. "What do you mean?"

"All that energy," he said, "it doesn't just disappear because it's not being fed. It'll drain slightly, but the energy of a building, it will still be there."

She shook her head. "That's not a thought I want to keep in my mind."

"Maybe not, but don't you want to find out for sure?"

"I don't know," she said, "but still, you're making me go back here."

He pulled the vehicle off to the side of the road. "Making you?"

She frowned, not liking that he was pressuring her. "I don't want to be here."

"Enough that you want me to turn around and leave?"

"Yes," she cried out. Then immediately said, "No."

He stopped and waited.

"I don't want to be here."

"You keep saying that," he said, "but how will anything change otherwise?"

"I don't know," she cried out. "I'm scared."

At that, he smiled and gently grabbed her hand. "I get that you're scared," he said. "I really do. I know that you went through something horrific that nobody should have to go through and certainly not on their own. That's why we're here. Together."

"But nobody's here to rescue," she said, "so no good can come of being here."

"But you don't know that no one is here. And you don't know what information we can find from here," he murmured. "We have to check at least. Maybe it'll be all for naught. Maybe we'll walk in, find an empty collapsed building that's not even safe to walk inside anymore, and it'll be all over."

"I wish," she said. "But what was that about its energy?"

"Buildings have energy too," he murmured quietly.

She stared at him for a long moment and then gave a decisive nod. "That makes sense."

He frowned. "You never considered such a thing?"

"Of course not," she said. "Why would I?"

He shrugged. "I was just thinking in terms of all that you've learned over time."

"Well, not anything that didn't come up," she said. "I didn't put any direct thought into that."

"Okay," he said, "that's fine. I'm not judging you for it."

"I'm just being supersensitive," she said, rubbing her face with her free hand.

"Take it easy," he said. "No right or wrong here. We'll just do our best."

"But that's not enough," she said quietly. "I can already hear the screams."

He looked at her with concern. "From here?"

She nodded.

"So we must be getting close," he said.

"Maybe, we have to be," she said. "I already said that."

"You did, but you didn't tell me which way we'll go."

"I can't see that as the problem," she murmured. "It should be here."

"I'm sure it's shielded in some way, don't you think?" he said.

"But that would take a ton of energy at this point," she said. "It makes no sense to do that after all this time."

"Another good reason we need to go find out what's so important here."

She looked at him. He was right. "It's a terrible place."

He nodded and squeezed her fingers gently. "I know it is," he said. "You're not the only one to have suffered like this in the world. Assholes have been doing all kinds of unimaginable things to people all over the world, and unfortunately it'll keep happening with the boss if we can't stop it."

"I don't even know if that's possible," she said quietly. "He's been operating for a very long time."

"He has been operating for a long time because people

allowed him to," he said. "We have to stop it. Now is the time."

She took a long slow deep breath. "I get that, I really do, but ..."

He nodded, with a smile. "And it always comes back to that. You're afraid, and that's okay."

"Well, it doesn't sound like it's okay," she said, disgruntled.

He chuckled. "Nothing is perfect in life."

"Nothing is perfect," she said. "Nothing is perfect in any way. This is just painful."

"And that's okay too," he said. "Listen. You want me to go alone?"

"No."

"So you want to come with me?"

"No."

He waited patiently as she had some internal argument going on.

"Yes."

"Good, we'll push through it and get to the other side. Now, can we continue?"

She nodded. "Okay, but I'm warning you," she said, "there won't be anything there to find."

"Then what are you so scared of?" he said. Hearing no response, he went on, "Regardless, we still have to try."

She nodded, and he started up the car again, looked at her, and said, "Now where?"

"Just go straight ahead," she said, "we'll be there in no time."

"And, if we aren't, it means they're cloaking it," he said, "and that's okay because that means something is more important here than we thought. But it also means we weren't expected to find it. And it *also* means," he said, with a smile, "that, when we do find it, which I'm sure we will, we'll find something very interesting."

And, with that, he drove forward.

HUNTER WASN'T SURE Beth would hold up when they got to the location. He felt the energy up ahead. Definitely something was in front of them, almost like a generator buzzing, which was an interesting thing to consider. Maybe they hadn't thought of energy workers finding it, and yet they should have because they were always looking at other people with similar skills to what Hunter and Beth and Stefan had.

But then the boss could also be complacent, cocky, and could think he owned the world, which in some ways, apparently he did. Hunter had to wonder what financial backing the boss had. Where had the money come from to run this place? Hunter sent a message to Stefan to get that in motion. Surely the boss had developed into a team of support people. With the energy amassed here, Hunter was sure one man was still in control, but this was more than what the boss could handle alone.

When you brought in somebody else, you took a chance of your whole system weakening. You had to learn to trust, and trust wasn't something these guys did very well. *Stefan, any chance we can trace employees, any team, to turn them?* Stefan agreed and would look into it. Except that the threat of death and other intimidation practices often worked wonders to silence victims and teams both.

Fear was like that; it could grip anybody but, for those dealing with difficult situations dominated by fear to that extent, could be almost impossible to let go of it.

He drove forward, and now they saw nothing but a black wall up ahead. The road showed no recent traffic. In fact, it was overgrown with weeds, as if no one had come this way in years. He slowly pulled off to the side, shut off the engine, and said, "We're here."

He looked over to see Beth, eyes wide and her bottom lip trembling, as she stared out the windshield. If he ever needed confirmation that they were here, that was it.

He grabbed her hand again and said, "Do you want to stay in the car?"

She immediately shook her head. "No," she said, "no, I really don't."

"That's fine," he said, "but it could get ugly."

"It will get ugly," she murmured, "but sitting here and waiting for something bad to happen, that'll never be a good thing for me."

"Why is that?"

"I've spent way too much of my life waiting for something to happen," she murmured. "I don't want to do that anymore."

"Okay," he said, "let's go then."

He opened up the car door and waited for her to slide out on her side. She did manage to stand, but she was trembling. He frowned. "I'm not so sure this is a good idea."

"If it goes wrong you can blame me, it was my idea originally," she said, looking at him sideways.

He quirked his lips at her. "Nope, I mean the part about you coming with me."

"You're not leaving me behind," she cried out, and he heard the pain of the ages echoing in her voice.

He walked over, put an arm around her shoulders, and

said, "That's not what I meant."

She took a deep breath. "Good," she said, "because I don't want to ever hear that come out of your mouth again."

"I won't walk away and leave you," he said. "You have to trust me."

"Trust is hard to come by," she murmured.

"Of course it is," he said, "and, for some people, it's impossible. But you have to start somewhere."

She frowned. "I don't even like the idea, much less the reality."

He laughed. "And that's okay too," he said, feeling some affection coming up between them. It surprised him, but he gave her another hug and said, "Let's walk. Surely that's harmless."

"You don't know," she said. "You just don't know."

"Are you ready to tell me?"

"No. Never. I'll never be ready for that."

"Okay then," he said, "in that case, let's go, so I can find out for myself."

"Nothing to find out," she said, "it'll all be hidden away."

"Hey, they don't call me a hunter for nothing," he said quietly.

She looked at him and frowned. "But are you really a hunter?" she asked. "We had guys who were beyond good," she said, "and anybody who wasn't didn't make the grade."

"And were they killed?"

"I don't know if they were killed, but they sure as heck didn't have much of a life afterward."

She believed that was the truth, but he had to wonder if she was right. "I get that," he said, "but it'll still be okay."

She shook her head. "If you say so," she said, "but it's

your funeral."

He smiled, nodded, and said, "Agreed." With that, he pushed her forward toward the black wall. Just as he was about to go, he heard the electricity snap and crackle off to the side. As he watched, an almost electric *zing* crossed the road in front of them. "Wow," he said quietly. "Is this electrified?"

"That's one word for it," she said. "That is how he kept us in."

"So that's also how he's planning on keeping us out," he said to himself. "Let me talk to Stefan." He immediately called on Stefan. *A massive electrical field is around the place.*

I can see it, Stefan said, and Hunter winced as Stefan crawled into his head, looking out of his own eyes. *Interesting*, he said. *An energy source is on the left.*

Hunter turned and walked toward the other side of the road. *I can feel it*, he said, *but I can't see it.*

I can, Stefan said. *Originally a generating station was here. It's on the other side of those bushes.*

But that surely can't be working all the time. No legitimate power service is around here.

No, it's apparently being charged from another power source, Stefan said. *This is fascinating.*

Well, we need to shut it down, so I can get in.

I think I can do it.

How will you manage that? Hunter asked.

You just have to interrupt the waves, Stefan said, but he sounded so preoccupied that Hunter wasn't exactly sure if Stefan was listening clearly to what Hunter was saying. Suddenly an odd crackle sounded in front of him, and then the field went out. Hunter turned to face Beth, who stood there, staring at the electrical field in shock.

"Did you do that?" she turned to him and asked.

"I think Stefan did."

Her eyebrows shot up, and then she slowly nodded. "He was always good at that stuff."

"Meaning?"

"Causing trouble," she said succinctly. "But he didn't handle electricity well back then."

In Hunter's mind, Stefan whispered, *I still don't.*

And then he winked out.

CHAPTER 14

BETH TURNED TO look at Hunter. "You know that they realize we're here now, right?"

A muscle in his jaw ticked, as he considered her words. "It would make sense that they would know something was different. It doesn't mean that they know we're here."

"It won't take him long," she said gently.

"Then we don't have much time." And, with that, he grabbed her hand and crossed the area where the force field had been.

"It feels strange just being two of us. I feel like there should be a whole team behind us."

"Well, we have a team in one sense," he murmured. "There's Stefan."

"But that's not a physical body here right now," she said. "I'm not even sure how it is you're talking to him," she murmured. "And I've seen some shit."

"And have you seen real psychic phenomena?"

"Definitely with Lizzy," she said. "Most of the others not so much but Lizzy was real."

"And she's the one who they worked on so hard?"

"Yes, she's the searcher, the one who can go out and hunt, like you've never seen before."

"So, can we expect her to come in our direction?"

She looked at him, terrified. "If she does, it's all over,"

she warned.

"Because she has the ability to kill?"

"I think everybody has the ability to kill," she said.

He waved a hand. "I meant, with energy."

She shrugged. "I wouldn't be at all surprised, but remember. I haven't been here for a few years."

"But she was their prize pupil?"

"Yes, and I was their prize failure," she said.

"That's a bitter way to put it."

"How else would you put it?" she murmured.

"How much older is Lizzy than you?"

"She's not, not by much anyway," she said. "We're pretty close to the same age."

He nodded. "Presumably she was treated better?"

"I don't know if she was or not because I wasn't in the same space as her. I would like to think so," she said. "I didn't hate her by any means."

"Good," he said, "if you don't put out energy into that kind of thought form, then it keeps your energy a little cleaner, a little less ratcheted, so it's a little easier to heal."

"Maybe," she said, "never was part of my makeup to feel that way."

"Good, that's all the more reason to keep going in this direction. Karma is a real bitch to argue with."

She snorted at that. "I don't even know that I believe in karma."

"Don't mock her," he murmured.

She looked at him. "Are you serious?"

"Absolutely," he said. "I've seen things come around and bite people in the ass, when it just seemed like there was no other rhyme or reason for it, except for something they'd done to hurt somebody else."

"But that would imply that somebody is out there, keeping a checks-and-balances sheet," she said, "in which case my side of that sheet is in a deficit."

"As long as you keep being the good person you are, then I'd like to think that good things will come to you."

She stared at him, shook her head, and said, "I can't believe anybody could have that Pollyanna attitude."

He smiled. "I've seen a lot of shitty things in this world," he murmured, "but I've also seen a lot of good. We can't forget that one doesn't negate the other."

"Maybe not," she said, "but it doesn't mean that the other exists either."

He smiled and said, "Where to?"

"We're here," she said, looking around. "This is it."

He stared at her. "What do you mean, this is it?"

"We already crossed the field. The compound couldn't have been much farther, and we've already been walking for ten minutes," she said. "Look. Just trees are here. Nothing is here. It's all gone."

"What's all gone?"

"The compound," she said. "I thought there'd be at least something left."

"Are you sure it isn't a case of something being hidden?"

"I don't think so," she said. "I would imagine that they blew it up, if nothing else." She pointed out some old darkened timbers. "Maybe they burnt it to the ground."

He gave a startled exclamation and walked over, studied the burn damage, and followed it. She followed behind, watching as he checked out a very large area burnt into the ground, new growth coming up around it.

"I thought you said concrete," he said, turning to look at her. "That doesn't burn."

She shrugged. "I thought so. But what did I know?"

"The concrete explains why Stefan may have had no connection to you all those years ago." He nodded, as he looked around at the area. "It's fascinating though."

"In what way?"

"So much damage," he said, "but Mother Earth has tried hard to regain her sense of balance here too."

She looked at him curiously. "You always talk about Mother Earth as if she's alive."

"Well, she is. She lives in the plants, the soil, the wind, the water. I certainly wouldn't want to make her feel like she wasn't alive."

She laughed at him. "It's so strange to think that you feel that way."

"Maybe," he said, not turning to look around. He stepped back. "Surely something is here."

"Well, the underground, if it still exists."

"What's in the underground?" he said, spinning on his heels to look at her.

"A basement."

He said, "Let's keep looking."

She twisted and turned, oriented herself. "Everything looks so different," she said. "I don't know if even that is here anymore."

"Well, we need to keep looking," he said. "That electrified black wall was guarding something."

"Says you. I'm not sure there is though," she cried out, looking around. "I feel like I'm completely turned around."

"How long were you driving with the blindfold on?"

She stopped and looked at him, her memories flashing through her brain. She stopped and said, "Longer than that little distance we just walked," she said, frowning.

"Any chance that you drove around in circles or that the compound was maybe bigger than you thought? This could be just an entranceway."

At that, she turned, looked at the roadway, and said, "You know what? You could be right. We saw signs of civilization, and I thought that would be it."

"But a compound like that," he said, "would have had an awful lot of buildings. Just for security, for people who worked there—their staff and their victims if nothing else."

"I never even thought of that," she said in amazement. "I always had it in my head as a single building."

"Well, let's keep walking," he said, and that's what they did.

HUNTER KNEW HE couldn't count on Beth's memories, couldn't count on anything coming out of her brain right now because she was too emotionally involved, and it had too much of a hold on her. "Did they do anything to your memory?"

"Of course they did," she said, "to my memories, to everything in my brain."

"Interesting," he murmured.

"No, not very interesting at all," she said in a snappy voice.

He caught himself holding back a grin. "I do appreciate your honesty," he said.

She shook her head. "I don't even know why we're here," she muttered.

He ignored that because she knew very well, just her way to pull back from the whole scenario. As they kept walking, he looked around with interest. "Did they have gardens here,

I wonder? Did they grow food, or did they bring it in?"

"I don't know," she said. "Sometimes I wondered if we had no food because we weren't ever given much to eat."

"And I would have thought that was a punishment," he said.

"It definitely was," she said, "but also times when there wasn't a whole lot, I think. But what do I know?" she said. "Everything is twisted up in my head."

"And that's to be expected," he said firmly, "so don't go getting upset because you can't remember clearly."

"Of course that upsets me," she said. "One of the things that they did was prey on my memories. They would lie to me, constantly telling me that I had family, then telling me that I didn't. They would tell me that I had siblings and then tell me that I had none. At one point in time they told me that I had actual siblings held in the compound, and I was terrified, thinking that they were right. Just more lies."

"That doesn't mean you didn't have family though, correct?"

She shrugged. "Who the hell knows what it meant?"

He stopped up ahead and said, "Now this looks much more promising."

The building ahead looked old and dilapidated but still stood. And appeared to be made of concrete. She stepped up to his side and said in amazement, "I never saw it from the outside, but it doesn't look quite so imposing as I had it in my head."

"It never is," he said quietly. "You've got to remember that you were looking back with a child's memory, and that has to be very different than the reality of what you were seeing before."

"All terrible," she murmured. "It doesn't matter what

the reality was. Nothing was good about it."

"I want to get inside and take a look." He led the way forward, barely stopping as they came to the actual entranceway. He pushed open the door, then he stepped inside. Holes were in the roof from years of disuse and decay. But partially standing, semisolid, and could, in fact, be fixed enough to be completely usable again, which was interesting since it was not being currently used. So, either they did have another place or they didn't want to come back here for a different reason. He watched as she walked slowly forward.

"While the decaying building might not have a whole lot of power over my memory, but just being here, even now, it feels pretty ..." And she stopped.

"Scary?"

"Scary, disheartening, upsetting." She shrugged. "All of the above. I don't know. It just feels so ... off. It's lonely. It's uncared for, but still, something is almost criminal about it."

"Criminal," he said, looking at her. "That's an interesting choice. Does something look criminal?"

"I don't know," she said. "What's that look for?"

Hunter gave her a head tilt. "Deciphering the energy you're picking up."

"I'm not sure it's energy at all," she said, "as much as it is feelings and emotions."

"And that's good," he said. "Keep picking those up because we need those too."

"Doesn't mean there's any validity to them," she said. "Remember. You can't trust anything that comes out of me. I'm broken."

He smiled. "You've been pretty-damn smart and right on so far," he said, "so I don't know how much in your head is broken after all."

She shrugged. "Well, I was broken for a long time," she said. "I would think it would take much longer to heal."

"Maybe, maybe not," he said in a noncommittal voice. "Keep pulling in whatever emotions you feel here."

"Despair," she said instantly. "Hurt, pain, loss, grief, frustration, anger."

He studied her and nodded. "Keep going," he urged. "Keep going."

She raised both hands. "I'm not even sure what to keep going with," she said. "Just so many emotions are here that it doesn't end, just waves and waves of it. So many people hurt, and so many people lost."

He nodded. "Can you get a sense of the boss here?"

"Well, something should be somewhere," she said, looking around, "but I spent a lifetime tuned into his energy in order to avoid wherever he would be," she said. "So the fact that I'm not even picking it up right now is odd."

"Maybe he's not even alive anymore. Did you consider that?"

"That would be wishful thinking," she said, with a broken laugh.

He looked around and said, "Let's keep walking." He walked through what was obviously a huge kitchen that looked institutional, like a big hospital kitchen, and nodded to himself. "Must have been a lot of people in here at one time, if they put this kitchen to good use," he murmured.

"Well, the headcount varied," she said. "At times there were a lot of patients. A few times there were only about six or seven of us, but sometimes as many as thirty."

At *thirty*, he turned and looked at her, his eyebrows up.

She nodded. "Remember? He was always hunting and looking for more of us."

"To find what though?"

"To find the talented few," she said, "since most of us didn't make the grade."

"Including you?"

She nodded. "I told you that I was the broken one."

"But you were broken because of them."

"I don't think they cared about the distinction. I just wasn't good enough to be one of them."

"Interesting," he murmured.

She shook her head. "Nothing interesting about it," she said shortly. "It's just all very sad."

He couldn't say anything to that, so he continued looking at everything energy-wise. He felt multiple energies, but old painful energy. Energy that was still screaming or had the power to scream. That said a lot about just how much pain had existed here because normally the energy would wear down over time, but this wasn't showing any signs of lessening. If anything, all that agony was all too interested in sticking around, as if it had a purpose, and it probably did. "The energy here is probably telling him something."

She stopped and looked at him.

He nodded. "It's almost like it's telling somebody something."

"Yeah, us," she said. "It's telling us to get the hell out of here while we can."

"And that's possible too," he murmured, feeling some of what she felt through his own soul. Definitely something was wrong in this place. The history was here, easy to read in terms of energy readings, but also the pain, the fear, and the torture was evident. He shook his head.

"I don't think I ever blamed anybody for what they did in there," she said. "How could I? Everybody was just doing their best to survive."

"Yet you continue to blame yourself."

"I do not," she snapped back.

He just gave her a small smile and turned away. "Every day you do it."

With that, she turned her back on him again.

He liked that she was getting more and more of a back-bone, fighting him, talking back. Something about this place brought out the victim, but, as long as he could keep her focused and keep her anger high, it would make her a little bit easier to work with.

She said, "I don't even know what this room was."

"I was thinking a commercial kitchen," he said.

She nodded. "Maybe. But I was never in here. Although something is a little familiar about that whole area by the washtubs."

"Did they—were you ever ... waterboarded?"

She nodded slowly. "Several times."

"Well, probably happened here then," he said, holding back the anger choking him. To have done such a thing to anybody was bad enough, but to do it to a child was unbelievable, especially one who was helpless and incapable of fighting back. He shook his head. "Let's keep looking around."

"Why? Isn't it enough for you yet?"

"We haven't found anything yet," he said. And he marched through the kitchens to the other rooms.

CHAPTER 15

Bᴇᴛʜ ᴛʀᴀɪʟᴇᴅ ʙᴇʜɪɴᴅ Hunter, hating the sense of being watched, being followed. All those different energies were poking and prodding at her. "We'll have company soon," she announced.

"I know. I feel them."

She raced to catch up. "What are you talking about? Why didn't you say something?"

"What would I say?" he said. "I felt them, and I know they're coming."

"Why are we still here then?" she wailed.

"Because we haven't seen what we need to see."

"And what is that?"

"I don't know," he said. "I'll know it when I find it. At least I hope I will."

She groaned. "How stupid this is. How insane is it to not leave while we still can?"

"I understand," he said, with a nod. "But we also have the opportunity to get to the bottom of something, and that is important."

"It's also deadly."

"Yes, it is," he said, "and that's why we're doing it. Remember?"

She took a long deep breath. She raced from room to room, looking for anything worth seeing, past one room of desks, various old papers crumpled on the floor, with years of dust and dirt on top of them. But Hunter appeared not to care. "I don't know what you're looking for," she cried out, after ten more minutes of searching.

He shrugged. "And I don't know either." He stepped into another room, full of filing cabinets.

"You know they'll be empty," she said.

He nodded. "Of course they are." But he went through the motions of opening them anyway. The bottom two drawers weren't empty.

She cried out and raced over. "Why would they leave this stuff?"

"Either it's not that important or they figured they'd come back later."

"So, you don't think it's an accident that they left it."

Hunter said, "If it were me, I'd make sure that we were out of here in one move."

"I heard many loud trucks before I was moved. I thought they were moving people, but they may have moved stuff first. Then the test subjects."

"Do you have any idea how many there were of you at the time of the move?"

She nodded. "Only seven of us at the time." But memories, distant and faint, crowded through her. "Yet I'm not sure on that number."

"So why were you in a separate vehicle?"

"I think we all were transported individually, as I heard a commotion near my room that seems to account for that recollection. So one of us to a vehicle, I guess."

His eyebrows shot up at that. "Were you all considered so precious?"

She snorted. "More like so dangerous." He opened his

mouth to say something, but she bent down to the bottom drawer, ignoring his reaction, as she rifled through the contents. "These are old files," she said, lifting up one. "This was Mitzi. She wasn't even here for very long," she said, staring down at a photo of a woman she barely recognized.

"But you did see her?"

She nodded slowly. "I think she was staff, although I don't know for sure."

"I guess you didn't have anybody clueing you in, did you?"

"Lizzy and I were pretty good about getting information out of the guards," she said, "but that was before we were separated."

"You two were friends?"

She nodded. "We were good friends. We had big dreams about leaving this place and renting an apartment together."

"And how did you know about things, like renting apartments?"

"We learned everything from the guards," she said. "And we were allowed some movies, which gave us a good idea of how the rest of the world worked. But, no, we didn't know enough to survive out there. I was a babe in the woods when I finally got free."

"You don't know that Lizzy ever got free, do you?"

She shook her head. "I hope so. I mean, otherwise it's just too much to think about."

"And yet you know for sure that she didn't?"

"Well, I sense and feel her energy, but I don't know if it's her reaching for me or if she's hunting me."

"Stop," he said. "I get that you want to believe that she made it, but you know that she's still working for them."

"Yes," she said, "definitely. But I keep hoping that inside

is the Lizzy I used to know."

He winced at that.

She said, "I know. Naive, right?" She reached for another folder. "These are all people I met who worked here temporarily," she said, "but I don't know anything about them. I don't know why these files would be here."

"Because they're not current obviously." He joined her and pulled out a few more, but most of them were covered in dirt and dust. He picked them up and laid them out along the top of the filing cabinets, then brought out his phone and took photos of the top page with the name, the information, and the photo, then sent them off to Stefan.

"Why are you doing that?"

"Maybe we can track down these people and see if they have something to say about it. These are actual connections to whatever the hell you went through," he said. "That makes them very valuable."

He looked around, spied an old bag sitting on the floor and collected all the files, putting them inside. Although initially it looked like a lot, by the time they were in the bag and stacked up, not that much. He looped his arm through the straps on the bag and motioned her forward. Just as he stepped past, he caught note of something and returned to the filing cabinet.

She followed and asked, "What's up?"

He pulled the filing cabinet away from the wall, and something fell. Another folder was back there. He pulled it out, opened it up for a look, then sucked in his breath. He held up the picture. "You know who that is?"

She stared at a picture of her four-year-old self. "Oh my God," she said, "that's my file."

"It is," he said, "but what's it doing here?"

"I have no idea."

She reached for it, but he said, "Come on. We don't have time." He shoved it inside the bag with the others and said, "We'll look at it later."

She stared at him in shock. "I don't want to lose that. It will have my family data. It'll have everything."

He hesitated, then brought it out and took pictures of the file. "We're taking precious time, when they are bearing down upon us now," he warned.

"I know, but it's everything to me," she said, feeling the impending sense of doom.

He flipped to the last page, taking several more pictures of the last few photos, charts, and notes there; then he shoved the file into his bag and said, "Let's finish our search, while we can."

"What if they closed the electrical shield?" she asked, looking around.

"That just confirms they're on their way. It doesn't mean we'll be here though," he said. He grabbed her hand and said, "Come on."

THE STUFF HUNTER had glanced at in her file terrorized him, and he didn't want to discuss it or to read through any details of that material. Just too damaging to be believed. But it did help to understand the terror she experienced right now. He immediately sent out energy, calming her down and soothing her system. He sent out a call to Stefan to help too. *We're being hunted*, he said.

Stefan murmured in his ear, *I can feel it, but they're a long way away yet.*

Presumably because we broke that barrier.

I don't know how advanced any of these people are or how they got that way, he said. *You can't just take any old somebody off the street.*

I need to keep going, to find more.

Or be satisfied with what you have, Stefan said. *We can come back later.*

We have a body here. We have to open an investigation, and I have files, Hunter said. *I want to make sure they don't get them. Although I sent you some photos, I also found her file.*

Hers? Stefan asked. *Normally they wouldn't have left hers behind.*

It was behind the filing cabinet, as if somebody had put it up on top, and it dropped down the back somewhere along the line.

Interesting, Stefan murmured. *Well, she needs that. It might help her to heal.*

I'm hoping so, he said. *She's a long way away from it right now.*

Of course, Stefan murmured. *Nothing like trauma to keep one constantly running and exposed.*

And, in this case, terrified, Hunter murmured. He raced through the building, looking at room after room after room. *Everything else is empty. I'm going out the back.*

Go, Stefan said. *Vehicles are on their way.*

I get it, he said. *I wish we could come up with something that would give them an alternate reason for why the energy popped.*

I might do something with that, Stefan said. *Give me a minute.*

As they came to the other side of the building, Hunter asked, "Is there no second floor to this building?"

She shook her head. "Not that I know of."

"Good, let's go out the back door." She bolted out ahead of him and into the woods, seeking the shelter of the trees.

He motioned to her. "Back to the car."

She hesitated. "They'll see us."

"And yet we need the wheels," he said, and he led the way, heading toward the car. She hated to, she really did, and he saw it on her face. "We don't want to be here when they arrive."

"They're coming now," she murmured, shaking her head. "This might not be the time to say, *I told you so*, but I will definitely tell you that later."

He burst out laughing. "Which implies that we'll still be here, so feel free," he said, laughing. And, with that, he chuckled and dragged her down the road toward the vehicle. He saw it up ahead, but he also heard vehicles on the way. He said, "I don't suppose you know how to create a smokescreen, do you?"

"Nope," she said, "I'm not even sure what you're asking."

"Yeah, I was afraid of that," he said. "Never mind. We'll make it." He rushed her toward the car and said, "Get in."

As soon as she was in, he started up the engine and turned the vehicle around, so they faced the exit. Turning his attention to Stefan, he said, *If you've got any good ideas, now would be the time.*

Stefan immediately replied. *Yeah, I'm bringing something to you*, he said. *But I can't hold it very long. Keep your lights off*, he said, *and get yourself farther into the trees, if you can.*

After following those instructions, they waited in the car.

She looked at Hunter and said, "Why are we sitting here? Why aren't we going?"

"We'll let them go past us," he said, "so we can get out

behind them."

And, sure enough, a large truck with lights on high came blazing through and raced past them.

"How come they didn't see us?" she asked in astonishment.

He turned the engine on again, pulled out, then heading in the opposite direction, he called out, "Thank you, Stefan. That worked."

She looked at him slowly and said, "Stefan?"

He nodded. "He created some screen to keep us hidden, but he can't hold it long."

"Can he hold it a little bit longer?" she asked.

"Well, he's working on it," he said, with a chuckle, and, with that, he raced out to the road and eventually onto the highway.

"Are we safe?" she cried out.

"We are for the moment, yes."

She took a long slow deep breath. "Dear God," she said, "that was a little too scary."

"I know. I get it," he said, "but we're free and clear now."

She shook her head. "But we've left our energy behind there. Anybody will read it."

"They could," he said, "but I'm not a hunter for nothing. I drew bits and pieces of all the other energies there to cloak our psychic footprints."

She looked at him in wonder. "I get that you think that's enough," she said. "I really do. But you're dreaming."

"Maybe," he said, "let's hope not. Let's hope it's enough. Now," he said, "we have to find a place to rest up and to go over these files."

She shook her head. "The cabin?"

"No, it's too far away," he said. "My own energy will crash soon. I need to hole up before that."

She asked, "Is a hotel or something close by?"

"I'm not sure," he said. He twisted his head and said, "Can you use my phone and see?" He tossed it to her.

She immediately snatched it up and found a motel not too far away. "What about the vehicle though?" she asked. "What if they saw it?"

"Well, let's hope they didn't," he said. "We'll have to take a chance on some of it."

And, with that, they raced to the motel.

CHAPTER 16

H UNTER CRASHED, STRETCHED out on one of the motel beds, having burned through enough energy that he needed to recharge. Beth, on the other hand, couldn't sleep. She sat here, staring at the folder that he'd retrieved for her, reading it through, and the tears dripped down her face at what those at the compound had done to her as a child. Without a thought to her well-being or her mental health, whatever they thought they could try with her, they'd done.

And not just her, she found, as she read the other files. Not that she'd read through them all by any means, but she had read several files, including Mitzi's. She was not staff, after all. She had been an adult, brought in as a hopeful, but, somewhere along the line, she hadn't survived.

"Does anybody even know, Mitzi? Does anybody even know what happened to you, or did you just disappear as yet-another random missing person in this world?" she murmured. The deaths at the compound were just scary, and nobody seemed to care. "How is that even possible?" she murmured.

She kept her voice low, not wanting to wake up Hunter. Even now, as she checked his energy, she noted his aura had pulled up tight against his skin. His face, his whole demeanor, was like he was in a very deep sleep, almost like a coma. He hadn't even moved, hadn't shifted not once. Kind of creepy.

She moved from the table, got up, filled a glass of water and took a sip. No way she would sleep. Not now, maybe not ever. She couldn't get past the thought that the boss's people had passed so close to her and Hunter. What must they have thought that triggered their arrival at the compound? They would surely be looking for her now. It had always been in the back of her mind that she would get caught, and she had long felt that no safety could be had for her anywhere in this world.

Beth wanted a safe place for her, really wanted it, but knew that would not likely happen—not now, probably not ever. The old memories overwhelmed her, a barrage of never-ending emotions, feelings, thoughts, fragments, and conversations. Bits and pieces of her old life slammed through her, reminding her just how terrible it had been.

Eventually she became partially dull to much of it but never all of it, not even close. Too terrible, never something anyone could adjust to, who could? But she'd done the best she could; they all had. Yet to see images of faces now in these stolen files, faces she had seen and known, faces that had come and gone, was just too much to handle.

She had no way to know why or just what these murderous people were up to. What had they done, and how much more were they still doing? Beth knew that Lizzy had been important to them and was the gifted child—even though, at the time, she hadn't been doing all that great. But those at the compound had such high hopes for Lizzy that everyone else had mocked her and wanted her gone because she was getting the preferential treatment the rest of them desperately wanted for themselves—but not to be because nothing would ever be good or right about any of this.

Distracting herself, Beth made tea and sat back down, desperately detaching from all the horrors to find something good in this nightmare. Otherwise, it would all be for naught, and she didn't want to live with that. Who would want to relive any of this? Not her, not now, hopefully not ever.

She flipped open Mitzi's file and read parts of the notes, listing her as uncooperative, undisciplined, and unwilling to work with them. She read that and snorted. "What did you expect? We were kidnapped, threatened with death or pain, told lies and more lies."

Why would anybody ever want to cooperate under those conditions? The real goal was to get out of there. Getting out was the only motivation anybody had to do anything, and Mitzi hadn't been any better. She'd done what she could, but that had been the end of it.

Groaning, Beth quickly read through the file, feeling some of the pain encroaching her system once again, as she thought about all the things she and Mitzi had lived through. *How had I even survived?* Finally she closed the file and sat back.

A rusty voice from the bed said, "Did you find anything?"

She said, "You should still be asleep."

"Well, I was," he said, "but you were thinking too loudly."

She laughed at that. "If only," she said, with a smile. She got up, walked over to look at him, and said, "How do you feel?"

"Better than I should," he said.

"Are you always this cheerful, accommodating? Even in bad situations?"

"No," he said, "and most people would say I wasn't that way at all."

"Well, they'd be wrong then," she said quietly. "So far, all you've done is everything you could to help me."

"But you don't want to trust in goodness and happiness, do you?" he said, with a smile. He sat up and shifted toward the back of the headboard, giving his face a scrub, and said, "I think I need a shower."

"Well, a shower would be lovely," she said. "I didn't even think of it."

"You were supposed to sleep," he said.

She looked away.

"You didn't get any sleep, did you?" he said, with a groan.

She shook her head. "Every time I close my eyes, it's just ..." she murmured.

He nodded. "I wondered."

She said, "Some things don't fade that easily, and we stirred up a lot of memories yesterday."

He sighed. "Food would be good too."

"Yeah, that I could use," she said, with a half laugh.

"Well, it's a motel," he said, "but I didn't see any signs of a restaurant here."

"No, it's a by-the-hour motel," she said. "Hardly high-end living."

"Do we need high-end living?"

She shook her head. "I've never had it, so I wouldn't know. But, no, I'd say anything that keeps us hidden and away from the public view is best."

"Agreed," he said. He sat up, stretched, then hopped to his feet and said, "I'll have a quick shower. Are you okay until then?"

"It's not like I'm going anywhere."

He tilted his head toward the files. "Did you learn anything?"

"Yes," she said. "Mitzi's dead. She wasn't staff. She was another victim."

He looked at her slowly. "Because of what they did?"

She nodded. "The experiments," she said quietly. "She didn't survive."

"What about the others?"

"I haven't looked," she said. "Only so much of this I can stomach at once."

"And your file?"

She frowned. "I tried, I really did but—" And then she broke off.

"Good enough," he said. "Give me five minutes, and I'll be back. Then we can go hunt up some food."

"In case you hadn't noticed," she said, "it's still very early in the morning."

"Well, we don't have to stay here," he said. "By the time we get somewhere, it will be time for food." And, with that, he walked into the bathroom.

AFTER A SHOWER Hunter felt a lot better. And he did need food. That happened when burning through a pile of energy like that. He'd felt his energy falter, when he was getting them safely away from the compound yesterday, but something, someone had helped. He wasn't sure if she did or if Stefan did. Hunter sent out a *Thank you* to Stefan.

Stefan immediately responded. *I've already contacted some local cops,* he said. *We'll get them up there to check out the body.*

Good, that's a start, but so much more needs to be done. Beth was looking at one of the files that I sent to you. It said the person died due to their experiments.

Which makes it murder, Stefan said.

I know. Not exactly something any of us want to think about, but it's hard not to. Obviously their experiments didn't always work out the way they thought they would, but, from what I've seen, I don't think they cared either way, Hunter said in a hard tone.

It's like they were building an army, but only the strongest made it through their testing, Stefan said tiredly. *We've heard of things like this in the past.*

Of course everybody wants to have that set of team players who can do the impossible, and that's why it's so hard to keep everybody quiet about gifted people, Hunter said. *This makes it even more difficult for us to stay hidden. And some of us never do. Look at you. You're always out in the public eye.*

Yeah, just so you don't have to, Stefan said cheerfully.

And I get that and thank you, Hunter said, *because I sure as heck wouldn't want to be dealing with the cops, like you do.*

No, he said, *but, at the end of the day, somebody has to do it, and I was on that path a long time ago.*

You were, indeed, he said. *By the way, we didn't find any file on you.*

I wouldn't expect there to be, Stefan said, *but it's interesting that hers was still there.*

I know, and I can't help but wonder if there was a reason for it.

I can't imagine they would have left something as important as that behind without a reason.

Bait?

And again, who knows? Watch your backs, and be open to

whatever possibility comes up, Stefan said.

I don't like these guys, Hunter said.

Nothing about them is good, that's for sure.

You're right about that, but it doesn't stop them from being dangerous to us all, and we have to watch that. We can't afford to have any more of our gifted people killed because of guys like this. Hunter paused. *I can't imagine being captured by them,* Hunter said in horror. *To think of them doing experiments like that on us, it's just*—and his voice broke off.

Remember. She's already been through it. Stefan's voice deepened with sadness. *As have many others.*

CHAPTER 17

BETH WOKE WITH a shock, sensing darkness within and without, voices calling to her, some familiar, screaming in the darkness.

"Beth! Help me! Help me!"

She shook her head, rubbing her face to hold back the memories, to hold back the tears.

Almost instantly Hunter was beside her. He gently covered her hands with his, pulling them away from her face. "Are you okay?"

She nodded slowly. "Every time I close my eyes, sleep never greets me."

"When we walk in the nightmare, in the shadows," he said, "it always seems more of the darkness crowds out the light."

She gave a broken laugh. "And yet that's not the way it's supposed to be. Supposed to be more light out there for everyone."

"There is," he said, "but you have to get far enough away from the shadows so you can see it. If you stay in the shadows, it obliterates the light."

"So how do I walk away from this?" she asked, bitterly staring at him. "Oh, you with all the answers, how do I possibly get away?"

His tone was guttural, as a hard laugh escaped, but he

pulled her into his arms and just held her against him, stiff and unyielding. "I don't have all the answers," he said quietly. "Nobody does. This is a journey, and nobody out there has a manual on how to walk on the psychic side. There should be instructions, but every person is different, and every experience is different, and even every event is different. I haven't seen the same thing twice yet, and I've been doing this for a long time."

"It's not fair," she said quietly. "I feel like everything was taken from me."

He nodded. "Your childhood and your younger teenage years, everything was taken from you. It's partly why you're so good at what you do."

She shook her head. "You don't understand though," she said. "I'm broken. Parts of me are everywhere, and I have no way to bring them all home again."

"I'm not sure about that," he said, pulling back slightly to look down at her. "You have to think that there's hope."

"And how do I even believe in hope?" she asked. "I close my eyes and hear voices calling me. When my eyes are open, I know they're still there, but I can't hear them."

His eyebrows slowly lifted. "That's odd."

"I don't know what I'm saying," she said. "Don't you get it? I'm broken. Nothing works as it's supposed to. Nothing has ever worked as it's supposed to. And, once they knew that, they just used me as one big experiment."

"Which was shitty of them in the first place," he said, "but it's not your fault."

She shrugged and settled back against the bed, pulling away from his words. She'd blamed herself for a long time. If she had been better, if she could have done more, she could have made her life easier, could have saved some of her friends, and could have made life easier for everybody.

"Stop taking the blame for all this," Hunter said in a rough voice, giving her hand and arm a shake. "You have to let that go."

"Well, that's easy for you to say, isn't it?" she said bitterly. "You're on the outside looking in. I'm on the inside, seeing where I failed. All the things that I couldn't do as well as I needed to. All the people who suffered because of it." That set him back slightly, which she noted with grim satisfaction.

"You're blaming yourself for others being hurt?"

"Of course. Remember? I was used to test others, and, even when I lied and said that the results were better than they were, I was the one who got punished."

"Because they had a way to find out if you were telling the truth or not?"

She shrugged. "Sure, the next time they tested that person, that child," she corrected, "it was obvious I had lied. But I would take the punishment in order to save them the punishment."

He groaned and sat back and said, "Beth, you can't save the world. You can't even save yourself some of the time," he murmured. "We can only do the best that we can do, and we do it to the best of our ability. But we can't do it all the time. Nobody functions at 100 percent for long."

She didn't want to hear what he had to say, although inklings of truth were there. The seeds of something that she knew, but had yet to grasp, were there. "Maybe," she said, "but this is not the guilt."

"Have you ever talked to anyone?" he asked cautiously.

She looked at him and smirked. "Like a therapist? Are you kidding? You know I'd be committed in no time."

He had to admit she had a point. "I'd like to think not, but you're right," he said. "Just aren't any tools out there, or anyone capable of handling this kind of scenario."

"Exactly," she said, "which is why we're still stuck where we are, … in the psychic Dark Ages."

"I'm sorry," he murmured.

She shrugged. "So am I, but that doesn't change a damn thing." Now she waved him off. "I'll try to go back to sleep."

He nodded and stepped back. "You can try," he said. "If that doesn't work, you can get up, and we can go get some food."

"Isn't it still too early for food?"

"In a way, yes."

She nodded and watched as he backed over to the small table. As far as motels went, it left a lot to be desired. But it was quiet and relatively safe for the moment. She felt them out there, hunting her. She felt them looking, that pervasive sense of being prey, while someone was after her. She knew an end was in sight but didn't know how it would work out. She could only hope that maybe, for once, she would be on the winning side.

She thought she'd done that before. She thought she'd been on that right side for once, but, when she took that bullet in her side, after all this time of freedom, she knew it had all been a facade, and all the years of staying on the move and getting away had worked, until it hadn't worked anymore. Which just broke her apart because she knew she could never stop looking over her shoulder. How was anybody supposed to get through life like this?

The alternative was for her to just give up and to walk away, knowing that safety would never be there for her.

This evil shouldn't be allowed, but, of course, nobody

monitored this. Nobody out there was capable of it. Maybe Stefan, but then he had his own trials. She didn't even know what he was doing with his life, but she figured he was doing some good because that had always been his bent.

But people changed, so maybe not. She herself had no idea, but she was at the end of her rope; yet she could only persevere, the same as always. Depressing, yet she didn't have a whole lot of choice. Forcing her eyelids closed to rest, she once again drifted toward sleep. She wasn't even under when she heard Lizzy's voice in her ear.

Beth, wake up.

She bolted upright with a soundless cry on her lips, as she studied the small room in a panic. Hunter was immediately at her side again. He raised an eyebrow, as she took a long slow deep breath and said, "Lizzy is here."

He looked at her sharply and then walked over to study outside the window. "I'm not so sure about that," he said. "I don't see her, sense her."

"You don't have to be sure," she said. "I'm sure." She stood, gathered her hoodie, called to Nocturne on the ethers to be prepared.

"And what does Lizzy want?"

"What she always wanted," she said. "Me. Lizzy's been hunting me all these years."

"Okay," he said. "What can we do about it? How do we throw her off our trail?"

At least he was asking her questions and not dismissing her concerns. A step forward. She looked at him and said, "We have to get out of here. Lizzy is not somebody to be trifled with."

"Okay, will she come alone?" he asked, studying the energy outside.

"No way to know. I don't know who is even left in that mess. I don't know who else is part of her team. I don't know anything," she cried out, "except Lizzy is hunting me."

"Why you?" he said urgently, turning from the window to face her. "Why? What is it about you that she can't let go?"

"I don't know," she said. "There has to be a reason, but I can't think of anything else."

He nodded slowly. "Well, it's possible. I've contacted Stefan. He's gathering people about us to protect us and to find Lizzy, so talk to me. Explain this Lizzy to me."

"I don't know what else to say," she murmured. "Anything is possible with these people. You don't know what they're like."

"No, I don't," he said, "and obviously we want to find them and stop them, if there's any way to do so."

"I would hope that Stefan could do it," she murmured, "or at least somehow be of assistance."

"And he would be if he could," Hunter murmured, "but we have to give him more information."

"Can't he track her?"

"How good is she? Can she hide her tracks?"

She slowly nodded, defeat sinking her shoulders. "She's the best at it," she murmured. "Nobody could ever beat her."

"Was she that talented?"

"She was talented, and she worked hard. We all did, but she was the best."

"Why was she the best?"

"Because she did so well," she said, looking at him. "Is that so hard to understand?"

"No," he murmured. "I just wondered if she had any tricks, anything that was different. Something that gave her an advantage over anybody else."

"Hard work was one," she said quietly, "not to mention she was fast, as in, she would panic because naturally she didn't want to be punished, and so many were punished and in the most horrible of ways. We all fought to do the best we could in order to avoid it."

"Of course, so the threat of punishment drove her to succeed?"

She nodded. "Isn't that how everybody functions in this world?" she murmured.

"Well, a stick is a heck of a good motivator in keeping people on the straight and narrow," he said. "It's just not too well looked upon."

"I don't think anybody at the compound cared one way or the other," she said quietly. "Let's get real. When it comes to people who want what they want, they don't care how they get it."

He nodded and said, "Do you have a way to communicate with her?"

She shrugged. "I've kept that channel closed since I escaped. Or tried to but being weak and disoriented I wasn't always successful."

"Why did you originally?"

She gave him a hard look. "Do you understand how any of this works?"

"Of course," he said, "at least I'd like to think so."

Just enough humor was in his voice that he probably did know. "I've kept it closed so that she can't track me."

"But she already has tracked you," he pointed out unnecessarily.

She glared at him. "Remember that part about Lizzy being exceptionally good?"

"I get it," he said, studying her.

"Can you see energy?" she asked suddenly.

He nodded slowly. "Most of the time."

"Most of the time?" she challenged.

He nodded.

"Can you see mine?"

"Yes," he said slowly, but he was obviously uncomfortable with the questioning.

"So, what is it you see?"

"Honestly," he said, "I see shards."

She stopped and stared. "What?"

"I see shards of energy, like a broken mirror."

"Well, that would fit," she said, with a hard laugh. "Because that's what I am, broken. I don't know that I ever mirrored anything, but I'm definitely broken."

"But you can heal," he urged. "There is a way to do this."

"And how is that?"

"Stefan," he said simply. "Or maybe Dr. Maddy."

"But this isn't normal healing," she said.

"Which is why it would take those two. Although we do have other healers in the group, it would take at least those two."

"And how does that work?" she asked.

"I'm not sure, but they have abilities that go way past anything that we know."

"Well, it would take somebody like that," she said, "because God knows I don't have a clue how to handle this. I've done the best I can, which is to stay out of the line of fire, but now that Lizzy has found me again?" She shrugged. "A part of me says I might as well just give in, tell them where I am, give up the fight, and walk."

"Wait, what?" he said. "Don't walk toward them."

"They'll be here finding me soon enough anyway."

"Is that what you want to do?"

"Of course not," she said, glaring at him. "Surely you know that much about me."

"Which is why I'm struggling to think that you would give up," he said in confusion.

"Because I'm tired," she snapped. "I'm tired of fighting. I'm tired of always being on the run. I'm tired of being alone in this world, with nothing to help me, with nobody to understand what this is like," she cried out.

"But you're not alone now," he said.

"No, of course not," she said, flailing her hands up. "I'm sorry. Don't listen to me. Obviously I'm more overwrought than I thought."

"You're being very hard on yourself again."

"Well, I don't know any other way to be," she stated. "So what difference does it make?"

He studied her for the longest time. "I'm not sure," he said, "but I'm pretty certain that we can do other things."

"Says you," she muttered and laid back down again.

"Don't we need to leave?" he asked suddenly.

"You're the hunter." She turned on him and said, "So, do we?"

He groaned. "Do you know that you are the only person who has ever made me doubt my abilities?" he asked. "For the last several years, I have been very content in knowing what I could and couldn't do. But, right now, I'm not exactly sure what's going on because I'm not getting the same reading out of any of this."

She gave him a cracked smile. "Now you know how I feel," she said. "Absolutely nothing is normal about Lizzy at all. She's way stronger than anybody could ever imagine."

"But is it just Lizzy or could it be more than that coming with her? What does she want with you?"

"I don't know," she said. "Maybe take me back. Maybe she is getting something special for hauling me back. I don't know," she said. "But, whatever it is, I don't want to go."

"And Stefan and I'll do everything we can to keep that from happening," he said.

She nodded slowly. "Thank you for that," she said, staring up at the ceiling. "But somehow I don't think it'll be enough."

"We won't worry about that right now," he murmured, "because sometimes we have to just trust."

She snorted. "Trust what?" she asked. "Trust that they'll get me one way or the other? Trust that my life will never be the same? Yeah, I trust in that all right," she said in a snappy voice.

"Come on," he said. "Let's upend this whole nightmare that's bothering you," he said. "Surely we can do something to switch up this energy."

"Yeah," she said, "we need to run like hell."

HUNTER COULDN'T BELIEVE how fast Beth was up and at the door. He barely grabbed her hand and said, "Stop. No point in running if Lizzy can continue to find us. We have to make sure she can't hunt us down."

"Too late," she said, staring at him and looking around wildly. "We've been here too long."

"We've hardly been here six hours," he cried out.

"Well, you should feel it," she snapped. "You should sense that somebody is pursuing us."

"Normally I would," he said, "but I'm wondering if I've been sucked into your own psychosis about this."

She stopped and stared. "Meaning, you think I'm making this up?"

He raised his hands, palms showing. "No, not necessarily."

"Not necessarily?" she said, glaring at him. "But maybe?"

"No, I didn't say that."

"But you thought it." At that, she felt his own his temper flaring up stronger and stronger.

"Stop putting words in my mouth," he said. "Look. Something's going on here that I don't understand."

"Well, goody for you," she replied. "I don't know why you think you should understand any of this, when I've been explaining how it's beyond understanding."

True. Confusing the heck out of him. "We have to get somewhere where you're safe."

"And where would that be?" she demanded.

"I'm not sure. We need a place where somehow Lizzy can't track you."

"Well, I don't know how to make that happen," she said. "I've been on the run for a long time."

"What did you do for those five years that she couldn't find you?"

She stopped, stared, and said slowly, "I hid."

"What do you mean, you hid? How did you hide?"

"Right under her nose. I stayed here in Oregon, knowing that they would all expect me to run away to Mexico or overseas or whatever."

CHAPTER 18

B ETH KNEW IT was useless to explain it to Hunter, but he had insisted on heading out once again. She sat in the front seat of the car, with the motorcycle still in the trunk, just wondering if she should make another run for it.

He looked at her and said, "Oh, hell no."

She glared at him. "What? Are you telepathic now?"

"Nobody needs to be telepathic to see the thoughts running through your head," he snapped. "Running away on your own will hardly help. They found you earlier to shoot you, and now they've found you again with me here, so they'll still find you, with or without me."

"So, what's the point of having you then?" she cried out, "if you're just dead weight."

He burst out laughing at that.

And she sagged into her seat. "Why don't you just let me go?"

"Can't do that," he said cheerfully.

"You should," she murmured, but, at the same time, she was damn glad he hadn't. It was new—this feeling of not being alone. But it would be dangerous to get accustomed to it.

"I suggest we pick up groceries and head back to the cabin."

As much as she liked the idea of going back to his cabin

on the lake, she didn't understand why he would retrace his steps. "Why there?"

"Because, based on your theory about hiding in plain sight, they won't expect us to go back to a place we've already been."

She frowned at that and then shrugged. "I guess that's a possibility," she said. "As long as you realize they will find us eventually."

"When they find us, what will they do with you?"

"If they don't immediately shoot me dead, they'll probably take me captive, back to the compound," she said. "I can't imagine why else they would want me."

"So, do you have any information that they're after? Did you run away with anything important?"

She shook her head. "No, I just ran away with myself," she murmured. "That was enough for them."

"So, they must see you as a continuous danger in order to keep coming after you."

"I imagine," she said. "If I ever got anybody in law enforcement to listen to me, I suppose there's always a chance they could be charged or have somebody shut down their operation."

"And yet the operations go on underground."

"Yes," she said, "underground is a good word for it." He was quiet for a long time, and she welcomed the silence. "I told you there are just no answers here," she murmured.

"There are always answers," he said. "We just have to get to the place where we can get a hold of them."

She laughed at that. "Again with the Pollyanna attitude."

"You're very well-spoken, you know," he said. "Did you go to school?"

"We were given all kinds of training and education," she

murmured. "Not necessarily what a normal curriculum would be like. But, if you're asking if I ever graduated high school, no, although we were taught in the compound to pass a GED test. I just hadn't completed that yet. So I got my GED pretty soon after I escaped. I needed it for getting a job. I could even do some of it online," she said, with a shrug. "Pretty simple, once I found a public library with free internet services."

"Good," he said, "and you're right. It's pretty important."

She nodded. "We were meant to function in society," she said, "so that was an important part of their plan."

"Right, so you had at least some schooling in the compound."

She nodded. "And it certainly made life a little bit easier for some of us, while being held there. Because school was something I took to quite simply. A way for me to hide— diving into the history of something else, you know?" she said with a half smile.

"Makes sense," he murmured.

"It doesn't matter if it does or not," she said. "Nothing else in that place did. We did whatever we could, when we could, and, if we were lucky, we survived. But more often than not, there just weren't any answers for us."

"No, of course not," he said. "Keeping you off-balance and isolated, out of society, kept you focused on them and kept you as a prisoner to their needs," he murmured. "That's pretty standard."

"Pretty standard for what, Prisoner 101?" she asked, with a snort.

"Something like that," he said, with a smile. "And it's good that you still have a sense of humor."

"Sometimes there isn't anything but," she said, "because all of this is way too ridiculous."

"Agreed," he murmured.

As they pulled into the same parking lot and grocery store they'd been at before, she looked all around and said, "I don't even feel them at the moment."

"Good, maybe they can't follow us through the ethers."

"I think she picks up some signature or something. I don't know."

"Did you work with her a lot?"

She nodded. "Too much, in a way. We became good friends, and that made this all the much harder for her, I'm sure."

"Because she has to hunt you?"

"Yes. It can't be that easy to turn around and hunt down a friend."

"Some people take to it without a problem," he muttered. "Not everybody is affected by simple things, like guilt."

She shook her head at that. "Our bosses certainly weren't."

"Tell me about them."

"Besides the boss, I only remember one other man," she said. "Initially there were a lot of different people, and then it broke down to just the one I dealt with primarily. He was ironically called my *caregiver*."

"What was he like?"

"A man lacking a conscience," she said succinctly. "I don't know." She gave a one-arm shrug. "It's hard to even know what to say. He was somebody fairly unique and fairly well versed in all this. But, at the same time, he is somebody I hated because my involvement with him included what this testing was all about."

"Well, that makes perfect sense though, doesn't it?"

She sighed. "None of it makes sense, so applying the standards of common sense to any of this mess is beyond any of us."

Hunter apparently didn't know what else to say to that, so he changed the subject instead. "You want to come into the grocery store?"

She nodded. "Yes," she said. "I need to get a few things."

"Like what?"

"Tea, for one," she said. "I'd love coffee, but tea is cheaper."

"We can get coffee, if you want."

"Good," she said, "I could use a cup. Maybe we can even pick up a cup to-go on the road with us."

"We can, indeed."

They walked into the store, and she searched around constantly.

"Can you sense her?"

"Out there," she said, with an arm movement toward the trees. He stopped and looked in that direction. She shook her head. "No, I don't mean there specifically but, as in, at the edge of my awareness."

"Ah, so she's just keeping an eye on you."

"Yes."

"So, why doesn't she just come in and take you down?"

She looked at him. "Well, I don't exactly stay in one spot. What would be the sense of that?"

He nodded slowly. "Did you ever see the person who shot you?"

She shook her head. "I just ran. I headed like a jackrabbit through the woods and never once saw the shooter. It's too bad though," she said. "It would have given me some confirmation as to who might be with her."

"Or it could have been her," he said.

She nodded. "I know it could have been, but I just don't have any way to know for sure."

"Which is part of the problem, of course," he said. "We're operating blind."

"Seems to be my thing," she said bitterly. "A lifetime of running without necessarily even knowing what I'm running from."

"That's a good way to put it too," he said, studying her face.

She shrugged. "I don't have any answers for you. I told you that I'm broken."

He didn't say anything but led the way through the store, as they quickly picked up a few items.

She stopped and said, "It would be nice to go for a swim in the lake."

He looked at her. "That's hardly the sign of somebody in hiding."

"Sometimes I decide that I shouldn't even bother hiding because I'll never get free of this anyway. On those days I think maybe I should just go out in a blaze of glory and enjoy myself anyway." He studied her for a long moment, and she just laughed. "I know. Everything that comes out of my mouth is something you're not expecting."

"Well, you got that right," he said. "It is definitely a bit of a surprise to hear what you have to say sometimes."

"And again, I don't know how much of that is even viable," she said, "but it just feels like everything is wrong all the time."

"I get it," he said. "Let's pay for these groceries and get

home. I need to talk to Stefan and do some research."

"I could probably help."

"Nope," he said, "I don't think so."

"Fine," she said.

"So, what were you doing in your last job?"

"Customer service. It paid cash at the end of the day," she said, with a smile. "A fast-food restaurant and nobody was keeping tabs on the paperwork."

"No," he said, "that way it's easier on them for taxes."

"Sure," she said, "and for me a lot better too. I could just stay on the move, without anybody knowing or caring."

"If that's better, yes," he said, "but sometimes you have to wonder what your definition of *better* is."

She laughed. "I'm not sure there is a definition of better," she said. "Sometimes it just is what it is."

Again, he didn't say anything but moved her through the check stand and paid for the few things they'd picked up. As soon as they got outside, she unwrapped the sandwich she'd bought and started plowing through it.

"You could have waited until we got home," he said.

"I didn't know how much farther that would be." When he frowned at her, she said, "I am not a very good judge of distance. It seems like I'm always walking one side in the dark and one side in the light, so it's a hard thing for me to judge."

"*Hmm.*" He motioned at the vehicle and headed back toward the cabin.

She was delighted to see it again, and honestly it was a perfect way to spend some time. Yet even that just felt wrong, like everything else in her life felt wrong. She groaned and stepped up onto the front porch, then said, "Maybe I should talk to somebody. If only there was somebody to talk to."

"There is," he said. "If nobody else, you could try Dr. Maddy."

"I'm sure she's got better things to do," she said instantly.

"Do you think so?" he said. "I don't. She's already been working on your system, so it'll be interesting to talk to her."

"Everything is interesting with you."

"Well, it is fascinating, isn't it?" he said. "We've got all these problems facing us and no solutions. I'm still intrigued by the fact that this person is always out there, yet, so far, we haven't seen any sign of anybody."

"You won't," she said in exasperation. "I was shot in the side, from behind me. Remember?"

He winced at that. "That's very true," he said. "Meaning that people will come and attack from the outside, without ever giving us a chance to discover any of the answers we're after."

"Exactly," she said. "Nothing's good about any of this."

"I got it," he said calmly, "but there has to be more in the way of answers available to us."

She shrugged. "Says you."

He laughed. "Yes. Says me."

"How can you always be so upbeat?"

"Because I've seen a lot in my life too," he said, "and, although we win some, and we lose some, we win a lot. I'm always confident going into a scenario, believing that we can get out of it, safe and sound."

"And there's that Pollyanna attitude again," she murmured.

He laughed. "Maybe so, but you have to keep trusting in something, so you might as well trust in me."

She shrugged. "If nothing is better, then why not, I suppose. But I'm telling you that it'll all blow up in our faces."

"And yet you don't seem to be too worried at the moment."

"I'm not," she said. "I don't know why."

"Whatever," he said, "just keep it up. It'll be much easier to function this way."

STEFAN STRODE FROM his bedroom and paced the huge living room along the expansive wall of windows. He wrapped his arms around his chest, as if his stomach was hurting. Not just his stomach but his legs, his arms, his back. His wife appeared in the subdued shadowy light, her voice soft as she called out, "Is there anything I can do?"

He gave her the gentlest of smiles. "Just being here is a help."

She nodded. "And yet it's very hard for me to sit and watch, knowing you're going through this purgatory every time."

"Not every time," he protested, then gave a self-deprecating laugh. "Okay, so maybe every time."

"It's different this time, isn't it?" she murmured.

He nodded. "I don't know why though."

"Do you remember her?"

He shook his head. "Sort of, but not really, and I hate to say that because obviously she held on to the image of me all these years."

"What about this Lizzy?"

"Vaguely," he said, "but honestly, it's hard for me to even remember that far back with any clarity. And then there's the part of me deliberately avoiding keeping those kinds of memories alive. I've done my best to shoot them down and suffocate them, so I didn't have to deal with that torment all the time."

"Which is a good thing," she murmured.

"A good thing except for now, when it rears its ugly head again."

"And that's not your fault."

"It doesn't matter if it's my fault or not," he said quietly. "There's still this sense that I should have done more."

"When she said she was broken, she meant it," Celina said.

"And I get that. I really do. But what are we supposed to do?" he asked. "Just so much is wrong in this world."

"There is, indeed, and you can't fix all these ails on your own," she said.

"No," he said. "I know that, and it's one of the hardest things I've ever had to adjust to, something that I am slowly coming to terms with."

"Just not fast enough," she said, with a half smile.

He shrugged. "That I've even gotten that far is something, and it's only to preserve my sanity that I'm staying here."

"Are you sure you can do nothing to help her?"

"I don't know," he said, with brutal honesty. "I've never seen this before."

"So much we've never seen before," she murmured. "And every time it seems like the evil just never quite goes away, and yet something good and new is even more shocking, more awe-inspiring than the case before."

"Isn't that the truth. What do we even know about this?"

"Only that a young woman has been in hiding for five

years, after she escaped an institution, where they imprisoned people, attempting to control and develop paranormal abilities. The people there, those in charge, were so dysfunctional—to the point that they tortured these people to discern and to strengthen those who had real abilities from those who did not, as well as to determine who was controllable and who was not. It's so scary to think that such a thing is even possible in this day and age," Celina murmured.

"It'll be a problem going forward, no matter what we do," Stefan said. "When you think about it, as soon as anybody knows of any kind of superpowers to control, everybody wants control of them."

"They shouldn't be able to."

"No, they shouldn't, but that's well past what any of us can do in this world," Stefan said. "It's scary to think that other people want to take possession of somebody because of what they can do with these gifts. I mean, it's not like any of the Mensa people are kidnapped because they have a higher brain capacity or intelligence than the common man—but that's only based on the IQ exams they're given at the time," he said. "That's where the problem is. Many people with a lot of intelligence don't do well on the IQ tests of today. So, therefore, we can't truly measure their abilities. In this case, somebody found a way to measure paranormal abilities and was using Beth to help with the test."

"But I don't understand how that works," Celina replied.

"I don't know either," he said, "but I don't doubt it. No, definitely something is going on. I don't even know if Beth remembers clearly. Like she said, she's broken."

"It broke my heart to hear her say that too," Celina said. "And it's just shocking that somebody could do any of that to a child."

"That was one of the things I did send out," he said, turning to look at her. "A request for information, hoping to find out who she is, but, so far, nobody has a clue."

"And it's not in her file?"

"I've been through the file that Hunter sent me photos of, and I've sent it off to a couple FBI agents, wondering if they have any information or another way to source out what we're missing in this. So far, I haven't gotten any positive responses."

"I suppose," Celina said, "if the mother had a home birth or something, there wouldn't be any need to register the child's birth."

"That's one way," he said. "The other way is that a lot of these kids just slip through the cracks. The parents could be homeless. The parents could be somebody who adopted them and then moved around between states. We don't know that the child has even been reported as missing," he said. "Just no real way to understand what happened with Beth's family."

"What I don't get is how she went from her parents to this institution guy," Celina noted. "He must have known, or somebody had some idea that she had these abilities, and it was passed on to him somehow, so that he would do something about it. A lot of things had to happen in a certain order for all this to come together, and that's what I don't get, I guess. The fact that it even happened at all."

"The fact that it happened at all," he said, with a nod, "and the fact that people are out there looking for more people like her."

"It is a scary thought," she murmured. "I mean, she didn't do anything to deserve this. She was just born."

"And, I think, in that case," he said, "that's all that was required. She was born and had this supernatural ability, whatever that was at the time, because I can't see any sign of what it is like now."

"Because she's broken?"

He nodded. "Because everything in her broke apart at some point."

"In that case, the very fact that she's even cognizant and functioning in the real world is an incredible feat."

"And somehow I worry that she'll flip and do something seriously odd," Stefan said.

"You mean, she could be dangerous?"

He turned to look at her and said, "Yes, I think she is dangerous. I think she has the potential to be very dangerous, but I don't know in what way."

"So then Hunter is in danger too?" Celina asked.

"Yes," he said quietly, "Hunter is definitely in danger, but is he in danger from her? That I can't answer."

She groaned. "I get it," she said. "I mean, I've been with you long enough to understand that frequently there are no answers, but I sure wish there were."

He gave a broken laugh. "You and me both, especially when it comes to things like this. Just no way to know where this will end up. We must protect her as much as we can and keep her safe. I don't want her to become another victim, and, if we can do anything to help her regain some semblance of normality, then I feel obligated to help with that as well."

"Is *obligated* the right word?" she said quietly. "That makes it sound as if you feel like you owe her."

"If she came from that place, and I missed getting her out, then I do owe her," he said, his voice harsh. "You don't know what that was like."

"No, I don't know what that's like," she said, walking steadily toward him. "But I know you can't fix the world."

He glared at her, and then his shoulders sagged. "I know that," he said. "I really do, and most times I manage it well. But—when it becomes personal like this—"

"You can't allow it to become personal," she whispered. "You can only save those whom you can save. You can't save everyone, and, in this case, this person, this woman, might be someone we can't help."

He shook his head. "Something is so very familiar about her, and yet at the same time I can't quite place her. Intellectually I know who she is, yet, when I think back, I just—"

"Is it because her energy is so different now?"

He nodded. "I think so. I just think that so much damage has been done to her energy that the sense of recognition is also damaged. She doesn't have the same pathways, the same wavey signature that I would have instinctively recognized."

"It's hard to imagine somebody being so damaged," she murmured, "that you can't recognize her."

"And it's disturbing," he said, "on so many levels."

She walked up, slipped her arms around him, and just stood gently with her head against his chest. "And remember," she said. "We can't save everyone."

"No," he said, "but I need to save this one."

She squeezed him gently, looked back up at him, and said, "Because you feel like that's the only way to save yourself?"

He looked down, smiled, and whispered, "Oh, once again, I'd forgotten just how wise you are."

"Oh, you can't do that," she said, with a beguiling look

on her face. "Because I'll just be here, reminding you all the time."

He burst out laughing, wrapped his arms around her, and held her close. "I am so grateful we found each other again."

"No kidding," she said. "Our lives were not the same without *us*. And that's what's wrong with Beth. Her life is not the same because she's not herself, and we'll do what we can to help her find those missing pieces," she said firmly. "Remembering that, we won't do anything that puts you in danger either."

He kissed the top of her head gently. "No," he said, "that's not on the agenda."

But he also knew that sometimes things happened, and sometimes nobody could do anything to stop it.

CHAPTER 19

EARLY THE NEXT morning Beth dipped her toe in the lake, wondering at the wisdom of diving in without a care if she were being hunted or not. She was just seizing the moment for the time that she had, and, if she failed, then at least she would have had these few glorious minutes. Yet it seemed so selfish and wrong to even think that way. She'd been on the run for so long, hiding, looking behind her constantly, always wondering when the boogeyman would pop out at her. And yet, when it had happened, all she had done was go into an automated mode, where she'd immediately gone on the run from everyone, preserving all the bits and pieces she could of herself, before the hunters caught up to her again.

The thing that had bothered her the most was that sense of defilement at the most elemental level. She wasn't who she was meant to be; she didn't even know who that was anymore—because of them. She struggled with it a lot. Her identity, her wishes, all felt like they mirrored Lizzy's because Beth and Lizzy had been through so much of a similar trauma. But Lizzy had come out stronger. Lizzy had come out whole, though that was probably not the right word either, but she'd certainly come out a very different person than Beth.

She wondered at the files that she'd seen and the little bit that she'd read. So much more information was in there. She would work on that later. However, she came down here first to heal her soul in the lake.

Nature had always been her salvation. When she had been locked away, sometimes the specks of dust in the air just danced in front of her. Sometimes that little shard of light that came through the tiny gun-slot windows high up in the wall would land directly on her. When she had lived on her own, just touching a leaf or bending down to feel the grass with her fingers, those moments had fed her soul and had kept her alive, kept her fighting, because, when she got locked up again, her interaction with Mother Nature would be taken away again, and she knew that her soul wouldn't survive.

With her legs dangling in the water, she turned her face to the sun above. It would be a gorgeous morning, yet cool enough that now she shivered, with just a towel wrapped around her shoulders. Deciding it was still better to be chilled and to fully enjoy the moment, she dropped the towel and slipped into the cool water.

She gasped as it hit her skin, before she sank underneath, striking out strongly toward the end of the dock, refusing to let the fronds of grasses growing deep underneath and touching her feet stop her from enjoying the moment. Something was creepy about those things below her in the darkness.

She'd spent her life in the darkness, and she wanted to find the sunshine as her main place to live, the place where she felt good, the place where she felt strong. She knew there would always be shadows, particularly for somebody like her. She just had to get to the point where she could live, knowing the shadows would be there, yet not be affected by them. She almost laughed at that because she was asking for a lot.

Her heart broke for Lizzy, who would never know the sun or the freedom out here. Even as Beth thought of it, she felt Lizzy almost turning in her direction, looking for her. Beth immediately shut down her thoughts, holding her breath tight, pulling in her energy. Anything to keep Lizzy from finding her. Beth loved her friend dearly, but this had to stop. Calmly she struck out for the center of the lake, before turning around and coming back toward the dock. As she neared the wooden piers, she saw Hunter standing there, his hands on his hips, glaring at her. She smiled up at him and said, "I needed this."

Immediately the condemnation on his face dropped away, and he nodded. "In that case," he said, "enjoy, just please stay safe."

She nodded. "I'm doing what I can," she said simply. "And, if it's not enough, then it's not enough."

He smiled. "And that sounds better to me."

She looked up at him and said, "I thought you would approve of that. But it doesn't mean that I can hold this thought, this belief, for long."

"You'll do what you can," he said, "and then you'll try again."

"Maybe," she said. "I'm always afraid that I'll give up trying."

"Not while I'm around," he said, "because I'll always be there to help bolster you and to remind you that the good fight is worth fighting."

"Is it though?" she whispered, as she studied him. "Sometimes I have to wonder."

"Ah, no more of that," he said. "Are you ready to come

out of the water?"

She remained in the water for a long moment and nodded. "I am getting chilled."

"No wonder," he said. "You don't have enough body fat to survive out here very long."

He reached down a hand, and she reached up, stunned at his simple and effortless strength as he hauled her onto the dock in front of him. He bent down and grabbed the towel and wrapped it around her. "Come on up, and you can have a hot shower, if you need it."

"I hope I don't need that," she said, "but I don't know. I was thinking I was doing okay, until I started back, and then it just seemed like I'd pushed the limit again."

"I think you do it all the time," he said. "You want to bite off more than you can chew. You want to live more than you've been able to. So your natural safeguards of what you can and cannot do don't apply."

"Well, I don't have any experience. I think those safeguards are something you learn over time, as you understand when your strength is waning and when it's okay," she said. "For me, I don't have those memories. I don't have that experience to draw on, you know?"

"But you're getting there," he said, "and that's what's important to remember."

She nodded again. "And, yes, you're right. I'm eager and, at the same time, almost self-defeated because of it all. It's just so much at once." She said it so simply that she hoped he'd realize it wasn't self-pity. She'd come a long way, and she knew that she had so much more to do, so much more to learn, and yet so much farther she could go. She looked around and smiled. "And again, you're truly blessed to have this place."

"I am," he said, "and that's one of the things that I do understand. When you have good things in your life, you should rejoice in having them. You should feel blessed. You should make a point of saying, *Thank you* to the world, because you're here, proud in your achievements, proud of what other people have done. They're all important," he said, "and too often people forget to celebrate the milestones as they hit them."

She grinned. "We're back to you being a good cheerleader," she said, chuckling.

He smiled. "Hey, whatever it takes."

"I got it," she said, "and, at some point in time, maybe I'll feel like I do have it."

"I hope so," he said, "because there's so much more to life, and you haven't had a chance to live any of it."

"But I'm getting there."

He led her up toward the cabin. "Do you want food?"

"Do we have anything? It seemed like we devoured it all last night."

"Nope, we have quite a bit left," he said. "I'm looking for a big breakfast, if you're up for a meal."

"I'll take anything you've got right now."

"Good. Go take a hot shower, and I'll get something ready."

She dashed up to her bedroom and then into the shower, gratefully standing under the hot water, wondering how she even managed to get into the lake, when it was so very cold. But something had been so absolutely freeing about it, something so gorgeously enlivening about being out there.

As she stepped from the shower and dried off, she heard him talking to somebody on the phone. Not wanting to listen in, and yet unable to help herself, she crept downstairs, only to understand that he was talking to Stefan. She frowned; she wanted to know what that conversation was about, but she also wanted Hunter to tell her honestly.

She stepped into the kitchen. He turned, saw her, and smiled, then pointed at the coffee and continued to talk to Stefan. Well, that was good because that meant he wouldn't hide the call from her.

"No, she's here right now," he said. "I can tell her when we get off. Sure, not a problem." He hung up and asked, "So you got some coffee?" He saw the cup in her hand and smiled.

"Was that Stefan?"

"Yes," he murmured. "He has contacted somebody in the FBI to track down your family."

She raised her eyebrows. "Wow, the FBI?"

"Yeah, when crimes cross state lines, they can get called in, and, of course, he has a few connections who get him information that other people might not get."

"What connections?"

"Remember Dr. Maddy?" she nodded.

"Her partner works for the FBI."

"Ah, interesting," she murmured. "And very convenient."

"Very convenient in many ways and not so much in others," he said. "Sometimes having that information at your fingertips is good. But, other times, once you know something, it means you must act on it. Not making change where change is needed means you're guilty of sitting by and doing nothing. And that's not something Stefan is capable of doing."

"Right," she said, "so, in many ways, this is a gift."

"Remember that about gifts," he said, quirking an eye at

her.

She smiled. "Yes, and we have to be grateful for them."

"Exactly, so just smile. Stefan is doing everything he can, and, when we have more information, he'll pass it on."

"Good," she said. "In the meantime, I shut Lizzy down from finding me, and, with any luck, we can stay here for at least a few days, while I regroup a little bit."

"Good," he said, "but you also have other injuries. So time to rest would help too."

"My body is full of scars," she said, "if that's what you mean." She let the cheerfulness in her voice guide the mood. "Remember that part about not always wanting to do what I should do and not always being good at it?"

He nodded. "They tortured you too, didn't they?"

"Of course," she said. "None of us were spared. Just one of those things we accepted. Not necessarily adjusted to but part of the process. If we failed, we were punished. If we didn't fail, we weren't punished."

"You don't remember any of their names, right? Nobody we could go after? No faces? Nothing tangible that we can find in the world out there?"

She shook her head. "Not that I can remember, no. And I've racked my brain about that for a long time—just the one guy I told you about that I dealt with the most."

"But no name."

"Well, I called him ..." And she stopped and frowned. "What did I call him? He wasn't the big boss. He was like the little boss, but I had a name for him."

"And yet you don't remember?" he asked curiously.

She shrugged. "At the moment it's slipped my mind," she said, with a shake of her head. "I feel like somebody has put safeguards in my brain to stop me from remembering a lot of stuff."

"Hell, even Stefan could have done that," he said.

She looked at him. "Without my permission?"

"All kinds of things can be done without your permission, as you should well know."

She stared at him and then nodded. "I guess that's quite true. I just hadn't thought that he might do it."

"And I'm not saying Stefan *did* it," he corrected. "Keep that in mind. Just because it's something he *could* do doesn't mean it's something he *did* do." She relaxed slightly. "Right, and besides," he said, "if it were done, it would have been done to aid in your healing, since all that trauma rushing back through your head won't help you heal."

"Maybe not," she murmured. "But, at some point, you want to stand on your own."

"Then you need to pick a time when that's possible." He turned and motioned at the pans. "Sausage and eggs are ready. Sit down with your coffee."

She looked at him. "Like, you can cook-cook?"

"I told you that I could." And then he remembered what her childhood had been like and the other conversation they'd had about cooking. "I can't imagine how much you had to catch up on."

"Well, we weren't as far behind as you might have thought. I was afraid of the world out there, afraid it would be much worse, but it turned out to be not as bad as I expected. Plus, I'm a pretty fast learner." She shrugged. "That was another thing that they needed from all of us—to pick up things quickly. And, when we didn't, we were punished."

"That's hardly a conducive learning environment."

"I don't think they cared," she said, looking at him.

"Not about us. It was about the entire team."

"You don't remember much of the team aspect though."

"Not in the last few years, no," she said.

"So, let me get this straight. When you were younger, you were with the larger group."

She nodded.

"As you grew older?"

"As I grew older, I was singled off to one handler, and I was led into rooms where I validated tests of other psychics."

"So, you would see those psychics."

"Sometimes, sometimes not," she said. "Often they were on the other side of a wall or a blacked-out glass window."

"The location we found looked like some major building had been destroyed there. Do you know anything about that?"

She shook her head. "I only saw internal rooms that they allowed me to see. So I didn't see the grounds."

"Do you remember the details of your surroundings when you escaped?"

"Not too much. I took the opportunity and ran. That's the only thing I remember."

"He went out to pee or something?"

She nodded. "But, as I think about it, maybe he went out to turn on that energy barrier. I don't know what he was doing, but I saw the opportunity and went for it."

"Understood," he said, but something odd was in his voice.

Still, she studied him and asked, "What are you thinking?"

"I just wish I knew how many other people were there at the time."

"Well, I assumed that all the other cars had left ahead of

me."

"Who told you that other people were there?"

"My handler."

"And he told you that you were the last one?"

She nodded. "Why? What difference does it make?"

"Maybe nothing," he said.

But obviously something troubled him. She hesitated, wondering what she should do about it. Then she decided that it would be in her best interests to leave it for the moment. "If you learn anything, I want you to promise you'll tell me," she said slowly.

He looked at her, as he lifted a forkful of sausage to his mouth. "Of course."

She shook her head. "No *of course* here," she said. "I need to know I can trust you."

"You can definitely trust me," he said instantly.

She smiled. "That means sharing information as you get it."

"Deal."

CHAPTER 20

THE NEXT FEW days settled into an uneasy truce. Beth swam, rested, healed, swam, ate, healed. On the third morning she woke up, assessed how she felt, and, for the first time, took a long slow deep breath, searching deep inside herself to see just how the pain was. She had put up a lot of blocks, so she didn't have to listen to her pain receptors. So many, so she didn't have to worry about cringing every time she took a breath or stepped wrong. But it seemed like everything was going pretty well now. She slowly stood, not even wincing with pain as she bent and twisted with her morning stretches.

After a hot shower she felt even better. Dressed, she headed down to the kitchen but saw no sign of Hunter. She put on the coffee and rummaged in the fridge, looking for food. They were running low again and needed to get more groceries, something they were both avoiding. They had just enough reasons to stay here, where it seemed like they were somewhat safe. She knew Lizzy was out there; no way she wasn't. And unfortunately Beth would have to step up and deal with that problem soon, but she just didn't know how to do it yet.

She didn't want to do anything to hurt Lizzy. They'd been best friends for the longest time; they were akin to sisters, and yet how could there ever be a friendship after being hunted by her? But Beth also knew Lizzy was hunting under duress and that Lizzy wouldn't have done it on her own. No way she would have. But who knew how damaged she was at this point, or whether she had a choice in anything anymore?

Beth kept racking her brain for any way to cut loose from the energy that she knew Lizzy was tracking, but it's not like Beth could simply excise it. Maybe, if they didn't know each other and hadn't spent years fighting against a common enemy, then maybe their energy wouldn't be so intermingled. Cutting that energy from her own system would probably kill Beth. She'd thought about it a lot; she'd even tried a couple times, but the pain in her body had been excruciating, and the similar loss in her heart had been almost as bad.

As she stood here, staring out the window, she whispered, "I love you, Lizzy. Please stop doing this."

She thought she heard an answer but probably just the wind. She tried hard to listen again, as she repeated her message twice and then a third time.

Hunter asked her from the doorway, "Is she answering you?"

Startled, she turned and stared at him, then shook her head. He frowned at her, as if knowing she was keeping something from him. She glared right back. "She can't be," Beth said. "It's just my imagination."

"And what is it that she's saying, that you think is your imagination?" he asked, taking a step into the kitchen.

She immediately stepped back, so she was against the counter. He frowned and stopped where he was. Not his intention to corner her. She shook her head. "I just keep hearing the same thing that I hear in my nightmares."

"And what is that?"

"*Remember*," she said. "That's all. Just one word. *Remember*."

"Fascinating," he murmured. He studied her carefully.

She shrugged. "I've looked at separating our energy. I've looked at killing off memories. I've looked at all kinds of things," she said, "but Lizzy and I were basically as close as sisters back then. We did everything together, and we were united against a common enemy. We even blended our energy and did the whole blood-swear thing," she said, with half a smile.

"And how would you ever learn about that?"

"From an old movie," she said, with a shrug. "Remember? Everything we learned was from everybody else."

"I am remembering that," he said. "So, if you can't separate from her, what can you do to stop her from seeing you?"

She frowned. "What I always did was hide in other people's energy."

"And that in itself is fascinating," he murmured, "and believe me. We'd all like to know a little more about your process."

She shook her head. "Too bad," she snapped. "I'm not up for being forced to do that."

"All we were planning on doing," he said, his eyebrows raising, "was asking you."

She immediately flushed and waved a hand at him. "Well, pardon me, if I don't quite trust you yet."

"We know you don't trust us yet," he said. "But it would be nice if you weren't quite so quick to judge us."

She frowned at that because this was just more evidence that she was a terrible person, which she probably was. But she was out for one thing and one thing only, and that was survival. "Don't you have something better to do with your time?" she asked him quietly.

He laughed. "Nope, you're not getting rid of me that easily."

She glared at him. "You know it's for your own health and well-being, right?"

"You've tried that line before too," he said, with a smirk.

She groaned. "Well, it's your funeral."

"Yep, and I've heard that a time or two myself."

She shrugged. "I can imagine. Are you always this irritating?"

He burst out laughing. "Glad to see you're feeling so much better. No more pain is cloaked in your voice either."

"Cloaked?"

"Of course, cloaked," he said. "You were struggling to hide it before."

She frowned in irritation. "Will you always read everything I do?"

"No, not always," he said, "but generally I can read a lot, yes."

"I don't think I like that," she announced.

"*I don't think I like that,*" he said in a mocking tone.

Immediately she glared at him again. "See? There you are. Making sure I don't like you."

"I'm not ensuring that you like me or not," he said. "I'd say it's irrelevant, but it is relevant in the sense that you do need to trust me."

"So you say," she muttered, "but sometimes you're just not someone I want to have anything to do with."

"Only sometimes?" he asked, in that same mocking voice again.

She flushed. "There you go again, laughing at me."

"Nope," he said, "that's where you're wrong. I'm not laughing at you. I'm just easing the tension between us."

She glared at him. "That just makes me feel worse."

"Why would you feel worse?" he asked in astonishment.

"Because it makes me sound like I'm the one who's not cooperating."

He shook his head and chuckled again. "Do you feel like you are cooperating?"

She shrugged. "Maybe not as much as I could, no."

"Well, then go by that," he said, "and hopefully other people will have other things to say."

She frowned. "It always makes me feel like I'm on the wrong end of the stick. I've had to play catch-up so much in the last few years," she said. "It's not a comfortable place to be."

"Of course not," he murmured. "Where you started, and now, with all that you've done, have tested your comfort zone, and you're still improving. Now you're growing and moving beyond all that."

"Growing where?" she said, with a shrug. "All I'm doing is running continuously, running away from Lizzy."

"Which is why we'll find a way to take a stand and to stop her from doing this. Presumably we can't talk her out of it because she's forced to do it, or it's become a burning passion of her own to hunt you," he said. "But we have to find a way to make this all come to a tidy stop, so you can go on and live a life. You haven't had the chance to have one yet, and we would all like to see you get that opportunity."

"When you say *all*—"

He chuckled. "Remember? More than just Stefan and I are out there."

"You mean, Dr. Maddy?"

"She's one of them, yes," he said, "but she certainly isn't the only one though."

"See? It's just hard for me to imagine that this whole group of people out there wants to do good."

"Was it hard to understand that this whole group of people in that compound wanted to do bad?" he asked.

She shook her head. "No, never, because I was living that. But to think that there might be a group in reverse, that's a bit hard to believe."

"Well, one day, when you truly trust us, I'm sure Stefan can set up a group meeting with the local people and a virtual meeting with the others, to prove that they exist and that you should believe it," he said calmly. "Whenever there's a negative, there's usually a positive somewhere to counteract it, but oftentimes you have to hunt a little harder to find it."

"See? That's the part I don't get. I mean, Stefan could be out doing whatever he wanted to, so why would he help me?"

"Because Stefan has made it his passion to help gifted people like us. Stefan is the go-between for us and the authorities. Like he says to me often, he deals with the police so we don't have to. Otherwise you'll have to ask him anything else beyond that."

"I'd like to," she said calmly, "but it's not like he's around for me to talk to."

"But he could be, if that's what you wanted."

"What do you mean?"

"I mean that he's available a lot of the time, and he does work with a lot of gifted people and helps them adapt to their abilities. Sometimes we win, and sometimes we lose."

"What do you mean by lose?"

"In case you hadn't figured it out, these abilities are not the easiest to control, and sometimes we get people who can adapt to that, and sometimes it's ... too much." He stopped, his voice drifting away.

"They go insane, you mean?"

"That's one of the possibilities," he said. "Some people can't handle the energy afterward." He paused. "You have to understand that your particular ability to cloak your presence from others who understand energy is pretty amazing."

"I'm sure Stefan can do it."

"He can, indeed," Hunter said, with a solid nod. "But I'm not sure he could do it for as long as you can."

She shrugged. "Desperation breeds all kinds of skills."

"And that's how you learned to do everything—to keep yourself safe, wasn't it?"

"Of course," she said, with a smile. "Nothing like knowing you'll get punished if you can't do something."

"And you watched others getting punished."

She nodded. "Are we getting food today?"

"Well, that's a valid question," he said, chuckling, as he walked forward and checked out the fridge. "Meaning, are we eating today at some point in time, or are we leaving the house and getting food? You were just changing the subject." She glared at him; he shrugged and said, "And I'll let you get away with it for the moment."

"How generous," she said, with half a snort.

"Not always," he said, "but sometimes there's a time to retreat."

"Which is what I was doing there."

"Now the question is, what do we need to do to keep

you safe, long-term? Because doing what you were doing worked great, until suddenly it didn't work anymore. Yet I suppose you have no idea how they found you, do you?"

"No, I don't," she said, "but believe me. I've been racking my brain to figure it out."

He nodded. "Of course you have, but there's never any easy answers in this psychic world about *do this and then you get that.*"

"Wouldn't that be nice," she said with a smirk.

"It would, indeed. If we do manage to find this Lizzy person, I presume she won't be easy to talk to, will she?"

"No," she said. "She'd changed in that last month or so when I was there."

"In what way?" he asked curiously.

"It's hard to describe," she said, "but it seemed like she was leaning more toward their side of life and away from me." She shook her head, then stepped away from the counter and said, "And you still haven't answered my question."

"Well, we have eggs and bacon," he said, "and we have bread, so we'll have breakfast sandwiches this morning," he said, rubbing his hands together with glee.

She looked at him. "I don't think I've ever had anything like that."

"You've been deprived of many of the great things in life," he said. "It looks to me like you've been starved for attention, for food, for safety, for comforts, for everything. You need a chance to have a normal life."

"Which brings us back to Lizzy," she said, nodding.

"Right," he said, "we keep coming back around to her."

"We don't have any choice," she said. "I know I can't be

free until I get her off my case."

"That's why we have to find something logical that will work to convince her to stop."

"My God," she said, "you can't believe it will be that simple."

"What's simple about it?" he asked, looking a little confused.

She studied his face to see if he was serious. "I think she likes being brainwashed just fine right now," she said, with difficulty. "I think she's so indoctrinated that she doesn't know logic, common sense, or the difference between this and anything else anymore."

"And that's possible," he said. "It certainly happens, way more than we would like to think it does, unfortunately. But that doesn't mean that she has everything she wants—like, maybe a chance to get off this crazy train to have a good life for herself."

Beth nodded sadly. "We used to talk about it a lot. About what life would be like, when we got free."

"And when you got free? Was it like that?"

"No," she said, "because, although my location changed all the time, I was never free."

"Because you were always being hunted."

"Exactly," she said simply. "Just no freedom in that."

"Nope, there never is," he said gently. "That's another reason we'll have to work hard to get you out of this scenario."

"Not just out," she said, sounding a little desperate. "I need to get all the way out. So they can't ever find me again."

He nodded. "Who in the group would have been a good

marksman?"

She stopped, surprised at the switch in conversation. "What do you mean?"

"You said you were shot."

"Yes, well, obviously I was shot," she said, half-jokingly, her hand automatically going to her side.

"Yep," he said, "I saw the bullet wound myself."

"And retrieved the bullet, right? I'm not going crazy."

With a big smile, he said, "You're not crazy at all. But would Lizzy have been the shooter?"

"I don't know if she shoots or not," she said cautiously, "if that's what you're asking."

"Well, it's not quite what I was asking, but I'm asking if it could have been a random stranger or somebody who was attacking you for a completely different reason."

"Oh, God, is the world that crazy? Do people attack each other for no reason?"

"Well, you'd hope not," he murmured, "but unfortunately it's certainly a possibility."

"Wow," she murmured, "we didn't see any of that in the movies. I mean, we did see a lot of horrible things, but, at the same time, we also knew it was made up for TV, and they kept telling us it was make believe. But they also kept telling us that the world was a dangerous place and that we needed looking after. And that the world needed protecting."

"And is that what you were being trained to do? To protect the world?"

"That's what we were told," she said firmly.

"Of course," he said, "because the world is a messed-up place, but it isn't *all* a messed-up place. Not everybody out here is trying to kill you."

"Well, that's good to know," she said, with a twitch of her lips. "But again, you know trust is a hard thing when you've had that information poured into your brain for God-only-knows how long."

"Right," he said, "you've certainly been repeatedly exposed to a ton of misinformation that isn't helping you."

"Not helping me or anybody else," she said, "and it's frustrating because I think I know so much and can do so much. Then I find out I'm nearly incapable of doing anything because of the way the world actually runs. Without money I have nothing, but, to get money, I need a job, which unfortunately requires skills, and, if I don't happen to have any skills, I'm out of luck."

"What job did you start with?"

"Cleaning," she said. "I did have skills for that."

"Why is that?"

"Because we cleaned our own rooms," she said. "It's not hard to move around a cloth with some chemicals on it."

"No," he said, "I imagine it isn't. And then what?"

"I started cleaning restaurants, and then I moved up to the front counter. I learned by watching the others, and I'm a fast learner," she said quietly. "It's not so hard when you're desperate, and, at the restaurant, at least I got food."

"Ah, that was a huge benefit."

"Just a small mom-and-pop restaurant at first, and I was part of the cleaning crew, who would go in at the end of the day, since they were too tired to do a cleanup. We didn't get paid that much but enough that I could survive while I learned a bit more."

"And where did you sleep?"

"In the brush," she said quietly, "for the longest time."

He just stared at her.

She shrugged. "What else could I do? It's not like I knew how to rent property."

"No, of course not," he said. "I keep forgetting how much you would have been missing in your education."

"Missing and yet not missing," she said, with a smile. "An amazing amount of stuff to learn is out there, an awful lot that I needed to get caught up on because we didn't learn it through real-life experience."

"No, of course not."

She saw that she'd surprised him. "Besides," she said, "nothing wrong with living out in Mother Nature."

"Absolutely not," he said. "I personally love it, but I do like to have a roof over my head when the weather gets ugly."

"Thankfully I didn't have too much bad weather when I was outside most of the time," she said.

"A lucky break for you, since so often the Oregon weather can be pretty ugly," he said.

"I agree with you there," she said, "but I was blessed to be in decent places whenever I needed to be. A couple times I got caught outside in the harsh elements, and once I got sick because I was soaked and couldn't get dry. But, after I found out about the public pools, that helped a lot too."

"Yes, you can always get showers there, can't you?"

She nodded. "And I needed that base for a while, until I could get enough money saved up to rent a room. Once I rented a room, I could rent a little bit bigger," she said, with a shrug. "I had some money. I don't think I even have any of it left now," she said, with a frown. "I guess I'll lose my place too, and all the money I earned," she said in outrage.

"Well, if you give me the address, we can get Stefan to send somebody there to collect it."

She looked at him. "Really?"

He nodded. "Why not? It's your money and your possessions. You can go there and pick it up again."

She immediately gave him the address. He wrote it down and sent a text to Stefan. "Do you think Lizzy would have found you there?"

"Well, somebody shot me there," she said, with that look again.

He nodded. "Do you think they would have gone in the house?"

"I don't know," she said. "Why?"

"I just wondered if there was any chance they would have hurt your landlord."

She stared at him in shock. "Well, I would certainly hope not," she said slowly, but the thought creeping into her mind made her terrified for the old lady who let out the rooms. "Her name is Sugar Mama," she said.

At that, he stared at her in shock.

She shrugged. "I guess she lived with sugar daddies all her life. When the last one passed away, he left her the house, but she had no way to make a living."

He chuckled. "Well, it sounds like letting out the rooms in the house made a living for her."

Beth nodded. "She's really sweet and good-hearted."

"Well, that's good," he said. "I'm glad you landed on your feet with her."

"Yeah, unless she was harassed or even worse because of me," she said. "Can you get Stefan to check?"

He nodded. "That I can do."

"And hopefully sooner than later?" she asked, worry in her voice. Because the last thing she wanted to do was ever cause Sugar Mama any trouble. "The only good thing is," she said, "that Sugar Mama is a pretty wise old lady. And I think she sees trouble coming a mile away. She's the one who took me in hand and warned me about some of the people around us."

"In what way?"

"One guy down at the end of the street liked kids too much. He had a record and was supposed to stay away from the playgrounds, but he didn't always," she said quietly. "And a couple other guys were pretty rough and ready. One had beaten his wife, and she disappeared, and, no, I don't know what *disappeared* means here."

He stared at her. "This Sugar Mama sounds like a very interesting woman."

"She is. She was good to me, and I do not want to have brought trouble onto her shoulders."

"We'll keep that in mind," he said quietly. "It's not always that way, you know?"

"No, but it sure seems like it," she said. "What kind of a world did you guys create that has such dysfunctional people in it?"

"Maybe we're all a little dysfunctional," he said. "Did you ever think that maybe that's just the way of the world?"

"Thanks for that," she said. "Remember? You're supposed to be making me feel better."

He burst out laughing. "Well, we can try to make you feel better," he said, "but that's not the easiest thing either."

"No," she said, "it isn't, but how distressing that so many of the things we had learned about in the compound were true."

"Of course," he said, nodding. "Always a bit of a shock, isn't it? You hope that everything bad was a lie, and then you find out—"

"That it is true and that, in some ways, the world is the nastiest place to be, where people do unimaginable things to each other and to children," she said. "Why the children?"

"Because some people are just sick," he said, "and they have unnatural desires."

She nodded slowly. "And that just takes me back to the boss, wondering whether he was one of them, or if he, in some twisted way, was somehow combating all the evilness out there."

CONSIDERING WHAT BETH had been through, her mental stability was absolutely amazing. And then Hunter wondered how much this Sugar Mama had to do with it all. If she'd seen in Beth that innocence and that desperate need to have a life, it's quite possible the old woman had been instrumental in setting her straight about a lot of the world. "Do you have a bank account?"

"Sugar Mama told me to get one," she said, "but I didn't trust it. I knew about banks, but again they weren't exactly something that I deemed trustworthy."

"I guess it depends on what information you are relying on," he said. "Most people nowadays would say they are safe."

"Sugar Mama didn't trust them," she said.

And he had an inkling into Sugar Mama's influence. "She taught you a lot, didn't she?"

"Yes," she said, "she taught me an awful lot, and I'll forever be grateful. Could you please get Stefan to check?"

"Yes," he said. "I already sent him a message. But remember, it won't be something he can run out the door and do."

"Why not?" she asked, staring at him.

"Well, there are laws stopping things like that too."

"Even if she's in danger?"

"Let's trust Stefan to check it out, okay?"

"I get that," she said. "We'll give Stefan time to do all kinds of stuff. But I want to do something in the meantime."

"And what is that?" he asked.

"I want to see if I can find Lizzy myself."

He stopped and stared. "What good would that do?"

"I don't know, but I know she's stronger than me and more skilled than I am."

"So going up against her is pretty much a suicide mission, is what I'm hearing."

"I don't know about that," she said, "but I was hoping maybe I could talk to her," she said, then raised both hands almost in a questioning movement.

"Do you think the friendship you had before still stands?"

"I would love to think that," she said, "but, no, you're right."

"And you never did tell me who would have any shooting skills in that group."

"I imagine any number of people," she said, tiredly studying him. "Don't forget the boss also had guards."

"Did you see any of those at the compound?"

"Not for a long time, not for years."

"Not for years? What does that mean?"

"Well, I was alone for the last several years," she said,

"with just my handler."

"Except for the testing?"

"Yes, the testing," she said, with a grimace. "Most of the time I didn't get to see people. I would just see energy. A lot of the time, Lizzy's energy. We were always working against or toward something."

"I'm sorry," he said. "That must have been very difficult."

"Well, between the loneliness, the sense that you're going crazy, and then the surety that you probably should be crazy so that the world out there isn't one you have to deal with," she said, "all definitely made for a strange way to live."

"It sounds devastating."

"I don't know about *devastating*," she said, "but *crippling* for sure."

"That's a good word for it," he said.

She shrugged. "It's easy to look back on all those years, but if I hadn't tried to break free—"

"I know. I get that," he said. "Let's not think about that right now."

She snorted. "How can I *not* think about that?"

"You're free," he said. "Let's keep you that way, and then we don't ever have to think about you being a captive again."

She smiled and said, "You know what? If nothing else, you do live in a pretty dreamy world."

He burst out laughing at that and continued to cook the eggs. She watched with interest. "Sugar Mama made something like that," she said, "but she always added these hot chili peppers and lots and lots of fresh tomatoes."

"Interesting," he said. "She liked hot food."

"She did. She would say, *hot man, hot food, and hot money* were all things she would love to handle."

He chuckled. "Don't tell me. Does she happen to be a large black woman?"

"Well, the only thing large about her is that chest of hers," she said, with a grin. "It's massive. She's only about five-six though, and she is running well past her sixties, if not into her seventies," she said, "but you wouldn't know it. She works hard to keep the wheels of time at bay."

He smiled. "I think I'd like her."

"You probably would," she said. "She'd definitely like you." And she waggled her eyebrows at him.

He chuckled. "She obviously had a big influence on you."

"Without her, I don't think I'd have survived," she said calmly. "She certainly is somebody I owe a lot of thanks to."

"And yet she probably wouldn't want thanks, would she?"

She shook her head. "Nope, that's not who she is."

"Exactly, and I'm grateful that she helped you, though I'd like to meet her when this is all over."

"She'd probably like to meet you too," she said, with a chuckle. "Anybody male is her type."

Still grinning at her and her comments, he quickly finished making up the breakfast sandwiches, and, when he placed the plate in front of her, he said, "There. Take a bite into that."

She looked at it and said, "Wow, that's huge."

"I thought you were hungry," he said.

"I was," she said. "I didn't realize something this big was in the offing though."

"If you can't eat it all," he said, "cut it in half. If you don't want the second half, I'll eat it."

She rolled her eyes at him. "That's not happening," she said, with a smile, then happily bit into the first half.

CHAPTER 21

*R*EMEMBER.

The whisper came with the same intensity that it always did, the energy floating out in the world around her.

Beth opened her eyes and bolted upright. Immediately Hunter, who'd been sitting beside her, laid a hand on her shoulder and said, "It's all right."

"*Remember*," she said.

His eyebrows shot up. "Remember what?"

"It's that same damn word again, somebody telling me to remember."

He groaned and said, "Now if only you knew what you're supposed to remember."

"I have no idea. I don't even know why there would be anything I've forgotten. Except, you know, a lot of things that I want to forget."

"Maybe something is in there that you want to forget, yet you shouldn't."

"Maybe, but I don't know what to say," she said. She hopped to her feet and said, "Did you get any news?"

"I did."

"You were supposed to tell me," she cried out.

"You were sleeping," he said. "Remember? Why would I wake you up for this little bit of information?"

"What information?" she said crossly, sitting back down

again.

"First off, Sugar Mama was injured, but we're not exactly sure what happened. She was found on the floor with a head injury."

She stared at him, feeling all the complacency about being safe draining away from her. "Oh my God," she said, "I need to go to her."

"Why?" he asked.

"Because it's my fault," she cried out. "I don't want anybody hurt. This is my fight."

"Well, that's just too damn bad," he said, staring at her. "This is a fight that involves a lot of people obviously, and you don't get to call the shots because you want to."

She glared at him. "You could do something about this."

"What do you want me to do?"

"I don't know," she snapped, "but stop people from attacking Sugar Mama."

"We don't know for a fact that she was attacked. She was lying at the bottom of a set of stairs. For all we know, she fell."

She glared at him and shook her head. "But you don't know that for sure," she said.

"No, of course I don't," he said, raising his hands.

"I want to go see her."

"That's not a wise idea."

"Why not?"

"Because, if she were attacked, they could be waiting to see if you show up."

"But you just said she wasn't attacked."

"No, I said that *maybe* she wasn't attacked," he said in exasperation. "Stop putting words in my mouth."

"Stop twisting the words around," she said.

He groaned. "Look. We can keep this up for a very long time, but we're not getting anywhere fighting each other."

"I want to go see her," she said, a mutinous tone in her voice. "I want to go get my money anyway." He frowned, looking at her. "It's a good way to see if they found me or if they went through my room."

"We know they found you," he said, "but it wouldn't be a bad idea to go back to where you were shot."

She stared at him. "What would that tell you?"

"Energy," he said. "It leaves a spore that I can hunt."

"Well, good then," she said. "Let's go." She bounced to her feet and raced to the door.

He got up much slower. "Wait a minute. We won't go without a plan."

"And yet we went back to the compound where I spent all those years without a plan."

He smiled. "Well, okay, I get that. That's one point to you," he said, "but it's still not the best idea."

"I'm not letting you use that anymore," she snapped. "I want to go see her."

"I get that," he groaned, "but let's not be stupid and impulsive about this."

"Is there such a thing?"

"Yes," he said, "there is, and right now we need to be a little more methodical in our actions."

"The method is simple," she said. "We go check up on Sugar Mama and for you to see where I was shot."

He looked at his phone, quickly sent Stefan a text, and said, "I'm telling him what we're doing."

"And we'll pick up groceries on our way back."

"Depending on how long we're gone for, yes," he said, with a nod. "I'm not exactly sure how many hours it'll take us to get there."

"Quite a few," she said, "but it doesn't matter because we need to go."

"I got it," he said, in frustration. "I'm getting there."

"Get there faster," she snapped. And, with that, she headed upstairs.

"Where are you going?"

"To pack," she said.

"Pack what?" he asked. "You don't have anything."

"So, it won't take me long. Make sure you're ready when I come down."

Upstairs, she sat down on the bed. She had to exit the room and not let him see that she trembled with fear. Fear for herself, fear for Sugar Mama. That woman didn't deserve anything that had come her way. Beth didn't want to believe that her friend had been attacked, but a "coincidence" was a little too hard to believe. Sugar Mama was all heart, and this needed to stop.

Beth couldn't stand the thought of even more people she knew getting hurt. It just wasn't fair, and, at the same time, she also knew that nobody cared, or at least nobody cared very much. So she had to do more than she was doing.

She got up and packed the little bit of clothing she had. "Hopefully somebody will understand what's going on," she murmured. "Hopefully somebody can do something about the nightmare this has become." Just so much was going on that Beth didn't understand. The whole premise of this was very simple: they needed to stop Lizzy from hunting Beth. And ultimately, Beth was afraid that would mean the death of her friend.

Yet … Beth wasn't even sure it was possible to kill her friend because Lizzy was one scary strong female. With that,

Beth took one last look around, wishing she could stay here indefinitely. But that wasn't a choice, and she headed downstairs with her small bag and with her head held high.

As she stood at the front door, she watched as he came to her, pulling on his boots and grabbing a jacket.

He looked at her and asked, "Do you want to leave some cat food behind for Nocturne?"

"You haven't bought him any yet?"

"I did," he said. "I put it outside because I never see him."

"Nocturne will be fine," she said briskly. "If not, we'll come back and get him."

"You're not planning on staying away permanently, are you?"

"I can't stay here permanently," she said, looking at him. "It's your house."

He frowned. "So you are looking at moving on?"

"Of course I am," she said, and, with that, she stepped outside onto the porch. She sniffed the fresh morning air.

He locked up and came behind her and laid a gentle hand on her shoulder. "Leaving doesn't have to be permanent, you know?"

"It feels like it does though," she murmured, staring up at the sky. "It definitely feels like it does."

HUNTER DROVE STEADILY through the day, but they were still hours away from where Beth had roomed at Sugar Mama's house. They traveled south on the coast, but eventually he shifted to a highway, taking them inland.

When she said, "We're about a half an hour away," he looked at her.

"Do you want to stop and pick up a coffee?" he asked.
She nodded. "That would be good."

The closer they got to the house she'd stayed at, the quieter she'd become, almost like a leaching of her energy slipped behind them.

He studied her carefully. "You're looking weaker."

"Sure," she said, with a shrug. "It happens."

"Why?"

"I don't know why," she said in exasperation, but then she shook her head. "Stress, fear, healing."

"Does it mean that Lizzy is closer?"

She stared at him. "I don't think so," she said slowly.

"So why then?" She shrugged and settled back into the seat. He drove through the next town, stopped at a coffee shop, and asked, "Do you want me to just run in?"

"That would be good."

But her energy was even now getting that much quieter again. He frowned as he got out, and he said, "I don't like anything about this."

"I know," she said, "but that's just who you are."

Not a whole lot he could say about that because he wasn't sure how she meant it, and he knew it was true to a certain extent regardless. But it was also clear that she wasn't explaining something. He headed into the coffee shop, keeping an eye on her. He placed his order and soon was served. When he stepped back out to the car with two coffees and a couple muffins, he was surprised to see her sitting up and looking a hell of a lot better. And even more surprised to see a black cat running away.

He got into the vehicle, looked at her, and said, "How did you recharge?"

She looked at him and said, "Would you believe meditation?"

He snorted at that. "If it were that easy," he said, "we'd all be doing it."

"Well, I'm sure Stefan would give you some lines about the universe is abundant, and no shortage of energy is anywhere."

"I've heard that," he said, "and obviously you have too."

"Of course," she murmured.

"But," he said, "that's not what you did."

"How do you know?"

He shook his head and said, "You want me to trust you, yet you won't trust me."

"It's nothing," she said, with a wave of her hand.

"If nothing, you wouldn't be looking like you just had a complete vacation in the time it took me to get coffee."

She shrugged.

"And yet you still won't tell me about Nocturne." When she turned away from him, he added, "You know something? For somebody who demands a lot of trust from other people, you're sure not very good at handing it out in the same measure."

She remained silent.

He knew there wouldn't be any winning that conversation, not with the way she was already sidestepping the issue. He went quiet for a long time and then said, "How much farther?"

"Not much," she said. "It's just up and around there."

He followed her directions, and they came up to an old farmhouse on a very large property. He pulled into the driveway, and she hopped out and stood at the side of the car.

He exited, walked around his car to join her, and asked,

"So where were you shot exactly?"

She pointed toward the backyard. "I had come down in the morning and was standing outside, doing some stretches." She showed him where, closer to the trees. "Right here," she said, and she pushed forward and walked to the place where she had been shot. "I'm sure my blood is still here."

He studied the ground and nodded. "Possibly. I see some stains. Did you turn and look?"

She shook her head. "No, I just bolted for the trees and through there and kept on running."

"And you know for sure he came after you?"

"I don't know anything," she said. "I just ran."

Hunter didn't respond, but he studied the ground with an intensity that made her pause.

"What's the matter?"

He looked up at her, shrugged, and said, "Nothing. Why?"

"Just the way you're looking."

"Well, it's my job," he said. "Let's take a look at your room."

Beth led the way, and he followed her.

CHAPTER 22

BETH TOOK AN outside set of steps and entered the second-floor bedroom she had rented, hating the feeling of almost being ashamed.

Hunter frowned that the outer door wasn't locked. Then he stepped inside and nodded. "Nice and clean."

She relaxed slightly, realizing no judgment was in his tone. "I was expecting you to laugh at me," she said lightly.

He studied her. "Why would I do that?" he said. "You survived, and that's worth everything."

"Maybe," she said, "but you don't realize just what a prize survival is until you're fighting for it."

"Exactly," he said. "No reason to be ashamed to live here. It's clean, rodent free. Plus you have lots of light and your own bathroom. It's all good." He nodded. "Now show me Sugar Mama's room and where the other renters stayed."

She said, "Well, that's the thing. A couple other tenants were here at the same time." She looked around, frowned, and said, "But I don't remember that I ever met them."

"How many people did she rent rooms to?"

"A couple. If she could, she preferred to only allow women, but Sugar Mama was down to just me for the last year. She kept looking for somebody else, and I know a couple people were asking, so she was a little desperate for money and considered bringing in men."

"Why didn't she like to rent to men?"

"She said they always gave her trouble, one way or another, so she tried to keep from renting to them." He didn't say anything, and she looked at him and said, "Don't you think men are trouble?"

"No, not necessarily," he said. "But I'm also male, so you know that I might be slightly biased in my view."

She chuckled. "I think the trouble was more sexual."

He stopped, looked at her. "Meaning that she felt they would attack her?"

"No, but that they always wanted favors from her or to strike up a relationship or something. She would say that she didn't want any more hot rods to play with, unless they were hot rods that she chose."

His lips twitched.

She smiled. "She's quite the character."

"I like that," he said. "And I can see her point. If you have a lot of single men here, and she's as much of a character as she sounds, I'm sure some of them would try their hand at a relationship with her."

"I don't think they wanted relationships so much as the odd *slap and tickle*, as she would call it."

He snorted and shook his head. "Like I said, she sounds like a hell of a character."

"Well, that she is but a good-hearted one too."

"Yeah, and that's important," he said. "Now whereabouts did she have her rooms?"

Beth led the way downstairs and said, "The whole downstairs floor is hers." She walked into the center.

"Did you have a key?"

"She never kept it locked. She thought, when you lock a door, it only made you feel like you were safe. The truth is, you were more vulnerable because you weren't expecting the predators outside to get inside. And, when they did, you were completely handicapped." He stopped and stared, as she shrugged. "Like I said, she's a character."

"With an interesting outlook on life," he murmured.

"Very," Beth said, as she showed him the lower floor areas. "I only had a little hot pot up in my room and that tiny fridge, so she would let me come down here and cook every once in a while and often invited me for a meal too."

"Interesting," he said. "It sounds like you were blessed."

"Yeah, she is more than a landlord. More like a friend, something I didn't expect to have."

"Of course not, but the good thing is," he said, "you did make a friend, and she helped you a lot." He wandered around the lower rooms. "No sign of a break-in, but, like you said, she kept the doors unlocked."

Beth watched as Hunter studied everything. "I see that you're looking for stuff," she said, "but I don't know what you're looking for."

"Something that looks familiar, something that feels familiar, something that could be familiar," he said, with a shrug. "Any number of things and typically, when I see it, I recognize it as being important."

She watched as he went around the main room and the kitchen and then headed into Sugar Mama's bedroom. Beth said, "I'm not comfortable having you in there."

"Hey, the woman is in the hospital. We have to find out what's wrong. I'm not snooping into her sex life or anything like that," he said in exasperation.

"Maybe not," she said, "and that she'd probably share with you quite freely."

He smiled and nodded, then went through everything

that he could and finally stepped back and said, "I want to go outside." His tone was abrupt, as if something bothered him, but he didn't seem to want to share. But then she hadn't shared a ton either. Something she would have to deal with. As he walked outside, he looked around the area and nodded.

"What are you nodding for?"

"She was struck," he said.

"So now we have it as an attack. And you're proof positive of that?"

He nodded. "I am, yes," he said, "but proof as far as the cops are concerned? No."

"Ah," she said. "So, spooky stuff."

"Always spooky stuff," he said, with a smile.

"Why is everything spooky stuff? You know what? For the longest time I thought I was the only one, but they kept bringing in new people to the compound, and then I thought the world was full of people like us. Yet, as I got older, I realized just how rare we are."

"Exactly," he said, "we gifted types are rare, and, as such, we have to look after ourselves because, all too frequently, there won't be enough of us around at any given time to help out."

"I guess," she said. He walked around the entire property and then looked again at the area where she had been attacked. But he wasn't saying anything. "Well?" she asked impatiently.

"Well what?" he said.

"Are you happy with this?"

"You mean, did I find anything? Yes, I did," he said. "Am I happy with what I found? Well, it's hard to be happy when a woman was attacked mostly because she knew someone. Now I want to go to the hospital and see if she's awake."

Beth stopped and said, "Wait. I need to go get my money and my clothes."

He turned, then nodded. "I'll be here."

She turned and raced upstairs. The money wasn't hard to find in a sock under her mattress. She grabbed it and her backpack, added her few belongings, then stuffed the money in there too. She loaded a couple little things that she had, including the one stupid pebble that she and Lizzy used to pass back and forth as a comfort stone. She looked at it, sighed, tucked it into her pocket, and raced back downstairs.

Hunter waited, leaning against the car, but he was on the phone this time. As she approached, he said, "Okay, Stefan, I've got to go." Then hung up.

"What was that about?" she challenged.

"Your Sugar Mama is awake, and she's talking."

HUNTER WATCHED, AS Beth tossed her backpack into the back seat of the car and asked, "Has that got all your money in it too?"

"Money and clothing," Beth said. "I don't have much."

He nodded, got into the vehicle as she did, turned it on, and drove carefully to the hospital. He'd definitely seen an energy he recognized, but they looked like different fragments of Beth herself. His long conversation with Stefan hadn't shed any light on it. He'd seen the same energy in Beth's aura, but then she had used other people to hide her energy, so hers was completely intermingled with everybody else's.

By the time they reached the hospital, he was still no

closer to figuring it out. He parked and led the way through to the administration desk, where he asked where Sugar Mama's room was.

The woman laughed. "You can see her holding court from a long way off," she said. "She's up on the second floor."

They made their way up the stairs and down the hall, and, sure enough, several people stood around an open doorway, laughing and chuckling.

As he approached, one of the other patients looked at him and said to Sugar Mama, "It looks like you've got company."

Everybody backed away slightly, as Hunter entered the room with Beth. Sugar Mama took one look at Beth, cried out, and opened her arms. Hunter stayed at the doorway and watched, as the smiling woman in the bed reached up and hugged Beth tight. If Sugar Mama had never had a daughter, she'd adopted Beth as hers, seeing Beth as an otherwise lost soul on the streets. Sugar Mama had obviously taken her in and done her a world of good. She finally released her, then looked at Hunter and said, "Wow, when you find yourself a man, you really find one, girl."

Beth laughed. "It's not like that with us."

"Good Lord," she said, rolling an eye at her. "Why not?"

He stepped forward and said, "Thank you for looking after her."

Her eyes narrowed, as she studied him. "I sure as hell hope you'll solve the problem that she has got herself messed up in, so she doesn't need people like me out there helping her, protecting her."

"Wouldn't that be nice?" he said. "You can count on the fact that we're working on it."

"Good," she said. "And, while you're at it, you can find that asshole who hit me."

"I would love to. We suspect it's one and the same."

"Well, he was asking about her."

"Do you remember what questions he asked?"

"He wanted to locate her," Sugar Mama said. "Then he was asking some weird questions about how she'd been and how she'd been acting for the last few years. I don't know what he was going on about. I said she was fine, and, just like always, I'd never had any problem with her. Which I haven't," she said, as she patted Beth's hand. "This child has got a strong brain in her head and a will to live, and I wouldn't do anything to take that away from her."

"Good," Hunter said, "because you do understand, for some of these men, that's exactly what they are looking at doing, right?"

She nodded slowly. "It's a sick world out there, if you're not careful. I tried to teach her how to be careful, but she's quite the innocent. She has a ways to go."

"I know," he murmured. "I wasn't planning on taking advantage of her."

She frowned, nodded, and said, "And I hear you. I'm just not sure whether I believe you."

At that, Beth burst into laughter. "I said the same thing to him."

She looked over, grinned, and said, "Good, I'm glad you were smart enough to at least worry about that much."

"Of course," Beth said, "and answers would be lovely, but apparently they're not that easy to come by."

"No," she said, "they sure aren't. But it's not all bad."

"No," Beth murmured, "it's not all bad. At the same time, it's pretty hard to find anything that's very good about it just now," she said, looking at him.

"I don't know what I can tell you," Sugar Mama said to them both, "but I sure hope they left my house alone."

"We were just there," Beth said gently. "It looks fine."

"Well, thank the Good Lord for that," she said. "I think it may be time I sold out and went somewhere else."

"Where would you go?" Beth asked her friend.

"Well, my sister contacted me not too long ago. She wants to share a house and to grow old together. We've always been the best of friends, but we never had the time or the energy to spend much time together," she said, whispering.

The two friends sat and quietly visited for a little bit longer, and then finally Hunter joined them. "We need to keep moving."

At that, Sugar Mama looked at him and said, "Who is the guy?"

"I don't know," he said, looking at her. "Any chance you could give us a description?"

"Sure," she said. "Five foot eleven, with long black hair, older than you—late forties or fifties. Looks after himself somewhat but was anxious, like he was seriously worried about Beth."

Hunter looked at Beth to see a puzzled look on her face, then she shrugged. "That could have been him. I don't know."

At that, Hunter froze, and he took several steps closer to Sugar Mama. "What do you mean by *worried?*"

"Well, that was the thing that I didn't get. I thought he was after her, and he was. He really was," she said. "Don't get me wrong. He was trying to find her, and he wouldn't leave any stone unturned. But he was also worried."

"In what way?" Beth asked. Stepping forward, she grabbed Sugar Mama's hand. "And I'm so sorry that he hurt you."

Sugar Mama waved her hand. "Hey," she said, "I learned a long time ago how to avoid a man's fist."

"Did he beat you?" she cried out.

"No, but he looked like he wanted to. He would step forward with that fist clenched of his because he was so frustrated. But he was frustrated because he couldn't find you."

"Did he say what he wanted?" Hunter asked her intently.

She shook her head. "No, he wouldn't tell me much, and, when I told him that I wasn't into throwing young girls up to get themselves beaten, he just looked at me in surprise. 'You don't know the half of it,' he said briskly, and then he backed away a little bit, and I thought he would take off, and everything would be fine. But then he turned around, and that fist was coming. I ducked but not fast enough, and I tripped backward and fell down the stairs," she said, reaching up to her head, and she winced. "You know it's definitely time to leave that old house. I think I'll put it on the market and move back to my sister's." Then she looked at Beth in alarm. "But what about you?"

"I won't be staying there any longer anyway," Beth said. "I've paid you the rent for the month, and I collected the rest of my belongings while I was there." She smiled, leaned over, and kissed Sugar Mama gently on the cheek. "Thank you for all you did to help me."

"Well, I'll tell you, honey, if you want one more spot of advice," she said, "you'll hang on to this guy."

Beth looked at her, then at Hunter. "Really?"

The old woman grinned at him and laughed. "Obviously we didn't spend enough time together," she said, "if you don't recognize a sugar daddy standing right in front of you."

Hunter snorted at that. "I'm hardly anybody's sugar daddy."

"No," she said, "you're better. You're a protector."

"What the hell does that mean?" Beth asked in confusion.

"He's somebody who always looks to do right and will defend the underdog," she said. "You can't go wrong with him. He'll look after you. Matter of fact, seeing him with you right now makes me feel all the more certain about leaving. I was worried about it before because my sister did mention living together a little while back. But I knew that you would still need a place and would still need somebody to keep an eye out for you. But now I can see that you'll be just fine."

"I hardly even know him," she murmured.

"Nope," she said, "I can see that, but, if you're smart, you'll get to know him a whole lot better." At that, she burst out with a raucous laughter that filled the hallway.

Hunter looked at the others in the doorway, huge grins on everybody's faces. He knew what they were all thinking, but he didn't think that Beth was in any way ready for that conversation. Although no way she could have been around Sugar Mama and not understood how life worked. That just brought him back to wondering what Beth's life in captivity had been all about when it came to relationships. He hoped that she hadn't been put in a position where that had been part of the punishment. He didn't want to think along those lines. But now that he'd considered it, hard not to.

"We need to go," he said. Sugar Mama was still grinning, when she gave a great big bear hug to Beth. And she pointed a meaty fist at him and said, "You look after that girl."

"I plan on it," he said, "but she's not being very cooperative."

Sugar Mama's smile fell away. "She's been through a lot," she said. "If she knows that she's in trouble or has a reason to be wary, you need to listen to her too."

"I got it," he said quietly. "I trust her instincts. Don't worry. But my instincts also need to be trusted, and right now they're telling me to get the hell out of here."

At that, Sugar Mama pushed Beth away. "Go on now," she said. "You only get one chance to listen to your instincts because, when you're wrong, it's fatal, so go."

And, with one final glance at Sugar Mama, Beth stepped out of the hospital room toward Hunter. He smiled, wrapped an arm around her shoulders, pulled her up close, and said, "She will do just fine."

"What if he finds her here?"

"No reason to now," he said. "Remember? She's already told him everything she knows. If she hadn't fallen down the stairs, she probably wouldn't have even ended up here."

Her shoulders sagged with relief. "You think he wouldn't have killed her?"

"I hope not," he said. "He hasn't killed anybody we've seen on this trail yet, has he?"

"Only my guard, when I escaped," she said. "I wondered about that."

"Why?" Hunter asked.

"Because I know that other people have died, just by reading some of those files we retrieved. So, the real question is, why hasn't he killed me?"

Hunter stared at her and asked, "What reason are you coming up with?"

"Because he needs me alive," she said simply. "He needs me for something, and, for that, I have to be alive."

AT LEAST BETH was thinking on her feet. Hunter just wasn't sure if it would be fast enough. Danger was poking him in the back, and he raced Beth along the hospital hallway, down the stairwell, and out the back door. He dragged her every step of the way with him. When they finally got outside, he didn't even duck; he bolted straight forward and headed for the trees.

"Why are we going out here?" she cried out.

He immediately tugged her into the dense brush, ignoring the sticks that poked at his skin. "Because," he snapped. He held her quiet, his finger against her lips as he waited, his eyes closed, senses on alert.

He felt that same creepy sensation of being followed. But not here, not outside. At least not yet. Hunter had mentally mapped out where they were and how far they had to go to get back to his car. It would entail a few minutes of being exposed. He wanted this guy to go inside the hospital, but, at the same time, he was worried about where he was going and what would happen. He sent a message to Stefan, asking him to contact the hospital on the off chance that their attacker was heading toward Sugar Mama. Just when some of the pressure nagging at him eased, Hunter moved along the tree line, around to where he saw the car in front of them. He leaned closer to Beth and said, "The car's up ahead. We'll run straight to it. Get in without a question, do you hear me?"

She nodded and didn't say anything. He held up three fingers, dropped one, dropped the second, and then, on the third, he bolted once again, dragging her forward. But she was running as fast as he was. They made it to the car. He turned on the engine, and they bolted out of the parking lot, now realizing he had a flat tire.

Swearing, he pulled off to the side of the road up ahead and said, "Grab your things." He broke out the motorcycle, still in the trunk. He handed her a helmet and told her to get on. He started it up and, leaving the car exactly there, tore off down the highway.

CHAPTER 23

Beth had never spent much time on a motorcycle. She understood in theory how they worked, which had allowed her to escape Hunter that one time on his motorcycle. Now she clung with her head flat against his back, her eyes closed, as he ripped down the highway, putting as many miles between them and the hospital as he could. And all she could think about was Sugar Mama. The woman had been a wonderful friend, and Beth didn't want to see anything more happen to her.

If this guy only wanted information, no need for him to clean up his tracks, but, if he were looking to do something further, then he wouldn't want anybody to know that he'd been asking questions. The fact that she and Hunter had been at the hospital at the same time likely meant that's exactly what he was up to. She didn't even know how to stop it. In her heart of hearts, she felt it was already over.

She closed her eyes and sent out a shot of energy. She didn't have very much to spare, but she had recharged rather well earlier in the day. She sent out a probe, looking for information from the hospital, but immediately hit some rebounding wall that slammed her back into her own energy.

You have to let her go.

She slowly sat up taller on the motorcycle. Had Hunter done that? Had Stefan?

I did it, Stefan said calmly in her head.

Beth wanted to rant and to rail at him, yet she was full of wonder at his abilities. *Why?* was all she could say. And then she followed it up with a confused *How?*

The why is because you don't dare let the attacker know where you are, and, if he can see your energy, he'll follow that probe of yours right back to where you are.

She gasped at that. *I should know that, shouldn't I?* she said, bewildered. *I just feel like everything's so discombobulated,* she said. *Everything is all over the place.*

Well, you definitely are scattered because, yes, you should have known that your energy can be traced, just as you know you can trace the energy of others. Anybody who has done the work you've done for so many years would have known that.

What work did I do? she asked bitterly. *I tested others for their abilities.*

Did you ever have anybody who was good?

Lizzy, she said instantly, *only Lizzy. Some were okay, and some were developing, but the boss was only after the best of the best.*

Of course he was.

Something odd was in his voice. *What's the matter?*

The old compound, he said, *the reason you saw so little of it. It blew up somewhere around the time that you left.*

What?

They destroyed it to make sure nobody could ever gain any information from it. Most of the lab area was blown up and a few of the offices but not much was left, according to the police report.

And it's hidden from the public, so nobody cared, I'm sure.

I think the police said something about a gas leak.

She frowned at that. *Was gas there?*

Well, they found oil heaters and gas heaters, he said.

It's so bizarre that we're talking this way.

I reached out many times, hoping people out there at the compound would respond.

Well, it's probably that beacon of yours that brought me to you in the first place then, she said, *and, for that, I'm sorry. You may want to consider taking it down, in case you get any more head cases, like me.*

His voice was gentle when he said, *I'm not particularly bothered. It did what it needed to do, as I intended. It brought in someone who needed help.*

Yes, but I don't think you were thinking about this kind of help, she murmured.

Help is help, he said. *It doesn't matter what kind. This is very much up our alley because it involves a person who is blessed to have an awful lot of skill.*

No. I probably had *skill,* she said, *at least at one point in time, but definitely not now.*

Says you, he said, with a chuckle, *but look who's talking to me telepathically.*

She frowned at that. *I'm also on the back of a motorcycle.*

Good, trust Hunter. He's good at what he does.

So far, he's mostly just been running, not exactly hunting anything.

Well, sometimes when you're a hunter, the best thing to do is retreat, he said. *You must trust him.*

Maybe, she murmured. *It certainly is a strange scenario that I find myself in right now.*

But it's better than where you were, right?

Of course. I was a prisoner back then, she snapped. *Nothing is like that at all.*

No, nothing is, he said, *and that's one of the reasons why you need to keep close to Hunter.*

You have a lot of faith in him.

We go way back, he said. *He has done a lot of work for me.*

For you?

Yes, he said, *we've helped an awful lot of energy workers who were in difficult straits.*

Are there that many in the world?

Too many, he said sadly, *and we don't get to all of them by any means.*

Well, you're not responsible for that, she said. *There is a limit to what even you can do.*

He chuckled. *Says the person who doesn't think she has any abilities.*

Maybe, at one time, though I don't recognize anything anymore.

Well, you are gifted, Stefan said, *but do you have any idea why this guy would want you?*

No, because I don't understand why they ever wanted me in the first place. I don't even know what my abilities were that they would care so much about. As far as I understand, I burned-out badly.

And what does that mean to you?

Well, I couldn't read people anymore. I couldn't see anything, couldn't do anything. I was just done.

Okay, he said, *and that's possible.*

Years of testing, years of being tested, years of experiments, years of drugs, years of silence, she murmured.

How long was the silence? he asked curiously.

It seems like forever, but I don't know.

Okay, good enough, he said. *Again we're not pushing anything.*

Everybody is pushing.

Stefan just stayed quiet.

I'm not bitching, Beth said.

Bitch away, he said. *You have every right to. A lot of your life was stolen from you. I'm still looking for the people in those files that you found.*

Well, let me know if you find them, she said. *They seemed like a long time ago.*

And I think they probably were, he said thoughtfully, *but that doesn't mean that they aren't still important.*

She smiled. *I get it, but, at the same time, I don't understand how any of this helps me get free of them. I was just going to hide and avoid being a prisoner for another millennia.*

True, he said, *but the fact of the matter is, you've been tracked down now. And you must do anything you can to keep yourself separate and away.*

Got it, she murmured, and, with that, Stefan disappeared.

When she refocused on her surroundings, they were heading toward the cabin. She frowned at that. Meanwhile he parked his motorcycle in a tree line near the cabin. She looked at him. "Do you think it's safe here?"

"I'm not sure," he said. "We're putting in as many safeguards as we can, but, of course, if they tracked you back to the hospital, it's possible that they'll track you here too."

She nodded. "It feels like they'll come here next."

He stopped, looked at her, and said, "In that case, we need to pack up and get out of here."

"And go where?" she said.

"I'm sure Stefan will have another safe place for us."

She looked at him. "Does he just keep a series of properties?"

"We have a network of locations that we can use. They

aren't ours, but they're mostly empty, and we can access them as needed."

"How nice for you," she murmured.

He smiled. "A lot of people out there are happy to help."

"I guess if it's nothing that they need to put themselves out about. An empty property can imply all kinds of things."

"Sure, most of these benefactors are wealthy and own multiple properties," he said candidly. "We don't count them guilty of anything just because they have an easier life, in some ways, than the rest of us."

"And I didn't mean it that way," she said, with a sigh. "I did find it a challenge learning to make a living when I didn't have any skills though."

"Which is why having skills is so important," he said, with a chuckle.

She nodded. "It's not like I was trained to have any decent ones though."

"Maybe not," he said, "but you did very well for yourself, considering."

"Mostly because of Sugar Mama." At that, her face grew distant.

He studied her. "What's the matter?"

"Stefan shut down my probe. I wanted to see if she was okay."

He faced her squarely. "Don't send out probes," he said immediately. "I don't care what the reasoning is. They are automatically trackable back to you."

She frowned, sensing her own back going up at his orders.

HUNTER SHOOK HIS head. "This isn't an argument about

power or control," he said. "This is too important to your safety. You can't have any energy work going on. You just can't. Otherwise it'll pinpoint your location."

She groaned. "That's hardly fair."

"Nothing is fair about this," he murmured. "Everything in life right now is something that you have to watch out for. Anything that you might have done automatically before, you cannot do now."

This was just so much different than what she had expected freedom to be. And, of course, she'd had a taste of what freedom was, and then it all blew up. She nodded slowly. "I get that," she said, "and it sucks."

"And hopefully we get your life free of these people. Then things can be different, better." He chuckled. "Let's get some food."

"You're always going on about food," she said immediately.

"Sure. Why not?" he said. "One of the best things in life is food. Whenever there's food, you better enjoy it because you don't know where the next meal is coming from."

She frowned at that. "I guess. And we didn't stop at the store again."

He shook his head. "You're thinking too much again. Let's get in, out of sight." He ushered her inside the small cabin.

This, oddly enough, felt like home. Something was so rewarding and peaceful about it. "Have you got some protection around this place?"

"Of course." He looked at her questioningly. "Can't you feel it?"

"Hell yes, I can feel it," she said. "I'm not exactly sure what it was, mind you, but yes."

"Interesting," he murmured, but he didn't add to that. She frowned, as he shook his head. "Remember. Trust is all about sharing, but that goes both ways."

She glared at him. "Seems like it's only ever one way though. And it seems like you're the one who's always winning."

"No winning in this," he said sadly. "This is very much a case of survival, and anybody who's still alive right now is on the winning team."

CHAPTER 24

AFTER A MEAL Beth felt her high energy completely drain away. She turned toward Hunter. "Any chance for a swim in the lake?"

Hunter frowned, got an odd look in his eyes, checking something; then he nodded. "We can probably do that, but we'll wait until dusk settles in."

She nodded at that. "Then I can go to sleep right afterward."

"Sounds good," he said, studying her. He glanced outside. "It's pretty close to that time, if you want to get changed."

She nodded and headed up to her room. She quickly changed into her only bathing suit and grabbed a towel. As she walked downstairs, she heard Hunter on the phone. She couldn't hear well enough to understand, but his tone was grim. As she came into the living room, he ended the call and faced her. "What's the matter?" she asked, and then she knew. She closed her eyes, swaying in place. "It's Sugar Mama, isn't it?"

He nodded ever-so-slowly. "Apparently I was wrong," he said, guilt twisting his voice. "He did go back."

"Well, we knew he was there," she whispered.

"I know, but I was hoping he was after us, not her."

"Chances are he was, but that doesn't mean he would let

an opportunity like that pass him by in the hospital," she murmured. She shook her head. "Life sucks. All she wanted to do was live with her sister."

"I know," he said. "She was just looking for a chance to do something else with her life. She was a good person and sure didn't deserve that."

Beth looked at Hunter. "Do we know for sure it was him?"

"No, not for sure," he said. "All we know is that she's dead. Looks like a heart attack."

At that, Beth was surprised. "So maybe not him. Maybe she died of natural causes. She did have a heart condition."

"It's possible," he said. "We don't have any way to find out at the moment either. I'm also not sure the hospital will do any checking."

She stared at him in shock. "You mean, they won't do an autopsy?"

"It's rare to have autopsies done without cause."

She shook her head. "But, in cases of murder, surely they do."

"Yes, but how do we explain to them that there's a good chance she was murdered? She died not very long after we were there."

"But you also know that *he* was there."

"We do, via our psychic abilities, but I surely couldn't give a sketch artist any details," he said. "Look. The idea of foul play has been presented, but we have no way to know what decision will be made at this point in time."

She sagged into place on the couch. "Wow, I don't even know how to feel about that."

"I guess it depends on your beliefs about life and death."

"I haven't had any experience with religious studies," she

murmured. "So I'm not sure I have any beliefs either way."

He looked at her. "But what about in our realm? Have you ever seen ghosts?"

"Not really," she said.

"What do you mean by *not really?*" he said. "That's a pretty clear yes-or-no question."

She looked at him. "Given the work I did, I spent a lot of the time in a haze, not sure what or who I saw."

"Right," he said. "I keep forgetting just how extensive your training was," he said. But a bitter note was there.

"Not just training," she said, "but recovery."

"I get that. I just wish I had some idea of what happened to make them think you could do whatever it is that they thought you could do."

"I probably made a mistake one day," she said candidly. "Mistakes are not something that you can get away from with them."

"Did you see something, like a person's aura, or did someone do something that revealed a psychic gift?"

"I could tell what people were gifted, what they were doing if they had any of those gifts, and if they didn't have any," she said, "and then the boss would start testing them to increase their abilities. I've told you all this, so why are you asking me again?"

"Clarity," he said simply. "I'm looking for clarity."

She glared at him. "And I don't know how many times I can tell you, but I don't remember anything. I don't remember a lot of things—let's put it that way," she corrected. "I mean, obviously some things are hard to forget, but a lot of other things were just never very clear at all."

"And I get that," he said in a soothing voice. "That just seems to make it worse." She glared at him. He raised both hands in surrender. "I'm not pissing you off on purpose."

"Good," she said, "because you're doing it without even trying."

He chuckled. "Let's go for a swim."

"And, just like that, we'll forget about Sugar Mama."

"No," he said, "that's never a good idea. Mourn them for a while, but then focus on the good memories. You should always honor and remember those who have passed. Remember them with a smile, remember them with joy that their life wasn't meaningless while they were here. That they did something of value while they lived and that we rejoiced in them. I think even you would agree that, despite the challenges, Sugar Mama enjoyed her life."

"Yes, she did," Beth admitted. "She enjoyed an awful lot in her life. At the end I think she enjoyed more peace and quiet than her *hot men*."

"Well, everybody needs to do things in their own way," he said.

"And, if that was hers, then fine. I don't have any judgment for her," she murmured.

"Neither do I," he said. "She was a fascinating woman, and I know that, no matter what I think or even what the world would say about her and her lifestyle, she was happy. As long as she didn't hurt anybody in the process, who are we to judge?"

"I would like to think more people out there aren't quite so judgmental."

"No," he said, "people out there are very judgmental. But nobody has to say anything. It's private. It's Sugar Mama. It's who she was, and she was a wonderful person to you. And what you need to remember is, when you needed a friend, she was there for you."

Beth smiled mistily at him. "Thank you for that."

"And thank her," he said gently. "She helped you stay alive, and that's worth everything to me."

Not a whole lot she could say to that, so she moved toward the window. "Sugar Mama would tell me to go have a swim, if that's what I wanted to do."

"Let's go then," he said, stepping up to her side.

She looked at him, still fully dressed, and frowned. "You're not coming in?"

He shook his head. "Nope, I'll be on watch."

She glared at him. "That's not guaranteed to make me relax."

"Maybe not," he said, "but it is a fact of life for now."

Out on the deck she smiled to see the cat food dish mostly empty. She pointed. "Guess we need to fill that, huh?"

He nodded. "If nothing else the raccoons will enjoy it."

She looked at him, but he gave her a bland look. Frowning, she headed down the steps toward the water. She wasn't sure what he was thinking when it came to Nocturne, and, even as soon as she thought about him, he appeared beside her. She smiled and stroked his silky fur. "Not a fun trip, not to or from the hospital."

He didn't say anything, just sauntered at her side all the way down to the water. The fact that he had stayed here was also good. He was very good at discerning which places were safe and which weren't, and having stayed here meant that Nocturne had decided he and Beth were safe here. If he continued to feel that way, then she would be more complacent about this place. Maybe she could keep her head on straight here.

She needed time to heal on so many different levels and,

so far, hadn't had any opportunity to do that. At the water, instead of giving herself a chance to get in slowly, she dove in off the end of the dock, almost crying out as the cold water closed over her head. It really was cold. She didn't understand that, yet found it also glorious. She relished in what such a beautiful feeling it was, as her head broke through the water. Gasping for breath now, she struck out strongly toward the center of the lake. When she heard a cry, she turned behind her. Hunter had his hand up. She frowned and called back, "What's the matter?"

"Don't go out too far," he said.

She thought about it, and he was probably right. Just because she had the energy right now didn't mean it would be there for the return trip. She slowly turned and moved back in his direction. Even though she was a long way from shore, she heard a sudden cry from Nocturne in warning. She called out a warning to Hunter, and then a sound carried on the air. Hunter was no longer there. She stayed in the middle of the water, worried at the sudden silence. She had recognized the sound as gunfire; she just didn't know where it came from or from whom. She wanted to call out to Nocturne to ask him what the hell. He'd just given her the okay that they were safe, so how could that change so fast?

Then she heard an odd sound, one she didn't expect. A rowboat.

She immediately sank under the water but couldn't possibly hide her position for long when she still needed to breathe. Drifting as silently as she could, she headed toward the dock. As she reached the safety of the wood, she heard Nocturne right beside her, urging her to safety. He hadn't seen it coming because the attack had come from the water. She looked for Hunter but still found no sign of him. She wasn't sure if she should stay in the water or get out but found it damn hard to stay in the cold water. Surely there had to be another solution.

She looked around, studying the long weeds off to her side; that was as good an answer as any. Moving under the water as much as she could, leaving no ripple, she headed toward the shrubbery and slipped up into the greenery. There, Nocturne waited for her. She immediately reached out to touch him, finding herself grounded immediately by the soothing touch of her hand on his fur. Something was so very special about that cat. As soon as she caught her breath, she peered through the grass, looking to see who was after her. But, of course, she couldn't see anything. The rowboat seemed empty, just jostling out there in the water, as if somebody had slipped in. Or out.

She hadn't heard him. And that was even scarier because, if somebody else could move through the shadows as easily as that, no way she could hide from him. She hunkered down and didn't move. Ten minutes passed, then fifteen, and she felt the chill set in further. Was the whole point of this to get her so caught up that she couldn't do anything, and then they would catch her?

Freezing to death was hardly the ending she wanted for herself, but maybe she had no choice in the matter. *Scary thought.* A splash sounded close by, and Nocturne froze at her side. Beth heard somebody climbing out of the water. Taking her cue, she slipped back into the water with a deep breath and pushed herself gently through the water, underneath the surface, out to the rowboat.

She stayed underwater as long as she could, coming up on the far side of the boat, vaguely outlined from under the water's surface. She came up gasping for air and tilted the rowboat ever-so-slightly. Empty, except for a backpack and a few other things in there. She wondered about getting in, but she didn't know how. She'd seen it done, but it didn't look like it would be very easy.

Instead she drifted along with the rowboat, until she was a bit closer to the shore. Still no sign of Hunter and no sign of the new arrival at all. Standing in the shallow water now, she pushed the rowboat up against the dock. There she slid up onto the dock, slipped into the rowboat, and headed across the lake again.

The shooter's getaway vehicle had to be somewhere close by that other shore too. So far nobody had shot at her, so she decided that the same man wanted her alive. She would leave Hunter to deal with him. If nothing else, Hunter could keep himself safe—if anything Stefan had said was true. She felt bad, deserting Hunter, but she also felt that he'd be the first one to tell her to run. She didn't necessarily want to run, but she wanted to get answers, and, for the first time, she was close enough to get some. With that, she kept paddling across the lake in the direction the shooter had probably come from.

REMEMBER, LIZZY'S VOICE called out to Beth in the darkness. *You can't forget. It's not allowed. We're too close. It means too much. Remember. Remember. Remember.*

Beth swatted at the air, as if to bat the words back at Lizzy.

Lizzy chuckled. *You can't get rid of me that easily.* And she droned on again and again and again, pushing Beth's memories forward. *Remember.*

Remember.

Remember.

Lizzy's voice was fainter and fainter, as somehow Beth managed to send those words back to her.

HUNTER WATCHED BETH, wondering what she was up to. When she slipped into the rowboat and headed across the lake, his eyebrows shot up. An interesting tactic on her part, as she'd left the shooter stranded here on this side. With any luck Hunter would find this person. However, if his wheels were over there, she could, in theory, take off on Hunter. Again.

He didn't even know what to think of that. Odd but a part of him cheered her on. She needed to do whatever it took to keep herself safe. And he needed to change his focus from her, now that he knew she was okay and not frozen in the water, turning his attention to this asshole, who had come to land at his place.

Hunter searched the darkness, aware somebody out there was using energy as a blind. That made him very dangerous, but Hunter was no fool, and he had recognized the technique. He waited, looking for the energy to shift with any movement. All energy left a signature, whether that person's energy or somebody else's. Even if the gunman utilized the energy from nature, that movement left a signature. And, sure enough, as Hunter carefully watched, he saw a slight haziness coming toward him.

Swearing slightly at that because it meant that Hunter was as exposed as the other guy, he crouched and slipped a little deeper into the woods, leaving himself an exit, if this guy managed to see him. As Hunter watched and waited, the newcomer slowly approached and then called out, "We want the same thing."

At that, Hunter stopped and stared. He doubted that— he really did—but an interesting tactic.

"I want her alive," the man called out.

Well, that was good, and it followed through on what Hunter and Beth had discussed. But not enough. Hunter hesitated.

The guy said, "I can see where you are. No point in hiding from me. I am also holding a weapon on you."

Of course he had a weapon. He had shot it earlier. And wouldn't have any trouble hitting his target in this lighting. Hunter stood slowly and asked, "Why do you want her?"

"None of your business."

"And yet you say that we want the same thing. I want her safe."

"So do I," the stranger said, "absolutely I do."

"Why is that?" Hunter asked curiously.

"I can't tell you," he said.

"Well then, I'm not helping you."

"Maybe I don't need your help," he said, his voice suddenly almost tired, as if he'd been working for ages toward a certain end.

"You've been after her for a long time."

"Since she left, yes," he said. "She's delusional, in case you didn't notice. She's also a great harm to those around her."

Hunter wasn't so sure about that being true, but he saw it as a tactic someone would use. "I haven't noticed that she's dangerous."

"Of course not. It's not like she just turns around and kills you. It's not that kind of a danger. But she will kill you, and she won't even know she's done it."

He froze at that. "Did you kill Sugar Mama?"

At that, he snorted. "I had to," he said. "But if she hadn't escaped I wouldn't have had to so it's her fault."

"BS," he said. "She's met lots of people in the intervening years, you didn't kill all of them?."

"No, but anyone she got close to yes," he said, his tone sad. "You have no idea what she can do, or why she's doing it and no one else can either. It's too dangerous."

"You do?"

"Yes," he said, "I do, and I'll help her."

"You shot her," Hunter cried out in outrage. "Do you think I'm a fool?"

"No, you're not a fool," he said quietly, "but you are disillusional, and you have no idea what you're seeing."

Hunter shook his head at that. "Nice try," he said. "And that's why we'll have a problem."

The gunman said, "You have to listen to me."

"No, I really don't. Nothing you've said has made any sense yet. Make some sense, and, fine, I'll listen. But otherwise, no way."

"Nothing I can say will make sense of any of this," he said grimly. "It would be nice if people would finally, for once in their lifetime, listen and do what they're told, but they don't. And just like the rest of them," he said, "you'll die trying."

Hunter wasn't even sure what the hell was going on, but no way Beth had killed Sugar Mama, and he could only presume that this guy didn't know that Hunter had been at the hospital and had felt this gunman's presence there, confirmed by the same energy Hunter tracked right now. "You haven't told me why you want her."

"To help her," he said in exasperation, "and it's getting

damn hard to do."

"Of course it is. You kill the people around her, and you hunt her down like an animal. That makes it hard for anybody to believe you."

The gunman shook his head almost frantically. "You don't understand," he said. "She has to be dealt with. She's dangerous."

"*Dealt with*? That's an interesting term." And not one Hunter liked the sound of at all. "I don't want anything to do with that," he said.

"No, of course not. That's where we end up with problems, each and every time."

"I still need answers," Hunter said.

"Well, you won't get them from her because she can't give them to you," he said.

"I know what happened to the compound."

"It blew up," he said, then stopped. "You know about that, huh?"

"Yes, she took me there." He had his target in sight, and his form became clearer and clearer. The shock on the other man's face was something else, and then it lit up with joy. Hunter was left reeling with the conflicting emotions roiling off the man's face.

"She took you there? Oh, that's wonderful."

"How in the hell is that wonderful?" Hunter asked.

The stranger laughed. "Like I said, you don't understand anything. But that's a true sign of progress."

Hunter looked around. "And, of course, she's gone again."

"Yes, but she won't leave you for long," the stranger said. "I just have to stay close to you, and she'll come back."

"She won't come back if you're here," Hunter said. "She

knows you're after her. You shot her. Remember?"

"Yes, but I had to."

Something inside Hunter wanted to squeeze this man's neck until it snapped. "You *had* to?" he asked, his voice deadly.

The stranger raised a hand and said, "Don't get all defensive. You have no clue. I've told you that you don't understand what's going on."

"Then help me to understand and stop talking in riddles," he barked.

"I wish I could," he said, "but you won't take it kindly anyway."

"You never know," he said. "You could try me."

At that, the guy laughed. "You're just looking for an opportunity to kill me, and I can't have you do that. She has to be stopped."

"One minute you say you want her safe, then that she needs help, and now you say she has to be stopped. How is anybody supposed to believe you?"

He snorted. "It's the same thing."

"What are you talking about?"

"She has to be stopped before she kills anyone else," he said. "Haven't you figured out that she's leaving a swath of dead bodies everywhere?"

"No," Hunter said, as the information didn't compute.

He groaned. "You don't understand, and that's why you have to let me help her," he said impatiently. "You'd think that psychics would be smarter, but somehow they've just got these big blind spots that make them stupid."

Hunter's back stiffened. "I don't even recall the last person who called me something like that and lived."

"Yeah, yeah, yeah, you're a big strong man," he said with

a sneer, shaking his head.

"You still haven't said how you will help her."

"I didn't tell you," he said, "because that's none of your business. But I will."

"You will what?"

"I will help her," he said, with exaggerated patience. "I just need you to help me get her."

"No," he said, "she suffered enough at your hands."

"Yes, she did," he said. "I didn't understand, and that's my mistake. I'll rectify it."

"You'll tell me a whole lot more before I give you any help," he declared.

"Maybe I don't need any help from you."

"Why so?"

"I suspect she'll be back here in no time."

Hunter said, "She's smart enough to stay away."

"That depends. Have you gotten into her pants yet or not?" asked the other man crudely. "Most men try to bind women to them sexually, and she's a complete innocent when it comes to that." The other man stepped forward, frowning, and asked, "Did you get her into bed?"

"That's none of your business," Hunter said harshly.

"Ah no, you didn't then. Okay, that's good. I didn't think it would happen that easily."

"She has been gone for a lot of years."

"Mostly because I've been hunting her for all those years," he said in exasperation. "If she had come in from the cold a long time ago, it would have been a hell of a lot easier. The fact that she took you to the compound though, that's encouraging."

"What about your new compound?"

He looked at him and gave a crafty smile. "What about it?"

"Why hasn't she taken me there?"

"Well, if she didn't tell you, I won't," he said, "but at least everything that comes out of your mouth tells me that she's for real again. And that she's making sense."

"Now if only you were," Hunter muttered.

The stranger laughed. "Yeah, it's confusing if you don't have all the answers, but believe me. You don't want all the answers, and I don't dare give them to you."

"And why is that?"

"Easy. You'll be dead before you know it."

"And you're saying that she'll be the one who kills me."

"Of course," he said, shaking his head. "Everybody always gives me that same disbelief."

At the term *everybody* Hunter frowned. Why was anyone else involved in this? She hadn't mentioned anything about it. "How many other people are involved in this?" he murmured.

"Not many now," he said, and then he laughed. "In many ways, she just killed them all."

"No," he said. "I'm not listening to that garbage."

"No, of course not," he said, with a smile. "She's got you firmly wrapped around her finger."

"No," he said, "but I understand lies and deception, and that's exactly what you're doing. You're lying."

The guy laughed. "In some things, absolutely I am," he said, "but don't doubt that it's for your own good."

"The last time somebody told me, *It's for my own good*, they were trying to shoot me," Hunter said.

"Well, look at that," the stranger said, lifting his weapon. "History repeats itself."

And he fired into the darkness, only Hunter was no longer there.

CHAPTER 25

BETH HEARD THE shot cut through the silence of the night, like an arrow of pain hitting her heart. She didn't want to be responsible for Hunter's death. She reminded herself that she trusted in his ability to evade a gunman like that and, even better, hopefully turn it around and make him pay. She sat here in the boat, cradling herself, burying her face in her hands, as she wondered what to do.

When the boat gently nudged against the opposite shore, she turned and, grabbing the backpack, slipped into the water and out onto the land. She had no idea how this intruder had arrived, but she suspected she would find a getaway vehicle of some kind. And she and Hunter could use it; otherwise she was doomed to the back of a motorcycle.

Which, in a way, had its own exhilarating feeling, but, at the same time, it hadn't given her the sense of control that she had wanted. If anything, riding a motorcycle was like being on the back of a firecracker shot into the air, with no idea where she would land or what the landing would be like. As she hunted through the darkness, she found a path that led up to the highway, and there sat a small old pickup truck. She nodded when she saw it; this would be it.

She opened the driver's door, surprised that it wasn't locked. As she hopped in, she found no keys in the ignition. Of course not. But she would do what she could, and she hunted high and low; yet she still had the backpack, and the keys were likely in there. She turned on the interior light, dug through the backpack, and found them. She quickly turned off the light and started the engine.

Then she sat here, wondering what she should do. Was it safe to go back to Hunter's place, or should she go somewhere else? She didn't have a clue where to go at this point. Only one person who she could ask. "Stefan?" she asked out loud.

Yes, Stefan said, his voice distracted, almost muffled in her head.

"Is Hunter okay? I heard a shot."

He's okay.

"Well, thank God for that," she said.

A note of humor was in his voice when he said, *Glad to know you care.*

"I don't want to care," she said passionately. "When you care, you lose. Everybody gets hurt. Everybody leaves. Everybody goes away and does something on their own, and it doesn't seem to matter who and what you are. You just don't matter to them, and you're left alone."

Being alone is not a guarantee in life, he said, *unless you do what you've been doing, which is hiding.*

"I had a reason to hide," she said harshly.

Absolutely, and you still do because, even now, this gunman is after you.

"Do you know anything about him?"

Nope. And I can't get very much of reading at all. Just a cloudy darkness all around him.

"*Hmm*," she murmured. "I don't recognize his energy or his voice or anything."

Which is interesting because he seems to know an awful lot about you.

"Interesting," she said, "because I don't recognize anything about him at all. At least nothing I can understand. But Hunter's okay?"

He is for the moment, yes, Stefan said. *You need to stay out of the way. Otherwise he'll have to split his energy, worrying about you.*

"He probably already has," she said. "I went across the lake and found this guy's vehicle. But now I'm sitting inside it, wondering what to do."

Stay where you are, Stefan said.

"Well, if this guy comes back for it, I don't want him to find me here," she snapped. "Not to mention I'm soaking wet."

Stefan thought about it for a long moment. *Do you have another place to go?*

"Not right now," she said. "I don't even know what time it is. I think it's like eleven o'clock at night."

Right.

"I also don't want to leave Hunter alone or for him to get hurt."

I'll keep track of Hunter, but he shuts off when he's out there, so that no energy can be traced to him.

"I get that," she said, shivering in the cool night air, "but I'm chilled because I came across the lake, and now I wish I were back home, with a change of clothes."

Well, you could try that, Stefan said cautiously, *but I wouldn't suggest it.*

"No. Well, maybe I'll search the truck," she said. "I'll also move it so, if he comes back, he doesn't find it where he expects it to be."

Good idea, Stefan said, *but please don't do anything stupid.*

"You mean, any stupider than I already have?" she said sadly.

You don't even know what you've done, he murmured. *That's the thing. This guy does seem to have answers, and I trust Hunter to capture him.*

"In that case," she said, "I'll see if I can find a towel or some clothing to get changed into. And then I'll go help Hunter."

And, with that, she was gone. She could still hear Stefan sputtering in the ethers. Even though she didn't have a phone, she had talked to him that way and had still managed to cut him off. She shook her head. "What the hell is wrong with me?" she murmured. "Hunter and Stefan are just trying to help me."

But then that's what this guy supposedly had told Hunter. She frowned. How did she know that? She closed her eyes and heard the gunman's whispers. Just bits and pieces in the ethers.

I'll help her. I don't want to hurt her.

She didn't believe him. Because, of course, all she did remember was the pain, the hurts of the long time she had been held at the compound. Was there any chance he was telling the truth? Not much. At least she didn't dare risk it. She checked the vehicle and found a couple towels and a change of clothes. She didn't want to wear his clothes, but she grabbed the towel and gave herself a good scrub down, hoping that that would be enough to get her warmed up. She put the heat on inside the truck, hoping she could dry off faster, and then drove up past the driveway to Hunter's cabin and pulled off into the brush. No way was she giving the truck up to this guy, and, at the same time, she didn't dare get caught by him either.

She shivered as the cold overcame her body. The heater was not doing enough to help warm her, but she also knew that, given certain times of stress, the cold would take over, and it would completely make her incapable of doing anything. She shuddered as she worked toward warming up, scrubbing her arms, trying hard to dry off with the towels and the heat. She wasn't that cold; she shouldn't have been. But nothing like a little bit of a shock to her system to freeze her inside. Just so much she could do. She sat and waited, and, the longer she waited, the more panicky she got.

Finally she hopped from the truck, grabbed everything that was useful and stuffed it into the same backpack, including the insurance registration papers, then slipped into the darkness around her. She couldn't handle that weird sense of being followed. She raced into the woods, still cold and shivering. Calling on Nocturne to give her a hand, it wasn't long before she calmed her breathing some.

She shifted to a large tree and climbed up to the top. She sat there, hugging the branches, waiting for the sensation of being caught to pass. She wasn't caught; she wasn't prey. She was here. She was free. Somewhere out there was Hunter, and maybe that sensation was getting to her.

She didn't know, but she did her best to shake off such an eerie feeling. And just when she thought she had calmed down, she heard a gentle meow. She smiled and reached out a hand to feel Nocturne, who was walking down the branch toward her. "You found me, didn't you, buddy? I'm so glad," she murmured gently in his ear, cuddling him close. "Is it safe out there?"

Of course it didn't feel safe; nothing felt safe right now. But that was part of the craziness of her life. She desperately wanted to go into the cabin and to have a shower and clean up, but no way to do that when Hunter was in trouble. And then the sensation of being followed had stopped, but now it shifted to a pressing danger—but not for her, for Hunter. She swore, then slipped down the tree, and, with Nocturne at her side, she raced in the direction of Hunter.

She couldn't even explain that weird sensation inside her. But she knew without a doubt that he was in trouble and that he didn't know it. Somehow she did. She didn't even know where that sense came from, but it was there, and it was strong, and she would not ignore it. She'd spent a lifetime listening to it. Even more important to listen to it now.

How invaluable to have somebody like Hunter in her life. She had no way to know if he would even survive with her help or not. But she would do everything she could to give him his chance to survive in whatever way he wanted. He'd helped her, and she could do no less.

REMEMBER, LIZZY CALLED out again, desperate for Beth to listen for once. *Remember.*

But, no, Beth had no intention of remembering.

Remember. Remember. Remember.

HUNTER SHIFTED ONCE more in the darkness, searching for the energy around him. This guy had skills, as in mad skills, some Hunter had never seen before. It made him question so many things about his life right now. Hunter thought that he'd understood and that he knew all the tricks that could happen, but this guy had showed him time and time again that Hunter didn't know it all.

This wasn't the time to be shocked or surprised. Far from it. This wasn't the time to find out that you weren't as good as you thought you were. But, of course, that is exactly when things like that happened. When people were tested and found out that there was more to life than what they thought. Still, he hunkered down and waited. In his experience, most people grew impatient and needed to move or to take that extra action because they couldn't just be still.

"You can't hide from me," the other man said. "I can see your energy."

The trouble was that didn't mean anything because Hunter saw his too. Although not as clearly now as he'd like to, which he didn't understand. Something was going on here that he'd never seen before. If Stefan had learned any lesson in his illustrious career, it was that there always was some asshole out there with a skill set that nobody could be prepared for. And it looked like Hunter had just found yet another one. "You still haven't said why you want her," he said, throwing his voice from another direction.

"I have told you. You just don't want to listen."

Hunter wondered why such fatigue was in the man's voice. If she were dangerous, why had she been a captive under his control? "You lost her, didn't you?" He felt the anger resonating around him. "This is all about you making up for losing her."

"You don't understand," he said. "She's dangerous."

"But is she dangerous to you or to other people? Because I'm not too bothered if she's a danger to you. You're the asshole who kept her locked up."

"She had to be locked up," he stated. "I've told you that she's a danger."

"Yeah, but you never give any details to support those

claims. Most people don't like listening to that BS, unless it changes the song."

"Doesn't matter if you believe me or not," he said, his voice suddenly deadly. "I'm not leaving without her. I've spent years hunting her down."

"It's that *hunting* part that I don't get. You say that she's a danger and that you want her alive. But now you're hunting her and make no bones about the fact that, as far as you're concerned, she's yours for the taking. With no consideration for what she wants."

"Of course not," he said. "You don't understand."

"No, I sure don't," he said. "Explain it."

"I can't," he said simply.

"Can't or won't?" Hunter asked. He got silence again, and he nodded. "*Won't*. Got it. So, you're keeping secrets about your intentions for this young woman. Intentions that will never go down well with anybody."

"They always do," he said. "You just have to find the right people."

Hunter didn't quite understand that, but what an interesting thought. He frowned, as he looked out at the darkness. "Why don't we go inside and talk about it?" he said.

The other man laughed. "Nothing to talk about. And you don't have anything to offer me."

"I thought you wanted her."

"Yeah, but she's gone," he said. "She's on the other side of the lake right now, probably stealing my damn truck," he said, completely nonchalant.

"And that doesn't seem to bother you."

"Nah, it doesn't," he said. "It's not mine anyway."

"If you're planning on keeping her as a captive again, no

way I'll condone that."

"Of course not," he said. "I was hoping to avoid more bloodshed, but none of you ever listen." And, with that, more shots were fired and peppered the ground all around Hunter. Swearing under his breath, Hunter shifted and moved yet again. This guy tracked him in unknown ways. He sent out a message to Stefan. *How is he doing this?*

I think he's following her energy to you.

Hunter froze at that thought. But it made sense. He stopped still and made a very deliberate attempt to shed any of her energy that may or may not have been cloaked in his aura. With or without your permission, when you spent time with each other, your two energies link automatically. And, if this guy knew how to read her energy, then he was following that right to Hunter. He quickly shifted, cutting ties, dislodging hooks, and cleaning his aura with a speed that he'd never expected. But, when done, he shifted, changing his position yet again.

"I'm getting tired of this," the other man said. "Show yourself."

"Why would I do that?" Hunter said, tossing his voice to where he had been standing.

"Because this needs to end," he roared. And he filled the air with gunfire, shattering the spot where Hunter had been standing moments ago.

But the good news was that Hunter was no longer there, and now he understood how he was being tracked. He came up behind the man, just as the gunman emptied the magazine, and, with a heavy blow, Hunter hit the gunman on the temple and dropped him to the ground.

Hunter had caught his prey.

CHAPTER 26

BETH SLIPPED THROUGH the trees in the darkness, racing toward the cabin, as soundlessly as possible, not an easy thing to do. She was pulling on her skills, but she was tired, cold, and her fragmented energy had dissipated again. She'd been healing and coming on so much stronger, to the point that she had managed to rebuild as much of herself as she could, but each time that had quickly dissipated with the next challenge.

Nocturne raced at her side, staying close, always wary, always sending out alarms, if she needed to be aware of anything. Finally she came beside the cabin and slipped down into the trees. She saw no sign of life inside the cabin, no lights on, nothing. But she heard voices. She crept a little closer, peering through the darkness.

"Lizzy, where are you, you bitch?" she muttered to herself.

Mocking laughter rippled through her mind. *Remember.*

"I can't remember anything, damn it. I don't want to remember anything. You and I are the only ones who know how bad the compound was. Why would you even want to make me remember?" she cried out softly. But there was no answer, never any answer. Lizzy only ever wanted Beth to say and to do what Lizzy wanted. How did one ever come back from something like that? They didn't. They went crazy or insane, except for people like Lizzy—Lizzy, who seemed to have absolutely no problem, no remorse, no conscience.

"How did we end up so different?" Beth murmured.

And this time Lizzy did answer, with more mocking laughter in her voice. *We're not different at all. You just don't want to acknowledge it.*

Beth shook her head, refusing to listen to that drivel again. She'd heard too much of it before, and she wouldn't get sucked in again. She'd spent a long time protecting herself from her old friend. Some friends one should never have, and, if one were unlucky enough to have them, they should do everything they could to split off from them. And, of course, saying that didn't change anything.

Beth slipped closer to the dark cabin, down toward the voices, wondering who and what was going on, petrified to get caught by this man and wondering why she was even here. Self-preservation said she should be far away from here, and she was pretty sure Hunter would agree. Even Stefan had made a point of her staying away. But what was she supposed to do? This guy had come after Hunter, and Hunter was here for her.

Once again, Beth was troubled by the awareness that Lizzy was not here for Hunter. Lizzy would have said, *To hell with it*, and then run, looking after herself. But, no, not who Beth was. She kept moving through the darkness, until she heard the voices a whole lot clearer. She climbed up to the cabin and peered around the corner.

"You will never stop me."

"Well, I can always just kill you right now, correct?" Hunter said, in a bored tone.

That stopped Beth in her tracks. Would he really? Or was it just a bluff? She had to believe it a bluff. She didn't think Hunter would kill indiscriminately like that. Although, if this asshole tried to kill them one more time, she might take him out herself. Where was that fine line? But, in this case, most likely self-defense. Still, if they let the gunman go, he would just come after them again.

"You still can't stop me."

"Meaning that you have a way to stay alive after death?" Hunter asked curiously.

At that, the other man laughed. "Wow, you're one of those far-out psychic people, aren't you?"

"And what are you?"

"I'm a scientist," he said proudly. "And I've seen things that you have no idea about."

Hunter nodded. "So have I," he said calmly. "And this isn't a pissing contest. I want to know what it is you want with Beth."

"I've already told you. I'm trying to save her."

"From what?"

He burst out laughing again. "From herself, but I don't expect you to understand."

"Good, because I don't have a clue," he said.

"Untie me," the other man commanded.

"That's not happening."

"You need to," he said. "She's a danger, I've already told you that."

"So why is it you're to rescue her then? It sounds to me like you just want to put her down, like a sick dog."

"More like a mad dog maybe," he said in an ugly tone.

"I don't like that," Hunter said. "I can't imagine that she's done anything to deserve that."

"That's because you're a fool," the other man snapped. "But, hey, it's your life, your death. I really don't care."

"Meaning?"

"She'll turn on you like the rabid dog she is. You won't know where, and you won't know when, but it will happen."

"I don't believe you," Hunter said in that same calm voice.

Beth listened intently, looking hard for any doubt in Hunter's tone, not finding any. Hunter seemed very sure of his answer. That revelation helped to warm her chilled body on the inside. She wondered how that unwavering trust Hunter had for her could even be. He didn't know her, didn't know anything about her. For all they knew, this guy was correct. Maybe she had hurt people in the past. Maybe she was a danger to the world. It would break her heart if she were, and she definitely didn't think it true. It didn't feel like she was a killer.

But so much in her world that she didn't know, that she couldn't remember, that just wasn't working for her. She'd been hiding and blocking out her past because that was the only way she was capable of functioning in her present. Just so many ugly memories, so much pain, and so much torture. Even now, if she let herself go in that direction, the thoughts and feelings and pain would overwhelm her, and she'd be completely incapable of handling what was to come.

She stepped through the back door into the dark cabin and said, "Glad to see you've caught him."

Hunter glanced at her. "How long have you been listening?"

She shrugged. "Long enough. Now that you've got him, I'll go get changed." Her teeth chattered with the cold.

"Looks like you need to go fast," he said. "Maybe have a hot bath."

"Wouldn't that be nice," she said, "but I can't say I feel

very safe with this guy sitting here." Even as she stood here, she felt the intensity of the stranger's gaze. She studied him, her eyes adjusting to the sparse lighting. "I don't even know who you are. Why do you hate me so much?"

"Remember," he commanded.

An inkling of something stirred in the back of her mind, a voice almost remembered and yet not. She stared at him. "I can't remember anything," she confessed. "Something about your voice is a bit familiar, but that's all."

"Only because you're choosing not to remember," he said. He gave her a hard smile. "I will help you to remember, if you let me."

"And why would I want to?" she said. "It doesn't sound like anything is in my past that I want to be aware of."

"Are you scared?" he taunted.

"Maybe," she said, with utter honesty. "I don't have a clue what it is that you think I've done, but none of it sounds like anything I want to own up to."

He gave a brutal laugh. "You never used to stick your head in the sand."

"No," she said, "but a lot of things have changed."

"Not that much," he said. "The reality is, you're not who you think you are."

"Yes, I am," she said calmly. "That much I do know."

"No," he whispered, "you are who you want to be now, but you're not who you used to be."

"Well, whoever I used to be," she said, "is dead and gone. I am me now."

"And who and what is that?" he asked. "Because it's not the person I see standing in front of me, content to be oblivious to everything in her world."

"You don't even know me," she said, "so you have no

right to make that judgment."

"I know you better than anybody else," he stated. "I raised you since you were a child."

She stopped and stared. "You? No." She shook her head. "No. I would know."

"And what is it that you would know?" he asked.

"I'd recognize you. Besides, if you were the asshole who kept me prisoner all that time, no way we'll let you go."

Hunter said, "You just became someone the police want to see."

At that, the other man laughed and laughed. "If you think I'm staying anywhere long enough for the police to show up, think again," he said. "There's a reason she was with me. She is extremely talented."

"And you wanted to utilize that talent?" Hunter asked.

"We wanted to study it," he admitted. "*He* wanted to study you. He wanted to see how much you could do, how hard and how fast you could progress."

She felt an inkling of truth to that because she did know the competitiveness inside herself. "And I wonder how much of that was you pushing me," she said calmly, hiding the fear inside her that even now stretched forward from deep inside.

"You can hide, but you can't hide from yourself."

"Sure I can."

"Not for long," he said and shook his head. "For a little while, yes, everybody can do that. Self-delusion isn't a brand-new phenomenon," he murmured. "You can hide for a while, but it doesn't do you any good."

"It feels like it does," she said, "because I don't know who and what you were talking about before, but I was not a danger to anybody." She stopped, wondering if she should ask that question. His gaze was steady and hard but full of enlightenment, and she knew he had the answers that she desperately wanted. "Where is Lizzy?" she demanded.

One eyebrow shot up, and he gave her one of the coldest, clearest smiles she'd ever seen.

The two men in this were a stark comparison of this evil man to Hunter—two extremes. Why had she been so uncooperative with him, with Stefan? Yet she knew this evil man from before. Should have initially seen Hunter and Stefan for the goodness that they were, that they put forth into this world. Why was this never so clear as right now?

"Where is Lizzy?" he repeated. "She's always around," the gunman said, with a careless shrug. "You know that."

"I don't know anything," she said calmly. "She talks to me sometimes."

He nodded. "She was always good at that. You two, were ..." He let his voice drop away.

"Close. Yes, I know," she said. "We were close. Up until she became a traitor."

At that, he didn't seem to know what to say. "All I can tell you," he said, "is that you need to come back. We need to help you find your memories again."

"I'm okay not remembering," she murmured. "Nothing from those days is nice enough that I want to remember."

Hunter, at her side, asked, "Will you live with that though?"

"I have to," she said, "because I don't trust anything this man says."

Hunter nodded in agreement. "I'm with you there," he said, "but that doesn't mean we don't have other ways to help you remember things."

At that, the other man looked alarmed. "You can't. Her psyche is very delicate. It has to be somebody who knows and understands what's going on."

"That sure as hell will never be you," she said brutally. "Not in any lifetime."

He glared at her. "You don't know that," he said, "and you need to watch your mouth. It seems like being free all this time has done nothing for your manners."

"Manners? … From you?" she said, with a snort. "No, it probably didn't help at all. But I'll listen to you about absolutely nothing."

He shrugged and said, "You'll know eventually. Whether it happens now or in ten years," he said, "the truth will come out."

"That's nice," she murmured, "but it still doesn't have anything to do with you."

"I am your truth," he snapped. "And, in time, you'll be eager for me to give you the answers you are desperate for."

"I'm not that desperate," she said. "I've survived without you all these years. I'll survive for a whole lot longer."

"I found you," he murmured, "so what do you think it'll take for Lizzy to find you?"

"She's already looking. I think she's already found me," she said, with a shrug. "As far as I know, she doesn't give a damn."

"Oh, she cares," he said, his voice quiet. "She cares a lot. You are just being difficult."

"I was always difficult to you," she said. "Some things just never change."

He laughed at that. "Isn't that the truth?" he murmured, studying her. He turned toward Hunter. "Where did you find him?"

"Maybe he found me," she said, tossing her hair in defiance.

"He'd be an interesting one to test, wouldn't he now?" he said, as if inviting her to share in the joke of their past.

She stiffened. "There was nothing fun about any of that testing," she said. "You hurt people."

"No, you hurt people," he said calmly.

"I had nothing to do with it. You forced me," she screamed at him.

Immediately Hunter reached out a hand. "Easy," he said. "Remember. This is what he wants. He wants you to lose control."

She pulled back, gasping for breath. "Too easily," she murmured.

The gunman taunted her. "Oh, but you always had a control issue. I helped you with it, but somehow you just never got smart enough to handle it on your own. I thought that, after all this time, maybe you would have improved, but it looks like you still have some of your inherent weaknesses."

"We all have inherent weaknesses," Hunter said immediately.

"Stop defending her," he said. "I know who she is inside and out. You haven't a clue."

"Says you," Hunter snapped right back.

She shook her head. "No. He's right, honestly. You don't know. He does. But I'm still not going back with him."

"Good," Hunter said, "and stop feeling like just because I don't know everything doesn't mean that I don't have a good idea of who you are at your core. He isn't the be-all and end-all of your existence."

"Well, that's good," she said, "because that would be beyond depressing. He's not a nice man."

"Of course I am," he said. "As much as any of us are. I don't worry about the social niceties that everybody else seems to worry about. Why should I? Scientifically speaking, that is simply not helpful."

"You mean, it didn't further your own agenda, so who cares?" Hunter said.

"Of course," he said. "It's not like being nice gets you anywhere, and it sure as hell doesn't help you progress in life," he murmured. "As you well know, Beth. You tried being nice. We ran all kinds of tests."

"No, they weren't tests," she said, bits and pieces filtering through her mind. Terrible scenarios. "You would be nice for all of five minutes, and then you would turn around and betray them."

"But, in that five minutes, you saw them willingly trying, hopefully grabbing that glimmer of hope that this would all end."

"But instead you'd end it for them."

"They were nothing," he said, with a casual wave of his hand, as if they were little more than dust on his leg.

Hunter faced him. "Did you kill them?"

"I wouldn't say I did," he said, with a half smile. "You just don't want to see the truth. The woman standing beside you is a killer, a serial killer at that," he said, laughing. "But she is my problem, not yours. And you need to back off and let me take her with me."

"And how do you plan to do that?" he asked.

Then Beth felt Lizzy's presence. "No," she screamed. "Lizzy, get away from him!"

Hunter instinctively took a step back, and she instinctively took a step forward. "Lizzy, go away."

Their captive laughed and laughed. "Oh, my God," he

said, "this is too priceless. You haven't a clue."

But there was that energy, that other energy here. She glared at him. "What have you done to Lizzy?"

"Nothing," he said. "But she misses you."

"Too damn bad," she said. She turned to Hunter. "You'll have to kill him."

He shook his head. "That's not my style."

"Then you won't be alive to try a second style," she snapped. "You don't know how dangerous he is."

"I can see that he's dangerous," Hunter said, "but something is going on here that we need to understand. Otherwise you'll never be free of this."

"They won't help us," she said, glaring at Hunter. "I'm not sticking around for Lizzy."

"I thought she was your friend."

"*Was* is the point," she said. "That woman is dangerous." She glared at the man on the chair. "What do we call you?"

"Well, you always used to call me Peter. I was a handler there."

"My *caregiver*." She shuddered at that. "I still can't believe it's you."

"Of course you can," he said. "Even if you didn't believe me, you know perfectly well that's what Lizzy called me."

"She was a sick person," she murmured.

"No, she was a survivor. Don't you remember what people would do to try to survive?"

"They'll do anything," she cried out passionately. "I don't blame Lizzy. But I do blame you for what Lizzy became."

"She's a hell of a weapon," he murmured. "Or at least she was."

"What? You burned her out too?" she asked brutally.

At that, Hunter spun on her. "Too? Did he burn you out?"

"If that's what you call it, yes," she said. "I told you that I ran away because I couldn't handle it anymore. I couldn't be his captive, his prisoner, and still deal with all the stuff he expected me to deal with."

"You don't have a clue again," Peter said calmly. "It's very simple. You just won't let us deal with it so that you can pull you together."

"Ha!" She thought his terminology apropos, when she was dealing with so much of this splintering of her energy because of her own health. She glared at him. "I used to be healthy, until you."

"You were healthy at one time," he said, with a nod. "You've also become quite sick, quite weak. And I told you that I could help you, but you won't let me. So, not a whole lot I can do to make things any better for you."

"You're a liar," she declared.

"You keep saying things like that, and you're just pissing me off."

Sure enough, he acted like he was in a temper. She glared at him. "You're the one who's tied up."

"So what? Have you forgotten how easy some things are to get out of?" he asked. And, just like that, he stood. She stared at him in surprise, and Hunter swore, stepping forward, a weapon in his hand. But the other man looked at him, smiled, and said, "Fight a battle that you're capable of winning," he said. "This is not it."

And, with that, he disappeared into the darkness outside. Hunter took off in pursuit, even as she cried out, "Hunter, no! He'll kill you." But darkness was all around her. And silence. An eerie silence. Almost like the absence of every-thing. Then she knew that Lizzy was here. "Lizzy, go away," she cried out. "I don't want anything to do with you. Leave us alone. I haven't hurt you. I haven't done anything to you. Just let me live!"

That same horrible laughter carried on the ethers. *Remember, just remember.*

And, with that, the energy disappeared. Now running full-bent into the darkness, panicked and screaming, getting away from whatever was chasing her, unsure if anything was chasing her at all or if only her own memories, Beth ran until she couldn't run anymore and finally fell to the ground and curled up into a ball, like a child, sobbing. Only Nocturne found her to curl up at her side. Always there. Always accepting. Always on her side.

BEYOND FRUSTRATED, HUNTER raced through the dark-ness, following the little bits of energy that he saw. Finally he came to a stumbling stop. "Stefan, he's gone," Hunter said out loud, as if this were easier than a telepathic conversation.

I know, Stefan said quietly. *Go back to the cabin, check up on her.*

"What do you think of what he said?"

I think we need to look into her history more.

"I thought that was already in progress."

It is, but we haven't gotten very far, he said. *I'll call Grant and see if we can get something a whole lot more in-depth. I'll call you later, once I know more.* And, with that, Stefan was gone too.

Tired, worn out, frustrated, and beyond angry at himself for having lost Peter, Hunter headed back to the cabin. As he stepped into the kitchen, he heard the shower water running. Had she gone and taken a shower, so nonchalant over the entire thing?

He couldn't forget what the stranger had said—that she was such a danger to herself and to others. Hunter didn't know if he believed that or not, but Peter obviously had skills Hunter hadn't seen before either. Troubling, in many ways. So much was out there that even Stefan didn't know how to deal with, and there was no training, no dictionary defining these abilities. Literally nothing. All very frustrating. Finally he put on the teakettle and stared out into the darkness, while he waited for the water to heat up. He'd rather have something much darker, but he didn't trust himself at the moment. Too many things to sort out.

When he heard movement behind him, he didn't turn around.

"I'm sorry," she said.

And that was the last thing he'd expected to hear. He turned slowly to look at her. "Why?"

"Why what?" she said. "Why am I sorry, or why did he show up?"

"We know why he showed up," he said, with a half snort. "Why are you sorry?"

"Because my ugly past is coming back to make your life hell. You should just let it go."

"Sure," he said, crossing his arms over his chest. "I'm supposed to just let him take you away?"

She winced at that. "Well, I hope you don't do that," she murmured. "But I also don't know in what way I can make this all go away."

"Well, you haven't managed to make it go away in the years that you've been on the run," he said. "I sure would love to know how they found you though."

"I don't know," she said. "I thought I was free and clear. Honestly I didn't see any reason why they would continue to come after me."

"And yet, even now, he won't let it go."

"Why?" she cried out. "I don't get it."

"Neither do I," he said, "but we'll have to find out."

She shook her head. "Then again, it's not something I've managed to find out in all these years, so what'll give us the advantage now?"

"Good question," he said. "We'll have to go into your past a little more."

"What past?" she said. "I don't have a past. Remember?"

So much bitterness was in her voice, so much honesty and pain, that he knew she couldn't be faking it. "I get that," he said, "and I'm sorry for you because this is way more trauma than anybody should have to go through."

"Yet it still doesn't change anything," she said, with a sigh.

"No, it doesn't. Yet maybe in some ways it does," he said.

"You're talking in riddles, and I'm too damn tired," she said. "I had a shower, and I'm somewhat warmed up. I only came down to say, *Good night*," she said, "and to say, *Thank you*."

"Thank me for what?"

"For looking after me again," she said boldly.

"I don't know how much looking after you that I did," he said, "since the guy got away."

"I expected him to, honestly. I think he's spent a lifetime figuring out how to blend into shadows. I just don't know if he'll come back tonight or not."

"Well, he knows where we are, so he might. He also was looking for his vehicle."

"He stole it anyway," she murmured. "Always his modus operandi, if I remember correctly."

"If you even remember that much, it might be a help," he murmured. "I mean, it seems like everything is up in the air as to what you remember and what you don't."

"Honestly, I don't want to remember anything that he's talking about. Part of me is terrified that I was such a bad person that I was killing people."

"Do you feel like you were ever a killer?"

"No," she said, shaking her head. "I don't, but I also don't know what I might have done when I was desperate to get away from them."

"True," he murmured. "That's one of those things that is hard to know. Life is not the easiest at any time, and we can all be pressured into doing things we don't want to do in order to get away."

She shook her head. "How is this even allowed?" she said. "How is it that people like this even get to exist?"

"Well, outside of the fact that you told me to go ahead and kill him tonight," he said humorously, "it's because we are a civilized society, where people like that get to exist until enough evidence is found to take them down."

She blew out a breath, a strand of drying hair flying off her forehead. "And I should apologize for that," she murmured. "The whole killing-him thing. In the heat of the moment, all I could think of was our safety and what we needed to do to get away."

"Oh, I understand," he said, "believe me, but killing in the heat of the moment is not the same as self-defense. I half-expected him to go for my throat again," he murmured, "but instead he took off."

"And I also think that," she said, "because he doesn't want to hurt me and because he wants to take me back to wherever," she said, "I don't know if he would hurt you right now, since you are protecting me. Or he could be of the opinion that you're more of a help because of the fact that you're here looking after me, and maybe I would be more cooperative if he kept you alive."

"Which implies that he's looking to take me prisoner and to use me against you."

"And he might," she said, with a shrug, "I don't know. I just know that he's obviously got an agenda that we aren't privy to."

"Very true," he said, "and people like that are dangerous."

"And, like you said, we're all dangerous given the right circumstances."

He gave her a lopsided smile. "You're pretty good at twisting words around."

"I don't want to be good at twisting words around," she said, with a half laugh. "I just want to be left alone in peace and quiet to live my life. I don't want to keep looking over my shoulder, and I don't want to be afraid of making friends that will end up like Sugar Mama."

"Sugar Mama. I still don't have a guaranteed answer for you there," he said. "I didn't get an answer out of this guy either. He said you're to blame for her death. You got too close to her. He couldn't take the chance of you having told her anything about the work you did."

"Well, I didn't," she cried in outrage. "He didn't have to hurt her. She wasn't a part of this in any way."

"I wish he'd been clearer but everybody seems to talk in

riddles when it comes to this crap."

"Because nobody ever wants to get caught," she murmured.

"Absolutely. It doesn't change anything though."

She shrugged. "I wouldn't mind going to bed now, if you don't mind. It's hard enough to get any restorative sleep as it is."

"Go," he said. "Get some sleep. You'll need it." She hesitated. He said, "Go on. I'll stand watch."

"The trouble is," she said, "even if you do stand watch, then what?"

"Hopefully," he said, "by then, we'll be in a position of getting free of him."

"Maybe," she murmured. "At least it's something worth trying for."

"And remember," he said. "The bottom line is that he doesn't seem to want to hurt you."

She was at the point of walking out of the kitchen, Nocturne following along as silent as ever. She stopped, turned, looked at him, and said, "He doesn't want to *kill* me," she corrected, her voice a mere whisper. "That's very different than not wanting to hurt me." And, with that, she left the kitchen.

CHAPTER 27

IN HER ROOM, Beth curled up on her bed, her knees to her
chest, and rocked gently on the bed. Her mind was a
kaleidoscope of emotions—everything from fear to pain to
terror to feelings. She didn't want or even know how to deal
with Hunter. Sugar Mama had left nothing secret about her
relationships with men, to the point that random sex seemed
normal. Beth had tried a few relationships herself. Even sex.
But outside of sweat, awkwardness, and pain, definitely not
the glorious feelings that books or indeed Sugar Mama had
promised. Beth had been left disappointed and even embar-
rassed.

And now she wondered if the partner made the difference.

As in Hunter.

She couldn't imagine feeling the same way with him but
wasn't at all sure, particularly in her condition.

Peter both terrified and reassured her. Terrified her that
he was somewhat recognizable and yet reassured her for the
same reason. Maybe some of her memories were intact. But
was that a good thing? Should she remember, as Lizzy kept
telling her?

Or live in the moment and try to find a way forward?
And then, what about Hunter? Was he part of her way
forward, or should he become something in her past? She

was conflicted. Emotions overwhelmed in both pro and con forms. She and Hunter were connected by their very actions, their very talents.

That something pulled at her, toward him of all things, which made her distrust him. And yet why? Other than she distrusted everyone.

But was that fair? And, if not, then why always look for a reason to get away from him?

Because, in truth, she wanted to go toward him—and was terrified of it.

That in itself made her angry.

"Beth? Are you okay?"

The words, the knock on her door, startled her. "Go away. … I'm fine." She added the last as an afterthought, so he wouldn't keep bugging her.

"You're not fine."

"Ha, what do you know?" she muttered. The door opened, and he stepped into the room, his gaze intent. She glared back.

"How are your energy levels?"

She wrapped her arms tighter around Nocturne. "Getting better." That was only a tiny lie. But he knew anyway. She upped the wattage of her glare. "I said, I'm fine."

"Just prickly."

What could she say to that? She was always this way. "I'm just being me."

"You are. And mostly to force everyone to keep their distance."

She glared at him. "Your point?"

He took another step closer, and a sudden heat filled her. "I don't want to always be pushed away."

"It's best," she murmured. "I'm not whole. We don't

know each other that well. There are a million reasons to stay away from each other."

"You might never be more whole than you are now. Will you always be alone? And we can always put issues between us. Do you want that too?"

"Yes," she snapped. "It's better."

He took a step backward. Then stopped. Then, as if making a decision, he moved forward and sat down on the bed beside her. "You don't have to be alone. I know you don't know who to trust. Who to listen to. But a lot of that comes with experience."

"Something I have no firsthand knowledge of," she muttered.

He opened his arms, whispering, "I'm not the enemy."

He might not be the enemy, but he was damn dangerous. She leaned ever-so-faintly in the direction of the promise of his warmth. She desperately wanted to be held, even for a moment. To let down her guard and to relax and to know everything would be okay. If only for a moment.

"You need rest."

"Something I don't get much of." She felt herself leaning closer and closer. His arms closed gently around her.

"Let your guard down once," he murmured. "You're safe."

"Am I?" she murmured, snuggling in closer. "I feel safe, but, like so much of my life, the feeling has no depth. As if it's a fleeting sensation and no more."

"You need to sink into it. Accept it as a possibility, before you dismiss it out of hand. I know much of this is out of the norm for you. But that doesn't make it wrong."

She tilted her head to look up at him. "Even being held like this is foreign."

"Because it requires trust." His voice was soft, gentle. A warmth that she'd never seen before was in his gaze. She desperately wanted to fully feel again.

He kissed her temple. "It's terrible to always be alone. It's not necessary."

"Are you seducing me?" She was curious to know what was going on, as she had had very little experience with men. At the same time she hoped he was. She wanted to know what that felt like. What a kiss from him would make her feel. And more. Warnings appeared in the back of her mind, but she was desperate to ignore them.

A low chuckle whispered against her ear, as he dropped yet another kiss on her forehead, then on her temple and finally on her cheek. "And if I am seducing you?"

"Well, I'm definitely interested." Nocturne let out a yowl and slunk away. She laughed.

He paused and eyed her carefully.

It was her turn to chuckle. "I surprised you, didn't I?"

"Very much so."

She twisted so she could sit a little higher and reached up, repeating his movements, and kissed him on the cheek. He stilled. She kissed him on the chin. Then stretching higher, she kissed him on the temple. When his gaze locked on hers, she sank against his chest and murmured, "Kiss me."

He lowered his head, his lips a hair's breadth from hers ... and waited.

She moaned lightly and stretched up and closed the distance, crushing his mouth with hers. His response was immediate; his arms wrapped around her, pulling her tight against his chest. She could barely breathe, and it had nothing to do with the crush of his arms, as she was frantic to get closer. He collapsed against her bed, pulling her with him. His mouth sultry, his kisses deep, he brought up depths of emotions she'd never felt before. Had no clue were even possible. A searing heat, a tension, coiled inside her, almost a pain from a need so dark and so frantic that she climbed his frame to assuage it.

"Easy," he murmured. "Take it easy."

She whimpered.

He kissed her gently, his tongue stroked her puffy lips. "It's all right."

"Is it?" she asked, her voice soft, her neck reaching up for more of his touch. "It doesn't feel that way. I feel needy, desperate. Like a hunger that won't quit."

"I'll fix it." He lowered his head yet again.

BETH HAD NO idea her energy was flaring, spitting out bits and pieces of herself, as she slowly unraveled in his arms. He'd wanted this from the first moment he had met her, had hoped she'd feel the same way—eventually. This timing likely wasn't fair, as she was a mess. But not of her own doing. And he wanted her badly. Felt like he always had.

Was it too much to ask for one night? At least one night to start. He would prefer a lifetime, but she needed to heal before she could fully make that decision. He just needed to be at her side long enough for her to want the same things, that she'd see him as a partner, a friend, a lover. And never as the enemy.

He shifted, so he could pull his shirt up and over his head—letting out a roar as she reached up and pinched his nipples. As he came back down, she struggled to take off her clothes. He quickly helped divest her of the little she had on and kicked off his shoes, shucking off his jeans, underwear, and socks all at once. When he turned to look at her, she was smiling at him. A real heartwarming smile of welcome, with her arms open.

He fell into them, taking her into his embrace, determined to make their time together something she'd never forget.

But all his sense of control was ripped away by her passion, as she rose to give as good as he gave, just as determined to make it a time he'd never forget. He barely had a chance to explore her exquisite body, to kiss the many scars that broke his heart, or to leisurely bring her passion to a slow burn, when she flipped him over and took him in her hands, then in her mouth, he was undone.

Now flipping her over, as he surged into her, she gasped and stilled, let out a cry. Then flipped him once again and rode him as a stallion rode a favorite mare. When he couldn't handle it anymore, he grabbed her hips and surged up again and again. He couldn't hold on, ... but he had to, ... the need building. ... He broke out in a sweat, his body shuddering, as it drove to an end he was trying to hold off.

Beth arched backward and screamed, as her climax ripped through her.

With one final plunge, his orgasm exploded inside her.

CHAPTER 28

W HEN BETH WOKE the next morning, she was surprised to find the sunlight shining in through the bedroom window. She'd slept surprisingly well, considering. She lay here for a long moment, assessing her body and energy. She was still weak but better. And sometime in the night Nocturne had returned to curl up against her side. She gently stroked his soft fur as considered how she felt.

Sated. Happy. Achy, but also warm and glowing on the inside.

Fascinated that she had somehow survived the night—no, more than survived, … thrived—made her want to find him and do it all over again.

She got to her feet, dressed, and headed to the kitchen. The unexpected visitor last night had kept her on her toes, and even now she suspected the stolen truck was still parked nearby. Just in case it wasn't this morning, she had retrieved Peter's backpack and had stowed it in the cabin. She hadn't even looked at the rest of what was in the backpack. She put on coffee, took the backpack, and dumped the contents onto the kitchen table. She wasn't sure where Hunter was but knew he wouldn't be too far away.

She sorted through everything in the backpack, an accumulation of bits and pieces—a wallet with some cash, and she certainly wasn't against using that. Man, she had certainly lost enough herself. There were several IDs, likely one he had taken from the truck he had recently stolen as well. She laid the three IDs, all of different males, off to one side and sorted through the rest. Found a small black book. As soon as she saw that, she snatched it up. "What the hell is this?" she murmured, as she flipped through it.

And, indeed, she read bits and pieces, little troublesome notes.

Appears to be in good health.

Still struggling.

No sign of improvement.

No awareness of memories.

She sat back and glared at it. "That's not helpful," she muttered.

"What is it?"

She looked up to see Hunter leaning against the door-jamb, his arms crossed. He was freshly shaved and showered.

She smiled, her heart lighting up at the sight of him. "I figured you'd be around somewhere."

"Not going anywhere for a while," he said. He looked at the backpack and items on the table. "What's this?"

"From the truck," she said. "Well, his rowboat, and then I brought it with me in his truck when I came home."

Home. He barely could take note of that, as his eyebrows shot up, and he walked over. "Would have been good to have known about this last night."

"Sorry, I didn't even think to show it to you," she said. "I saw it this morning and just now started going through it."

"Anything interesting?"

"Some IDs. I suspect he's just kept whatever he's picked up from vehicles that he stole."

"Well, it's convenient that way, isn't it?"

"Absolutely," she said. "Maybe if he gets lucky, one's close enough in appearance to use."

Hunter nodded. "A couple credit cards are here in different names, but, after a certain amount of time, mere hours in some cases," he said, "they won't be good anymore."

"But they can be used immediately though," she murmured, studying them. She set them off on one side, and she said, "This notebook is what I immediately glommed on to, but it doesn't help."

"What's it about?"

"Me, apparently." He stopped and looked at her, then reached out a hand. She put the notebook in it and shrugged. "It's just his notes, and it doesn't seem to say anything positive or negative either way."

"Well, maybe that's a good thing."

"Not if it doesn't give us answers," she said in frustration.

He flipped through it and said, "Your memories appear to be the big blocking point."

"Yes. At least according to him."

"Do you want help getting them back?"

"Hell no," she said immediately. "I told you. Everything he said about my memories suggests I don't want to remember something."

"Will you be content to stay in the darkness though?" he murmured.

"If that's all I have, then that's all I have." He frowned at that, and she shrugged. "What am I supposed to say? You're asking me if I want to find out information that potentially shows me to be an incredibly bad person. I'd just as soon stand in the darkness and forget about it. I've reinvented my life for the last many years. I'm okay to stay this way."

"Are you though? Really?"

Something was oddly intimate about the question, but she didn't want to go there now. Better to leave last night in the past. She waved a hand at him. "Forget all that woo-woo psychiatry stuff," she said. "I'm surviving just fine."

"You're surviving, but you are not thriving."

"Come on. Does anybody really thrive in this world?" she asked curiously. "Seems like everybody I talk to is in survival mode one way or another, as if they've got so many problems and so much pain that they aren't thriving anyway," she said. "I think thriving is a misnomer."

"I don't know about a misnomer," he murmured, "but I certainly don't see that it's something you have to hide from."

"But we're all hiding."

"Yes," he said, "but I think, at some point in time, you'll want answers."

"Maybe, but that time is not now." And, with that, she returned her attention to the rest of the stuff from Peter's backpack and raised both hands in frustration. "Nothing is here."

"No," Hunter said. "Did you expect there to be?"

She frowned. "He has to make a mistake sometime."

"Maybe. But it looks to me like he's been doing this just as long as you have been running," he murmured. "Tell me more about Lizzy."

"Why?" she asked, clamming up and glaring at him.

"Because Lizzy seems to be a big part of this."

"I told you. She was my best friend. If we could have any friends in a place like that, then she was it. I struggled with hurting people, and she didn't seem to have a problem with it."

"Is that what broke up your friendship?"

"What broke us was that I was punished for not following orders, and she stepped up and followed the orders to avoid being hurt again. And I couldn't handle it."

"You couldn't understand why she would do such a thing?"

"Of course I could understand. I just didn't like the fact that she did it."

"So you judged her for it."

"Ouch," she said, glaring at him. "That's hardly fair."

"The truth isn't always fair," he said, right back at her.

She waved a hand. "So, instead of this talk, is there any food?"

"Sure," he said, looking at her steadily. "Where was Lizzy when you guys were being relocated?"

"In one of the cars ahead of me," she said.

"Was she ever used as a weapon against you?"

"I knew it was guaranteed the minute I left," she said. "Lizzy is by far the strongest of them all." She looked at him and said, "And you'd better watch it because you do have some abilities, and it would be abilities that Peter would thwart."

"I hear you. He more or less made a threat to that extent last night."

She nodded. "If he sees any value in you, he will do what he can to utilize it, then throw you away again."

"Interesting that he would throw it away afterward."

"Most of the time," she murmured, "the abilities are pretty well done for."

"Meaning, they are burned out?"

She nodded. "If you want to use that phrase, yes."

"*If I want to use that phrase*," he said, studying her close-ly. "What abilities are we talking about?"

"Anything and everything," she said, "including a lot of wannabes or people who had minor abilities. People would pretend to have better abilities than they had, until they were tested. Then, of course, the truth would come out, and it would go badly for them."

"He sounds like a nice guy."

"I've already told you that he isn't, and I've warned you," she said. "I can't do any more than that. You'll proceed at your own risk."

"Of course," he said. "Thanks for the warning."

She glared at him. "This isn't funny, you know?"

"No, I get it," he said. "You've seen some pretty rough things. These things just never seem to get any easier, do they?"

She shook her head. "No, they don't. Peter's an asshole, and he's never changed. We gonna eat anytime soon?"

"Food won't change the conversation," he interrupted.

"Food needs to change the conversation," she murmured.

He stepped into the pantry and froze. She followed him and gasped. "Where did that come from?"

"I don't know," he murmured, "but I can guess."

In front of them was a painting, faded, but a portrait of her. She stepped closer. "I almost feel like I remember this," she murmured.

"It's an interesting painting, isn't it? Multiple images of you."

"Yeah, it's one of those receding images," she said. "I remember playing with that."

"Did you paint it?" he asked.

She frowned and shrugged. "I feel like I had a hand in it, but I don't know," she said. "Why would Peter leave this though?" She turned to look at Hunter.

"To trigger your memory, I would guess," he said. "That appears to be the biggest issue on his mind."

"Well, if that's what he wants, then it's the last thing I want," she said forcibly.

"Got it," he said, in a calm voice, "but that doesn't mean that isn't what ultimately needs to happen."

"Don't push it," she muttered.

He walked around the painting and checked the doors. "Everything is locked."

"He used to be good at picking locks," she said. "I didn't see him ever fail."

"Well, in that case, no point in locking them again."

"Why?" she asked curiously.

"Because he was obviously here already, so what's the point?"

She wasn't sure what to say about that but nodded. "Fine. Does that mean we can still have food?"

"Of course." He looked around the kitchen to see if anything else was different, while she watched.

"If he came, and he added something, does that make him a thief?"

"No, it means he broke in and entered a property that's not his. Even if not locked, he would still be entering illegally."

"I get it," she said. "I just wish I knew where I was supposed to go from here." An uneasy feeling rode deep down into her spine, that constant memory of Lizzy telling her to remember. "I think they want me to know what I'm like on the inside because I did such horrible things," she said.

"They're jogging my memory, so I'll go back to being like them."

"In that case, then I hope you never remember," he said quietly.

She looked at him with relief. "I'm glad you said that," she replied, "because I've been racking my brain, wondering if I'm supposed to confess to some crimes that I don't even know if I committed or not."

"Well, you can't confess to crimes you can't remember," he said. "Which just supports the justification of not remembering. Unless not remembering is hurting you."

"I'm fine," she said immediately.

He nodded and didn't say anything, as he brought out eggs and bread. "A little bit of bacon and eggs are left," he said, "and I can make some toast. You okay with that?"

"It's edible," she said, "so absolutely."

He smiled at her and said, "Food ought to be more than just edible."

"When you're on the run, *just edible* works."

"But you're not on the run anymore."

"No," she said, with a confused frown. "We're holed up here, but Peter has the run of the place, so I'm not sure why we're still here."

"Where would we go that he couldn't find us?"

"Nowhere," she said, with a shrug.

He nodded. "So, I'm not sure running will help us."

"No, but it would make me feel better."

"That's because action over inaction always feels better," he said quietly. "In this case, we would just be burning our energy but not necessarily improving the situation."

"So, what do we do to improve it?"

"Well, let's find out some more about your history. And

his."

"How is it possible to even find out what his real name is?"

"I did get some photos of him when he was knocked out," he said quietly. "I sent them off to Stefan, and the FBI is looking into it."

"Right. You have friends in high places."

"I do. And it's not so much that it's the FBI but a special division of the FBI that is looking into these types of crimes."

"What crime did he commit exactly?" she said.

"Well, on the surface, it's just plain stalking and, of course, entering the house illegally. When you leave a painting behind, it's hardly theft, but I'm sure the FBI could come up with something for it. He was discharging his firearm last night several times, and I think he would have quite cheerfully killed me."

"Which goes against what he was saying."

"Oh, I think he would have killed me in a temper but would prefer to utilize me to his advantage to get you to remember."

"That would not make me happy," she said calmly. "I don't like being used as a pawn, and I don't want anybody I know to be used to make me do something."

"Oh, I hear you. But that doesn't mean we'll have any choice though. We don't know what his end game is."

She replied, "So we need to leave here, so that he can't play his end game."

"Maybe. Or maybe we should just stay here and see if we can come up with a few devices of our own to get clear of this."

"You're talking in circles again."

"Maybe," he said, "maybe not. Let's eat up first, recharge our energies, and come up with a game plan."

"You keep saying things like that, but I feel like it's just to throw me off the scent."

"And what scent would that be?" he asked her curiously, as he cracked eggs into a bowl.

"The fact that there isn't anything we can do," she said calmly. "The fact that he's got our number, no matter what."

"That doesn't mean he'll win," Hunter said quietly.

"How can he lose though?" she murmured. "He's got all the cards in his hand."

He grinned at her. "Does he?"

She frowned. "Yes, I think he does. He disappeared quite easily last night."

"Sure, but do you think I didn't let him?"

At that, her jaw dropped. She leaned forward and said, "Seriously?"

He nodded. "He's not a whole lot of value if he's a prisoner and won't talk. What we need to know is what he'll do next, where he went, and what he's planning on doing from now on."

"But how will you figure that out? He's gone. It's not like you can track him."

"That's exactly what I did. I put a tracker on him," he said. "So hopefully, when I go check it again, which is where I was just a little bit ago, we'll have a better idea of where he is."

She shook her head in astonishment. "I didn't know you had access to that stuff."

"Most people just don't know where because they don't care enough to look," he said. "In my business it's something I do all the time."

"But you can track him otherwise too, can't you?"

"I can, if you're talking about energy. Yes, that's what I do. It's my bent," he said, "but I'm also caught between that and keeping you safe."

"Well, I wouldn't worry about that so much," she said. "Again, we know that he doesn't want to kill me."

"True, but do we want you to get caught?"

"Well, if we did," she said, "and you could track me, then it would take us back to his home base and whatever else he's got planned."

"I thought of that too," Hunter said calmly, "but I'm not up to using you as bait. You've been used enough in your life."

"And what if I told you to use me? Just make sure you come rescue me."

"I've already considered that," he murmured, "and I've discarded it."

"And if I want you to anyway?"

"It's too dangerous."

"Too bad," she said in exasperation, "because we need to put a stop to this."

"We do, but we don't have enough information yet."

"And where will we get the information from?"

"Stefan is working on it."

"Right. Stefan and the FBI."

"Exactly," he said, tossing her a quick grin. "Remember? Trust is a problem for you."

"Of course it is," she said, "because in all those years that I needed somebody to rescue me, nobody was out there to do it."

"Maybe nobody knew you needed a rescue, and maybe your cries for help weren't getting through because of whatever scenario they had managed to wrap around you. Maybe you were in a steel building or another construction capable of blocking radio waves, which can stop telepathic messages, even on the ether. Our minds still need a way to get loose in order to send messages."

"And somebody has to be listening," she said calmly.

"Indeed. And I wouldn't guarantee that nobody was listening, but that doesn't mean that your message was coming through loud and clear."

She frowned at that. "All the things that have to happen in order to make life a little easier on some of us," she said, with a shake of her head. "You don't think about it, do you?"

"No, because nobody wants to believe it's as shitty a world out there as it is."

"It's not all shitty."

"What! Is this you saying that?"

She laughed. "Okay, fine," she said. "So a lot of it is shitty."

"A lot of it is, indeed, shitty, but it's not all like you said. Come on. Eat up." He put the plate down in front of her.

She sniffed the air. "I never could make bacon look like this," she said, staring at the crispy strips. "It was always burnt or looking like half-raw fat."

"Lots of people don't care which way it ends up, as long as it's cooked enough not to make you sick. Bacon's bacon. It's always a treat."

"Maybe," she said, "but I like mine so it doesn't have fat jiggling all over it."

"Then it's a good thing it's not got any fat jiggling all over it today," he said, with a chuckle.

She smiled. "I don't understand how you can be so calm about this whole thing."

"Because," he said, "I've seen assholes like him before. I know he's dangerous, and I know that he's hunting you, but I believe that we will get through this."

"It just seems so far-fetched." She wanted to believe Hunter; she really did.

"All of it is far-fetched," he said.

She laughed. "I know, and when I think about all the things that I went through, well, that all seems severely far-fetched too, especially now that I've got some distance from it."

"Of course," he said. "When you're in the middle of it, it's so darn close it almost chokes you because you have to live it so intensely, but, as soon as you get a little distance, you can see how different it truly was. Even then you'll always have it colored by your perception of what you went through."

"It would be nice to think that everything that I feel and am afraid of is wrong," she said, frowning. "That would make me very happy, but it doesn't feel like it's wrong."

"We won't worry about right or wrong either," he said. "We'll let it go and just believe in you."

She shook her head. "Believing in me has got to be the hardest thing."

"Nope," he said, "but it is the most important thing. You have to trust who you are right now, and, if we find that you did some terrible things back then under duress and via torture, we'll deal with it."

"No," she said, "I don't think I can."

"You don't have a choice. This is what's upon us right now. No walking away from it anymore."

"I could," she said. "I could get into that stolen truck and just run."

315

"You could," he said, "but you won't run far or fast or for very long."

"Because he's found me?"

"He's found you, and he's tracked you once. Now he's got a good idea of your energy again, and he won't be letting you walk for long."

"Then let him catch me," she said impulsively. "Use me as bait. Come on. You know you want to."

He looked up at her, as he put another bite of eggs into his mouth, shaking his head. "Just like you know where your moral code is, I know where mine is too," he said gently. "Crossing that line is not something I can live with."

"But being hunted for the rest of my life is not something I can live with," she said, "and what if I'm not the only person he's got his eye on?"

"I definitely got the impression that you were his primary focus," Hunter said, looking at her calmly.

"But maybe that's wrong. Maybe he's not just after me. Maybe it's me and half-a-dozen others. Maybe that's why he took all these years to find me," she said, waving her fork in the air. "Maybe he went and collected everybody else first."

Hunter studied her for a long moment. "Maybe."

Just then his phone rang.

HUNTER PULLED OUT his phone, looked at it, smiled, and said, "It's Stefan. I'll be back soon." He snagged the last bite on his plate and popped it into his mouth, as he dropped his fork, picked up his coffee, and walked out of the room. "Hey, Stefan. What have you got?"

"Is she around?"

"She's in the other room, eating breakfast," he said,

stepping out onto the deck and closing the door behind him.

"Good. Make sure that you're someplace she can't see you."

"Fine. So what's going on?"

"Well, we found something about her birth."

"And?"

"Well, it's not completely clear—we don't have any legal documents. But we found an article, from way back when, regarding two girls who were sold by their mother ... to a cult—"

"Sold to a cult? Well, that could explain some things."

"Exactly. Twin girls."

"Twins?"

"Yes."

Then it hit him. "Oh, my God! Lizzy."

"That's what I'm wondering," Stefan said. "If they were twins, it would make a sad kind of sense and would also explain why it's easy for Lizzy to keep track of her. It would also explain why Beth's deliberately forgetting her history. If she can block off all that, she can block off her sister's access to her."

"Exactly." He sat down on the armchair farthest away on the deck and said, "Wow! Poor Beth."

"Poor both of them. Apparently they disappeared somewhere about ten days before their fourth birthday."

"And what about the mother?"

"They never found the mother, and that's why the case remained open but cold, which could be related to the fact that the mother received a large chunk of change, supposedly from a friend, just a few days after the disappearance."

"So the mother was investigated?"

"Not right away. She professed to not know what friend

had given her the money, and the authorities had trouble tracking it back then. They had no direct evidence of any illegal wrongdoing on the mother's end, and the funds came from a private anonymous offshore account. The authorities thought she had sold the twins, but that was as far as they got, when she upped and disappeared. But the money was never touched. So they are presuming she's deceased."

Hunter shook his head. "Just when you think you've seen the extent of the depravity of the human condition—"

"We haven't seen a fraction of it. So many of our recent cases have involved horrible abuse that preyed on kids, all in the name of various religions and motivations," Stefan said. "We could be looking at that scenario here too."

"How sad for Beth," Hunter said. "It would explain that sense of loss she always feels."

"I wondered about that too because, if you think about it, losing a twin is never easy—whether separated by death or by geography. And, if Lizzy is her twin, but Beth's not in contact with her, there would always be that sense that Beth has lost her, but not necessarily that she'll ever get her back again."

"No, I know. I hear her talking to Lizzy sometimes. I'm not even sure if she's completely aware of it."

"She probably is, whether she thinks she is or not. I don't know. She could be just calling out, like to see if she's listening in or not."

"I get that," he said, "but I think there's more to this than we know so far."

"Absolutely there is."

"Beth suggested today that we set a trap and let Peter take her, as long as we follow along and save her—even though she acknowledged having a problem with the fact that she spent no small amount of time crying out for help and nobody came."

"What she's volunteering for is her own worse nightmare," Stefan said.

"Well, it's a nightmare for anybody, but yeah."

"Interesting that she would suggest it though." Then Stefan asked humorously, "And yet she doesn't want to recall her own memories?"

"No, she's afraid she was a terrible person in that previous life, and she doesn't want to remember it, if she was."

"Even though most likely under terrible duress, so she wouldn't be responsible."

"I don't think that matters enough to let herself off the hook," Hunter said.

"What do you think about her idea?"

"I think it's a terrible plan," Hunter said immediately. "She's one scary female, and she's got abilities that we don't know and understand, but no way will I let Peter have her. I don't want to see anything bad happen to her."

"Of course not," Stefan said, "and, after all this time you two have shared, I'm sure there's even more of a connection between you and her."

"Sure, there is, but it's not something I want to talk about."

Hunter could almost hear the smile in Stefan's voice as he replied, "If you say so."

"I've got other things to deal with. He left a portrait in the pantry overnight."

"Who did?"

"This asshole, Peter. A painting of Beth, years ago as a child. Like a, ... it's got multiple pictures of her."

"Take a photo of it and send it to me," he said. And,

with that, Stefan rang off.

Hunter walked back inside, noting Beth was gone from the kitchen table. Hunter headed toward the painting and took several photos, sending them to Stefan, texting, **It's a weird painting, but she remembers doing it herself but thought that somebody else was helping her.**

When he didn't get an answer, figuring that Stefan would still be studying it for a while, he walked from the kitchen area into the other first-floor rooms, only Beth wasn't there. He cleaned up their breakfast dishes, still looking around for her, and, when he didn't see her, he walked upstairs to her bedroom—empty as well. Unfortunately more than empty. Like it had been cleaned out.

With panic in his voice, he called out for her, "Beth, where are you?" He called over and over again, searched inside, then outside, before finally calling Stefan on the phone. "She's gone."

"Yeah, she's gone," he said, his voice grim. "I'm sorry you didn't show me that picture before."

"Why is that?"

"Because it's a very special painting," he said. "I don't have time to explain, but, in many ways, it illuminates so much. We have to find her, and we have to find her now."

CHAPTER 29

B ETH HADN'T GIVEN Hunter the slightest indication
that she was leaving. She was already off the property
and racing for Peter's stolen truck that she'd left hidden. She
had everything with her hopefully, so she wouldn't leave any
trace, but she had also taken everything from her stalker's
backpack as well. Reaching the truck, she slid inside, turned
on the engine, and headed for the highway, as fast as she
could.

She was heading back to—the word *home* even came to
mind but was immediately discarded in favor of *cell, captivity, compound,* or any other number of depressing and scary
names. Bits and pieces circulated through her brain, letting
her know that something stirred deep inside. She wasn't sure
how or why. Maybe seeing Peter again. She didn't know.
But, as she kept driving forward, following her instincts, she
was at a crunch point.

She didn't want to live like this, constantly looking over
her shoulder. She had fooled herself into thinking she could
do it for a while, but that wasn't lasting. Not effective. Not
soothing. And everybody around her was getting hurt. She
knew in her heart of hearts that Sugar Mama would still be
alive if not for her.

And, if she stayed around Hunter, it would be the same
thing for him too. And the last thing she wanted to do was

bring these predators to Stefan and his wife. None of this was a good scenario, and Beth was at the root of it all. She didn't know why Lizzy kept telling her to remember. She didn't know why Lizzy wouldn't leave her alone. Beth called out from the truck, "I'm coming, and I want to have this out, one way or another."

A mocking laughter floated through the inside of the cab. Even Nocturne straightened at the sound then relaxed on the seat beside her.

Beth gripped the steering wheel firmly, hating that her palms were already sweaty. "I'm hours away," she said. "You can just calm down and let me get there."

Again, the same mocking laughter came.

Beth shuddered, hating what she was heading for, her stomach already revolting. Part of her said to return to safety, to Hunter, that he would help. Another part of her said there was no help for it, and Hunter would just get hurt, like Sugar Mama. Beth hated to admit that she cared.

She'd spent a lifetime not caring, a lifetime pushing people away, keeping herself locked away, hidden, particularly after Lizzy had made such a point of betraying her. Beth just couldn't do some things. And she knew that Hunter, with his caring attitude and that smooth deep husky voice had hit her at a time in her life where she was at a point of no return. She could deal with this and have a future, or she could deal with this and have no future, or she could just not deal with it at all and still have no future.

The clarity of that scenario helped her to decide, come what may. She could have had Hunter on her side, but he'd already refused to let her become bait, and, since Peter wanted only her, it made no sense to involve Hunter any further. He'd kept her safe somewhat so far, but she could require only so much of him. Just then Stefan's voice crept into her head.

You are being foolish.

Well, that's on me, she replied.

It doesn't have to be this way.

If you know where I am, then I'm sure you're about to tell Hunter.

He knows you're gone.

Good luck following me, she stated. *This can't go on. You know that.* Silence came from the other end, and she smiled and nodded to herself. *I know you agree with me,* she said, *but Hunter won't.*

He doesn't want to see you hurt.

No, and I don't want to see him hurt either, she said. *They killed Sugar Mama. You know that.*

I know, he said, his voice soft and gentle, almost the barest of a whisper in her mind. *They couldn't leave any witnesses.*

I can't have that happen to anybody else, she said. *Every time I get close to anybody, it's either betrayal or death.*

You can't blame yourself for this.

Why not? she said.

Do you have any family?

What's that supposed to mean?

Do you ever remember, even way back when?

No, she said. *Remember the memories? Remember that voice in my head? Surely you've heard it, telling me to remember.*

I wondered, he said, his tone thoughtful. *I heard something, but I wasn't sure who it came from.*

I'm not sure who it's coming from either, she said, *but I think it's Lizzy, and I don't know why she wants me to remember anything.*

I think it's important that you do remember.

Why? So I can remember all the people I've hurt, the things I've done, the horrors of my world? How will that help me at all? she cried out in frustration. Not having anybody to hit out at, she slammed her fist against the steering wheel. *I just want this to stop. I want to go away and live the life of a good person, not that horrible human being I was.*

So, it's not that you don't remember but you're deliberately not remembering.

She frowned at that. *Sounds like splitting hairs to me.*

He chuckled. *We have all kinds of safety mechanisms*, he said. *And yours is to not remember.*

If that means safety for me as a person, then it's all fine, she said. *I had a shitty upbringing. I had a terrible childhood and an even worse adolescence,* she said. *Surely now that I've got a chance for a clean slate, I should be allowed to have a future.*

Absolutely you should.

Then don't stop me.

I'm not planning on stopping you, he said. *I was hoping to help you.*

And how do you expect to do that?

How about backup? he said. *And that's just a start.*

Everybody who comes will get hurt, she said. *Can't you guys understand that? You don't know what you're facing.*

Maybe we don't, he said, *but you're not explaining it either.*

Because I can't, I don't even know myself, she said, the frustration once again spilling outward and over. *You don't know what it's like to not know.*

No, I don't. But I do know, he said, *that there's always more than one option.*

No, there isn't. Not this time, she said. *In this scenario the best option is the only one I'm willing to look at, and that's for nobody else to get hurt.* Especially Hunter.

Ah. What about yourself?

I've been hurt so many times before, what is one more? she said, tired, fatigued, with a sense of who-gives-a-shit overwhelming her. *It's hard for me to even realize everything that's gone on in my life, but I know I can't have it continue like this. I need to be free, and I need to know that something is out there.*

Something for you?

Some purpose to living. There. She'd said it. *If this is all there is,* she said, *I don't want it. I need it to disappear.*

And if it doesn't?

Then no point in going on.

So simply put and yet clear as a bell.

I know you don't understand that, she said, *but I would prefer death over this.*

Don't do anything foolish, he ordered.

Foolish? she said. *You mean, anything else foolish.*

You have help this time.

Supposedly I had help all those years ago too, she snapped. *You got away. I didn't.*

His voice broke when he whispered, *I know. I didn't even know you were still there.*

Well, I was a new recruit. Remember? she said, with bitterness. *I wasn't given a whole lot of choice.*

No, that's true, he said. *Anybody who was there didn't get any choice.*

But you managed to get away.

And so did you, later, he said. *You don't have to go back.*

I do though because only part of me got away. The rest, the memories, are still there.

You said you didn't want to remember.

I don't, she said, *but I don't think that's a choice any longer.* And, with that, she slammed him out of her mind, then closed and locked the door. "Take *that* message, Stefan."

And, of course, there was no response. There couldn't be. She'd made sure of it. Groaning, tired, sad, and feeling more alone than she ever had in her short life, she drove steadily on into the night.

"WHAT DO YOU mean, she's going back to the compound?" Hunter was stunned. "It's a destroyed building. What is there to go back to?"

"I don't know," Stefan said. "You did say one building is still standing, right?"

"Sure. The part with the offices and the files that were pretty well destroyed."

"Well, they'd taken everything they wanted, but something still draws her back there," Stefan said.

"And that's pretty sad," Hunter said, turning to look around him. "But nothing is there."

"Something is—something that's important—and she has to go there."

"Well, that's easy enough," he said, grabbing the keys to the motorcycle and shoving them into his pocket. "I'll be hours though."

"She's not that far ahead of you. You'll catch up in no time."

"Sure, but catching up isn't the same thing in this case. She doesn't want me around, so I'll have to stay hidden."

"And I get that," he said, "but you can't be too hidden. She's heading for whatever crunch time there is. She did say a couple interesting things though."

"Yeah, like what?" Hunter said, his mind consumed with packing a few things that he would need. One of the things he wanted with him was his weapons. He quickly slid a knife into his ankle sheath, then a small handgun that he kept in an ankle holster. Then he put on a shoulder holster and grabbed his leathers.

"You're going loaded for bear," Stefan said, his voice quiet.

"Sure. In this case we're going grizzly hunting, from the sounds of it."

"I think you're going nightmare hunting."

That made him pause. "There aren't any physical weapons for that."

"No, there isn't, but that's why it's important that you understand what she said."

Hunter, finally clued in, stopped, and he said, "Okay, what did she say?"

"She said something about everybody around her gets hurt, and it's either that or they betray her."

"I presume she's talking about Sugar Mama."

"Yes. And Lizzy."

"Which makes sense, but one person getting hurt is hardly a be-all and end-all. I'm sorry for Sugar Mama obviously, and I'm sorry for Beth because of the guilt that'll rack her soul over it, but there wasn't anybody else—well, the guard who was killed because she escaped—but no one else, or at least nobody she's told us about."

"I think *not having told us* is more likely. She thinks that she spent a lifetime with the testing, where people got hurt because of her."

"Right. That folder on Mitzi spoke of her death. Plus, those two people, one kid, one adult, who were killed in front of Beth. But again she's not responsible for that. The assholes who forced her into this are."

"Exactly. But she also said that she couldn't stand it if you got hurt. And I read her thoughts. She's also worried about me and Celina getting hurt."

Hunter stopped, and a slow smile broke across his face. "Well, I knew I was making headway, but I didn't expect to make that much headway."

"Oh, she cares," Stefan affirmed, "but I think she's scared to care."

"Of course. Still, that's not her decision."

"Well, it is," Stefan said humorously. "And she's already made it, and she's keeping you out of it."

"Good luck with that," he said. "This girl needs a friend in this life."

"She needs more than that," Stefan said.

"True, but, hey, friends is a good place to start."

"Yes, it is," he murmured. "Now it's a matter of making sure you don't get hurt because there'll be no forgiveness in her soul for herself if you do."

"And again, she's not responsible for that. She kept me out initially, but I'm here now," he said. "Anything else?"

"Yes." Stefan paused. "You won't like this."

"What?" he demanded.

"She wants to find answers."

"So do we," Hunter said, frowning.

"She's blocked me now. And you could never reach her telepathically. She's already chosen to die to save us."

"Not acceptable," Hunter roared. "She has yet to live."

"Listen," Stefan barked. He heard a frustrated groan from Hunter's end of the call. "She thinks confronting this issue will give her, ... us, answers. And finally she's seen enough of our side of living free that she won't accept anything less. That means, we may be there for her—you physically, me in the ethers—but she wants to go through hell to get it done. Meaning ..."

"Meaning, I can't interfere? ... Damn it, Stefan. You're asking too much. *She's* asking too much."

"I know it hurts you to stand back, but I agree with her on this one."

More cursing from Hunter followed.

Stefan let his friend work it out himself. "Shit." He sighed loudly. Then exhaled again. "I hate to ask, but is there anything else I need to know?"

"No," he said, "I'll come along with you."

"Well, phone me in a couple hours," he said. "You need rest. I don't know what's coming up, but one of us needs to recharge. I haven't had any sleep since I met her. I'll check in with you in a couple hours."

And, on that note, he headed out the front door, locked it, checked the fuel on the bike, and nodded. With that, he took off.

CHAPTER 30

W HEN BETH FINALLY made the series of turns to get to the compound, she took a moment at the crossroads, and then, determined to follow through, she hit the gas and turned off the main road, heading down the gravel road toward her final destination. "I'm sorry, Hunter. I should have said goodbye at least. I'm sure you're coming behind me, thanks to Stefan, and I'm so sorry. You don't have a clue what's coming."

She did though. She just didn't know how bad it would be. She didn't know how bad any of this could be. But she knew her memories held the answers, and she knew those memories, the ones she didn't want to recall, would be the ones that broke this wide open. Whatever that meant.

She drove carefully in the darkness, feeling a sense of gloom hovering over her soul the deeper and deeper she went. She didn't even know why she was here, not really. At least all the arguments had been tossed back and forth over the last few hours, but she didn't know for sure.

"Stop it," she yelled at herself in the vehicle. "You know exactly why you're here." She came upon the same corner, where they'd found the guard's body hidden. She wanted to get out and check to see if it was still there but hoped that somebody would have done something about it by now, though the site didn't look like it had been touched. And that just said more about the power of those who had been part of this nightmare. Shaking her head, she drove on.

"Nocturne, don't you get caught with me. You know better right?"

He rubbed against her thigh giving her a huge sense of relief. "Sorry buddy. Of course you do. I might need your help in there too."

He meowed softly. He knew exactly how dangerous her trip could end up being. He'd been there with her back then. Hell, he'd been there with her since forever. At least as far back as her memories of him went.

Approaching the edge of the compound, she parked the truck and hopped out. She stood here for a long moment, hating the feeling of needing to go in, battling that same existing warfare that told her to stay away. But she'd come this far, so, in for a penny, in for a pound. She took several steps forward and didn't even hear the movement, but, all of a sudden, she knew she wasn't alone and stiffened. "Who are you?"

"The better question," said the man, possibly Peter, "is why are you here?"

But she never got a chance to answer. Darkness raced toward her, and she collapsed to the ground.

BETH WOKE TO her worst nightmare all over again.

She lay here for a moment, seeing the same dripping nasty concrete walls. She was chained to a bed, and she couldn't even begin to move. She stayed quiet, years of practice holding her in good stead, as she allowed every horrible thought to play through her mind as she remained a captive. Is this what she had thought she would do when she got back? Had she not expected this? Of course she had. So what the hell was she doing here?

Nocturne?

A soft faint meow responded. Still there was no sign of him.

She wanted to close her eyes, yet she wanted to cry out at the same time. She did nothing. She lay here, as always, her body completely relaxed in the bed, as she stared all around her. Years and years had given her the will to live through this. She was not that scared child anymore. She was an adult who understood another world was out there, a world that was a better place to be than here, but a world that required her to make peace with her past before she could move on.

"Good, you're awake," he said.

She nodded. "I am." She yawned. "I didn't sleep too bad. Thanks for knocking me out."

An odd silence followed. "Are you sure I knocked you out?"

"Well, someone did," she said, rotating her neck. "I don't remember sleeping that well when I was here before."

"You didn't sleep well at all," he said calmly. "You kept fighting it all the time."

"Yeah, captivity will do that to you."

He laughed. "That had nothing to do with it, but I'm glad to hear that you're in a good mood."

"Why not?" she said. "I've been here before."

"That you have."

"So why the chains?" she asked, lifting her wrists and looking at them.

"Safety precaution," he said.

"Mine or yours?" she replied.

"Both."

That was a surprise. She kept calm, sending out a message. *Well, Stefan, I'm here and chained up. Not sure if that's what I expected, but it's sure as hell what feels normal.*

She couldn't sense anything in the ethers, but then she was the one who had sent out that last little message and had slammed the door behind it. Not a whole lot she could do but blame herself now. She opened the door just in case, but also knew Stefan had no reason to even want to cross that threshold. She hadn't treated him nicely, and all she had done was bring him more pain than he deserved. Such was her life.

"What are you thinking?"

"Isn't that your domain?" she asked curiously. "Aren't you the one who always decided what we were allowed to think or do?"

"I wish," he said, with a harsh laugh. "Then I could have controlled every aspect of your world. But, no, you had a mind of your own, and one that you would not share."

"I wonder why," she said.

"I get it," he said. "You're still angry at me."

"You think?" But she didn't explain further.

"It won't be bad," he said. "It's just important for you to remember who you are."

"Maybe the question should be, why did I think it so important that I forget?"

"Because you blamed yourself," he said, "and that was wrong. You weren't to blame."

"I feel like you would … let me blame myself," she said quietly, searching her mind, her memories, looking for whatever was at the bottom of this.

"No," he said, "you took it on very easily on your own."

"And you let me?"

"Of course," he said, "not like we could ever do very much to stop you."

"You make me sound like I was always in control."

"Have you convinced yourself that you weren't? That you were a victim?" He asked, "Wouldn't it be nice to absolve all your own guilt that way?"

And, of course, that just reaffirmed what she had been afraid of, that she was guilty. And guilty of some heinous crime for which she got absolutely no salvation. If that were the truth, it would be very hard to deal with, but she was long past treating herself like a victim. "Then let's get on with it," she said.

"Why so eager all of a sudden?"

"Since when wasn't I anxious to get started?"

He thought for a long moment.

She wanted to twist to see his face, but he kept himself out of sight. "And why are you hiding anyway?"

A moment of startled silence came. "You're the one who would never allow us to stand in your view," he said. "You said it made it much worse."

She raised her eyebrows at that. Because she didn't remember any of it, didn't remember the orders that she supposedly had given, didn't remember any of those kinds of instructions, or why would she have chosen something like that. That didn't make a whole lot of sense.

"Hey, they were your instructions," he said, with a mocking laugh. "We were all just forced to follow along."

"I highly doubt you were forced to do anything," she declared.

"So much spice and vinegar," he said. "I wonder how you'll feel when you find out the truth."

"Probably lousy," she murmured, "but then that's also

335

partly why you're here, isn't it? To make sure that I do."

A long moment of silence came; then finally, he said, "Just rest." And then he disappeared. She heard his footsteps echoing in the distance.

"Rest," she murmured. What was she supposed to rest up for? She knew she wouldn't want to know, but it also felt oddly familiar, as if all this was something she'd done before, many times over. She wouldn't like it, but that didn't stop the fact that she'd survived it before, so she could survive it again. If only she could remember what the hell all of this was about.

She knew that the torture was partially self-inflicted because of her own guilt. But also a huge part of her understood something else was going on here. Peter seemed content, happy to have her back. And she understood that too. It just made her feel even more disenfranchised from everything. She wished she had a better understanding of how this was all supposed to go, but, as she had walked in blind, she was still blind. There wouldn't be any answers until this started. So be it.

She closed her eyes and rested. Even in the darkness, she hoped against hope that maybe her dismissive attitude to Stefan hadn't completely blocked him from helping her.

Although she didn't know what help he could give, she was still hoping he could do something. If only to make sure she didn't stay here for the rest of her life. And knowing he would at least do that much, then she could believe that she wouldn't be stuck here forever. And that was enough to keep her buoyed attitude from collapsing.

HUNTER WAS IN the shadows, watching in shock as two

men came up behind her, knocked her out, bundled her up into the back of a truck, and left. *That's not what he had expected at all. Hey, Stefan,* he called out to his friend. *They've knocked her out and taken her away.*

Good, he said, *maybe this will work after all.*

Hunter frowned at that but kept a little distance back, noting they were going farther up that same road past the compound. *They're taking her someplace close by, but she still won't know where she is because they've knocked her out.*

Exactly. So it's all part of the disorientation process. Bastards, Stefan said without rancor.

Hunter wished he understood more, but he was willing to go along with this—he hoped.

It's important you stay hidden, Stefan reminded him.

That's the plan, he said. He watched as they pulled off to the side, where another vehicle was. *They've stopped. We're only maybe a few hundred meters from where she was. They just drove around in a circle.*

Partially to disorient her, if she were awake, Stefan said. *That's an old technique for keeping her lost and separated and isolated.*

I get it, he said, *but they're going through an awful lot of trouble for that. I don't think they have a whole lot available to them. So they're doing whatever they can.*

I don't know, but we need to follow through and figure it out, before she becomes so lost that there is no future for her.

"Which is another scary thought," Hunter muttered to himself, and not one he planned to entertain. He kept watching from the darkness, keeping his energy tight, close against his body, in case these people were the scary energy workers she thought they were. The jury was still out on that, as far as he was concerned.

So far, Hunter hadn't seen anything scary about them, just irritating and frustrating—aggravating, as they preyed on children. Children who became women who were vulnerable to whatever particular brand of poison they were serving. These guys were assholes, no doubt about it; the question was whether any answers could be found here, or if there would only be more questions.

As he watched, she was lifted and carried inside a broken-down building that looked to be barely standing. Whatever had happened here had left them without much of a home base. Good or bad, Hunter didn't know, but they were still utilizing it—surely not permanently. It would likely only be for whatever purposes they were dealing with right now.

Hunter watched as they carried her in. He parked the bike in the shadows, out of sight, camouflaged it with branches to give himself an exit when the opportunity arrived, then cloaked his energy, as Peter was probably here, and followed them inside. As soon as he got to the doorway, he stopped, looked around. They were a long way away. They'd gone down a hallway that had almost no roof, even above the structure. This wasn't the records building that he and Beth had searched earlier. This was a second building still standing that had obviously been damaged by whatever blast had happened here.

As he looked around, everything coming to a central courtyard, but the damage looked like it happened somewhere there and had blasted outward. The buildings on the outside perimeter were still standing, but the ones on the inside circle were just piles of rubble. He shook his head, and, instead of going inside the building, he crept along the outside, down to where she had been taken.

He was horrified, as he watched through cracks in the building, when she was placed on a bed and quickly clamped in place and locked, and then a door, whatever part of a door that remained, was closed behind them. The two men spoke quietly for a moment and then disappeared down the last remaining hallway.

Hunter hesitated. His natural instinct was to rescue her before they could hurt her more. But, damn it. He had to let this play out here.

Noting exactly where she was, he followed the two men down to the far side and lost track of them, as they exited the building. He saw no other building or part of a building here. He saw a generator and a battery system, where somebody had attempted to make coffee. He shook his head at that. Obviously this was not a permanent setup, so what the hell was going on?

Just as he turned to slide back around, he caught sight of somebody coming toward him. Even though his energy was cloaked, he remained visible to everyone. He raced into the woods, keeping his presence a secret. And that's where he stayed until the morning light broke through the sky. At that, he felt her stirring and waking up.

He smiled. "Keep fighting the good fight, little one."

Too bad he couldn't be in there and fight it with her. But she had brought this on herself, and clearly she needed to bring this to some conclusion. All he could do was hope that he was around when the time came to help her out. But he couldn't do it right now. It wouldn't achieve the results *she* needed, so he had to wait. He had to be patient and see just what the hell would happen.

Patiently waiting was never his gift.

CHAPTER 31

B ETH REMAINED QUIET, knowing this waiting game was part of her test. When she heard a voice again, she thought it was Hunter. She frowned and called out, "Hunter?" But there was no answer. She shook her head, wondering just what was going on. She heard Lizzy's voice in the background.

Remember. Remember. Remember.

But now it sounded like a broken record, as in, seriously a record player just on an endless loop. A horrible thought came to her mind. What if that's all Beth had been hearing all this time? Was it Lizzy's voice on a recording? Maybe Lizzy wasn't haunting her after all. Maybe Beth was haunted sheerly by the fact that she couldn't get Lizzy's voice out of her mind. Maybe some of their bloody testing had gone wrong, and something had been emblazed into Beth's brain instead of somebody else's. She frowned at that because that would be an easy answer. She could get up from here and walk away, and she would be fine.

She looked at the bindings holding her fast and shook her head. They would never hold her. People just didn't understand that, and, when desperation hit, it took an awful lot to keep somebody secured. Once they were secured, not so bad, but getting them there? That was a different story, especially in her case. She didn't get held easily. And, with that revelation, she had to study her whole scenario going in.

If they could not hold her here at the compound, if that were truly the case, why was she here? Why had she been here at any point in time? It made no sense. Unless she was a willing participant in all of this. Her stomach sank, as she thought about all the pain she'd been part of, wondering if that was even possible to consider. And, of course, impossible *not* to consider it once it hit her brain. Yet … she had been a child. A child can't be held responsible for this. She took a long slow deep breath and let it out, then did it again and again.

"Good," he said. "You're calming down."

"I haven't been very upset," she murmured.

"No, but enough. We need you to get started."

"And that would be fine," she said. "Let's get going." After a moment of startled silence, she shrugged. "Obviously that's the next step."

"That's true," he said cautiously. "I just wasn't expecting this much cooperation."

"Well, I'm tired of it," she snapped, "and I want this over with."

"I get that," he said. "Glad to hear it."

She nodded. "Here?"

"No, we'll go down to the lab."

"Good enough," she said. She lifted her wrists. "Do I need the chains?"

"You always did have the chains, so let's keep everything the same then."

She could tell that, once again, she'd floored him with that. "Do you expect me to fight my bonds?"

"Well, you always did."

"Which means you had a way to keep me here."

"Of course, but mostly by choice."

"Mostly only afterward."

"True," he said cautiously. "What do you remember?"

"Nothing," she said. "That's why I'm here."

"Good," he said. A whisper of voices came behind her that she didn't understand, but she heard someone.

A stranger approached and unlocked her bonds. He assisted her upright and then said, "Follow me." She followed him, wondering who he was. She looked over to see Peter, the same man who had followed her to Hunter's cabin.

"Glad you got away," she said.

He nodded slightly. "Takes a lot to keep me down."

"I remember." And she did remember. He had a huge will, and sometimes she'd wondered if he was even human because of it. He looked at her steadily, and just more unsettled confusion was inside him. And that was good. If she could keep him off-balance, maybe she could get out of this alive.

She still didn't understand anything, and maybe that was her own fault, but she was here right now, and they needed to do whatever needed to be done to get this nightmare over with. She followed as directed, and she sat where she was told to. And, when she finally sank into the seat, it felt oddly familiar. She looked around, but nothing in the actual location felt familiar. But the seat? She shifted in it and then frowned. "This is my old chair."

"It is."

"Good," she said, settling back. "That'll be easier." And again she could sense that she'd unsettled him. She waited.

"Okay, we'll start now."

"Fine. What are we starting?"

"You don't remember, do you?"

"I've told you that before."

"Well, I've understood that you haven't, … that you don't remember a lot," he said cautiously, "but I don't understand how much you do remember."

"Basically nothing," she said, with a wave of her hand. "So let's get on with it, and do whatever we need to do."

He nodded and stepped in front of her. He looked at her closely and said, "If you don't remember, it won't work."

"Well, it needs to work," she stated.

"But you've tried to remember, haven't you?"

"Didn't work," she said, with a nod.

"In that case," he said, "what makes you think it'll work now?"

"Well, I assumed you had some ability to make me remember," she said, staring at him. "Are you saying, after all of this fuss to get me here, that you don't?"

He hesitated, and then he said, "I do." And, without warning, he lifted his hand, holding a handgun, and he shot her.

She cried out, as the pain racked through her shoulder.

"Remember," he called out, his voice harsh. And he fired the gun again. This one went into her arm, and the third hit her thigh. By now she was screaming at the top of her lungs, and he was roaring, "Remember. Remember."

Then finally she passed out. And remembered nothing.

HUNTER HEARD THE first shot and then the second and third, followed by the screaming. He raced to the building, with no idea what the hell was going on. It took him a while to find where she was because they had moved her, but, even as Hunter raced through the hallway, the gun went off one more time. In the distance, he heard her scream, and then it suddenly cut off to a horrible silence.

Determined, he made it through the barrier to see the guard standing there and staring in shock. A quick scan of his aura showed no psychic gifts in him. Hunter turned to look and there was Beth, tied to a chair, strapped down and bleeding all over the floor. He could hardly rein in his anger, his need to act.

Stand down, Hunter, Stefan said. *This is her show. Let us give it a bit more time. She's seeking answers and we're definitely learning more about her own gifts.*

Peter stood in front of her with a handgun, screaming at her. Hunter completely froze for a long moment. The guard remained off to the side, his arms crossed over his chest, completely ignoring the scenario.

Well, that's one thing Hunter couldn't do. As he raced forward to Peter, he heard her screaming back at her abuser.

"Remember what?" she roared. "Remember what? I can't remember anything!"

"Well, it's the only way to do this," he said. And he lifted the handgun.

Hunter turned immediately to Beth, standing there, completely free of her restraints, blood pouring down her body, as she glared at Peter, the gun still in his hand.

"Remember," Peter ordered her.

And Hunter saw something in the expression on her face, as the horror, everything, rolled together.

And she snapped, "Oh, I remember." She reached up a hand, and just that movement had Peter bracing for it, as he saw the energy, a firebolt, that shot him backward.

He screamed at her, "No! Not that. Remember what happened to you."

345

"I remember," she screamed back at him.

"No," he said, "you don't. Remember Lizzy."

She stared at him for a moment, then seemed to crumple in on herself. "I killed my sister," she burst out, bawling.

Peter stood up on his feet, still holding the handgun as she collapsed, completely unconcerned with the injuries he'd given her. "No," he said, "you didn't."

She stared at him through her tears, shaking her head. "I don't understand. I don't understand."

"Your sister, *Sarah*, died, yes," he said. "She died not long after you got here. You were both very little, but she was weak, and you were strong."

"I could have looked after her," she said, glaring at him. "You wouldn't let me."

"You did look after her," he said calmly, quietly. "You looked after her as long as you could. But it was not to be."

"It could have been. We could have had a good life."

"No," he said. "She wasn't strong enough to survive."

"Only because of you."

"No," he said, shaking his head. "I know you want to believe that. I know you want to blame me," he said. "But, if you'll blame somebody, blame your mother who sold her."

"Sold her," she spat out, "to you."

"Yes, to my boss at least," he said, "and that was a good thing. Sarah would never have survived there anyway. I tried hard to keep her alive. She was special."

"So special," Beth said, shaking her head. "I still don't understand."

"That's because you won't remember," he said.

So much frustration was in his voice that Hunter didn't even know what to do. The guard looked at Hunter and whispered, "Don't stop this."

"Says you," Hunter said in an ugly tone, "he just shot her."

"But do you see her?" he asked. "Do you see that she's not bothered by four bullet holes?"

And, of course, that's the part that Hunter needed to zero in on.

"She's stronger than anybody I've ever seen," the guard said. "But she's so very disconnected from everything."

"Of course she is. Look at the abuse. Look at what she went through."

"But it's not what you think," the guard said. "Just wait."

Hunter realized that may be a viable answer, just that patience wasn't his strong point, as he stepped back into the shadows and watched.

She stood up once again. "My sister was precious."

"She was precious, and she survived for those first four years, but then she couldn't survive anymore. No matter how much energy you poured into her, she couldn't survive any longer."

She shook her head. "That's not true. You wouldn't let me do any more."

"Because nothing more could be done. It was killing you to help her."

Some of what was going on here could be the truth because Hunter had heard and had seen things like that before. And, if that were the case, then it could be quite true here. Beth would have hurt herself; she would have put herself in the grave in an effort to help somebody who was dying anyway.

"I had to stop it," Peter said.

"You didn't have to do anything," she stated. "She was

doing fine."

"No, she wasn't. And that's not what this is about."

"No, you took my best friend, and you turned her into my worst enemy," she roared. "You made me do things that I would never have done before."

"That," he said, with a nod, "is true. And, for that, I'm sorry. I thought that our research justified the means, until I realized what it did to you, and even then I couldn't see. I wouldn't allow myself to see. I wouldn't let anything stop us because I saw the value in it."

"And now?" she asked bitterly.

"Now I know I was wrong. Now I know some things have value that we don't always understand," he said, "and I pushed you too far, too hard."

She stared at him in shock. "That's almost like an apology."

He gave her a ghostly smile. "I don't know about that," he said. "That would be taking it a little too far, but I definitely did not push the line of what I *should have* done."

She shook her head. "Then why am I here?"

"You tell me," he said. "You came voluntarily."

"But you were the one hunting me."

"Yes," he said, "you need to remember."

"You keep saying that. I've been trying to remember. I can't. At least not what you say. I remember the years of abuse, all the testing, all those people we hurt."

He nodded. "And again, that's unfortunate."

"Unfortunate?" she said, staring at him. "That's what you call it? All those people dead?"

"They didn't all die," he said. "And lots of them were sick anyway. Many of them were mentally unstable."

"And what happened to them?"

"Some had to be terminated, yes," he said. "They were obviously very damaged and wouldn't survive. Some of them died on their own. Some of them had to go to a hospital and have since passed away. Doing this energy work took a toll that we didn't realize." He said, "I wouldn't have done it if I knew everybody would suffer so terribly."

"Yes, you would have," she said, staring at him. "You definitely would have. You didn't care. It was always about your results."

He winced. "I know. And that's what I'm saying. That's why you're here. That's why I'm trying to save you."

She shook her head. "No. It makes no sense that you would even try."

"Yes," he said. "I'm making this right, but you're the last one for me to deal with. And you're the hardest," he said. "I want to go to my grave, knowing that I at least tried to fix what I did wrong."

She stared at him. "You're dying?"

"I am," he hesitated.

She nodded. "So you want me to pour life into you?" She shook her head. "I can't do that."

"You don't know that," he said. "If we can help you to fix yourself," he said, "you can. I know you can because I saw firsthand everything that you were capable of doing."

"And you want me to do it for you?" She laughed. "Too bad you spent all those years abusing me, forcing me to hurt all those people."

"You weren't hurting them," he said. "We were running experiments."

"And they were being hurt through the experiments," she said, glaring at him. "And you wouldn't let it stop. You wouldn't let me stop. I had to do it. You didn't give me any other choice."

"You were very powerful," he murmured. "You were by far the best of everyone. We couldn't let you stop."

"Couldn't let me stop?" she said, with a headshake. "Every person I touched left a little bit of their tortured soul with me to deal with. And you couldn't let me stop? Not even to keep me sane and whole?"

"No," he said, "and then everything blew up."

"And that's the part I don't get," she said.

"That's because you won't remember," he said in frustration.

"Did you ever think that maybe I can't remember because something in me is damaged to the point that it can't heal, that it can't be fixed?"

He took several long deep breaths and said, "Yes, I considered it, but then I thought about you and all the things that you've done in your life, and it's quite possible that you could fix this. You may be quite capable of doing what needs to be done to fix yourself. Even if you can't help me."

She stared at him. "I think you're putting too much on me," she said. "There's a reason all of that is buried."

"Yes," he said, "because it's unpleasant, because you don't want to listen, because you don't want to believe. But that doesn't change the value of it."

She stared at him. "What is it that I'll find?" And she turned, looking around. "Where is Lizzy? In your horror chamber here?"

"Maybe that's what's missing," he said, staring at her. "Why don't you want to talk to Lizzy?"

"Why would I want to?" she said, staring at him. "Lizzy betrayed me. She hurt me."

"She didn't mean to hurt you," he said. "Again, you can

blame me if you want."

She spun to look at him. "What do you mean, *if I want?*"

He took another slow breath and said, "She was following my orders."

At that, she glared at him. "Of course she was. Everybody followed your orders. We had no choice."

"No," he said. "Some people had a choice. Some people didn't. You had less choice than others."

She stared at him. "You're still not making any sense."

"First, remember. Then heal yourself."

"And if I can't remember?"

"Then this is what your life is," he said. "You'll always be wondering, always be chased, always be hunted."

"Why?"

"Because I can't stop Lizzy," he roared. "Only you can."

CHAPTER 32

BETH STARED AT him in shock. Disbelief. Horror. She'd shut off all sensations to her wounds, shutting down in emergency mode. She could only keep it up for a little while. "That can't be," she said, and then she shook her head. "Did Lizzy go rogue?"

"That's one word for it," he said. "You have to stop her."

"And how do you expect me to do that?" she said bitterly. "Lizzy is …" And then she stopped, raising her hands in frustration. "Lizzy is Lizzy."

"Exactly," he said, "and we need you to stop her." He looked at her, at the guard, and then back at her again. "You do want to stop her, don't you?"

"Well, she has to be stopped," she said. "She's dangerous."

"She's out of control, and she's very dangerous," he said.

"Exactly," she said.

"So, if you can't remember, at least give us a hand at stopping her."

She frowned and said, "I don't want to do this, but I know that it needs to happen. Lizzy does need to be stopped," she admitted.

"Good," he said, "that's progress."

She shook her head. "No, I don't think it is—because I don't understand or trust in what you're after here. But I am willing to not look at that end game until I can help stop her."

"Fine," he said, "just do that much."

"And then what?" she said.

"And then, I don't know," he said. "That's up to you."

"I won't help you any further."

"Fine," he said, exhausted. "You don't have to. Let's just deal with this."

"Fine. But, when you get Lizzy here," she said, "you know there'll be hell to pay."

"There'll be hell to pay no matter what," he said. "I'm dying. I don't give a shit. But let's at least bring this to a conclusion. Bring her here."

She groaned and said, "And how do you expect me to bring Lizzy to you?"

"Call her," he said. "She always used to listen to you before."

"Before she moved to the dark side and became your puppet," she snapped.

He glared at her. "Just do it."

She looked down at her wounds and said, "I need to wash up."

He turned to the guard and said, "Bring her a bowl of warm water."

With that, the guard disappeared. She stared at Peter. "Why did you shoot me?"

"I was hoping the pain would cause you to remember."

"It's just pain," she said. "I've lived with it for so long that it's useless." She reached into one of the wounds and popped out the bullet and threw it on the floor. Then she did the same with the other three. "You know that most people would see me as a freak, right?"

"If they saw you right now, yes," he said, but still that same old fascination remained in his voice. He looked at her and said, "You're a marvel. You know that, right?"

She shook her head. "I am not a marvel in any way, shape, or form," she said. "I'm just one busted-up, broken-down, crazy-ass female, who's one step away from death. The only way I can do this right now is because I healed from the last injuries and had time to rest."

"No," he said, "I don't know about the rest of it, but you're not one step away from death. That was the one thing you could always keep at bay."

"And yet my twin sister died."

"She did, indeed," he said, "and, for that, I'm sorry, but she was always sickly."

She nodded. "She was at that. So much pain always gets very confused in my head."

"Mostly because everything's a mess in there," he said. "That's why you need to stop Lizzy."

"Because she's making it worse?"

"Yes, she is, and she doesn't mind doing it. It's fun for her."

"Well, that's because she's a mess herself," she said, "and you made us that way."

He groaned at that. "Well, let's leave off all the blame for now and get down to work."

Beth closed her eyes and called out, "Lizzy, it's time for us to settle this. I need you to come back again." The same laughing voice was in her head. "She's just telling me to remember. That's all she ever does."

He looked at her and said, "Remember? *That* recording?"

"I heard it earlier," she said. "Was Lizzy telling me to

remember, or has it been that recording?"

"Most of the time it's been the recording," he said. "I've been playing it for a long time. That was Lizzy's suggestion."

"Of course," Beth said, "it's also like some Chinese torture, hearing that thing over and over again."

"So deal with it."

She closed her eyes and called out, sending her energy as far out as she could. "Lizzy, come to me." When she heard nothing but laughter, she frowned and said, "She's not listening."

"You used to make her listen."

She nodded. "At one point in time I could, but she's being difficult."

"It's a part of who she is now."

"Yeah, rogue," she said, shaking her head. She closed her eyes and roared outward, "Lizzy, time to come home, time to deal with this problem. The two of us, we can meet and hash it out. We can finally be friends again." She didn't know about the friend part, but she thought she'd toss it out there. She had no idea why and how they'd become so estranged, but obviously there had been some horrific upset, something Beth had willingly blocked—mostly because, as far as she understood from the bits of memories that she had, Lizzy had done something Beth had totally disagreed with. Maybe time to look at her own judgments.

"Lizzy, I'm sorry," she said quietly. "I don't know what the hell's going on, but I'm a mess, and I need help." That was the first time she had admitted that too.

At that, Lizzy whispered, *Say you're sorry.*

"I'm sorry, Lizzy," she said immediately. Now she felt rather than saw the presence around her. "I recognize your energy now."

Peter nodded slowly. "If you've even remembered that, it's a good start."

"Maybe not," Beth said. "You weren't even the boss."

"No," he said, "I worked with the boss. I was part of the scenario, but I wasn't the leading part."

"Right," she said, "you were doing some fellowship."

He nodded slowly, but he eyed her carefully, as if he were more worried about what she would do.

"What's the matter?" she whispered.

"I'm just waiting," he said. "I know how volatile the two of you are when you get together."

She nodded. "That's because we were best friends, then separated by betrayal, and it just bites. Particularly considering we didn't get much of a life."

"I get it," he said. "But it wasn't me who kept you captive."

"Apparently not," she said, looking at him and really seeing him. "I didn't recognize you. I still don't."

"No. Life hasn't been all that easy for me."

"What happened to him? The boss."

"He died," he said, eyeing her carefully again.

"Great. I can't say I'm sorry."

"No, of course not. He did a lot of terrible things that made your life hell."

"Yes."

"But he didn't kill your sister," he reminded her.

"Apparently not," she said, frowning. "All of it is rolled up into one great big jumbled mess in my head."

He nodded slowly. "Keep that in mind."

She nodded. "Lizzy should be here soon."

"Good," he said. And in a move that made her completely stop and study him, he moved backward several steps.

She took a close look at her surroundings, oddly noting Hunter without comment. "What happened to this place?"

He frowned. "Well, let's talk about that, after Lizzy shows up."

"Did she have something to do with it?"

He nodded. "Yes, she did."

"Is she close physically?"

"She never leaves this area," he said. "So, yes, she's close."

"Did you have to pick her up?"

"No, she didn't want me to pick her up."

Beth nodded. "Lizzy was always independent."

"She was. She was also quite difficult."

"Of course she was, particularly after you guys treated her that way."

"Yes," he said diffidently. Finally a rustling in the shadows was heard outside. "There she is." He looked at Beth and spun away from the window almost fearfully.

"She's got you running scared, doesn't she?" Beth said with a smirk.

"Lizzy is very scary."

"Yeah, she is. So are you ready to face her?" she asked.

"I am," he said. "Are you?"

"Of course," she said, with a wave of her hand. "Lizzy and I were friends more than we were enemies," she said. "I'm hoping she'll talk to me. I think it's because she was jealous."

"You think so?"

"I think so," she said quietly.

"We'll see," he said. "Bring her in."

She shrugged and said, "Did you open the door for her?"

"It's open. I left it open for her," he said, "but, like you, she's also powerful."

"That's true. She wouldn't have to worry about a door, if she didn't want to."

"Exactly."

She smiled as she felt Lizzy's energy nearing them and said, "Lizzy, come on in."

After a moment of silence, then the partial door slowly opened wider. And in stepped Lizzy. Beth stared at her for a long moment.

"Oh, my God."

HUNTER CREPT OUT of the shadows, back up beside the guard, who reached out and grabbed him by the arm with a warning look. Hunter nodded. Again, the guard obviously wasn't here to hurt him, and Hunter had certainly heard enough so far to understand that something dramatic was happening here. But when the door opened and Lizzy stepped through in her ghostly form, he couldn't do anything but suck his breath back in shock.

The guard gripped Hunter's arm hard in warning.

Hunter stared at Lizzy. Back to Beth. Then again to Lizzy. Lizzy *was* Beth. He whispered, "Triplets?"

The guard shook his head. "No."

At the no, Hunter stared at the guard in shock. And then, riveted to the scene playing in front of him, he studied Lizzy's faint form. If not her twin—or a triplet with the addition of Sarah—Lizzy had to be a ghost. *Had* to be.

But Beth studied Lizzy with a sense of detachment and finally said, "You don't look so good," her tone blunt, as if uncaring.

Lizzy laughed. "Neither do you."

Beth frowned at that. "I guess that's true, isn't it?"

"Of course it is, and you should know by now that, if I don't look good, you don't look good."

"Well, you shouldn't have done this," Beth said.

"I haven't done anything," Lizzy snapped. "You're weak."

"No, you were hurting people."

"No, I haven't. I haven't hurt anybody." And she stared at Beth.

Something trickled down her spine, making Beth uneasy. She looked around to see Peter standing there, staring at her. "Oh, my God," she said. The room spun, and she blanked out.

Hunter stepped forward.

Frowning, Peter spun, extended his hands, yelling, "Don't touch either of them. You must stay out of this."

Hunter looked at him, at the Lizzy form, still standing, then visually checked on Beth, who had fallen to the floor, and said, "What the hell's going on?"

"You'll find out," he said, "but the only hope of saving Beth is to let this happen." He walked forward, picked up a bucket of water, and threw it on her. Hunter stepped back, even as his instincts drove him to shake Peter and stop his abuse.

But when Beth burst awake again, she glared at Peter. "Water treatment? Really?"

He said, "It's necessary."

She turned to look at Lizzy. "What did you do? Put him up to this?"

"I didn't put them up to anything," Lizzy said, crossing her arms over her chest. "You're the one who's dangerous as hell."

"No," Beth said. "I'm not."

"Why do you think he's torturing you like this then?"

"I don't know," she said. "Why?"

"Remember."

CHAPTER 33

B ETH STARED AT Lizzy, for the first time seeing how vapid and pale her energy was. "Are you a ghost?" she demanded.

"No, of course not," Lizzy said. "I need you to think back to that night."

"What night?"

"The night you escaped."

Beth nodded slowly. "Okay, what about it?"

"Do you remember the explosion?"

She frowned. "Vaguely. Noise and chaos, with screaming and some kind of ... explosion. Like a bomb going off. What was that?"

"Well, you could say it was almost like an atom splitting," Lizzy said, "but not so much an atom splitting as you splitting."

Beth stared at her in shock. "What are you talking about?"

"Do you know who I am?"

"You're ... You're ... You're Lizzy. My best friend."

"Of course," she said and gently smiled. "And the fact that you're here now is really good."

"Sure," Beth said, giving her an odd look. "You guys are worrying me."

"No, we aren't worrying you," Lizzy said. "We're making you feel better, to be better."

"This way?" she said. "With water torture?" she asked Peter.

"It's necessary. Remember that night?"

"Yes, the one with the explosion. I know," Beth said, "but I don't know what caused the explosion." She turned to look at Lizzy. "Was it you?"

"It was *you*," Lizzy said firmly. "You're the one who caused it."

"What did I do?"

"You were hurting, and another person had died, and you'd just had it. It was your last straw, and you lost it, screaming as long and as hard as you could." She paused for a moment. "think of the cat you loved more than life itself. It died that night too."

"Ouch," she said, staring at Lizzy, but the memories rushed back. Nocturne. Memories rushed in on her. Her beloved pet. Only allowed on sufferance as it kept her calm and his life always held over her head to keep her compliant.

"My God, you were testing somebody." She turned to look at Peter, who immediately shook his head.

"Not me. The boss, yes. And you were testing the male subject, being used as a backdrop for him, and the test subject couldn't handle it. He went insane, but the insanity just carried on right into death."

"Oh, my God. I remember. His eyes rolled into the back of his head, like he had had a heart attack right in front of us. Only terrible convulsions and a terrible scream coming from his mouth."

"Yes," Peter said, nodding. She stared at him. "That was terrible and the last straw for you," Peter said, smiling with encouragement.

"Yes," she said, "I remember that." She turned to Lizzy. "I remember screaming at the top of my lungs."

"And that's what happened. As soon as you started screaming, you did something, and the whole place blew."

Beth stared at Lizzy in shock. "I caused that blast?"

Lizzy nodded. "Yes, you did. You caused it."

She sagged in the chair. "Oh, my God. Did I kill anyone?"

Slowly Peter nodded. "You killed the boss."

She stared at him, shaking her head. "No, no, no. I couldn't have."

"You did," he said, "but that may have been something that needed to happen. I don't know. But you did something else that night too."

"What did I do?" she asked.

Peter hesitated, turned to Hunter and the guard standing there. "Your scream," he said, "it's like you couldn't handle another death, so you split everything apart, into what you could handle and what you couldn't handle."

She stared at him, uncomprehending. "That doesn't make any sense."

"And until I saw it happen," he said, "I'd never seen anything like it before. But it's true."

"But what did I do exactly?"

He took a deep breath. "Your complete energy split. It's like it blew apart with the explosion."

"Okay," she said, "but I obviously pulled myself together enough because I escaped."

"You did because one of the guards was running to get the hell away, and you got into the vehicle with him. He stopped and got out when he realized you were in the car with him, and he ran away and died."

"What do you mean, he died?" she asked, staring at him. "He wasn't killed?"

Peter shook his head. "His body is still out there in the woods. We didn't do anything because we weren't sure what to do or who to tell or how to even explain it."

"Then how did he die?"

"I think at the time he had a heart attack. He was running flat-out into the brush, and we never saw him again. Apparently you just found him, during your last trip here."

"The skeleton that Hunter and I found?" She stared at Peter in shock.

He nodded. "Yes."

"Okay," she shrugged. "Well, I don't remember that. I remember escaping."

"Yes," he said, "you did escape, or at least part of you escaped. The other part took an escape route that you didn't expect."

"What do you mean?" she said, staring at him, bewildered.

"He means me," Lizzy said, stepping forward.

Beth stared at Lizzy. "You escaped?"

"I did," she said. "But it isn't exactly the way I expected to."

Beth stared at her for a crazy moment, saying, "I don't get it."

"That's because you don't want to get it," Lizzy said quietly. "But it's simple." And she stepped closer and closer and closer.

"Wait," Beth said. "Don't hurt me."

Lizzy stopped. "I don't intend to hurt you," she said. "What I'm hoping to do is pull you back together again." And then she stopped, looked at her, and said, "Or maybe I should say pull us back together again."

Beth gasped, then stared at her old friend in shock, with a terrible awareness. "Oh ... my God," she said.

Lizzy nodded ever-so-slowly. "Yes," she said, walking closer and closer, until she stood before her. "I am you, and you are me. And, in that explosion, you divided your energy into two separate existences. An existence you have spent a lifetime hiding from, and I've spent a lifetime chasing. We are one and the same." And, with that, she stepped into and through Beth.

HUNTER WATCHED IN shock, as a weird *poof* sound could be heard around him, followed by a blending of colors and light, almost in a kaleidoscope, and then, just like that, it stopped. He took several steps forward, watching as Beth slowly opened her eyes. He crouched down in front of her. "Beth?"

She stared at him, both a worldly shock and a knowing inside her. "Dear God," she whispered.

Peter stepped forward from behind and asked, "Now do you remember?"

She looked up at him and slowly nodded, her gaze going from Hunter to Peter. "Yes," she said, "I do. So much of it." Tears filled her eyes. "I kept asking everyone to stop the testing. I knew that the man was suffering terribly, that he wasn't handling it, and that it was killing him. But nobody would stop."

Peter nodded. "That was the boss. A man so full of his own goals that nothing else and nobody else mattered."

Tears filled her eyes and slowly dripped down her cheeks. She wiped her eyes, then turned to look at Hunter.

"My name isn't Beth."

Peter stepped forward again.

Hunter looked at him, then at Beth, asking, "What do you mean?"

"My name is Lizbeth," she said, her voice so very faint. "I always had this part of me that argued with me all the time, telling me to stop this and to do more to fight back, and then this other part of me was saying I couldn't and that there was nothing I could do. I was in a situation that I could in no way win, and, if I did fight back, it would just mean more pain and more torment for us all."

Hunter understood. "So when you did fight back, this person died."

"You mean, I killed him," she said bluntly.

He winced. "That was hardly your doing and not your fault."

"It felt like it was my fault," she said, the tears now a steady stream down her cheeks. "And when that happened," she said, "it was like a scream going off in my head of 'No more! Stop this!' And the only thing I could apparently think to do was to split my energy in two. Nocturne got caught in the blast at the same time. He's still caught. Neither here nor there. Or maybe he just stays because he loves me." She gave a shudder and lifted her hand. "I feel weird."

"Of course you do," Hunter said quietly. "It's been a long time since you've had this collectiveness around you."

"It's why Lizzy always followed me, why she was always hunting me."

"She wasn't hunting you. She was getting back together again with you, but, at the same time, she could never leave because she was you."

"That's why she always found me," she said, with a ghost

of a smile, "because she, ... she was me."

"Exactly," he said quietly. He shook his head and turned to look at Peter and the guard, studying her carefully. "You're looking like she's still a bomb about to go off."

"If you'd seen what she did," Peter said, "then it would be something you'd be wary of too."

"It was pretty scary at the time for me too," said Lizbeth.

"Of course," Peter said. "I guess I'm just not sure that you won't blow up again."

She smiled. "Oh God, I hope not." But she looked at Hunter. "I can't make any guarantees."

"Of course you can," Hunter said, "because the thing is, you won't be in that testing scenario anymore. You'll be free, and we'll get Dr. Maddy to help heal you and give you the time you need, so you can function properly."

"I'm not a test case or a sacrifice case," she said, "so you don't have to look after me."

"No more of that talk," he said. "I think you've been through enough."

"Well, she has, and she hasn't," the guard said, staring at her.

"What do you mean?" Hunter turned to face him.

"You see? One of the reasons why Peter used Lizbeth all the time was because she was so powerful, and sometimes she would hide away and pretend to be unconscious or incapable of working. She was very good at hiding her skills."

"And how do you know this?" Hunter asked the guard.

The guard gave Hunter a ghost of a smile. "Because the boss was my father."

She gasped at that. "Now I remember you," she said, staring at him. "You've changed."

"We all have," he said. "I grew up watching you."

She shook her head. "That's not healthy. What your father did wasn't healthy."

"No," he said quietly, "it wasn't. But he had his reasons."

"Such as?" she challenged.

"He thought you could do so much good."

"Good?" she cried out, staring at him. "What good did I do? We tested psychics constantly. I was forced to push them to their limits, otherwise get punished myself," she said bitterly. "And most of them couldn't handle it."

"No, they couldn't, but the ones who did became very strong."

"I don't even know who they are," she said, with a wave of her hand. "I don't even know where they are."

"He worked with them closely for a long time. He was just driven. Possessed with figuring out how to make somebody stronger and better. You were the strongest that he had, and every time you worked with somebody, you became better, so he kept pushing you, more for your sake than for the other person."

"And that's just wrong," she said, staring at him bitterly. "Because it wasn't for me, it was for himself."

"Yes," he said, "that's true."

She slowly rubbed her face.

"It'll take a while," Hunter murmured, gently reaching out a hand to touch her, feeling the shock and tingling as his energy touched hers. Weird, a sensation of … everything.

"It's also why Peter found us." She nodded slowly. "Because he was always in tune with me back then, weren't you, Peter?" She looked at him and smiled. "And, of course, you were there when Lizzy became her own person."

Hunter sat back, looked at her, and said, "When Lizbeth

became Lizzy and Beth."

"Yes," she said.

"And your twin sister?"

She smiled. "*Sarah*. She didn't survive very long. I have very little recollection of her. At the time I just remembered needing to keep her safe, but she was always sick," she said sadly.

"I'd been wondering if Lizzy was your twin sister," Hunter said. "Or a triplet even."

She stared at him and then slowly shook her head. "I wish she were," she said. "I'm afraid it's even stranger. Lizzy was a part of me I always talked to, as if she were my best friend. I was so alone and lonely."

"And yet now," Hunter said, reaching out a hand and sliding it over hers, gently caressing her skin, "you're whole again."

She took a long slow deep breath—once, twice, three times. She shifted, almost like struggling into a suit that had become misaligned. "Yes," she said, with a bright smile. She looked around at the broken-down building. "Did I really do all this?"

Peter nodded. "Yes, you did," he said. "It happened so fast. And, yes, people were caught in the blast, a lot were injured. It went down in history as a crazy phenomenon."

"And the police?" Hunter turned and looked at Peter.

He shook his head. "No. We took care of our own, and everybody scattered. Obviously the project, along with the boss, was dead."

"And where is he?"

Peter hesitated. "He's buried out back," he said, with a shrug, "as are a couple lab techs, who were here at the time and didn't make it."

She stared, feeling terrible at all she had done.

Hunter looked down to see her bottom lip trembling. He squeezed her fingers. "It's not your fault. Everything that had happened to you built up to that point."

"And how do I stop it from happening again?" she whispered.

He pulled her close and said, "You don't get into that situation again, that's how." He smiled, leaned over, kissing her gently on the cheek, said, "And I can help with that." She wrapped her arms around him, and he felt her slight frame shaking. He closed his arms securely around her and whispered, "It'll be okay."

"Maybe not," said the young guard.

Hunter turned to look at him. "What do you mean?"

The guard held a gun pointed toward all three of them. He motioned at Peter. "Go stand over there with them," he said.

Peter looked at him. "Harry, what are you doing?"

"I didn't think you'd get her back together," he said, "but, now that you have, do you think I'll lose this opportunity?"

"What are you talking about?" Peter said in shock. "The whole goal was to save the one person who needed saving."

"Who said she needed saving?" Harry asked. "We should have just caged her. Do you think I didn't understand what my father was doing? He was controlling the most powerful person we've ever seen."

"Exactly," Peter said emphatically. "*Control.* She's a human being, her own person. We've done enough to torture her."

Hunter agreed, but he saw that Harry wasn't having it. "So you're interested in carrying on the boss's work, are you?" Hunter asked calmly.

Harry laughed. "I've got a new lab all set up," he said in a conversational tone. "I have all his notes, all his history. I did all his computer work and backed up everything."

"And what? You think I'll be taken prisoner again?" she asked in astonishment.

"Sure," he said. "Why wouldn't you? Bullets may not kill you easily, but they'll kill loverboy."

She stiffened in his arms. "So, you plan on hurting him to get my cooperation?"

"Why not?" he said. "It's a system that works over and over again."

She glared at him. "Maybe not," she said. "I think I've had enough of hurting other people."

"You're only good if you can do something with that energy," he said. "Otherwise you might as well be dead. Because you're a danger if you're not."

"I'm no danger to anybody anymore," she said. "I just want to spend the rest of my life learning what life is really like."

"Well, that'll never happen," Harry said. "So you're coming along as my prisoner or loverboy dies. What'll it be?"

She stared at Harry in shock, then looked up at Hunter.

"Yeah, loverboy won't get you the answers you want because I'll take him out," Harry stated.

She stared at Peter. "Harry's been helping you all this time?"

"Yes," he said sadly, turning to look at Harry. "You don't have to do this. Look at what she did to this place," he said, in horror and shock and wonder. "She blew it up all at once."

"What makes you think I won't do that again?" she

asked Harry curiously.

"Well, I won't push you as hard or as fast. I have my father's notes. I won't make the same mistake he did."

"So you plan to create an army all of your own?"

"Why not?" he said. "It sounds good to me." He waved the handgun. "Now, move away from her, loverboy."

HUNTER SAID, "NOPE, not happening."

"Really?" Harry said, with a big grin. "I'm the one holding the gun. Remember?"

"And I've seen assholes like you before," Hunter said, with a calmness that he didn't feel. He sent out probes, looking for anything in this guy's energy that Hunter could track. If he could track it, he could possibly shut it down. "I'm checking out your energy," he said. "And all kinds of energy are in your aura, especially your father's."

"Sure, we've always been close."

At that, Lizbeth—and he was struggling to not call her Beth—whispered, "No, you're right. Something else happened in that blast, didn't it?"

Harry looked at her. "What are you talking about?"

"When did you feel like you needed to do this?" Hunter asked.

"Right from the beginning, of course." Harry turned and looked at Hunter funny and said, "What are you talking about? Did you do something to me, Lizbeth?"

In Hunter's arms, Lizbeth shook her head and said, "Nothing. I didn't do anything."

"Are you sure?" Harry said, staring at her, but fear was in his eyes.

She gave him a fat smile. "You'll never know, will you?"

He raised the gun.

She smiled and said, "If I can do what I did, who knows what else I can do?" she said. "Maybe I left some of Lizzy out there. Maybe I left part of her and part of me all over the place."

Hunter looked at her. "That's what happened at Stefan's, isn't it?"

She nodded. "Every time I get exhausted, I fragment," she murmured. "So, at that point in time, it wasn't any surprise that bits and pieces of me are everywhere."

Hunter said, "You could do that again. You're probably tired enough."

She looked at him and asked, "What do you mean?"

He said, "I'm pretty sure if you think about it ..."

She looked at him, turned to look at Harry, and said, "Harry?"

"What?" he asked, waving the gun around. "I don't like this," he said. "I feel like you're ganging up on me."

"Well, you could check behind you," she said, her eyes glowing with an unearthly light.

"Why?" Harry asked, taking several steps back, and froze, spun around, and cried out. "No, no, no," he said.

"Put the gun down," Lizzy cried out, a fragment standing behind him, in the same form of Lizbeth who talked to him. He turned to look back at Beth, and he fired, but at the images behind him. Immediately Hunter pulled her out of the way and tucked her and Peter behind a wall, where they were safe.

Harry cried out.

Another Lizzy fragment showed up on his left, asking, "What good will screaming do?"

Now half-crazy, Harry turned to shoot again. But, as the

bullets never reached his target, Harry just looked at Hunter, as he stepped closer and closer.

"Oh, my God," Harry said. "You're one of them."

Hunter nodded. "I am, indeed. What will you do about it?"

As if realizing he could do absolutely nothing, Harry turned the gun to his own head and pulled the trigger.

Hunter rushed forward, as the other two raced up to Harry's side.

"That's not what I thought he'd do," Lizbeth cried out.

"No, but maybe it's the best thing after all."

She nodded and said, "Well, it's an answer. I don't know about the right one." She looked at Peter. "However, thank you for getting Lizzy back to me."

He gave her a sad smile. "Don't thank me," he said. "I just needed it to come to an end, so I could move on."

Hunter understood. "It's quite something when you're part of it and when you can see the damage done."

"So much damage over the years," he said. "I hated that I was involved, but it was supposedly science, supposedly all in the name of science." He shook his head. "The boss had grants, big-money grants. Private companies were paying for all that research to find psychics, others as powerful as Lizbeth was. He just didn't ever respect the limits that a person could be pushed to—before they cracked."

"Well, that's a good one," she said, "because that's what happened, isn't it? I popped. I feel like there are cracks in me even now."

"No," he said. "There *were* cracks. Just before you and Lizzy joined again," he said. "Yes, there were cracks, but your skin is smooth now, and, given some time for you to blend again," he said, "you'll be fine."

376

She nodded ever-so-slowly and whispered to Hunter, "Thank you."

Hunter leaned over, kissed her gently, and said, "No. Thank you for showing me something else in life that I'd never seen before—and for being who you are. An honest, trustworthy, beautiful soul."

She opened her mouth to protest, and he placed a finger against it. "Stop," he said. "What you went through was horrible, but you are not to blame. And now we'll spend the rest of our lives moving forward together, where you'll learn that lesson over and over again. That is, if you want to."

She kissed him gently and said, "I'm all for that." She focused on Peter. "And you?"

"I'm good. I'm going back East to my family," he said. "I've learned a lot of lessons," he said, "and the biggest one is what is really important in life. And it's not science." He gave them a sad smile and said, "Now, if you don't mind, you need to get out of here, while I deal with the rest of this."

She looked around, winced, and nodded. "What will you do with Harry?"

"I'll bury him with his father, and he'll be another cold case, a missing person nobody will ever know what happened to," he said. "No other way to have this make sense."

"Yes, there is," Hunter said. "Let me handle it."

Peter looked at him. "Are you sure?"

Hunter nodded. "I have people who can handle this."

"In that case," Peter said, "I'm out of here. I don't have much time left, and I want to spend it with those I love." And with a hand lifted, he took off.

She looked at Hunter. "Stefan?"

He nodded. "Yes, Stefan. We have quite a law enforcement network that can handle this. Just give me a few minutes." He pulled out his phone, sent a text message, and said, "We'll have to stick around here, until it's cleaned up."

"That's fine," Lizbeth said. "I wouldn't mind exploring and putting some of the memories into the right places." At that she heard a meow.

"Nocturne." She bent down to her huge black cat winding through her legs. "I was afraid I lost you in that nightmare."

He jumped into her arms and rubbed up against her. She hugged him close tears in her eyes. *Thanks for being here my friend.*

His engine kicked into high gear. *Always.*

She gripped him tighter, delighted to be able to keep the one constant thing in her life.

"As long as Nocturne will keep an eye on you," he said with a knowing look at her arms, "and as long as you stay close. No more running away?"

She looked up at him, laughed, and said, "I'm not planning on running away again. Unless it's running toward the bed in the cabin for an encore."

"I'll lead the way, if that's your destination. As for disappearing, well, as long as you know," he said, "even if you do, I won't be far behind you."

And he gave her a big smile, wrapped her up in his arms, and held her close.

This concludes Book 19 of Psychic Visions:
Snap, Crackle….
Read about What If…: Psychic Visions, Book 20

What If...: Psychic Visions (Book #20)

Detective Abigail Cartwright has earned a reputation for solving weird homicide cases, but, when she's called to a lecture hall at the local university, she faces the oddest one yet. During a What If ... lecture, run by soon-to-be-retired Professor Gertrude Milligan, two students died. Without any signs of how or why.

Confused, Abby digs in to solve the mystery, only to find several old cases connect—or do they? Were the two students murdered, or was something else going on?

Professor Leon Wellington is worried about his aunt Gertie. Their personal history was bad enough, but to have two of her favorite students die right in front of her has left her shocked and grieving. How can she not be a prime suspect in this case? Then she goes missing ...

When the past collides with the present, the stakes are higher than ever, as a killer realizes how close he is to losing everything ...

Find Book 20 here!

To find out more visit Dale Mayer's website.

https://geni.us/DMWhatIfUniversal

Sneak Peek from What If...

Professor Gertrude Milligan strode down the stairs, studying the empty amphitheater. She was ready for her class, but, as always, she was a few minutes early. She liked to settle into the space alone, before the doors opened. It helped. After all these years, teaching was getting longer and harder, and she just wanted to sit down, have a cup of tea. But this philosophy class called What If? was one she enjoyed teaching, and she was here, bright and early.

As she approached the main platform area, she walked to the podium and dumped her paperwork on top of it. She rolled her neck slightly and stretched her shoulders back. She was coming to the end of her reign. She wasn't quite ready to give up, but, at sixty-five, she knew it was time. Giving up her research would bother her the most. She absolutely loved the research. She didn't mind the kids. Some of them were even incredibly intelligent and kept her hopping. They kept her mind going.

And the rest of them were just here because they needed the credits, before they moved on to the rest of their dull, boring lives that had absolutely nothing to do with the *what ifs* in the world, and that was a damn shame.

She walked to the chalkboard, wincing, because of course nobody had cleared off the last lecture. She quickly took the eraser and wiped down the board, wrote the name of her current lecture at the top, and underneath it wrote WHAT IF? in large bold lettering. Then, just as the doors opened, she turned toward the class. She walked back and forth on the platform, keeping her mind open, thinking about the million things in her day, until slowly the trickle of students came in.

After a glance at her watch, she called out, "Two minutes." And it always seemed like, in that last minute, about half of the class poured in. She frowned at the noisy group. All of them knew her by now. They'd been in her class for at least three months, and they were coming to the end of the term, and exams were coming up. She was ready, but she didn't think they were.

A class like this was supposed to make you think, to keep you on your toes, and to keep your brain nimble. Instead it seemed to have the opposite effect and put so many of these kids to sleep. As she looked at some of the older students, they were hardly kids anymore. A couple were under twenty, but most of them were in their early twenties, midtwenties, late twenties. She knew at least one was in her midforties. She even had a couple in their sixties here.

"Time," she called out.

The two students closest to the doors got up, let in a few scrambling students, and then closed and locked the doors. She was strict on that. There were to be no interruptions. If you couldn't be here on time, you couldn't be allowed to disrupt the rest of her class. She waited a moment for everybody to calm down and to stop shuffling. And then she started.

"Good morning, everyone. Glad to see you could make it so early." They all cracked a smile. "I know. Lots of final projects, lots of exam studying to do as we begin next week," she said. "This is our last lecture class, but don't worry. You've come this far, and you'll make it." A twitter of laughter echoed through the group. She smiled and said, "As always, we're talking *what if*s. We already discussed in this class, *What if aliens arrived? What if Armageddon happened? What if a third world war happened?*

"Today, as in some of the other topics, this one will be completely different. We'll discuss psychic phenomena. But not just any psychic phenomenon, because, of course, it's a very wide field. There are psychics, and then there are mediums, who don't necessarily consider themselves psychics, like the aura readers, the healers, all kinds of different classifications and groups. But I want to talk about something completely different today because, of course, my mind always thinks in terms of *what if,*" she said, looking around at the class, noting that everybody leaned forward with interest. "Say, for example," she stated, pointing to the row in front, where three girls sat together. The same three who'd sat there all semester. They were fun loving and she had a soft spot for each of them. She smiled at them. "Say these three girls were targeted."

At that, the girls straightened up and one asked, "Targeted for what?"

Gertrude laughed. "I don't mean *targeted,* targeted. I don't mean to be stalked or with a target on your back or with a gun or something. But let's just say, what if you had a back door into your mind? What if other people had a way to put ideas in your head? What if people could control your thinking? What if people not only controlled your thinking but your actions? Has anybody ever thought about this?"

A couple students put up their hands.

She continued, "And you're thinking more of the movies, aren't you? Like, you know, mind control and other things like that, right?"

They both nodded.

"Right? So think about psychics, think about energy,

think about people who can heal somebody else just by waving their hands over the surface of an injury and pouring supposedly loving energy into that area. What about people who can stand here and look at you and see your past life all in your energy?" she said, waving her hand around one of the male students standing off to the side. "They can check out your history. They can go into something called akashic records—the Book of Life—and see all kinds of stuff.

"And then we have others, energy forms, where people have hooks into each other because, of course, we either love or hate them. These can form at birth, and they can continue right through your death. Sometimes people say diseases can be caused this way because you're so full of other people's negative energy that you poison your own soul," she murmured. "But what if—now think about this," she said, "what if there was a back door to your mind? And somebody else had access?"

She looked at the three girls and said, "I mean, just what if somebody stood up here today, without you even knowing it, and could get into your mind, while you sat here in class. What if that were possible? Now think about it, and then raise your hands and toss out the possibilities of what we could be looking at."

After that, it was a little slow to start, but then people came up with myriad ideas about how to run countries, how to control somebody's love life, how to gain access to bank accounts, how to control relationships. She nodded and wrote a lot of them on the board.

"Think bigger. Think World War Three," she said. "What if somebody was controlling somebody else from a distance? I mean, just because we have a back door to the mind, does that mean the person has to be sitting right beside you in order to control your mind?" She looked at the girls and said, "What if the one in the middle could access the two outer girls of this group?"

The girls just looked at her, and the one in the center, Carrie, said, "I don't think I like being here."

Gertrude laughed. "Think about it. What if somebody from somewhere else in the world had access because energy ..." and she turned to look at the class and said, "Energy ..."

And the class cried out, "Has no boundaries. There is no life. There is no death. Energy is forever. Energy only transforms. So what if?"

By the time the hour-long class was more or less done, it had been a very animated session, and she was delighted. She readied the last of the homework for her next class and said, "It's that time, and it's been a pleasure, everybody. Good job. Feel free to take off, to get ready for your exams, and we'll see you next term, maybe," she said. "If not, have a good life."

And, with that, everybody gathered up their stuff.

She walked over to the board, grabbed the eraser, and started clearing off all the notes that she had put there. A small shriek and a weird silence had her turning to look. She asked, "What's the matter?"

While everybody else was still streaming out the doors up at the top, an entire group of people around the front row just stared at her and then looked at where the group of girls had been sitting.

"We forgot one *what if,*" said Carrie in the middle, who now stood, her voice high and strained.

"What's that?" Gertrude asked.

"What if the back door to the mind," she said, "could

kill someone?"

Gertrude shrugged and said, "Well, if anything else is possible, that is too. Why?" she asked.

Carrie looked at her professor in shock, then turned to look at the girls seated on either side of her and said, "Because both of them are dead."

Find Book 20 here!

To find out more visit Dale Mayer's website.

https://geni.us/DMWhatIfUniversal

Simon Says... Hide: Kate Morgan (Book #1)

Welcome to a new thriller series from *USA Today* Best-Selling Author Dale Mayer. Set in Vancouver, BC, the team of Detective Kate Morgan and Simon St. Laurant, an unwilling psychic, marries all the elements of Dale's work that you've come to love, plus so much more.

Detective Kate Morgan, newly promoted to the Vancouver PD Homicide Department, stands for the victims in her world. She was once a victim herself, just as her mother had been a victim, and then her brother—an unsolved missing child's case—was yet another victim. She can't stand those who take advantage of others, and the worst ones are those who prey on the hopes of desperate people to line their own pockets.

So, when she finds a connection between more than a half-dozen cold cases to a current case, where a child's life hangs in the balance, Kate would make a deal with the devil himself to find the culprit and to save the child.

Simon St. Laurant's grandmother had the Sight and had warned him that, once he used it, he could never walk away. Until now, her caution had made it easy to avoid that first step. But, when nightmares of his own past are triggered,

Simon can't stand back and watch child after child be abused. Not without offering his help to those chasing the monsters.

Even if it means dealing with the cranky and critical Detective Kate Morgan …

Find Simon Says… Hide here!
To find out more visit Dale Mayer's website.
https://geni.us/DMSSHideUniversal

Author's Note

Thank you for reading Snap, Crackle…: Psychic Visions, Book 19! If you enjoyed the book, please take a moment and leave a short review.

Dear reader,

I love to hear from readers, and you can contact me at my website: www.dalemayer.com or at my Facebook author page. To be informed of new releases and special offers, sign up for my newsletter or follow me on BookBub. And if you are interested in joining Dale Mayer's Reader Group, here is the Facebook sign up page.
http://geni.us/DaleMayerFBGroup

Cheers,
Dale Mayer

About the Author

Dale Mayer is a *USA Today* best-selling author, best known for her SEALs military romances, her Psychic Visions series, and her Lovely Lethal Garden cozy series. Her contemporary romances are raw and full of passion and emotion (Broken But ... Mending, Hathaway House series). Her thrillers will keep you guessing (Kate Morgan, By Death series), and her romantic comedies will keep you giggling (*It's a Dog's Life*, a stand-alone novella; and the Broken Protocols series, starring Charming Marvin, the cat).

Dale honors the stories that come to her—and some of them are crazy, break all the rules and cross multiple genres!

To go with her fiction, she also writes nonfiction in many different fields, with books available on résumé writing, companion gardening, and the US mortgage system. All her books are available in print and ebook format.

Connect with Dale Mayer Online

Dale's Website – www.dalemayer.com
Twitter – @DaleMayer
Facebook Page – geni.us/DaleMayerFBFanPage
Facebook Group – geni.us/DaleMayerFBGroup
BookBub – geni.us/DaleMayerBookbub
Instagram – geni.us/DaleMayerInstagram
Goodreads – geni.us/DaleMayerGoodreads
Newsletter – geni.us/DaleNews

Also by Dale Mayer

Published Adult Books:

Bullard's Battle
Ryland's Reach, Book 1
Cain's Cross, Book 2
Eton's Escape, Book 3
Garret's Gambit, Book 4
Kano's Keep, Book 5
Fallon's Flaw, Book 6
Quinn's Quest, Book 7
Bullard's Beauty, Book 8
Bullard's Best, Book 9

Terkel's Team
Damon's Deal, Book 1

Kate Morgan
Simon Says… Hide, Book 1

Hathaway House
Aaron, Book 1
Brock, Book 2
Cole, Book 3
Denton, Book 4

Elliot, Book 5

Finn, Book 6

Gregory, Book 7

Heath, Book 8

Iain, Book 9

Jaden, Book 10

Keith, Book 11

Lance, Book 12

Melissa, Book 13

Nash, Book 14

Owen, Book 15

Hathaway House, Books 1–3

Hathaway House, Books 4–6

Hathaway House, Books 7–9

The K9 Files

Ethan, Book 1

Pierce, Book 2

Zane, Book 3

Blaze, Book 4

Lucas, Book 5

Parker, Book 6

Carter, Book 7

Weston, Book 8

Greyson, Book 9

Rowan, Book 10

Caleb, Book 11

Kurt, Book 12

Tucker, Book 13

Lovely Lethal Gardens

Psychic Vision Series

Tuesday's Child

Hide 'n Go Seek

Maddy's Floor

Garden of Sorrow

Knock Knock...

Rare Find

Eyes to the Soul

Now You See Her

Shattered

Into the Abyss

Seeds of Malice

Eye of the Falcon

Itsy-Bitsy Spider

Unmasked

Deep Beneath

From the Ashes

Stroke of Death

Ice Maiden

Snap, Crackle...

What If...

Psychic Visions Books 1–3

Psychic Visions Books 4–6

Psychic Visions Books 7–9

By Death Series

Touched by Death

Haunted by Death

Chilled by Death

By Death Books 1–3

Broken Protocols – Romantic Comedy Series
Cat's Meow
Cat's Pajamas
Cat's Cradle
Cat's Claus
Broken Protocols 1-4

Broken and... Mending
Skin
Scars
Scales (of Justice)
Broken but... Mending 1-3

Glory
Genesis
Tori
Celeste
Glory Trilogy

Biker Blues
Morgan: Biker Blues, Volume 1
Cash: Biker Blues, Volume 2

SEALs of Honor
Mason: SEALs of Honor, Book 1
Hawk: SEALs of Honor, Book 2
Dane: SEALs of Honor, Book 3
Swede: SEALs of Honor, Book 4

SEALs of Honor, Books 20–22

SEALs of Honor, Books 23–25

Heroes for Hire

Levi's Legend: Heroes for Hire, Book 1

Stone's Surrender: Heroes for Hire, Book 2

Merk's Mistake: Heroes for Hire, Book 3

Rhodes's Reward: Heroes for Hire, Book 4

Flynn's Firecracker: Heroes for Hire, Book 5

Logan's Light: Heroes for Hire, Book 6

Harrison's Heart: Heroes for Hire, Book 7

Saul's Sweetheart: Heroes for Hire, Book 8

Dakota's Delight: Heroes for Hire, Book 9

Tyson's Treasure: Heroes for Hire, Book 10

Jace's Jewel: Heroes for Hire, Book 11

Rory's Rose: Heroes for Hire, Book 12

Brandon's Bliss: Heroes for Hire, Book 13

Liam's Lily: Heroes for Hire, Book 14

North's Nikki: Heroes for Hire, Book 15

Anders's Angel: Heroes for Hire, Book 16

Reyes's Raina: Heroes for Hire, Book 17

Dezi's Diamond: Heroes for Hire, Book 18

Vince's Vixen: Heroes for Hire, Book 19

Ice's Icing: Heroes for Hire, Book 20

Johan's Joy: Heroes for Hire, Book 21

Galen's Gemma: Heroes for Hire, Book 22

Zack's Zest: Heroes for Hire, Book 23

Bonaparte's Belle: Heroes for Hire, Book 24

Noah's Nemesis: Heroes for Hire, Book 25

Heroes for Hire, Books 1–3
Heroes for Hire, Books 4–6
Heroes for Hire, Books 7–9
Heroes for Hire, Books 10–12
Heroes for Hire, Books 13–15

SEALs of Steel

Badger: SEALs of Steel, Book 1
Erick: SEALs of Steel, Book 2
Cade: SEALs of Steel, Book 3
Talon: SEALs of Steel, Book 4
Laszlo: SEALs of Steel, Book 5
Geir: SEALs of Steel, Book 6
Jager: SEALs of Steel, Book 7
The Final Reveal: SEALs of Steel, Book 8
SEALs of Steel, Books 1–4
SEALs of Steel, Books 5–8
SEALs of Steel, Books 1–8

The Mavericks

Kerrick, Book 1
Griffin, Book 2
Jax, Book 3
Beau, Book 4
Asher, Book 5
Ryker, Book 6
Miles, Book 7
Nico, Book 8
Keane, Book 9

Lennox, Book 10

Gavin, Book 11

Shane, Book 12

Diesel, Book 13

Jerricho, Book 14

Killian, Book 15

The Mavericks, Books 1–2

The Mavericks, Books 3–4

The Mavericks, Books 5–6

The Mavericks, Books 7–8

The Mavericks, Books 9–10

The Mavericks, Books 11–12

Collections
Dare to Be You…

Dare to Love…

Dare to be Strong…

RomanceX3

Standalone Novellas
It's a Dog's Life

Riana's Revenge

Second Chances

Published Young Adult Books:

Family Blood Ties Series
Vampire in Denial

Vampire in Distress

Vampire in Design

Vampire in Deceit
Vampire in Defiance
Vampire in Conflict
Vampire in Chaos
Vampire in Crisis
Vampire in Control
Vampire in Charge
Family Blood Ties Set 1–3
Family Blood Ties Set 1–5
Family Blood Ties Set 4–6
Family Blood Ties Set 7–9
Sian's Solution, A Family Blood Ties Series Prequel
  Novelette

Design series
Dangerous Designs
Deadly Designs
Darkest Designs
Design Series Trilogy

Standalone
In Cassie's Corner
Gem Stone (a Gemma Stone Mystery)
Time Thieves

Published Non-Fiction Books:

Career Essentials
Career Essentials: The Résumé
Career Essentials: The Cover Letter
Career Essentials: The Interview
Career Essentials: 3 in 1

www.ingramcontent.com/pod-product-compliance
Lightning Source LLC
Chambersburg PA
CBHW060307100726
47907CB00002B/324